PRAISE FOR NANNY AT NUMBER 43

WHAT THE MEDIA IS SAYING

"A nanny emerges to chill the blood and set pulses racing in this thoroughly gripping and entertaining tale" *Sunday Independent*

"Nicola Cassidy has a talent for pacing and also has a real talent for speech and tone" *Books Ireland Magazine*

"I can't put it down" Gillian Nelis, Managing Editor of *Sunday Business Post*

WHAT BOOK BLOGGERS ARE SAYING

"Another gem from Nicola Cassidy" *Simply Homemade Blog*

"A character driven novel and a plot driven novel which is exactly what I always want, but don't always get. This book entertained me from beginning to end" *Between The Lines Blog*

"A gripping, chilling read which I just couldn't put down. Found myself reading far too late at night as I desperately wanted to see what would happen next" *Over the Rainbow Book Blog*

"Dark, gritty and full of utterly life-like characters. Nicola's attention to detail in her dialogue, description and character building is truly wonderful" *Madwoman in the Attic Blog*

"Nicola Cassidy writes so beautifully, just gorgeous to read" *Bad Mammy Blog*

"Grabbed me from the very first page. Perfect for fans of Hannah Kent's *Burial Rites*, *The Nanny at Number 43* is an accomplished historical novel that blends elements of crime fiction with a compelling domestic drama" *The Shelf of Unread Books Blog*

"Thoroughly engrossing, filled with atmosphere and a sense of menace. Mary Poppins this is NOT....I can recommend this for anyone who loves historical fiction with a thrilling edge"
The Bookwormery Blog

"At times it felt as if I was watching a movie" *The Wolf Pad Blog*

"I absolutely loved this book!!
Five stars from me!!" *Donna's Book Blog*

"Nicola Cassidy has created a wonderful character. The Nanny is a very dark and mysterious individual. *The Nanny at Number 43* is an emotive read. It's a fascinating interpretation and twist of historical facts and is another impressive novel from Nicola Cassidy" *Swirl and Thread Blog*

"This is a wonderful example of good historical fiction, but it also has an engaging cast of characters that wouldn't be out of place in *Rebecca* ... Short chapters combined with an addictive writing style meant that I fell prey to the 'just one more' habit that so often purloins my sleep, but it was entirely worth it in this case. Start it at your peril – because you won't want to put it down"
Behind Green Eyes Blog

"A must read for fans of historical fiction"
Not Another Book Blogger

"Cassidy's writing is ... evocative.
This is a highly recommended 5-star read!" *Jan's Book Buzz*

ADELE

A NOVEL

NICOLA
CASSIDY

POOLBEG

This book is a work of fiction. References to real people, events, establishments, organisations, or locales are intended only to provide a sense of authenticity, and are used fictitiously. All other characters, and all incidents and dialogue, are drawn from the author's imagination and are not to be construed as real.

Published 2020 by Poolbeg Press Ltd
123 Grange Hill, Baldoyle
Dublin 13, Ireland
E-mail: poolbeg@poolbeg.com
www.poolbeg.com

A catalogue record for this book is available from the British Library.

ISBN 978-1-78199-740-6

Typeset by Poolbeg Press Ltd

www.poolbeg.com

ABOUT THE AUTHOR

Nicola Cassidy grew up in the quiet countryside outside Drogheda, in County Louth, and started writing stories at a young age. Once she'd learned to love books without pictures (it was a difficult step), she devoured her local library's stock and was particularly drawn to historical fiction and memoirs. Encouraged by her English teacher, she chose to study journalism at Dublin City University, and worked for a short time in local and national newspapers, before turning to political PR and marketing management. She studied creative writing at the Irish Writers' Centre while living in Dublin and set up her popular and award-nominated lifestyle blog www.LadyNicci.com. She wrote her first novel while on maternity leave for her first daughter and started planning her second ten days after her second daughter was born. She lives in Termonfeckin, County Louth, with her husband and two daughters.

Her historical suspense novel, *The Nanny at Number 43*, was published by Poolbeg in 2019.

ALSO BY NICOLA CASSIDY

December Girl

The Nanny at Number 43

ACKNOWLEDGEMENTS

To Kathleen Riley for her kind assistance and enthusiasm and for her wonderful 'Astaire Bible', which made writing this book so much easier. I urge anyone with a keen interest in the history of Fred and Adele Astaire to seek out Kathleen's book *The Astaires*.

To the staff at Howard Gotlieb Archival Research Center at Boston University for welcoming me and helping me sort through the Astaire archives, especially to Katie Fortier who was most kind and helpful.

To Ava Astaire and Richard McKenzie who donated the archives in the first place. I thoroughly enjoyed Richard's memoirs *Turn Left at the Black Cow* and I have Ava's *At Home in Ireland, Cooking and Entertaining* on my bookshelf for reference. I am hoping her knowledge will somehow rub off on my rather lacklustre homemaking skills!

To Denis Nevin at Lismore Castle who met with me and gave me a tour of the castle. This was vital in being able to authentically recreate the scenes there. He also gave me a number of contacts, most notably his sister Kathleen Penny who also met with me and provided a wealth of anecdotes, much of it hilarious, about the wonderful Adele.

To Iris and Derrick Mathews who run Le Tremblay

Loire Writers Retreat. It was there that I first began the real work on this book and what nicer setting than under the warm French sun, accompanied by the even warmer Northern Irish hospitality.

To my family who continually support what I do. To Ronan who not only supports financially but emotionally – it was he who practically posted me to Boston himself to do the research. To Trish our childminder, Mags at afterschool care, and Sam, an adopted member of our family.

Thank you to my writing friends, Sheila Forsey and Andrea Mara, for always being at the end of the phone whenever author doubt strikes. (Often!)

Finally, a thank-you to Paula Campbell at Poolbeg Press and the team behind her who loved the book from the day I mentioned it on our first ever meeting. It's wonderful to have an enthusiastic team willing the book well. Thank you to Gaye Shortland for making the editing process so easy and to Tracy Brennan my agent.

DEDICATION

For Ronan, my own dancing partner through life

PART ONE

AUDITION

MONOLOGUE

There's a feeling when you walk out on stage. A moment of silence. A collective intake of breath. And in that moment, in the gap between your appearance and their eyes on you and that breath in, that is when I feel most alive.

It doesn't matter the setting. The size of the stage. The darkness or the dimness of the lights. It is always the same. The anticipation, the waiting. For you.

And when Fred is with me, I feel even more on show. The two of us, together, entertaining as one.

Fred. The pride in him I feel, the pride we all feel, particularly Mama. Though she would never say. In that tight-lipped, proud way of hers. And Father too, I suspect.

I do think of it now, often. That moment, those moments, just as the lights come up, that silence.

And that is when you capture them, you see. That very first moment. You must learn to hold them.

Because audiences like that. They like to be held, played with, sparkled to. And not everyone can do it – not everyone has the power I have … had.

What is the point now? When you think of it?

It is Fred who is the star and I am happy for him. He has worked for it and it is so much easier for a man, of course.

But he has never forgotten and neither have I.

That before Fred Astaire, there was Adele, the cheeky, chirpy hold-the-audience-in-the-palm-of-her-paw girl.

I came first. And I am still here.

Watching. Waiting, for that moment, when you step on stage, for the space where everyone breathes in and holds it until you speak.

Let the show begin.

CHAPTER ONE

LOS ANGELES, CALIFORNIA, 1978

"Miss Morgan?"

"Yes?"

"Good morning, this is Ben Sanchez from Porthouse Books."

"Oh, hi. Hi!"

"It's not good news, I'm afraid. We had our meeting this morning."

"Oh."

"I'm sorry to report that it didn't go your way."

"Oh."

"Yes, unfortunately the rest of the board didn't feel it would sell. I'm disappointed myself. Perhaps you could submit elsewhere? I still believe it could be published. It's such a story."

"Yes. Oh, I'm so disappointed, Mr. Sanchez."

"I know."

"Is there anything we can do – a rewrite – I could rewrite the ending perhaps again? What if I spoke with some bookshops myself? I have some good contacts."

"It's not a runner for us, Miss Morgan. I'm truly sorry we couldn't move forward on it. But, please, if you have something else in mind, I'd love to read it."

"Oh. Right. Well, I … no, I don't have anything else."

"Take some time. Hopefully we can talk again. You have our address. And our phone number."

"Yes."

"Goodbye, Miss Morgan."

"Goodbye."

The phone receiver clicked, sending a tiny echo through the tiled hall.

Ellie Morgan, who was sitting in the small seat of the wicker telephone table, folded her hands into her lap and slumped forward.

"Goodbye," she said into the empty hallway, past the kitchen, to no one in particular but herself.

CHAPTER TWO

OMAHA, NEBRASKA, DECEMBER 1902

ALL OF THE EYES ARE ON ME.

It is a funny feeling, everyone looking at me.

I see Daddy and Mama and they are staring real hard like they are waiting for something to happen, something big.

The big thing is me, me and the song I'm going to sing and the little dance I'm going to do here on the table – and when I've finished I will curtsy at the end and then do a little bow, because that feels like the thing to do.

I close my eyes for a minute and I breathe in through my nose, quick, and when I open my eyes again they are all still waiting and the music is at the right spot now and so I launch into the dance, all of my moving bigger now than when I do it at home.

I remember all of the words. It is easy. They are just there, coming out of my mouth, without me even thinking about it.

Like the steps. My feet move, and my arms too, just the way they should.

All of the eyes keep staring at me, big smiles coming on their faces now.

They like what I am doing, I know it, they really like it.

When the piano player gets to the end of the song he thumps the keys real hard and so I sing louder because I am finishing and my voice needs to come out stronger.

Everyone is standing now, clapping, even the people who were sitting down, the old men in the chairs who have bad backs and don't even work for Storz anymore but Mr. Storz invites them to the Christmas party every year at the offices of the brewery because he feels kind of sorry for them and Daddy told me once they look forward to it all year because they miss working at the brewery and meeting with all the folks all day long.

I see Daddy and Mama standing close together and they are clapping all wild, like I do when Daddy brings home something nice for us from work, like a cream bun he picked up in Fischer's bakery that day or even better some paper I can use to cut up for my paper dolls.

Freddie is at Mama's legs, standing beside her, his arms wrapped round her knees as if they are a tree trunk.

He doesn't really like the noise and he looks scared.

Silly Freddie.

He doesn't know that they are clapping for me and that I have made everyone happy with my singing and my dancing and my curtsying.

He wrinkles up his nose and I wonder if he might cry after all – he sure looks like he wants to.

Oh Freddie.

I get down off the table – a man reaches out his hand and I hold it and step onto the stool they've pulled up to it like steps.

I go over to Mama and Daddy and everyone is still clapping and Daddy squeezes my shoulder and bends down and pulls me in and hugs me.

It feels nice. He smells of beer and cologne.

He stands back up and I look at Mama's face and she is smiling, but she doesn't touch me or hug me like Daddy does.

But I know that she is pleased. She has a pleased look on her face.

Freddie hides behind her skirt.

There is a table with bowls of food on it, that anyone can just go up to and eat. They have little plates stacked high and Mama helps us take what we want from all the bowls to put onto little plates.

I choose sliced apple and small parcel pastries which have meat in them. Freddie gets Mama to dig her spoon into a blancmange and it wobbles on his plate. There are even sugar-coated plums and lumps of fudge and I ask Mama for some because I know she will give them to me on account of the good singing I did.

I have been to the Storz Christmas party every year except the year I was born but I only remember last year's when I was five. This year I am six. It is even better this year with all the people shaking my hand and pinching my cheek and patting me on the head.

After we've eaten the food on our plates, we go play with all the other children who have gathered in a place over to the side of the party hall, where there are some hoops and games.

I think it is all a lot of fun and I make best friends with a girl who has brown hair like me only her hair is in ringlets and mine is short.

When we grow tired Freddie and I go to find Mama and Daddy. They are sitting at a table and Daddy is laughing very loud and I see that his face is red and Mama has a frown on hers.

"Are you ready to go home?" Mama asks and I say yes, even though it is fun and I would kind of like to stay.

Daddy throws his hand down at Mama when she says it's time to go as if he doesn't hear her and after a few minutes she asks him again and he shakes his head.

When she asks him another time he gets angry and stands straight up and breaks off the talking he is doing to the man who is leaning close to him and says, "Looks like it's time to go home, Nelson, so says the wife!"

He comes around to our side of the table and grabs me and Freddie by the arms and pulls us and I let a yelp out because he has startled me and now he is walking very fast and our legs are all running.

I look behind to see Mama stand up and say goodbye to the people at the table and grab for my cape and hers.

Then we are outside in the cold, standing at the door where you go into Storz Brewing Company and Daddy is waiting for a minute.

"*Ow!*" says Freddie and he tries to pull his arm away from Daddy but he doesn't let him.

When Mama comes out she says, "Fritz" but he ignores her and walks off again very fast pulling us and she has to run to catch up.

Freddie starts to cry and Daddy drops my hand and grabs at him roughly and swings him round so that he is carrying him now, and then he grabs at my fingers again.

Only the sound of our footsteps on the sidewalk near the brewery and then our footsteps on the muddy hardened path outside the street of the town can be heard as we make our way home.

When we get to our house Daddy takes us in and puts us in our beds, only taking our shoes off, and tells us we are to go straight to sleep now.

Freddie doesn't find it hard to sleep because he is small

and tired but I hear Daddy shouting at Mama and she shouts back and I can't sleep for a while until they have stopped fighting and Mama goes to bed, slamming the bedroom door, and then it is quiet.

At Christmastime the Storz Brewing Company gives everybody who works there a little diary with crisscross pages and this year Daddy gave it to me. I take a pencil, rub it across the pages and look at the marks in grey. I would like to be able to draw something, something real nice. I would like to be able to draw Mama.

My drawings are no good, but I don't really mind. It is fun to use the pencil in that diary and I do it every day in the afternoon when there's not much else to be doing.

For Christmas Day we have a nice dinner of half a turkey that Mama got to share from our neighbour two doors up who has connections to a woman who rears birds for eating on the other side of Omaha. It is so nice with the gravy and the potatoes and I eat it all up.

Mama has also made baked apple strudel and I am almost so full that I can't eat it but I do a good job at trying.

We got a small green Christmas tree and Daddy planted it in a bucket of mud and it is in our front room where we all sit and it smells real nice. I think it is funny that we have a tree in our house but Mama tells me it is a *tradition* and that means that it's something you do just because.

I helped put a star on top of it that we made out of paper ourselves, Mama and me. Daddy held me up to do it and told me I was a great girl for doing that.

All of the houses around us do the same thing and I check to see what kind of stars they have when we go in and out to say hello to the people who live there. When we go in, there is great laughter and 'hellos' from the grown-ups, and then we are told to play and after a while we are given root beer in cups and sponge cake.

The daddies drink the bottles of beer given to them by Mr. Storz and they hold up their glasses and bash them off each other and say 'A toast!' and 'To Storz!'.

I like toast just like Mr. Storz, but I don't see any toast when they are holding up their drinks. Mama puts margarine on mine but I prefer when she uses marmalade with the little bits. Grown-ups are very funny sometimes.

The best thing about Christmas is that you get a present and when I woke up on the morning of Christmas I found that my present was pencils that make different colours when you put them on the paper. I use them so much Daddy has to keep paring them with the knife Mama peels everything with and he tells me to 'go easy'.

It is hard to go easy. I have never had so much fun in my life.

Everyone has three days off for Christmas and then they are back to work for Mr. Storz.

It will be another whole year before we can go to the Christmas party again and have turkey and get a lovely present.

It is a very long time to wait, I think.

A short time after Christmas Mama tells me that I will be going to a class at Willard Chambers Dancing Academy.

It is for girls and boys who want to dance.

Mama tells me I want to dance.

I didn't know this.

She says I was so good at the Christmas party that everybody kept saying it to Daddy and that she had been thinking about it for a while and that it was true. I was very good at dancing and this class would teach me how to dance properly.

I thought that this was fine.

The academy was near to where we went to the Storz Christmas party, on West Farnam Street.

Mr. Chambers was clapping his hands at girls of all different ages when I came into the class.

He was telling them to get in line.

He smiled at Mama and came over to greet us and he said that I was very welcome. I felt a little bit shy then.

He took me over to another little girl who looked like my age and she held my hand and showed me how do to the dance steps when Mr. Chambers went back to the top of the class and counted out the numbers.

Mama sat in a seat with all the other mamas at the side of the class. She had a smile on her face, which made me feel happy.

We did three dances and the last one was the hardest because there was a lot of different moves and I didn't know them at all.

Mama said afterwards that I would learn.

Mr. Chambers said I was 'a natural' and that I would do well.

I noticed there was a smell of something in the hall, like the cupboard in our house where Mama keeps the sweeping brush and the dustpan and cloths for cleaning.

I liked it, that smell.

CHAPTER THREE

OMAHA, NEBRASKA, JULY 1973

ELLIE MORGAN PULLED HER FORD FAIRLANE into a wide space right outside Chambers Dancing Academy. A large window was dressed with US flags and paper fans in red, white and blue for the fourth of July. They looked like children had made them.

She grabbed her bag and pulled down the visor to check her reflection in the small rectangular mirror embedded in it.

Her stomach lurched.

She had her work cut out with this interview.

She slammed the door with a hefty push, telling herself that she had nothing to be afraid of. The woman sounded like a battleaxe on the phone but she knew, from having met so many interviewees before, that people in person were different.

The door that led into the hall of the academy was loose, pushed open so often by many small hands. She could hear the roll of *trump-trump* music, the type a band would march to, coming from a room next door.

She peeked in the window of the door to see a line of young girls and boys who were indeed marching up and down the wide dance hall, parting to carry out various somersaults and flips. It reminded her of cheerleading practice.

A young woman was standing, watching, shouting at intervals. Too young to be Miss Chambers.

She walked down the corridor looking for an office of some sort and found a woman, her back to her, holding a coffeepot, in a small room with a sink and cupboards in it.

The kitchen.

Ellie knocked gingerly on the door.

From behind the woman looked in her fifties perhaps. She was small and lithe, and her shoulders were straight, her posture rigid.

When she turned round Ellie was taken aback at the woman's face. This woman was in her late seventies, eighties perhaps.

It had to be her.

"Miss Chambers?"

"Yes."

"Ellie Morgan – we spoke on the telephone?"

She walked forward and held out her hand. The woman took it limply, still holding the coffeepot in the other hand.

"I hope it still suits to chat?"

"Yes," said Miss Chambers, looking her up and down. "Would you like a cup of coffee?"

"That would be lovely," said Ellie.

She chatted about the drive to Omaha, how long it had taken, things she had seen on the road, while the woman went about setting out another cup on a saucer and pouring brown-black coffee from the metal pot.

"Such flat landscape, you can see for miles – it really is beautiful."

"This way," said Miss Chambers, handing Ellie her coffee cup and saucer and walking off ahead, not acknowledging any of Ellie's compliments about her homeland.

She followed her down a corridor past another smaller studio into a room the same size as the kitchen, with two desks set up. Miss Chambers had a comfortable handsewn cushion on her chair and a typewriter at the desk. Pictures adorned the walls, various brown frames against the patterned wallpaper.

Ellie wanted to study them, or at least catch a glimpse.

"So," said Miss Chambers, sitting down lightly on the chair.

Ellie sat in front of her – her chair, she noticed, had no cushion at all.

"Thank you for seeing me. I really do appreciate it. Do you mind if I use this?" She took a Dictaphone recorder from her bag and laid it on the desk.

"I do actually."

"It's just for my notes, it's not for other ears."

"I'd prefer not," said Miss Chambers and she shook her head.

Ellie's stomach lurched again. Nerves.

She put the Dictaphone back in her bag and took out her notebook, uncapping her pen, looking up to see if there would be a protest about this too, but the woman stared and said nothing.

"Well, as I explained on the phone, I was wondering if your father had any memories of Miss Astaire, any that you can recall him telling you?"

"It is such a long time ago – I don't really remember him saying much."

"Can you tell me what he did say?"

"He just said that she was talented and that she went to New York."

Ellie waited. Miss Chambers opened her hands in a 'that's it' gesture.

"Were there any school records of her, anything like that?"

"No, not from back then. It was so long ago."

"Was he happy, that she made it? Did he feel … proud?"

"Of course. But he was a quiet man. He didn't brag too much."

This wasn't going well. Had she really driven all the way from California for this? Seventeen hundred miles and two days of hard driving and this interview could be over within a minute.

"Yes … I understand. Could you tell me about your father? What he was like?"

"He was a nice man. A good teacher. He taught hundreds of girls and boys to dance. As I have."

"Yes, you must be legendary in these parts."

Flattery might work.

Miss Chambers pursed her mouth.

Ellie glanced about the room.

"Do you have any pictures of her?"

Some of the frames on the walls looked old.

"Yes," said Miss Chambers.

Ellie turned to look at her in surprise. Progress.

Pushing back her chair, Miss Chambers stood and walked to the wall opposite, near the door, where two rows of photos hung.

"Here," she pointed, standing on tiptoe.

Ellie got up and came to where Miss Chambers was standing and pointing.

And there she was. Her face, familiar from the photographs

now, smiling, a happy youngster amongst a group of other similarly aged girls and boys.

"And this is me," said Miss Chambers, pointing to a girl who was not smiling, right next to Adele Astaire.

"You!" said Ellie. "You knew her?"

"Oh yes. We were in class together. We are the same age actually."

Ellie looked at the side of Miss Chamber's face. "I … I didn't know. Oh, that's wonderful. You didn't tell me."

"You didn't ask. You only asked about my father."

Ellie felt a bit silly. Still, the woman could have offered the information if she had wanted.

"We were friends," she said. "I liked her. I used to hold her hand for the steps. I was so familiar with it all. Daddy loved her. He said you could see she was a dancer, the first day she came in those doors, the way she held herself. You can always tell, I think. It's in the bones, in the back. This is Daddy."

Miss Chambers pointed at another photo, of a man on his own, staring at the camera, a slight smile on his face.

"It was he who told Adele's mother to take her to New York. He said that's where she needed to be, if she wanted to make it. So I guess we have Daddy to thank." She went past Ellie to make her way back to her seat.

"Did he follow her career?" Ellie asked as she sat again.

"Everybody did. She came home a few times. Total sell-outs, those shows. But I never really spoke to her again. Their father was here for years. He was a very proud man. A very presentable man. My father always joked to my mother that if she didn't marry him, she would have chased Fritz about the place. A lot of women did, you know."

"Oh?"

"There were rumours. But it's not my place to say. It was so long ago. And I was only a child."

Ellie looked down at her notebook. It was blank. She didn't need to write down the word *rumours*. That would stick.

"You know, we didn't think much of it at the time, but Freddie was talented too. He could stand en pointe. Up he'd go, no problem."

"Really?"

"Oh, yes. His mother enrolled him in the school too. But they went to New York for Adele. It was Adele who was to get the training."

"Were you happy for her? That she made it?"

"Yes. Of course. We all were. Not many famous people from Omaha."

She let out a tinkly laugh, surprising Ellie. "They sacrificed a lot. They worked hard. They did a lot of touring. I had a very nice life here with my parents and the studio. I don't think I would have liked all that touring, even though I was talented too. I like to teach. That is my calling."

Outside in the corridor a rush of pounding feet. The music had stopped. The class must be over.

Ellie leaned over and took a sip from her untouched coffee cup.

"Can you remember where they lived? The street?"

Miss Chambers frowned for a moment.

"Yes, I do. Would you like me to show you?"

"Oh, that would be wonderful."

"You are driving?"

"Yes."

"I'll get my coat."

CHAPTER FOUR

OMAHA, NEBRASKA, JANUARY 1905

MAMA SAID WE WERE GOING ON AN ADVENTURE. She got very busy organising everything for this adventure and we even had to go to get new clothes made for it. I needed a new dress and a jacket and Freddie was getting new shorts, two shirts and a pullover. We went to Mama's favourite tailoress to be measured and I liked the tickle of the tape and Mrs. Butler's fingers as she pressed them quickly against my back and down my legs and I had to hold out my arms for them to be measured too.

She talked non-stop to Mama while she worked.

"Oh, you are very brave, Mrs. Austerlitz," she said. "But what an adventure. You are right, taking the chance now, while they are young."

Everyone, it seemed, knew that we were going on an adventure.

At our last class at Chambers Dancing Academy, Mr. Chambers spoke with Mama for a long time and they talked about the different dance schools that were in New York and the new one we would be going to which Daddy had cut out of *The New York Clipper* that he had specially on subscription. *The Clipper* had all different articles about theatre folk and adverts for new musicals and sheet music.

The new school we were going to was *Alviene Master School of the Theatre and Academy of Cultural Arts.*

I liked the sound of it for sure.

Everybody had gone home and it was just Freddie and me and my friend Lola then, whose Daddy was Mr. Chambers, sitting on the chairs, swinging our legs. Then Mr. Chambers came over and took my hand tightly and shook it and wouldn't let it go.

"The very best of luck, Adele. The very best of luck."

Mr. Chambers was excited about our adventure too.

We got up to leave and I waved to Lola and she waved back and smiled.

I wondered if she could come on the adventure with us too.

I would have liked that.

The night before we were going on our adventure all the neighbours came over and they poured drinks and made clattery noises and did a load of high talking.

Freddie got real tired and he was on Mama's knee and she put him to bed before me because he was grumpy with everyone patting him on the head.

People kept saying, "You'll miss them," to Daddy and I didn't know what they meant.

Daddy was coming on the train to New York with us too, so how would he miss us?

When most of the neighbours had gone home, back to their own houses where their children were sleeping, Mama took me to the bedroom I shared with Freddie.

"Why will Daddy miss us, Mama?" I said.

She sat on the bed and said, "Because we will be in New York and Daddy will be here."

"But I thought he was coming to New York too?"

"He is," she said. "We are going on the train together. But then, when we are all set up, he will be coming back here."

So we would be in New York on our own, just Mama, Freddie and me. I didn't know what to think about this. I guessed that was what happened on adventures.

"But I want Daddy to stay with us," I said. Tears came to my eyes.

"Daddy has to work, here," she said. "If he doesn't work here, then we wouldn't be able to stay in New York."

I was too tired to ask why. I put my head on the pillow and Mama patted my head and told me I needed to get my rest because I would need all my energy for our adventure which was starting tomorrow.

I was looking forward to seeing what an adventure was. There sure was a lot of fuss before you went on one.

Mama and Daddy were in bad moods the next morning and they were running around a lot and were flustered. We got dressed in our new clothes and I felt so nice, even though the collar on my dress was a bit stiff on my neck and I kept scratching at it to try and get my skin used to it.

Freddie was very excited because today we would be climbing on a train, not just standing at the station looking at it like we had done before. We had tickets and everything.

Daddy got the horse and buggy ready and Dorothy, our help, put three suitcases in the back of it and a carpet bag. When it was time to go we waved to Dorothy and the neighbours who stood at their doors to see us off. Freddie and I waved for ages, giggling.

It was fun in the buggy. We sailed along the streets, so fast, the horse clip-clopping all the way along the road.

When we got to the station, a porter helped us with our cases and they were brought in and put on the platform. The train was there already, steam going all up in the air, and it was noisy, spewing out smoke at us.

The train conductor took us all onto the train and put us in our seats which were a seat for me and Freddie facing Mama and Daddy. Mama told us that these would be our beds also and we could not believe that this is where we would be sleeping too.

The conductor brought other people onto the train too but they were mostly men and women, not children like Freddie and me.

It took a long time to get everyone on, and when the train was ready, it blew a big long whistle.

When it started to move off I got so excited I wanted to do a pee but Mama told me I had to wait. We waved out the window, sticking our hands out at all the people on the platform who were waving hankies. I don't know why they were waving at us, but they were. Some were crying. Probably because they weren't going on the adventure themselves.

We would be on the train for two whole days and two nights. Freddie couldn't stop jittery-jumping up and down. We had never been inside a train before but we had often watched it coming in and out over the tracks. The big freight trains took all the beer we made in Omaha all over the country Daddy said.

But this was a different train. This was a train for people and there were no big vats of beer on it at all. This was a train for adventurers like us.

It took a while but soon the engine got going real fast

and we enjoyed just sitting there and seeing all the fields go by. There were houses and huts too but not too many. I liked to see the horses, especially the ones who started running alongside us like they were in a race.

We had cards and dice and Mama had a big picnic basket, but she said we had to wait to eat as we had a long journey and we had to make everything last. She said we would have our dinner in the dining car in the evening time.

After a while, when we had settled down a bit, after we had played Rummy twice and a game of Switch, we got a little bit tired and I curled in against the window and felt my eyes close. Mama took out a blanket and laid it over me and Freddie and said we should try to rest as we were going to be on the train for a long time.

"Mama, what will our house be like in New York?" I said, watching a tall wooden house fly by before it was gone.

"Probably an apartment," she said. "Everyone lives in an apartment in New York."

Daddy told us that New York was very big and had lots of people and there were so many people that they lived in apartments, which were like rooms all piled up on top of each other.

Daddy knew a lot about New York because when he first came to America he lived there for a while and he was a musician playing the piano and he was very good at it but there were so many other people playing the piano too that he went to work for the International Portrait and Picture Company and that's how he came to Omaha.

I thought it was a good job he did because that's where he met Mama.

"Why don't you stay in New York with us, Daddy, and play the piano again?" I said.

Mama and Daddy laughed.

"I would like that," he said. "But I don't think Mr. Storz would be too happy."

I could see why Mr. Storz wanted to keep Daddy for himself.

I wished he could live in New York in the apartments all piled up on top of each other, with us.

"You could ask him?" I said. I thought that he was a nice man and he might not mind, if Daddy explained.

"I will come and visit," he said. "Don't you worry. And besides, you will be so busy learning dancing and singing that you won't even notice I'm gone."

I didn't think that was true. But Daddy seemed to think so and he smiled and looked out the window at another tall house that flew by.

CHAPTER FIVE

OMAHA, NEBRASKA, JULY 1973

NOT HAVING EXPECTED TO BE transporting her interview subject in her car, Ellie asked Miss Chambers to wait just a moment while she moved two newspapers, a folder, brown paper wrapping from a sandwich she had picked up in a small diner on the road and a large flask of water from the passenger seat.

Not for the first time, she was glad she had made the decision to hire a car. Had she taken Kirk's, she would have been dealing with a dirty ashtray and suspicious food stains all over the front seat which, she assumed, Miss Chambers would not have been too happy about.

Not that Kirk would have lent her his car. She hadn't even asked.

She pulled out onto the street. There were cars parked haphazardly along the street, outside a diner, a launderette and an ice-cream parlour.

Miss Chambers was quiet, giving only instructions to "turn left here" and "next turn coming up".

"This is the street," she said as they turned into a narrow road with grassy banks on either side.

Along the sidewalk, a low wall ran in front of the banks, cement blocks painted white.

"I think it's here," said Miss Chambers, stabbing a finger at the window towards a row of neat, wooden-boarded houses.

Ellie pulled her car in and they both got out and stood, looking up the bank to where the houses sat.

"It's hard to remember," said Miss Chambers, walking now and shading her eyes in the glare. "But I feel it's this one. My father always mentioned it whenever we passed. '*The Austerlitzes, remember them?*'"

The house was small and porched, a square bay window jutting out to the left.

"Should we go up for a look?" Ellie asked.

Miss Chambers shrugged.

Ellie put out her arm instinctively as they climbed the path on the hill. It hovered near Miss Chambers' back; the woman was lithe, but she was aged.

Up closer the house looked dishevelled, an unfinished paint job now obvious all along the posts supporting the porch roof. Two rocking chairs and a small folding table with a tin of paint on it sat on the porch. A torn screen covered the door.

"It was neater in my day," said Miss Chambers.

"Should we knock?" Ellie asked.

Miss Chambers nodded.

Tentatively, Ellie opened the screen door and knocked on the wooden door behind it.

They waited. There was no movement inside, no noise. No one home.

Disappointed, Ellie walked along the porch and looked towards the side of the house.

"Did you ever visit her here?" she asked.

"Not that I can remember," said Miss Chambers. "Maybe

my father did. I would have just seen her at the school."

"Your father was very helpful to them?"

"He was a helpful man."

"Was she born here, would you say?"

"Maybe. People moved around a lot in those days. It was easy to find a house. We were a community, we all knew one another, all helped each other. It was different then, we were up against a lot of ... anti-sentiment, you could say. Being German."

"You're of German descent too?"

"Yes. Most people are around here. When I was a child most people still spoke German. That's why the breweries are here. We brought it with us."

Ellie looked at more debris that had been piled beside the house on the lawn. A damaged fender of a car. Another two old, rusted paint pots. A broken mop. And a bird cage, a little swing set right in the middle. She feared if she looked more closely she would see a tiny avian skeleton.

"When Freddie was born he nearly died."

"Really?" said Ellie.

"He was all blown up like a balloon and then he shrunk. Their mama nursed him. I remember my own mama telling me that."

"Wow."

"Course there were lots of things like that back then, babies being sick. Not making it. Different now with the hospitals and all. I haven't got any siblings. Not alive anyway."

Ellie wondered whether Lola Chambers had any children of her own. There was no wedding ring, she'd noticed.

"It's a good thing he lived, though, isn't it?"

"Who?"

"Fred Astaire. You wouldn't be here otherwise, would you?"

"No. I guess not."

They walked back to the car, Ellie putting her arm out again in case Miss Chambers wished to grab it. She didn't.

On reaching the car, she pulled open the door and got in, her posture never changing from ramrod straight.

CHAPTER SIX

SOMEWHERE IN PENNSYLVANIA, JANUARY 1905

ON THE SECOND DAY, THE TRAIN WAS NOT AS MUCH FUN. We were bored sitting in our seats, not able to move round much. Mama wrote the names of the States down on a piece of paper and when we passed through different stations or the train made a stop, we marked it down on the page, Mama tracing the letters and sounding them out so that I could understand. *Iowa. Illinois. Indiana.* They all started with the letter I, a big I, not the one with the period on top. It was the same I that you used for I, like in 'Mother May I'. Mama liked to teach us things and I could read lots now.

The first night had been fun, taking down the beds and pulling the little curtain around us. There was a closet where you could go to wash your hands and face and go to the toilet and I liked the smell of the small soap on the sink. I washed my hands twice with it.

It was funny to be sleeping on a train with other people around us.

Freddie said being on the train was the best thing that had ever happened in his whole life and I guess, at five and a half, it probably was.

Back home, he used to make Mama take him down to see the tracks all the time – it was his favourite walk to do. Now that we were on our own sleeper train, Daddy brought him into all the carriages we were allowed go. The viewing car at the end was nice with lovely velvety seats like armchairs but there wasn't much to do there.

The dining car was where you went for dinner and you had to go at a special time because there were so many people to be fed. They had menus and I was able to read most of it and I had potatoes and fish, which tasted real nice, with lots of salt in it.

There was one car where you could go to get your hair cut and Daddy took Freddie in and got him all smartened up and Freddie thought this was the greatest thing even though he wasn't really a fan of getting his hair cut normally. He was afraid of the scissors chopping his ears off, I think.

We didn't go into the smoking cars or the drinking cars because they weren't for children, Daddy said. He left Mama though to go there on his own and when he came back you could smell it all off him. I kept an eye on Mama because I didn't want her getting angry on our adventure.

Whenever George the train man came by, to help with the beds or the garbage or anything we needed, Freddie would ask lots of questions and George loved to answer him because he liked trains so much too. All of the train men were called George and all of them were black like Mr. Roberts who owned the barber shop on Maple Street back home.

We were on the train so long I thought the *chug-chug* was part of my blood. We got so used to it that when it stopped at a station it made us feel strange and wobbly.

I liked the *chug-chug* noise, especially when we were

trying to sleep in the pull-down beds at night. They were a bit shaky and they bent towards the floor so you thought you might fall. The *chuga-chug* helped you sleep.

Chug-chug, chug-chug.

On the second night I found it easier to go to sleep, now that I was used to everything around me. The voices of all the people talking faded in and out of my ears. I opened and closed my eyes.

Freddie was curled up in his bed, underneath mine, his hand out over the blanket, his fingers tapping along to the train: *chug-chug, chug-chug, chug-chug.*

And then I fell asleep.

When I woke up, we were in New York.

I was so glad Daddy was with us now. He knew how to do everything, like how to fetch the porter and get us all out of the station which had the most people I had ever seen in one place, ever. Even more than at the Storz Christmas party and at church.

We had pulled into Pennsylvania Station with our faces right up against the window and now, outside the station, our eyes were stuck to the skies. Except there was hardly any sky in some parts, only buildings, like great big towers, stretching up and up and up.

"*Wow-wee,*" we said, over and over again, the words slipping from our mouths – we just couldn't help it.

Even Mama was impressed and she had a smile on her face, a look of wonder.

"How did they build them?" Freddie asked.

Mama shrugged and said maybe they must have very long ladders in New York.

Daddy led the way and I think Freddie was scared he

would lose us, because I could feel him, the bottom of his shorts touching off my legs, as we walked. There were so many people about, all different types of people, some real funny looking wearing very strange clothes. I couldn't help staring even though that's rude and you're not supposed to do it.

It took us an age to get to the Herald Square Hotel where we were staying for a few days. It had a place called a lobby where you waited while they got you your keys and I had never seen anything so fancy, except in Mr. Storz's house and he was fancy because he was rich.

There were coloured rugs on the floor, marble pillars and huge big trees with rough bark and spiky green leaves, tall like the buildings outside. Except these trees were inside.

And they weren't Christmas trees either.

There was a lovely smell in the air, like perfume.

We sat in leather chairs and waited while Daddy spoke to the man at the desk and then we all walked over to a door where another man was and he pressed a button and waited until a light came on and he opened a door and behind it was a small room with a cage door, and he was able to fold the cage door backwards.

"This is an elevator," said Daddy. "Wait till you see what happens."

We all went inside the tiny room and the man folded the cage door back again and pressed a button on a panel of buttons and number four lit up.

And then, the biggest, worst feeling ever happened and the whole floor shook and we were moving upwards and I didn't like it at all.

I gripped Mama's arm tight and she gripped mine back.

It didn't take long before the feeling stopped and there was a jolt and we stood, watching the man unfold the cage door again and push open another door and we were in a completely new place.

We got out and Daddy said, "See, that was an elevator. It saves you the stairs."

I thought it was magic.

We were all staying in one room. Two beds with Mama and Daddy in one and Freddie and me in the other. They were right up close to each other and we had a window down onto the street. On adventures you spend a lot of time together like on the train and now in this hotel room.

Freddie and I looked out the window for an age while Mama and Daddy fussed around with our cases.

We all had a wash in the basin, which was not like the basin at home, but shinier with lovely, lovely soap. I wondered when we left here if we could take the soap with us.

Daddy said we were going to meet Monsieur Alviene and we had to be on our best behaviour. If we were good then we were going to go to a proper restaurant, Daddy's favourite.

We had to be on our best behaviour there too.

"There's a lot of best behaviour on adventures," Freddie said.

The meeting at Monsieur Alviene's dance school was very easy. We barely did any dancing at all. He talked to Mama and Daddy and he asked me to do a twirl around and he looked at Freddie and said, "And who is this cute little fellow?"

I thought this was a funny thing to say because it was me Mama and Daddy had brought all the way to New

York to see Monsieur Alviene, but it pleased Freddie no end and he went up en pointe, just to show Monsieur Alviene and he thought it was wonderful.

After more talking with Mama and Daddy, Monsieur Alviene showed us some steps and asked me and Freddie to repeat them with him. I followed them easy enough, but Freddie made some mistakes. I guess it was because he was only five, but Monsieur Alviene didn't seem to mind. He laughed a lot, which was a bit funny for a dance tutor. He had a lot of white hair.

Our lessons would be at two o'clock every day at Monsieur Alviene's school and in the morning time Mama would give us our schooling. Monsieur Alviene told Daddy that he would also help us with our apartment and he knew just the place. We would be able to see it tomorrow.

When it was time to go Monsieur Alviene shook my hand and patted Freddie on the head.

"We're going to make a big star out of you," he said to Freddie and everyone laughed, even me.

We left the school and Daddy said to Mama, "Well, isn't that just fine?"

Mama smiled and looked happy with everything.

It was the evening time then and Daddy said it was time to go to Luchow's which was a very fancy place and somewhere that would give us a taste of 'home'.

Home didn't mean Omaha, it meant Austria which is where Daddy is really from. Now that we were in New York he was talking about home a lot because New York is the place he first came to when he left Austria and I think it was bringing back a lot of memories for him.

"Why did you leave Austria, Daddy?" I asked as we walked along the street.

"To see the world," he said. "And," he looked down at me, "because my daddy, your grandpa, was very strict, much stricter than I am. If you think I am strict, you know nothing!"

"He wanted to be famous," said Mama. "A famous music man."

"Yes," said Daddy. "That too."

Luchow's restaurant was dark, a bit like how the Herald Square Hotel was dark in parts too. It made it nicer to go into, like somewhere secret. We waited in line behind a man and woman. The woman was the prettiest lady I had ever seen before in my life and she was young too. I thought maybe they were just married, they looked so happy.

I wondered if we had the right clothes to come here. Mama had changed her dress especially, but I still felt we were not up to scratch. I felt New York dressing up was different to Omaha dressing up.

It had been many years since Daddy had been in Luchow's and he told the man at the front who took you to your table that he used to come here all the time and it was his favourite restaurant.

The man smiled.

"What lovely children," he said.

He had a singsong voice. Like a lady.

"And what has brought you all the way back to New York?" he asked.

Daddy told him that I was enrolling in Monsieur Alviene's stage school on the corner of Eighth Avenue and Twenty-Third Street.

"Oh, she is, is she?"

The man stared at me intently, right into my eyes.

I stared back.

Then I gave him a big smile.

He laughed.

"Well, I can see why," he said and laughed.

Daddy put his hand on my shoulder.

The smell of food was strong, all different smells. I saw a man tuck into a big plate which had black shells all lined up like a mountain. Mama told me they were called mussels.

I was worried they might not have food for us because this looked like such a grown-up place, but luckily the waiter who came could tell us lots of nice things we could eat and we chose mashed potato with sausage and gravy.

Daddy ordered wine.

"Are you excited to get started at Alviene's?" Daddy asked.

I nodded. It felt like the right thing to do. But I didn't really know if I was excited or not. Everything was so busy at the moment, I was just trying to keep up.

"It is a good school. I think you will do well there."

The waiter brought two plates of food for Mama and Daddy which were called starters.

They brought bread rolls for us because children didn't have starters.

I watched another plate of mussels sail by my head, steam rising out of it and thought that Freddie and I could make a good game out of them if we divided them up and hid behind the armchairs at home and flung them at each other like pebbles.

"Papa, Monsieur Alviene said he's going to make a big star outta me!" said Freddie.

He looked up at Daddy with a toothy smile on his face.

We all laughed again.

"That's right, son," Daddy said.

Freddie. He could be so silly sometimes. Everyone knew it was *me* that was going to be the star.

But I didn't mind him tagging along. It would give him something to do anyways.

I just wished I could go up en pointe too. Maybe Monsieur Alviene would teach me?

CHAPTER SEVEN

OMAHA, NEBRASKA, JULY 1973

"ARE YOU SURE I CAN'T TAKE YOU for lunch, Miss Chambers? You've been so helpful, I really would like to offer – my treat."

"No, thank you," Miss Chambers replied as the car pulled to a stop in the same parking space they had left less than an hour before. "It's a kind offer, but I really need to get back now."

"I'd like to leave my number with you and my address," Ellie said, reaching for her bag to take out her notebook and pen. "If you think of anything, any other stories or anything you remember your father said, even in later years, I'd love to hear from you."

"Actually," said Miss Chambers, "there is one thing. I wanted to see what you were like before I gave it to you."

She opened the car door and Ellie opened her own quickly and hurried round to the passenger side to assist.

Inside the dance school, she followed Miss Chambers back down the corridor into the small office. The school was eerily quiet now, bereft of its pupils.

She watched Miss Chambers go to her desk, open a drawer and lift out a bulging brown paper folder.

"There weren't many students who left this school and made it to Broadway. There were plenty good enough, but none who made it. Myself included."

Miss Chambers eyed Ellie as though she were about to divulge a secret.

"My father was very proud of Adele and Fred Astaire. He followed their career for years. Cut out every article he ever saw. When they came back to town in the early days, he went to see every show, sat right up front. He was so proud of them."

Ellie felt her eyes light up, a thrill rushing through her as she realised what might be in the folder.

"I wanted to see what your intentions where. I wanted to make sure you weren't out to make a quick buck. Truth be told I didn't know what you wanted at all. But I can see that this project means a lot to you and that your intentions are honourable, I hope, and so I am happy to lend this to you. When you are finished, I would like it back. I guess in time to come they might frame the contents."

Ellie wondered who 'they' were.

"Thank you. Thank you so much. Don't worry, I will take good care of it."

Her voice belied the excitement she felt inside. She took the file from Miss Chambers and hugged it to her chest.

"Thank you for your help. I really am very grateful."

"You are welcome," Miss Chambers said, still sitting at her desk. "Good luck with your endeavours."

Promise me that you will endeavour to do all that you can: her mother's words written down, the beginning of this mission she had assigned herself.

In the car, Ellie opened the folder at the steering wheel, yellowed paper clippings slipping down towards her lap.

She felt her heart soar, more than it had risen in a very long time.

Ellie drove along the street, her heart still beating at the thought of what the folder might contain. She had wanted to empty it out onto the passenger seat and start sifting through the contents. But she wanted to savour it.

Lunch. She would take lunch and have a look then.

She drove along another two streets before finding a diner that looked at least a little appetising and pulled the car into a parking space outside. With all the nervous energy before her interview this morning her stomach had felt full. Now she realised she was ravenous.

A group of girls, their hair held high in beehives, gathered around a table inside the door. They had dark eyes and lashes. It was a striking look, she would give them that, though it was far from her own bohemian fashion sense. Her mother couldn't understand where she had gotten her hippie streak – *Certainly not from me*, she could hear her saying in her Irish accent.

But the laid-back look suited her. Her blonde hair looked soft and bright, hanging by her face. She loved the freedom of comfortable, flat sandals, the swish of the long skirts that hovered above her toes.

It was the Californian landscape perhaps that had lent itself to her way of life, her style. It was too hot to wear buttoned-up blouses and tight skirts. It was silly to wear heels when the beach was calling and you wanted to go for a long walk in the setting sun.

She pictured her mother now, her light hair silver in patches, ashamed that she had not got it coloured in so long. But she had become so weak, so immobile, that it had been impossible. And she found it hard to trust others in later years, to let them into her house, to give anyone but her daughter access.

She chose a table near the back and slid into the blue-leather diner seat. A waitress approached immediately, all smiles, and handed her a menu.

"Special today is toasted ravioli and dip. And the chef has just cooked up a nice batch of chicken soup, should that take your fancy."

Chicken soup. Something she had fed her mother, spoonful after spoonful after the surgery.

She didn't think she could face chicken soup now.

"Thank you," she smiled and turned her eyes to the menu.

A group of young men came into the diner, choosing the seats directly opposite the gang of girls.

She felt the atmosphere rise as the two groups called out to each other in greeting.

One of the boys went straight to the jukebox and switched off the Johnny Cash number that had been playing. After a few seconds of silence the loud *bomb-bomb* sounds from the start of the song he had chosen echoed through the diner. The girls squealed in delight.

Ellie watched as the young man walked back to the girls and held put his hand out, palm up, towards a girl who was right in the corner. She threw her head back and laughed and her companions made way so that she could climb out and take his hand. He pulled her to him and they walked back up the diner floor and began to dance.

Ellie smiled as she watched them grinding against each other.

Two of the other members of the group moved towards

the girls and pulled two more up to dance. Someone else ran up and turned the dial on the jukebox up.

"*Hey!*"

Ellie watched as the waitress who had met her with smiles thundered past and turned the music right down.

"*This ain't no dancehall, y'hear!*"

The couples moved back towards their seats but did not stop dancing.

"If you want food, order, if you wanna dance, find somewhere else!"

"Keep your panties on," said one of the seated young men.

To Ellie's left, a large, shirted man slid out of his seat and stood. He walked down to the group.

"Have some respect," he said, in a loud, calm voice.

The girls stopped dancing and pulled their partners back towards the seats and sat into them, the group now mixed.

The music stayed turned down low.

"Now, what I can I get you, sweetie?" said the waitress, arriving back to her table, a wisp of hair now fallen at her forehead.

"Trouble?" asked Ellie, her eyes flicking over the shirted man who ambled slowly back to his seat.

"Oh, you know, kids. Think they own the place. They're nice kids, but I let them have one dance, the next thing I know there's a whole horde of them blocking up my diner thinking it's some kinda dance hall."

"They like to dance, huh?"

"*Love* to."

"You ever get to dance yourself?"

The waitress raised her eyebrows in surprise.

"Me? Well. I do actually. Love me a bit of jivin' half

chance I get. Over at Ronnie Drake's every Saturday night. Don't even need a beer, the dancing keeps me going."

"I can't dance at all," said Ellie. "But I was just in with Chambers Dance Academy, with Lola Chambers."

"Oh," said the waitress. "Yeah, they do all the proper dance, ballet and that. For kids mostly. You putting a kid in there? Haven't seen you around."

"No. No. I'm a journalist. I'm working on a … a story."

"'Bout Chambers?"

"No. Someone else. Say, you know anything about the Astaires? Fred and Adele?"

"Well now, there's a blast from the past. Not much, I'm afraid. Just that they were born here. Came back the odd time, I think. Now my mama, she knew some of the family, I think – didn't their daddy work at Storz?"

"Yes, I think so."

"You should talk to Liz-Beth – she's my cousin on my mom's side. Her daddy worked at Storz, used to collect all sorts of memorabilia. Maybe she could help?"

"Oh, do you think I could meet her today? Or tomorrow?"

The waitress shrugged. "Don't see why not. Gimme your order there and I'll give her a call for you."

By the time Ellie's plate of ravioli arrived, her waitress had come back to deliver the news that Liz-Beth was at home today and would be happy to talk to her. She was currently in the process of finding her father's boxes of 'Storz crap' and would have them down out of the attic by the time she arrived, under the hour, if that suited.

"Oh, that's just wonderful, thank you so much," said Ellie.

She couldn't help but smile at her good fortune today. She had been anxious about meeting Miss Chambers, ever since their arranging phone call. She was used to conducting interviews with all sorts, but this whole project was personal. It was different.

Now she held that precious folder as a result of that meeting in her hand. And, in less than an hour, she'd be looking at more materials that would help fill out her whole story.

She lifted the folder cover and peered at the first news article that lay on top of the pile.

It was a picture of Fred and Adele, Adele dressed in a ruffly dress with a flower in her hair, Fred in a white dicky bow and dark suit, his pocket square echoing the flower.

A little bride and groom.

She smiled, looking at their sweet faces, their innocence and youth.

This would make everything easier, give her the colour, the background she needed.

She decided she would wait to look at any more – for now, she wanted to concentrate on Omaha, on their beginnings.

She finished her food and left a $10 bill under her plate.

As she left the diner, she couldn't help but slide the dial up on the jukebox, letting the sounds of the Supremes echo just a bit louder down to the smiling, laughing youngsters.

CHAPTER EIGHT

NEW YORK, JULY 1905

MAMA IS A LOOKER. I NEVER KNEW THIS until we came to New York, but she is. You see it when we walk down the street. She has a fox fur that her mama, my grandma, gave her and with the green coat she wears and us in our coats, which are good wool coats she bought when we got our first stage wage, we look like a fine family as we walk down the block.

Men turn their heads. I even saw a man stop one day, stare and watch her walk all the way till we got to the door of the studio.

"That man is looking at you, Mama," I said.

"Never you mind him," she said.

"Why is he staring?"

"Because he has absolutely no manners," she said.

Mama thinks manners are very important. It is bad manners to stare. It is bad manners to eat your food quickly and without grace. It is good manners to be polite. You can be polite by being quiet until someone speaks to you and asks you a question.

"Don't speak out of turn," she likes to say. "Smile."

When you meet someone you have to hold out your hand and say, "How do you do?" or "Pleased to meet you".

You always look people in the eye when greeting them, but not a stare, more a hello to the eyes.

Mama says you can tell a lot by how a person says hello and goodbye.

Because she was a looker, sometimes men stood too close to her and if they did that they had better watch out! It happened during rehearsals sometimes or in theatres. Men, all different types, would come up and lay a hand on her shoulder, or sit too close while watching us.

"Kindly remove your hand," she would say. And she wouldn't even glance at them, just look ahead at us. Sometimes the men scowled. Other times they looked embarrassed.

Mama was a married woman. She had no time for men with feeling hands.

Always they came up to her, to be near to her, to touch. Sometimes I thought they might swoop in and kiss her.

I didn't like it. I don't know if Freddie noticed but I definitely did not like it.

They wouldn't do it if Daddy was around.

The boarding house where our apartment was had redbrick on the outside and brown windows. It looked to me just like a big house, but this is what apartments looked like. It was all divided up into rooms on the inside, a bit like the hotel we stayed in when we first came to New York, only apartments were bigger than hotel rooms and had cupboards and a table for doing your lessons on.

When we first came to see it, I noticed there was a funny smell, like from the garbage can we had at the back of our house, the way it smelled in summer. Only this was winter.

Daddy thought it was a bit small and worried that we wouldn't have enough room but Mama said it would suit just fine and she liked that it wasn't too far from Monsieur Alviene's school.

There were other performers living in the apartment block too. Across from us on our floor there was Carlos the Great, who was an illusionist and could make things disappear. He was a bit grumpy though, especially in the morning time and Mama said he was a big drinker and to stay away from him. That was fine by me. I didn't like getting my head bit off, thank you very much. We renamed him Carlos the Grouch.

We were on the second floor and below us were three women who all shared an apartment together. I thought they were very beautiful. They were dancers and singers and you could hear them practising sometimes. They could sing opera. They were sopranos, Mama said, and sometimes we'd hear them do harmony and we all thought it was lovely.

There weren't any other children in the building except us, but we could go downstairs during the day out onto the street and find our neighbours to play with. Freddie liked that, being out in the air and not all cooped up in the apartment, but I kind of liked being cosy up there.

Daddy spent four days with us in New York before it was time for him to go back to Omaha. He was pleased that we were all set up and said he could rest easy now. He gave me a big hug on the platform at Grand Central station and told me that I had to be a good girl for Mama and a good big sister for Freddie.

Freddie held onto his hand and didn't want him to go.

When the train blew out a big whistle he kissed Mama on the lips, real quick, and took his bag and walked off backwards, waving to us.

We were all sad that he wouldn't be with us now.

It was strange to walk back to our apartment without Daddy and get ready for bed and know that he was going to be sleeping on the train again tonight and that now and for all the rest of the days before us, he wouldn't be with us.

I thought Mama was a bit sad too but she said that we were going to be so busy with our new school and our lessons and getting used to our new life in the big city that there wouldn't be much time for missing Daddy.

That night I lay in my cot, which sagged in the middle and was tucked under the window in the corner and listened to all the sounds around me. I could hear a cat squealing, like somebody was strangling it, and I didn't like that noise at all. I heard horses go by pulling cabs, sometimes shouts coming from different men and a woman too.

Just before I fell asleep, I heard Carlos the Grouch come up the stairs and he stumbled and hit off the wall and started singing in a loud voice as he tried to find the key for his door. Mama sighed and turned over in her bed in annoyance.

Back home we didn't have to listen to people all around us up close like this. Back home, it was peaceful, except when Daddy came in late and sounded just like the illusionist did now, happy, making groaning noises, clearing his throat and being very, very drunk.

CHAPTER NINE

NEW YORK, OCTOBER 1905

Crack.

Tap.

Crack.

Tap.

One two three, one two three.

Sigh.

I am tired. So tired. *Crack*. I wish I were at home in my cot.

Freddie is still dancing. He never stops. Not for a moment. He doesn't even take breaks.

I like to take breaks all the time. Mama says I am the queen of breaks. But I think that she is always on a break, sitting and watching, doing her knitting. She is not standing, dancing, back and forth, up and down, like us.

The wedding cakes are very fine-looking. I was enormously happy when I saw them first. I thought, these will look so good on stage – we will be up high, we will be noticed!

But I am tired of the training now.

Crack.

Freddie is on the lower step and I am higher, we go up and down, back and forth, performing the 'Dreamland

Waltz', over and over, *one two three, tap, one two three, crack*. There are electric lights built into the cake – they look magnificent – and bells that we can tap with our feet.

Monsieur Alviene loves to use that big wedge of stick to keep time. I don't know where he got it from, it looks like the leg of a chair. He whacks it off the back of another wooden chair, one foot propped up on the rung.

Crack.

Freddie says it's easy to keep in time when Monsieur Alviene is tapping out the beat.

But it echoes in my dreams at night. Before I go to sleep, even when I waken in my cot, across from Freddie in the cold of the room where we all sleep. It makes my head ache. My legs ache too, my feet sometimes, from the tapping and dancing, the twisting and turning. I think they ache more than Freddie's who seems to have bones of lead in his toes. He must not feel the same crushing, burning as I do.

We are different, Freddie and me.

One day we measured and saw that our feet are different. I have a lower arch, his is much higher. That is how he can stand en pointe without the pain I have, even Mama said it.

Today we are rehearsing our new act, the Wedding Cake, our first one that will take us to the stage in a real, live show. The theatre where we will be performing is right down the pier at Pavilion Beach at Keyport and it is a big deal.

I am excited. It is what we have been working towards all this time. Monsieur Alviene thinks we are ready.

But I am tired. And Monsieur Alviene says we still need to practise.

Again! One more time!

The whole act was Monsieur Alviene's idea. The carpenters

built the wedding cakes for him – they look like steps made from wood, painted pink and white with tiny blue flowers, and icing. It looks like icing. But it could be snow. We come out the top, Freddie and me, a bride and groom.

I love the dress I wear for the act. It is flowy with ruffles and it is as though I am really getting married. I am like a princess.

Freddie is much smaller than me so Mama had a great idea of putting a big tall top hat on him and now we are more or less the same height.

Now, we look even.

We dance up and down the cake, the stairs are the layers. We tap out the beat of the song with our feet.

Freddie looks cute in his costume of tails.

We make a nice bride and groom, I think.

When our first dance is over, we have to go off and change into our second costumes. I am a glass of champagne, Freddie is a lobster. I laughed when I saw him first, but now we are just tired of the dancing up and down.

Mama is seated on a chair in front of us, watching.

She nods her head in time to the waltz and smiles when we are finished.

She likes it. It is a good act for us.

It has been worth it to come to New York.

And just when I think we are probably nearing finishing, Monsieur Alviene tells us that we will run over the whole thing once again and even the woman who plays the piano for us slumps forward.

When will we ever finish?

I think of the cookies that Mama might buy for us in Macy's on our way home.

I think that the Wedding Cake is a very fine act indeed,

but that we could come back tomorrow and start again, instead of staying on now.

Freddie is at the top of the cake, ready to tap, his foot pointed, hands behind his back.

Sigh.

Crack.

And off we go again.

We are so used to life in New York now that it's almost hard to remember what it was like back home in Nebraska. It is hard to think of the quiet, of the dusty roads, of the slow walking everywhere and people dropping by and hardly any big stairs anywhere.

We don't hear the whistle of the big trains coming in and out or the church bells ringing on Sunday. What we do hear are the sounds of everyone up close, cooking, banging doors, running feet and shouting. There's a lot of shouting.

Mama gives us lessons in arithmetic, geography, history and writing and reading. I like reading the most and I'm getting really good at it now. We joined the library so that we can take out books but it's a long walk so we don't go every week.

Freddie is learning his letters and he sticks his tongue out when he's writing them. I keep pushing it back with my pencil and he goes to hit me but Mama doesn't like that and so I try to do it when she's not looking or else we both might get a clout to the head.

We have dinner when we come home from our lessons in the dining hall downstairs.

On Saturday and Sundays we sometimes take the trolley car to the park and see the little boats on the lake. Sometimes we go to museums.

We might go to a matinee show too but, more usually, if we can afford it, Mama takes us to an evening show to see a play or a ballet or an opera or a vaudeville act we've heard is good.

Our seats are always up high, but even from up there we can study the different dancers and singers, what they are wearing and how they move. We get to know all the words and we practise what we hear when we are just joking about.

We especially like Adeline Genée, who is a ballerina, probably the finest in the whole of the world. We study her from our seats.

I suppose that I will be a famous dancer one day too. Mama thinks so.

I think it is probably a very nice job, even though there are the rehearsals and the long hours at the studio and costumes that are sometimes scratchy, but I still think it is probably a very nice job, compared to others.

Like the meat man, for instance. I watch him go by in his cart sometimes, a skinned animal on the back. I know that he will carve it up and there will be blood and I think dancing is a much nicer thing to do than have to cut meat, or sweep out the meat-packing house or clean out the slops, like I know that old woman has to do who attends to the back of our block.

In Omaha, when we lived there, our little town was full of meat houses and breweries. I hated the smell, the mix of blood and hops, all cooking and congealing and puffing into the air.

Sometimes I think of our little white house and Daddy all alone there. We always say our prayers to him at night, but I miss talking to him and I miss him kissing me goodnight with his big hugging arms. Mama doesn't give us hugs.

Mama said that Daddy always doted on me because I looked like him. I have dark hair and dark eyes, but Freddie has fair hair and blue eyes, like Mama.

I miss the tricks Daddy used to do with us, like taking off his thumb and putting it back on.

I miss his piano-playing, how he'd play after work and I would sit beside him on the stool. He showed me how to play it too and even though I play the piano sometimes at Monsieur Alviene's, I don't like to practise. Practice is tiresome and boring and there is so much of it, always.

We write letters to Daddy as part of our lessons, about everything we are learning and all the things we are seeing. He writes back and I read them out to Freddie because I am good at reading now. He writes separate letters to Mama, but she doesn't read those to us.

They are for her eyes only, she says.

I think Mama is happier in New York. Here, there are no fat rows, roaring back and forth. Sometimes I think, as I watch her sit in her chair in the evening, knitting and sighing, after all the work is done, that she is happy to be here, with just us, away from Daddy. Here, she doesn't have to worry about Daddy's drinking, because we can't see it and we don't have to know about his cheeks that will be shiny and red and glowing.

She doesn't have to say things like *Why can't you stay off it for one evening, one evening?*

And he doesn't have to say *This is my job* and she doesn't have to answer *Some job! I'm sure Mr. Storz thinks you're doing a FINE job drinking all his product!*

But Daddy is a very good salesman. He is funny and smiles a lot and the customers like that. He is so good at his job that one year the company gave him a special present at Christmas, a big basket with liquor in it and shortcake biscuits, all laid out in straw. Daddy brought it home, a big smile on his face, and we clapped our hands when we saw how nice it looked, but Mama didn't look too happy. She said we had enough bottles in the house. Daddy got mad and they had a fight then and he told her that nothing he did was ever good enough for her and he went off with the basket and slammed the door and we knew he was going to get out the whiskey bottle, and sit in his favourite chair, pouring slugs of it out into a glass, drinking them one after another, until he was drunk.

I didn't like Daddy being drunk. It wasn't that I minded him, it was more that Mama got very mad. I hated to see her so upset and have all that badness in the air in our house.

I wish Mama accepted Daddy's drinking just a bit more. He is happy when he is drinking. She says he is just like her father and that liquor killed her father in the end.

I don't want Daddy to die.

On the nights and days after Daddy had been drinking a lot, he would stay in his bed and Mama would cook just for us. You knew she was mad when she laid out the dinner, only three plates, one for her, one for Freddie and one for me. None for Daddy. When she was stopped being mad at him, she'd lay out the fourth plate. I always watched to see how many plates there would be at dinner.

Now, Mama doesn't get mad at Daddy but sometimes she gets mad at us. If we are being very noisy, and jumping around and not being quiet, Mama gets really mad and shouts, 'That's it!' and she leaves and slams the door.

Freddie laughs but I don't think it's funny. What if she doesn't come back?

What if she is hit by a cab and no one comes to get us up here?

I go to the window and I look out and I am quiet then, watching, waiting for her to come back.

Sometimes it is quick, sometimes it is a while. If it's in the winter, the tip of her nose will be red from the cold. If it's in the summer, she'll come back, sweaty from walking.

She is usually sorry after that, even giving us a quick hug when we are getting ready for bed.

I think that she probably can't help it, that we are annoying her, all stuck together in that little room.

But we can't help it either really.

And so we all get on, going to bed and sleeping then, thinking of Daddy all the way at home in Omaha and of our next day rehearsals as we near our first official performance of the Wedding Cake act at the end of the pier in New Jersey.

Everyone says it's going to be great.

CHAPTER TEN

OMAHA, NEBRASKA, JULY 1973

OUTSIDE A DOG BARKED. HE WAS A MUTT, a collie mixed with a German Shepherd, she thought. She didn't want to get out of the car.

She wondered should she honk the horn, alert Liz-Beth to her arrival.

The last thing she wanted to do was cross the threshold into the jaws of the woman's protector.

She waited, staring at the house, and saw a flicker of the blind at the window and then the front door open.

A small, dark-haired woman came out and put her hand on the dog's head, letting her fingers move to its snout.

It stopped barking.

Ellie got out and made her way to the porch, cautious.

"Don't mind him," said the woman, smiling. "Bark worse than his bite." She held out her hand. "Liz-Beth."

Ellie shook her hand and smiled.

"I'm a bit afraid of dogs."

"Oh, he looks fierce, but really he's a baby, aren't you?" she said, and she bent down and put her face in the dog's. He greeted her with long flashes of his tongue all over her face.

Liz-Beth invited Ellie into her home, which was a neat,

carpeted abode, the kitchen set into the same living space where Liz-Beth watched TV and did her ironing by the looks of it. The smell of hot fabric hung in the air and a pile of folded coloured dresses and tops were half toppled on the settee.

"So you're writing a story about the Astaires?"

"I am."

"Well, isn't that something!"

"Yes," Ellie said.

"Well, I don't know a lot, but I do know about Storz. Fritz was friends with my daddy, see? Oh, great pals. I remember him being over a lot. Not so much in later years, mind. I'm younger than Adele and Fred though, so I never really knew them. Just their daddy. So, what would you like to know? I got down the boxes of stuff, Daddy's pride and joy. He'd be so happy to know someone wanted to take a look. Always said this crap would end up in a museum. I dunno, who'd be interested in all these old letters and stuff, huh?"

Liz-Beth sat down on the settee, behind two cardboard boxes, which were displayed on the small brown coffee table.

Ellie sat down beside her.

They each put their hands on a box and opened the lid.

The smell of must filled Ellie's nose and she felt her heartbeat rise.

Another treasure trove.

Inside were papers, pictures, beer mats, invoices, labels and, proudly, Liz-Beth produced an actual bottle of beer.

"Don't know why he put this in here – I mean, if it burst open everything be ruined, but here you go. I wouldn't sample it if I were you. Poison you now it would, it's so out of date!"

Ellie turned the brown bottle over in her hands. The

label was a fawn colour and it said *Mugs Pale Ale*.

"That's named after a dog," said Liz-Beth. "A spaniel. Can't remember whose spaniel, but someone's!"

She laughed, showing uneven teeth, yellowed with age.

"Wow," said Ellie. "This is really something."

"Sad now that it's gone," said Liz-Beth. "Such a big employer in its day. So many families reared on Storz, you know. It wasn't just the brewing and all those workers, it was all the off-shoot businesses. My mama had a cleaning job in there, that's how she met my father. All the little cafés and businesses that supplied into them. Some of my aunts worked in the offices too. A great place it was in its day."

"What can you tell me about Fritz?" asked Ellie, putting the bottle down and leafing through some of the papers in her hands.

"Let me see, there might be a photo here," said Liz-Beth and she delved deeper into the box in front of her.

"Well, he was a nice man. Nice-looking, had a nice moustache. He was different to my daddy. Had a cane. I don't think he needed a cane but he carried it just the same. He looked smart, you know?"

Ellie nodded.

"He was Austrian too, you see. Like my daddy. Probably why they hit it off. It was mostly Germans around here then, but they had that connection. Probably could talk about home. Fritz was very musical. Wanted to be a musician – he was a musician, I think, but it didn't pay. And so he ended up at Storz. Ah!"

She took out a small black-and-white photo of two couples.

"There's my daddy and mama. And that's Fritz and Johanna."

Ellie took the photo and peered to where Liz-Beth's finger had been pointing.

"Oh my," she said.

Four smiling faces looked back, pale in the black-and-white photograph.

Johanna was the more glamorous of the two women, her hair wound up neatly, her waist pinched, her lips full.

"Married very young, they did. I think Johanna was in the family way. Not that I was ever told that, mind, but why else would you get married at fifteen, huh?"

"Fifteen?"

"Oh yes, not that unusual then."

Ellie tried to do some math in her head. Was the baby Adele?

"Do you know when this was taken?" asked Ellie.

"Well, it was before my time. I'm not sure. I know Johanna went away with the kids when they were very young so maybe before they went? Or on a trip home? They did come home sometimes, I think, when they were younger."

In Ellie's hands she held a small card. It said: *The finest beer you ever tasted. Just like the beer they made in the 'old country' ... so smooth ... mellow ... refreshing.*

"That would have been a calling card. For the salesmen. Dropped them in everywhere they went. Sampled the stuff everywhere they went too, if they were anything like my daddy." She laughed.

"Was he a drinker?"

"They all were. Came with the territory. Everyone drank beer back then – it was the way. Nothing thought of it until the prohibitionists started with their moaning." Liz-Beth grimaced in disgust. "Do-gooder good-for-nothin's. That was the start of the end. It was never the same after that."

They sat in silence for a minute, Ellie scanning the documents as fast as she could.

"Would you like a cup of tea? I have lemon. Or a beer? Seeing as we're talking beer!"

Ellie smiled. "Lemon tea would be lovely. Do you mind if I take a look through these boxes? Properly? I'd love to have a read of everything."

"Sure. Take your time, honey. I've some housework to be getting on with. You get comfy. And if you want to wash your hands, that stuff is so dusty, bathroom's down there on the left."

"Thank you," said Ellie. "I really do appreciate it."

"Not a worry," said Liz-Beth. "Daddy'd be delighted to know someone was finally interested in all this junk."

CHAPTER ELEVEN

NEW YORK, OCTOBER 1905

FREDDIE AND I GOT OUR PICTURES DONE. Monsieur Alviene said it would be a good idea for the Wedding Cake act and it took an age while the man behind the camera told us to hold still and smile. We stood beside a plant with spiky green leaves. Mama said we looked very fine in the photographs when we collected them in a big white envelope a week later.

Even though it was tiresome, I quite liked having our portrait done. It was funny seeing myself and Freddie all dressed up and how we looked. It was different to looking in the mirror. And you could hold the picture in your hand.

I thought of Daddy, how he used to take people's portraits too. Times were bad when he first came to Nebraska. The portrait job he came out for disappeared with the crash of '89. It was a bad time for business and everyone lost loads of money somehow. He had to find a job just to pay the rent and he took up in a saloon as a cook. That must have been how he learned all about liquors and cigars, and that is the job he does now, going round the state, selling. He says it's one of the finest jobs in the whole state and it probably is. Though I'm not sure if Mama thinks so.

Mama has been working on a new name for us.

Austerlitz sounded too German, she said. It had no 'star quality'.

She thought the 'Austers' might work. And we tried it out, Adele and Fred Auster.

I liked it. But Mama said it wasn't right.

Next she tried 'Astiers'.

I liked that too. But still she said it wasn't right.

One day, she tried 'Astaire'.

Fred and Adele Astaire.

"I like it," Mama said. "I really like it."

We were having our French lessons and I thought it sounded chic. Like the French word for a star, even though I know that's 'etoile'.

Mama liked it so much she changed her name too. She was not to be called Johanna Austerlitz anymore – from now on she was the shorter, better, Ann Astaire.

We made a great trio, Mama, Freddie and me. We were happy going to school to learn to sing, dance and act, taking our lessons in the morning with Mama, to keep up with our schooling. Back in Omaha we couldn't have gone to the theatres to watch the big acts, to see what we could learn for our act too.

One of the newspapers printed our new picture, ahead of our performance on the pier.

It said: **Brother and Sister Duo Set to Debut in Wedding Cake Act**

Mama cut out the article and pasted it in a big scrapbook she bought. She dated it and wrote about it in her diary, about our progress. She had a big diary though, not like the small pocket one Daddy gave me from Storz Brewing Company.

Because she had a lot to write about, she said.

The day came for our first performance. We had practised and practised and performed in front of the other students at school a few times, but this was the first time we would be getting paid to do it and we wouldn't know anybody in the audience at all.

Mama was nervous. Fred and I were not. What was there to be worried about? We knew every step. Every word. All we had to do was think of Monsieur Alviene cracking that stick off the chair and we would be in time.

We arrived at the theatre at Keyport at eight thirty in the morning but there wasn't one person there. We had to sit and wait outside on the bench and Freddie and I went down to the sand and scratched around and found pennies and quarters.

"Look, Delly!" Freddie said, holding up a quarter.

That was so much fun, digging in the sand, like pirates searching out treasure. We could have stayed there all day.

But after a while Mama called that the theatre was open now and we could go in and see about getting our act all set up.

Oh, those stagehands were not happy with our set. Not at all. It took an age to get it all in place, to get the lights working. They'd never seen such a contraption, they said, and then Freddie and I had to organise our costumes and run over the number. The other acts were arriving, and they were a bit put out, making faces and saying it wasn't fair that we got all the rehearsal time.

Mama told us it was OK. But we felt bad for everyone else.

Because our set was so big, they put us first on the bill.

Mama and Monsieur Alviene were not happy with this. It was the worst place to be, Mama said.

I didn't really mind. We would still be getting to dance, to wear our lovely costumes for everyone to see.

The matinee opened at three o'clock and there were no queues or anything outside.

Actually it was very quiet.

When we got up on stage, I could see why Mama said it was the worst place on the bill.

There was hardly anybody in the audience at all. People were still coming in when we started and they weren't paying attention while they sat down.

We went through our whole act, doing our steps, going up and down that wedding cake, just like we were supposed to.

When the music came to an end, a few people clapped, but it wasn't that loud.

I didn't think it had gone too well.

When we came off Monsieur Alviene said we did a fine job, all considering. He told Mama we needed more training.

"They have it," he said, "but they need more training."

He suggested ballet and the Metropolitan Opera.

When we left the theatre, walking up the pier with Mama I asked her if she was sorry it hadn't gone so good.

"Did we let you down, Mama?"

"No, Adele," said Mama. "You most certainly did not let me down."

I hated to think I'd let Mama or Monsieur Alviene

down. It gave me a really bad feeling in my stomach.

I looked out at the pier and the water and thought how it would be so much nicer if we could just go down to the beach and play again for a while and maybe we could find more quarters and pennies and give them to Mama to help pay for things because living in New York was expensive with three mouths to feed. That would cheer her up, I was sure.

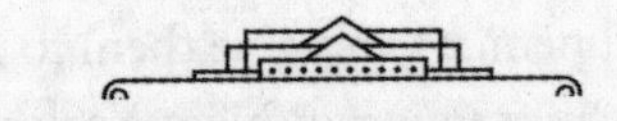

INTERVIEW WITH NED WAYBURN SCHOOL OF DANCE, NEW YORK

Research on: **The Evolution of Dance in Modern Theatre, A History, *by Larry Coleman***
Archive Located: New York Public Library of Performing Arts
Status: Unpublished

Gee, Ann Astaire was a looker. I remember her coming in with Adele and Frederick and, well, she caught my eye, I can tell ya that. I was in the middle of demonstrating a buck step and I stopped and looked at this lady, because she WAS a lady. She just came in and sat down and watched us.

When she spoke, I remembered – it was her husband Fritz who had written to me. He asked would I take a look at his daughter and son who were graduating from Monsieur Alviene's dance school and had an act all ready to go.

I'm a sucker for a kids' act. I just love that innocence, all that energy, real potential, and fun!

Alviene is a real good guy, a real teach-them-the-basics, you know. A good start. But they'd done the course with him. Done a few tours. Now they were ready for the next step up. They were ready ... for me.

I took them through a few steps. Freddie was really great, light on his feet, very slight, but very charming. I thought he could go far, with the right training, with the right encouragement. He was shy, you see, very shy.

Adele now, well, she was a real sparkly little lady. No shyness there – you could see she was well used to being in front of people, being 'on'. She liked to tell her brother what to do.

She was a good dancer. She had grace and the steps were no problem to her. I liked her. I liked them both.

Ann spoke to me, asked me what I thought. Well, there was no other answer but yes.

This pair would suit the Ned Wayburn School of Dance, absolutely.

That was our motto, you see: health, beauty, fame, popularity, independence. Hell, they had it all. They would fit right in.

I told them from the start – "It's all about personality. If you got no personality on stage, then you got nothin' – no charisma, no nothin'."

They had it in buckets though – with Freddie you had to tease it out of him a bit, but with Adele all you had to do was give her the stage.

I encouraged that – I told them, "Kids, if you want to leave an impression, bring your personality up to that stage and leave it behind. Never let the audience forget who you are. Be true to yourself. It's OK to be shy, like Freddie, it's endearing. It's who he is. But he's smart, let them know that too. Don't get pushed around on stage, Freddie, talk back to your sister."

Adele was like a smart clown. Funny, clever. She could deliver a joke in that high-pitched voice of hers and she'd make such a face, such an earnest face the whole theatre would be laughing.

I told them not to forget their arms. To work on their arms. You can learn all the steps you want, but if you don't learn to use your hands and arms, to express what the dance is all about, to put across the feeling, well then, you ain't a real dancer at all.

They were quick to learn, those kids.

I was pleased to see them off on their first tour. It would be good for them, start building the stamina in them, the strength they'd need if they really wanted to be a success in this business.

Because it's hard graft on the road. There's no break, no time for sickness, it's where you learn your trade. Up, out, smile, dance.

They knew if they did well, there'd be another tour next year and the year after that.

They were lucky to have their mom to look after them. She was a great mom, very caring, always there to tend to their every need. She was one of the most unlikely stage moms I'd ever seen, not too pushy but, wow, what a looker!

She could have been a star too had she been a dancer herself.

But she put everything into those kids, all her time, all her learning, all her love.

Those kids were born to be on the stage.

Anyone could see that.

CHAPTER TWELVE

OMAHA, NEBRASKA, DECEMBER 1908

SHE IS PURE WHITE WITH FEATHERY FUR and eyes like dark chocolates. She follows my hand in the window, yapping.

"Can we go in and see her, Daddy?"

Daddy shrugs. He is letting us do what we want now that we are home. Now that we are here for just two days.

Inside Sak's Cigar Store, the smell of seed and hops, the same smell as in the beer factory, hits our noses. Budgies twerp in their cages. On the counter, orange fish swim round and round in glass bowls, flitting between green plants that grow in water.

We go to the window which has a wooden fence against it, to keep the puppies in. Sawdust flies up in the air as the animals start jumping when we approach.

The white dog goes crazy when she sees us, yapping, trying to get to us and I lean over and pet her.

The owner of the shop comes over. He's called Mr. Moller and I remember him because I used to be in school with his son, who used to tease me and pull my hair.

He speaks in German to my father, greeting him, and then he turns to me and says, "Our little stars return."

I shrug shyly. I don't feel that shy, but it is nice to seem so.

Freddie stands back, watching, his hands in his pockets.

"She's nice, *ja*," Mr. Moller says and he bends over and lifts the puppy from her pen, handing her to me, sawdust falling from her paws, the smell of her little velvety belly filling my nose.

I rub her head and cuddle her to my face. She licks my nose and I laugh.

He asks if I am all ready for tonight and I say I am.

Mr. Moller says he and the whole family are going and his son, Ernst, is especially looking forward to seeing me.

I shrug shyly again and smile.

"The whole town is going," he says. "Very exciting. *Du wirst fantastisch sein!*"

"Look, Freddie," I say, holding up the puppy. "Isn't she sweet? Have you ever seen such a sweetheart?"

Freddie is not behind us anymore – he is over at a little cage and I walk over to show him the dog and I see that he is poking his finger in at a little white mouse, tucked into a wooden box.

"I'd love a pet mouse," he says, kind of under his breath, his eyes following the snow fur as it moves from his poking finger, the pink eyes bright.

"Yuck," I say. "Mice are just vermin."

"They are not!"

"Are too."

I turn back to the dog and hug her once more and I put her back in the pen beside Mr. Moller and Daddy who are still deep in conversation.

We leave the shop and continue up the town, stopping at the bakery to buy pastries to bring home to Mama who is resting, but more likely going through drawers, ready to point out to Daddy how badly he is keeping the house.

"At least I could keep a mouse in my pocket – where would you keep a dog?" Freddie says.

"In a basket," I say knowingly. "Or in a bag – haven't you seen those ladies in New York who carry their puppies in their bags?"

Freddie scoffs and shakes his head.

He thinks I am stupid.

But I'm older than him and more worldy. I'm way ahead and I think differently. Who'd want a dirty old mouse running round the train with us on tour?

"I would step on it," I tell him. "When you weren't looking."

"You would not."

"I would too."

And he knows that, indeed, I would.

After our first performance in Keyport, Monsieur Alviene booked us tour dates in New Jersey and Pennsylvania. We continued like this for the next two years, taking our lessons, touring, performing anywhere we thought we could learn something or earn a decent wage. We got used to performing in front of crowds.

When Mama and Daddy realised we had come as far as we could with Monsieur Alviene, they started looking for a new school for us. Daddy had been coming to New York as regularly as he could and between him and Mama they had some good contacts in the theatre now. Mama read *Variety* and *Vanity Fair* and all of the newspapers that reported on Broadway. She read them quick, because she needed to post them on to Daddy.

They wrote letters back and forth about which new school would be best for us, who the teachers were that would suit us and what we needed to be learning now that Monsieur Alviene had taken us so far.

Daddy wrote letters to his contacts and someone wrote back to tell him about Mr. Ned Wayburn.

When I saw Mr. Ned Wayburn first, I thought, how can this man teach us to dance? Because he was a big hulk of a man. He had wide shoulders and long legs and meaty weight all around his behind and stomach.

On the first day, he took our hands to show us the steps and my hand felt real small in his, curled up. I watched him move and realised that he danced light as a feather. His weight meant nothing at all.

I could follow the steps alright. They were tricky, but he had a real easy way of showing you, he made it simple. We saw him on the first day, but after that we had other teachers. Mr. Wayburn was in charge, he oversaw everything, but he wasn't there to teach us every day.

He was a real important man.

Fred's new favourite step was the buck-and-wing step, all dipping and elbows out. That was fun, he said, it felt like real fun. And it suited him – a joy came on his face when he danced like that.

It felt like we were going places now that we were enrolled with Mr. Ned Wayburn's School of Dance. We were more experienced, and we understood what touring and performing was like.

With all Daddy's letters back and forth he managed to secure us an agent too, Mr. Frank Vincent on the Orpheum Circuit. He offered us $150 a week and our train fares to book a twenty-week tour.

Mama was very excited. Daddy too. I think Daddy even more so. Right at the end of the tour we'd be landing in

Omaha, our hometown. This was a big deal for Daddy, his kids coming home, stars from New York.

We packed up a big trunk to go on tour. We put our costumes in it and all our normal clothes and our books too because Mama said we still needed to learn, even when we were on the road. The wedding cake set was packed up into trunks too and it went as part of the tour, on a train, with us.

It was exciting to get out of New York. I felt like we were going on an adventure again. It was fun to see where we were staying each night, to check out the little guesthouses where we were booked.

Mama organised all of it with Mr. Vincent, our agent.

We travelled with other acts and sometimes we joined native acts in a hometown too. There might be a girl who was a good singer, or a boy who could do magic, and sometimes dogs even came on stage to do tricks.

Cha Cha.

Cha Cha.

Cha Cha.

The sound is there in the daytime when we're awake, playing cards, or drawing or scribbling in our notebooks and it's there when we fall asleep on Mama's shoulder or curled into the window.

Cha Cha. Cha Cha.

The sound echoes through our bodies. When we get off the train to go check into our boarding house, then straight to the theatre for the show we're doing that night, I feel it is still in my body.

Cha Cha, Cha Cha, Cha Cha.

It is so strong that I think we've started dancing it on stage. It's like there's a new rhythm to our dance. Our *tap-tap* is right in rhythm with the train we just got off.

When we're on board I watch Freddie and see that his fingers are always tapping to the beat of train. *Tap-tap. Tap-tap. Tap-tap.* He drums them on the table, so loud sometimes I roar at him to shut the hell up.

And his foot goes too. Usually to a different beat. While his hands are tapping his feet are doing something else, like a double tap, in time.

It's a syncopated rhythm.

Mr. Wayburn taught us that.

And it drives me absolutely nuts.

Sometimes the guesthouses are not that nice and smell damp and are cold. Mama always grumbles when that happens, but usually we are so tired we don't even notice.

Sitting on a train, getting to a new theatre and doing our performances makes us very sleepy.

Mr. Vincent has squashed in a lot of dates and venues. We play lots of different halls. Usually it's a town hall, but sometimes it's a larger theatre in town. We like the larger theatres because they are able to handle our set and have people there that can help, but sometimes it's hard to fill all the seats. The town halls can be more fun, but they don't feel the same as the theatres. They don't have proper lights or somewhere nice that we can go before we start to get changed.

We used all our stage tricks on this tour. Some of the crowds were so big we had to raise our voices real loud to be heard. To do that, you had to use a special part of your throat, the bit that sits just under your mouth, to throw your voice up and over, but you're not shouting.

It's called projection.

We used our clown and comedian tricks. You could do all your steps to the music but what the audience loved most of all was if you had a joke with them. Throwing your eyes up towards the ceiling was a good one if somebody did something silly. Giving someone a look if they made a noise or walked by the stage to go to the bathroom was another favourite.

We worked on the Wedding Cake act so that it was as perfect as could be and we became so confident with it that we could get up any place and do it, without even thinking.

The audience laughed. They smiled at how cute we were. They gave us rounds and rounds of applause and if we were on later in the bill, they would stand up and clap too. That was called a standing ovation.

I'd been learning a lot from the other entertainers that we came across in the theatres.

The biggest thing was that you needed to look the audience in the eye, don't take no crap. I learned that word backstage. Crap means shit. I learned that too.

Sometimes I say it in my head when I'm on the wedding cake, in my fine, ruffly dress.

No crap. No shit.

I say it to the beat.

No crap, no shit, no crap, no shit.

It makes me giggle. Freddie has no idea what's going on in my head and he'd be horrified because he's such a gentle boy. He doesn't use any cuss words.

But I like the sound of those cuss words. They're powerful. They make me feel like I know what I'm doing, because I do know what I'm doing.

And when I say those words in my head, I stand up taller and I look out to the audience, especially if they're chatting and talking and not watching and I think, *Hey, you guys, I'm not taking any of this crap, you watch us and you watch us good.*

I wouldn't mind wearing some make-up. All the older girl entertainers do their make-up before they go on stage. They powder their faces with white stuff and it makes them look porcelain and then they use a pencil and draw in their eyebrows real dark. Some wear lipstick, painting it on with a little brush and I think they look just fine. I'd like to wear make-up too but Mama says no, that I'm too young and I'd only end up looking like a lady of the night, whatever that is.

I said, "What is a lady of the night?" but she said, "Never you mind."

Mama doesn't let us hang around for too long backstage. When we rehearse she sits and watches and comes and gets us straight after. And after the show, when we're feeling full of energy after the applause and enjoying the atmosphere that comes alive as other performers get ready to go on and glowing, beaming acts come off, she is there to get us too.

Mama says it's not good for children to hang around theatres too long and maybe she is right. She always talks about how we need to know how the world works, that the theatre is a very special world and not the 'normal' world where other folk live. She says we need to be children.

If she heard me say the word 'crap', she'd spank my ass.

And she probably wouldn't like the word 'ass' either.

But 'bottom' is very posh, don't you think?

At the end of our tour, we reach Omaha, just before Christmas. We've been on tour since July. It is nice to be home.

Our show is a sell-out. All evening carts and buggies pull up outside the Creighton Theatre on South 16th Street.

For the first time in a long time, butterflies flit round my tummy.

There's something about playing to our home crowd, to an audience where everyone knows us, or at least know of us.

Mama and Daddy are given front-row seats, the best in the house, in the middle.

"Just enjoy it," says Mama backstage when we are getting ready to go out.

We have done this act so many times. Up and down the wedding cake, *tap, tap, tap*, ringing the bells with our feet.

Freddie dancing, me joining in, waltzing.

I don't know if it means as much to Freddie as it does to me – he was so young when we left Omaha, only five. I'm not sure if he realises what a big night this is.

Still, he puts on some show, and so do I – we are the top of the bill and we bring the house down. The curtain closes but they have to raise it twice more the applause is so great and the cheers so loud.

We bow over and over again and I laugh and giggle and then, over the footlights, I see a basket of flowers. It is handed all the way up from the middle of the audience – it appears to be floating above the heads.

I take it, it feels heavy and when I look in there inside the basket is the white Pomeranian puppy, excited, jumping, her little paws scraping against the bunches of petals and the wicker.

"Oh!" I say. "Oh my!"

I drop the basket and scoop her out and I say "*Thank you so much, thank you so much!*"

Mr. Moller stands up tall in the audience. People turn to look at him and he takes a little bow himself and sweeps his hand up to the stage and blows us kisses. I see Ernst beside him. He is taller now and he stares at me, a funny smile on his face, and I make sure to catch his eye so that he knows I remember him and that I am thankful for what his father has done.

We are the stars that night.

All eyes are on us.

As the curtain falls for the last time, I see Freddie grasp the basket and look into the bottom of it, searching.

He looks back at me and the puppy and says nothing.

I know he is looking to see if Mr. Moller included the mouse.

His head dips and I feel sorry for him.

CHAPTER THIRTEEN

OMAHA, NEBRASKA, JULY 1973

ELLIE DROVE BY A LARGE REDBRICK BUILDING and slowed.

She recognised the shape of it from the photos she'd just seen at Liz-Beth's. Storz Brewing Company.

A long modern building sat attached to the older, more classical structure, ugly compared to the crafted brickwork and inlaid windows of the original factory. Rows of square-cut chimneys turreted the top of the building, and a tall, round-tower chimney could be seen behind, far back from the street.

The windows along the bottom had been boarded up with wood. The higher, harder-to-reach windows were spotted black, cracks leading from the pebble-shaped holes in the glass.

She thought of the photos she had just seen of an era gone by: delivery carts and horses lined up on the street, boys in caps and men too, standing, smoking, staring. Other photos with smiling, moustached men leaning against crates and boxes of different brews: Pale Ale, Triumph, Gold Crest, Pilsner.

She brought the car to a halt, pulling into a wide parking space near what looked to be an entrance to the factory.

There were no other cars on the street. Weeds sprang along the footpath, dotted along the wall.

She got out of the car and let her hand trail the brickwork. It felt rough and sharp. At the door, the entrance had been completely boarded over with a metal plate. Somebody had spray-painted the words '*boyz*' and an illegible squiggle.

The factory had only been closed since last year, but it looked as though it had been closed down for decades. She imagined the inside of it, all the machinery dismantled, the tiled floors dusty, birds nesting in the roof. The hum of the vats, the crush of grain on metal, voices on the production line, ringing out, all now ghosts of the past. She sighed in her nostalgia.

She didn't even drink beer. She barely drank at all. Sometimes, when dining with friends she'd have the odd glass of Californian white if it was offered. But she didn't like the mist that came to her head when she drank, as though everything had a veil over it. She'd never even had a hangover and looking at how Kirk often was when he woke up, she had no desire ever to acquire one. Kirk could drink anyone under the table. He loved his shorts, whiskey shooters, brandy sometimes, anything with a bite to it, that gave him a kick. He, of course, thought she was a bore because of it. He called her Sensible Sally, which was endearing at first, but lately he'd been saying it with a bit more menace. As though it really bothered him now.

She spotted a telephone box at the end of the street and walked to it while rooting in her handbag. She put two quarters into the slot.

The phone answered after two short rings.

"Hi, honey," she said.

"Hi!"

"How's everything?"

"Good, good. Great. How are you? How's it all going?"

"Oh, so good. You won't believe the stuff I've come across. I met Lola Chambers. I was worried she was going to be a bit of a battleaxe, you know, because of the way she was when I called, but she was so lovely – she's a tough nut to crack, but once you get in there, wow! She gave me this file, it was her father's and it literally has everything in it, all these cuttings, all these photos from the newspaper, it's going to take me ages to go through –"

"That's nice, honey."

"Yeah, it's amazing. I just can't believe she had it all this time, you know, sitting there, gathering dust. And *then* I went to a diner and got talking to this waitress and she sent me to her cousin and just like that, again, big boxes of stuff, all about the brewery – you know, where Fritz worked, that's their father – I'm right outside it now actually. I couldn't take that with me though so I had to –"

"Eh, honey?"

"Yeah?"

"Someone's at the door."

"Oh."

"I gotta go."

"Oh, OK ..."

"Call me later. Actually, I'm out later. Call me tomorrow, OK?"

"OK."

"Bye! Love you!"

"Love you ..."

She wanted to say 'too' but the line was already cut off.

She stepped out of the phone box, folded her arms and decided to walk the block around the factory. Her stomach felt strange, an uneasiness settled there – something about the tone of Kirk's voice.

He was too breezy. Surprised that she had rung.

Maybe this trip was a bad idea.

But he had encouraged it, after everything that had happened. Said it would do her good.

Stretching her legs would help. Bring her back to the project at hand. She needed to relax and not think the worst of everything, which was a bad habit of hers. Inherited from her mother.

When she got back to the car, she'd look up the map and find the best way through the streets to the guesthouse she'd booked. She could take a nap there maybe. Rest her head. And her mind.

Most of all, she needed to rest her mind.

CHAPTER FOURTEEN

SAN FRANCISCO, FEBRUARY 1909

OUR TOUR IS SO SUCCESSFUL WE ARE BOOKED for another twenty weeks in the New Year. Mr. Wayburn makes some changes. He takes away the awkward wedding cakes and puts some new dances together for us.

Freddie has some good ideas and Mr. Wayburn listens.

I do what they say, I don't much care for making up dances. I'm happy to be shown what to do and, once they decide on the steps, I learn them, remember them and perform them, in rehearsals, on stage, ready for our shows.

I feel like a seasoned performer now.

It was lovely to see Daddy at Christmas. We didn't have a house girl anymore, now that it was just Daddy at home. But Mama said the house was very neat and you'd think there'd been a woman around all the time. She said it with her hand on her hip.

There were new curtains up. And a new blanket stretched over the bed.

"Where'd you get this?" I heard Mama say when she was unpacking her case.

"Oh that? The store."

"Which store?"

"Eh ... jeez, I can't remember now? Schmidt's?"

"It's a very pretty design. Not something I'd have thought you'd pick out. Why did you need a new blanket anyway? We left plenty."

"Jeez, woman, it's a blanket. No need for the Spanish Inquisition!"

Mama went quiet then.

It was strange to stay at home for a night after all our time away. I wished we had longer, time to rest, to get out onto the street to see who was still hanging around.

All too soon it was time to head back east, for the rehearsals Mr. Wayburn had arranged ahead of our new tour. We were looking forward to next year, because we knew now what kind of touring we'd be doing and we had a guaranteed income which was a great relief for Mama and Daddy.

We decided we would leave the puppy with Daddy for the moment as being on tour meant it would be too difficult to care for her properly. I called her Trixie. And I cried when I had to leave her.

Freddie was worried about the new dance routine and how we'd get some of the trickier steps right, night after night on stage.

"Stop moaning," I said to him one afternoon during rehearsals. "You're such a Moaning Minnie!"

But Freddie was always worried. It's what he did best.

Worry, worry, worry.

Me? I don't care a jot. If I forget the steps l hop over them, turn to the audience and smile. That always works. And how would they know if we missed a step or two anyways?

"Can you see?"

Freddie is peeking through a tiny slit in the curtains.

He shrugs.

"Let me look," I say and I push him by the shoulder to move.

My eyes scan the audience.

A lot of women up front. It wouldn't be a woman.

I move to get a better view, heads appearing as I peer deeper through the crack.

"I can't see," I say and I turn back to Freddie.

The man in charge of the theatre comes up and stands behinds us. He gestures for us to follow him.

He takes us backstage, where Mama is standing.

They are discussing whether or not we should go on.

"Are you sure?" Mama asks the theatre manager. "You could be mistaken."

"They've done three theatres this week, ma'am. Our staff are sure. It's him."

My stomach leaps.

"What should we do, Mama?"

Mama sighs. "Go on," she says firmly. "You will not let all these people down who have come to see you."

"But ..." I say.

"We will deal with it."

On stage, I find it hard to concentrate on our routine, as my eyes scan the audience again, looking for him, for them.

Gerrymen.

I spot one man who stares at us curiously, stroking his beard lightly. His face looks different to the rest. Everyone else is watching us with smiles on their faces, he instead is looking at us like you might an animal in the zoo.

"I think I see him," I whisper to Freddie, but he doesn't miss a beat and keeps on dancing.

Christ.

We come off after our act and go to get changed quickly. We are hoping to escape out the side door, before he can come backstage, but it is too late.

There, standing in front of the room we are to get changed in is the man with the beard, looking very solemn. I knew it! God in damn it, carnation.

"Hello there," he says. "You were very good in your performance."

"Thank you," I say quietly.

Freddie stands beside me, breathing deeply after our routine.

"Is there someone who looks after you, a manager? Your mama or papa?"

"My mama is here," I say.

"Let's wait for her," he says, and he opens the door of the dressing room so that we can go ahead and get changed.

Inside Freddie and I remove our dance costumes and change back into our regular clothes.

"What does he want, Delly?" asks Freddie.

"Probably to shut us down," I say.

"Oh no!"

We are silent, listening, waiting to see what was going to happen next.

As I tie up my boots, I hear it happening.

Mama has arrived.

"Mrs. Astaire," says the man outside. He introduces himself and I hear the words "San Francisco Society" and "Prevention of Cruelty to Children".

I go up to the door and stand real close, trying to hear better.

Mama's voice is raised. She is angry.

"Nothing of the sort!" she says.

The man talks over her.

"Improper treatment … neglect … lawful protection …"

The door opens and I almost fall as it moves. I stumble and right myself, embarrassed to be caught eavesdropping.

"Children, get your things," says Mama.

"We're ready, Mama," I say.

She takes Freddie by the arm and pushes me out and we walk down the corridor, the man following us.

"Mrs. Astaire, this is serious," says the man in a loud voice. "Your bookings will be cancelled. And you will be fined!"

Mama pokes me in the back to move faster.

"*A disgrace*," the man says now, loudly. "Exploiting your own children like this! A disgrace!"

Outside the light makes our eyes water. It always happens when you come out of a matinee show.

We race down the street, Mama in silence, her face like thunder.

I don't ask what this all means, because I think I know.

This is not good.

Our twenty-week tour is cancelled.

Mama writes letters to newspapers to plead our case. She writes out the words carefully and uses carbon paper to copy two at a time. I read one of them and see she says very nice things about us, about our talent, our training, our love for the stage. She says we have worked hard for these opportunities to perform. She writes that while the Gerrymen's intentions may be good, they have no idea what sort of life she provides for her children.

I love, care for and adore my children. They are never happier than when they are on the stage. As a schoolteacher myself I see to it that their education does not suffer and if you question my children you will find that they can speak and write superb French due to my extra tuition. My children fail when they are not on stage, they live for it. Please, I implore you, do not ban my children from performing.

But our bookings remain cancelled. The money we were relying on is gone.

Mama goes quiet.

"Why are they doing this, Mama?" I ask one day, when I see her slumped over the kitchen table, like a woman broken.

"I don't know," she murmurs into her arm. "They think they are doing good, I suppose. If only they knew."

The newspapers carry lots of coverage of the Gerrymen's campaign. They started with the children who worked down the mines, in factories, slaving day in, day out. And when they finished with those, they turned to us, the stage children, working our hours in rehearsals and on stage.

Exploited.

But I don't think dancing and singing, and getting paid to do it, is the same as cutting rock in a mine. I don't feel sad when I am performing, when the audience is clapping and laughing and I am taking my bows.

I think the Gerrymen have it wrong.

Mama doesn't relent. She continues with her campaign, writing every day, even meeting with some newspaper men to tell of our plight.

It feels very strange not being able to perform. Since we came to New York it is all we've worked toward: lessons every day, extra classes in singing and toe-dancing, wonderful theatre shows to watch at night, our own shows to perform in between.

Freddie is a bit lost too. He takes to going outside, into the street and he has lots of friends. They play chase and marbles and kick the can.

I don't go outside. Instead, I sit inside and read, and do my hair in ribbons and draw pictures of costumes I would like to wear one day.

Everything feels subdued. Like we are on hold.

"I'm sure it wasn't this short last week!"

Mama is muttering, pins sticking out of the corner of her mouth.

She pulls at the hem of my dress. It now floats above my knee. She is right. Only a few weeks ago, it was not as high up, it was definitely longer, sitting at the knee. Which can only mean one thing.

I've had a growth spurt.

Because I am older than Freddie, I was always taller than him, but now I tower above him. He looks up at me and I feel like a grown-up. Other things have been happening too. My hips seem to have widened and, much to my embarrassment, my chest has grown and swollen and Mama has to bind it for our wedding act.

I am not supposed to be a young woman. Freddie and I are children in our performance, innocent. It doesn't work if Freddie, as a young boy, is married to a girl who looks much older than him.

It just doesn't work.

Mama is not happy at all about this, but I don't know what do about it.

"Hurry up and grow, will you?" I scowl at Freddie.

He shrugs his shoulders and goes out to play.

One Tuesday a letter arrives and Mama yelps.

"I've got a meeting! With the local branch!"

The Gerry society have agreed to see her. She is very excited but nervous too because she wants the meeting to go well.

On the day of the meeting she dresses beautifully, putting on powder and lipstick, pinning up her hair and putting on her fox fur.

"Wish me luck, children," she says, and we give her a peck on the cheek before she leaves.

While she is gone, I take out my pages and draw the styles I see on ladies walking below our apartment. From up here I can see their hats from the top, so I know what colours and flowers are in this season. I've been noticing that the most fashionable ladies have shorter hems on their dresses and they are narrower, straight down. I like this look. I draw all my dresses the same. Maybe it is not so bad that I am growing?

When I'm finished, I cut them all out and leave little paper jut-outs which I fold to hang the dresses on my stiff paper doll. I think this is my favourite thing to do in the world ever.

I am reading to Freddie when the door opens and Mama arrives home, a great big smile on her face and a brown-paper parcel with the unmistakable tag from Macy's bakery.

"I showed them the French verse you wrote," she says to me, smiling. "I think that's what swung it – they could see what clever children you are."

We eat our buns and have hot chocolate and I am so pleased that Mama managed to get us permission to go back on stage.

But something small is eating at me inside, a tiny niggle that I know is going to grow into a big worry.

It's about my body and how it's changing and how I am growing up.

I know that we can't go on for much longer, me towering

above Freddie, trying to be cute, singing innocent songs about a bride and groom in love.

I look over at Freddie, at his little shoulders and roundy head.

Why couldn't he grow up quicker, put a bit of meat on his bones, stretch out those little legs to help meet with me? There's less than two years between us, so why does it look like there are four or five?

He looks up and he annoys me with his face, just being there, not even doing anything.

And then I feel sorry for thinking such thoughts when he is such a sweet boy and none of this is his fault anyway.

We go to sleep, Mama happy in her dreams that she achieved a victory today, Freddie happy that Mama is smiling again and me worrying about what will happen to us all now.

CHAPTER FIFTEEN

NEW JERSEY, DECEMBER 1909

FIVE, SIX, SEVEN, EIGHT.

Step heel, step heel, turn around, kick! Step heel, step heel, turn around, kick!

"Well done, Adele," says Miss Haughey and I smile back at her.

She's nice. She's no Ned Wayburn, but she's nice.

After rehearsal Margo comes up to me and asks if I want to go and get an ice cream.

"Sure," I say.

Margo is nice too, thinks she has a good voice, but she doesn't really. I wonder if I should tell her she hasn't a note in her head, that I should know because I've been to stage school and have had plenty of singing lessons. But it seems like it would be cruel. She is very excited about our Christmas show. I just don't want her to embarrass herself, I don't think it would be fair.

The school theatre is small, it only fits about a hundred and fifty. It smells of old running shoes and polished wood. Down the back is a pummel horse and a springboard, but I've never seen anyone use them. They'll need to be cleared out, ahead of the show, which opens tomorrow night.

I say open, but this is only a three-night run. Three nights of the theatre packed out, with school students who aren't taking part and the parents of everyone else who is.

I'm looking forward to the show, even if it is not such a big deal as the days when we got paid to perform. If anything, this might be more exciting because I will know so many people in the audience. Maybe it'll be like that time we played in front of our home crowd in Omaha.

Maybe.

Margo and I leave the theatre and walk from the school out onto the sidewalk, and amble slowly down the road.

I like going to school here in New Jersey. I can't really remember my old school in Nebraska – just that it was a small schoolroom with lots of different-aged kids. Here, we are all divided up by our proper ages, although Freddie was put a year ahead, on account of Mama's schooling, which was very good they said. Not me, though – I'm with my age. Guess I didn't work as hard as Freddie!

Mama thought we might find it difficult, settling back in, but it wasn't at all. It was just another world to get used to and in this world there are a ton of girls my age. It's nice to hang out with girls who look like me.

I met Margo on the first day. She spotted me and came right up and started asking me all sorts of questions. She was real interested in me. I didn't have any friends my age so I started asking her questions too. She was different to me in that she had a lot of sisters and brothers, both younger and older. She had lived in Weehawken all her life. So had her dad. And her mom. She thought it was very exotic that Freddie and I had seen so much on our travels.

Margo introduced me to her friends. It was clear that

she was the leader and they looked up to her. They hung on every word she said. When I started talking, they listened to me too. At lunch we sat and talked about the boys we liked, ribbed about who fancied who and discussed in detail the boys we'd like to date ourselves and what it would be like to be married and have to do 'it'.

I have recently found out what 'it' is and I just can't believe that is what happens. Jane told Claire and she told Margo. Now we all talk about it in the group.

Margo says she would like to get married when she is sixteen. Jane says she will wait till she is eighteen.

I say I'm going to wait until I'm thirty and they all laugh.

Margo's daddy works in a factory near to the school. She doesn't realise how lucky she is that she gets to see him every day, that she is not separated from him, like Freddie and I are from ours.

Today, after rehearsals, the street is quiet where we walk. We stayed an extra hour to go over our final rehearsals for tomorrow night's show. Everyone will be back out though, later, in the evening time, to sit on the grass-ways that meet between streets, to gather at the ice-cream parlour, to sit in the café with the good gramophone.

Sometimes when I go there, if there's a song on that I know well, I'll get up and do a little dance. It's to teach the girls – they love to see a routine – but sometimes it's to impress the boys, who sit there, apart from us, looking.

I don't really miss the stage.

But I miss the eyes on me.

That feeling of being watched.

"You know, I gotta say," says Margo as we walk, our satchels against our chests, "you've got a talent, Adele. A real talent. I'd give anything for what you have."

I shrugged. "It's all my training. I've been training for so long."

"But you're a talent. It's not just the training. It's the … I dunno. It's the way everyone wants to look at you. I'm so jealous of you sometimes!"

"It's not all it's het up to be, you know," I say. "It's hard work, travelling, rehearsing. Moving all the time, going to all those boarding houses. And you gotta go on, no matter how tired you are, even if you're sick – there's no days off, it's just the way it is."

"But what a life, Adele! What do I have to look forward to? I'll be outta here next year, out to work, in the same factory as Daddy. He says to enjoy this last year, because this is it. This is my last year of freedom."

"You can't stay on in school?"

"Nope."

"But you're so young."

"We need the money. I'm just another mouth to feed. Gotta earn my keep."

I think of the factory where her daddy works. The building is grey with large doors that sweep open to let the workers in and out. Like a big prison, I always think when I pass, with its grilled windows and smoke billowing out the tall, skinny chimneys.

I think of Margo working there all her life. Going in young, coming out old. Her days spent inside the factory walls, on the packaging line, sealing, stamping, checking, getting old.

They'll do a play at Christmas. A cabaret. And it will be the highlight of her year.

"I'm sorry, Margo."

"Sorry for what?"

"That you have to go to work. That you can't ... you know ... follow your dreams."

"What's the point?" she says as we get to the ice-cream shop, a blue-and-white sign over our heads. "I can dream all I want, but unless I have talent ... like you ..."

We go in to order our ices, to sit over them and watch everyone else in the parlour. We talk about tomorrow night, about our make-up, about the socks we have sewn ribbon onto and the small handbags we're going to bring.

But I can't help lingering on what Margo said.

Why have I been picked to have this talent for the stage? What is it that makes me special? What is it that means, whatever happens, I won't spend my life sewing thick thread through canvas or packaging up boxes on an assembly line?

I feel lucky. And blessed.

It's mostly down to Mama, I think.

Our house in Highwood Park is very comfortable. Mama rents it from an old lady who lives two doors up and she's forever passing by, nosey, hoping to spot one of us or Mama outside so she can ambush us and pass all the time of day. It has a porch, and it's nice to sit out, in the evenings, with an iced tea, just like we sat outside in Omaha, when I was very young.

Daddy is still at work in Storz, but he comes east whenever he can and it's nice, now that we have the house and more room for everyone.

The first time he came he brought Trixie with him and I was so happy to be with her again, even though she arrived all grown up and fat. I told Daddy he didn't walk her enough and so I walked her every day, round the block a few times, and I played with her too. I decided that when I'm a grown-up with my own house I'm going to own lots of dogs, even if they do pee on the good rugs and chew skirting boards just for fun.

We are retired for the moment. Mama and Daddy said our wedding act had run its course. We're at an in-between stage, they said. We've got some growing up to do. Or at least Freddie does.

"Take a break," said Mr. Wayburn. "Let Freddie catch up. Then we'll work on something new."

Retirement meant moving out of our boarding house in New York City away from all the performers who lived there, out to the suburbs.

I'd never had so many friends.

Freddie got into a fight his very first day in school and came home with a bloody nose which annoyed Mama no end. It was hard for him being small and put in a class ahead. I knew by him, some days, by how quiet he got, by the temper that would sometimes come out at home, that things were harder for him, with the joking that boys do to each other, the name calling and the fooling around.

But after a few weeks he settled in too. He even made friends with the boy who punched him on the first day and he was forever out on the street, playing baseball now and catch. Freddie was good with people, they liked him. He had a lovely way about him.

Mama relaxed a lot, wearing cotton dresses and cooking for us. Sometimes we'd come in from school and she'd have a whole batch of brownies out of the oven or an apple pie when the apples were in season.

I think she enjoyed the break from the stage too, not having to school us or to take us to rehearsals each afternoon.

No longer did she have to organise costumes and shoes and stockings, our transport and our timetables. No longer did we keep our entertainment schedule, seeking out the best shows to go and see and learn from. Still, she would take out our scrapbooks often, finger the articles, and remember little stories about the theatres we played.

My mind would wander as she read, thinking back to the dusty behind-the-scenes, the heavy curtains as they rose up and down, the draught from the stage door that swept in and out.

On sunny afternoons, when we had done our homework and chores, we would take a wander down to the Jersey Shore, taking a small picnic to munch on in the sand. I loved those trips, the breeze in our hair, the sun on our faces, Mama all tied up in her big bonnet no matter what. Mama wouldn't remove a scrap of clothing, even if the temperature soared and sweat ran down her face.

Me and Freddie went barefoot in the sand, feeling all the time like we were on vacation even though we were just living.

When we were travelling and on the road, when we were rehearsing and working on our shows, there were very few boys around my age. In school, I was surrounded.

I liked the cheeky chaps, the brave boys who would come up and try to pinch me or tickle me, who would make a joke, who would mimic me or laugh about me, but not unkindly, to their friends.

I gave as good as I got, hand on hip, daring them to say their quip again.

My girlfriends enjoyed this, and we would gather in groups to have a bit of a stand-off, girls against boys.

My favourite boy was Jeffrey who had brown eyes and sallow skin. I liked the way he held my head in his hands, as though it were the world, the very globe between his fingers.

Scott Beakey was the worst, he kissed like a big slobbery jellyfish and I told him so. I said: "Scott, you need to practise and when you're finished go practise some more." Oh, he was the worst.

Mostly I enjoyed kissing boys. But I didn't want to get a reputation either. So I had to pick one. I picked Jeffrey. Because he was tall and I was petite, it made me feel quite grown up, walking around, his arm in mine, having to look up to him like a real man.

I didn't tell Mama because she might have stopped us going places. Instead, I said I was going out with Margo and I would meet him at the end of our street and we would go walking ourselves, holding hands, going wherever we pleased. We liked to go to the pier, to ride the Loop the Loop and it made my stomach turn so much I felt giddy all day.

Jeffrey wanted to do construction, like his dad, on skyscrapers in the city.

"Can you imagine, standing on top of one of those towers into the sky?" he said. "What you'd see? How it would feel, the wind in your hair, one wrong step and *BAM*! *Splat!*"

I told him I wanted to be a princess.

"A princess?"

"Sure."

"How?"

"What d'ya mean, how? I want to be a princess, in a castle, with servants. And beautiful gowns."

"Yeah. Right."

"Yeah, right, nothing. What's wrong with having a dream?"

"Nothing wrong with dreaming. Just … well, it ain't a very grown-up dream."

"Who says dreams have to be grown-up?"

"I mean it ain't realistic, is it?"

"Not with you, it ain't."

His face fell and he looked a bit hurt.

"Oh, give me a kiss, Jeffrey Dawson. You can do construction. I can be a princess. You can come and rescue me and build a ladder up to my tower."

"I'd like that."

"You would, would you?"

We kissed, legs dangling on the pier, arms entwined in each other, the two of us, all mixed up.

Margo looked like she was going to puke.

"Are you alright?"

"No."

"You'll be alright."

"I won't."

"Of course you will. Listen to me. Deep breaths. Pick one person in the audience, concentrate on them. Catch their eye. You'll be fine."

"It's alright for you, you're used to this."

"Exactly, so I know how to handle it. Listen to me and you'll be fine."

We stood in the wings, smoothing out our costumes with our hands. Margo was pale, so pale she looked kinda green, even under the stage powder they'd puffed all over our faces in a shower of dust.

"*You're on!*" A stagehand pushed us forward, a girl

from the grade above who delighted in her clipboard and power in telling us what to do.

Five, six, seven, eight.

Step heel, step heel, turn around, kick! Step heel, step heel, turn around, kick!

The boy on the piano was playing the music too fast. The excitement of performing live was getting to him, the tempo far ahead of the routine we had planned. I moved with the beat but when I looked across at Margo she was behind in the steps. She shot me a look of despair in between waving her hands out of time.

I tapped out the dance, my ankles sweeping back and forth. We had practised but not enough. Damn the boy on the piano anyway! What an amateur!

I looked up to catch Jeffrey's eyes. He was sitting in the middle, to the right. I could see him staring, his pupils boring a hole into my costume, into me.

Tap tap tap. Side step side step. Turn around. Kick!

I turned to face Margo, for the kicks we were to do facing each other, but she had yet to turn to me, so far behind was she on the beat.

I looked to the audience and gave a little shrug – one that said, I know what I'm doing but look at *her*.

Everyone erupted, in on the joke, enjoying that I was on time, on the beat and able to clown around.

When Margo turned, her face had fallen, the sound of the laughter making her shrivel.

When the music finished I turned to bow, but Margo walked straight off into the wings, without waiting to see what the audience thought.

I guess there was no need to wait.

We all knew exactly what they thought.

INTERVIEW WITH AURELIO COCCIA, CHOREOGRAPHER, NEW YORK

Research on:* The Evolution of Dance in Modern Theatre, A History, *by Larry Coleman
Archive Located: New York Public Library of Performing Arts
Status: Unpublished

If I was not Italian, then I think I would be Argentinian. Yes, that would suit me, I think.

I have met some Argentinians in my time and they have been forceful, like the dance, tight.

I would not be French. They are colourful, but I would prefer to be Argentinian. Definitely.

It was Paris probably that brought most success, yes. Paris and Rome, two of most beautiful places on this world. I tell everybody, anybody who will listen, I say you must go to Paris, you must go to Rome.

It is hard to describe unless you have been there, smelled it, felt it.

There is no place in America like those two cities.

But, of course, this is where the work is. This is where the success can be found.

I and my wife, we found success with Paris, with our show about Paris, with a dance from Paris. But the 'Apache' it is not my first love, it is a show dance. It is no way to treat a woman. To toss her around like that, throw her on the ground, pick her up, shake her like a rag doll. But, you know, people like it. Of course they do. It's the sex appeal, you see. Put sex appeal into your dance et voilá, like that, mwah, people will stand in their seats and say, more, more, por favore, more!

Our act brought us so much fame at vaudeville right across America. A lot of people approach us, to ask, "Hey, Signore Coccia, can you show me how to do the Apache? Can you show me how to dance? Can you show me what to do with my body? How to catch the lady before she falls?"

If I had time and if I thought they had talent I might take them on. But usually not. It is a difficult thing to take an older person and try to teach them. They know what they know.

They have learned so many bad habits already.

Young people, they are different. They are like sponges, ready to take on the movement, the rhythm, the feeling of what it is I am trying to teach them. I have always enjoyed working with young people, passing on what I know to them.

Fritz Astaire was very forceful when he called me. He said, "Mister Coccia, you are one of the greatest dancers in New York. I know you could teach these kids. Please. Meet with them, talk to them. They are good kids. And they have talent. But they're lost, they need help. They need you."

I met with them. I watched. Their Baseball act, sheesh, outdated. No wonder they were struggling. Ovviamente.

I know Mr. Ned Wayburn put a lot of time into it, it was their first act back, they had taken a break. And they had a good performance somewhere – where was it? I can't remember ... a big performance and it went down great, everybody loved it. But it was a charity show, lots of friends. They took on Proctor's then, that was a very big booking and it did not go well. Wiped from the bill. Poof! After just one performance.

Heart-breaking for them. They were very down when I met them. Lost. No idea where they were going.

I told their mama, I said, "There IS a lot of talent there, but they need coaching. Training. If they promise to work I'll take them on, but they need to bring their hearts and they need to do as I say. It will take a long time. They'll have to forget everything they know and start all over again."

She nodded, she said, "Yes, yes, of course, Mr. Coccia," and we agreed that I would take them as students for six months.

Well, they weren't happy with all of that, let me tell you.

When they trooped in with their sad faces and sad little hearts, I said, "What is the matter with you kids, huh? Why so down?"

I got them to put all of that sadness into their waltz, all that pain into tango.

I showed them the steps but I also showed them

how to act, how to get the feeling out of that music and those movements and put it across, for everyone, anyone to see on stage.

"Heart," I say. "Feel your heart! Feel his heart. Feel the beat. The passion. FEEL it."

They began to feel it. They were good students. They listened. And they practised, they did practise. Fred, oh, he went over it again and again and when he came back each week, he was better and better, they both were.

We worked on the act, we took out the dialogue, the talking, the bits that no one was listening to. And we put in proper songs, proper dances, we made it a showpiece!

They got happy as they learned, more confident in themselves.

One day I said to Adele, "Your footwork is very good" and she said, "But, Mr. Coccia, this is from before, from before we met you. You said we had to forget everything we knew and start again?"

"Yes," I said. "It is a figure of speech. Did you really think I meant forget everything?"

"Yes," she said.

"Yes," said Fred.

Poor kids. They take everything so literally. You have to be so careful how you say things to them.

And when they had perfected the tango, the waltz, the foxtrot and their tap, I told them they were ready and their time was up.

In those six months they became dancers. Really. Truly. Dancers.

And they were ready for the world.

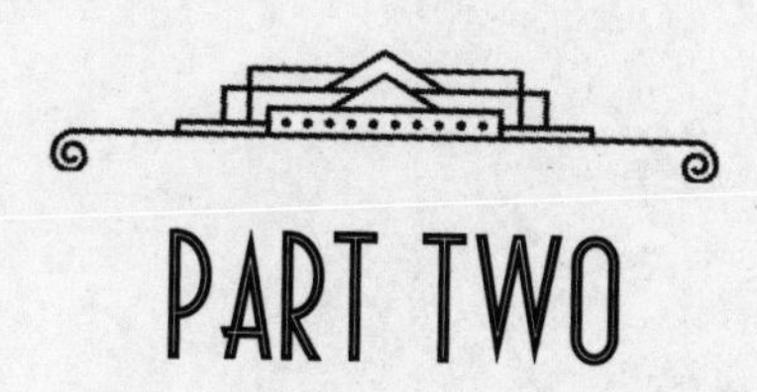

PART TWO

DRESS REHEARSAL

INTERVIEW WITH GEORGE GERSHWIN, COMPOSER, NEW YORK

Research on: **Modern Composers, Their Influences and Desires, *by Jeanette Riley***
Archive Located: New York Public Library of Performing Arts
Status: Published 1938, out of print

Adele Astaire was real kooky. I had my eye on her, you know.

She had her eye on me too!

She was lovely. Great big smile.

I sat in with the orchestra one day for Apple Blossoms *– they were stuck for a piano player for rehearsals.*

Fred and I were buddies. We hung out at Remick's, you know, messing around. Remick's was a song house, down at Tin Pan Alley. I was a piano-plugger, selling sheet music. He had a real ear for a song, Fred. Great way of taking something and making it into something else, something popular. You know, he could hear potential, something else no-one could hear. That's what Tin Pan Alley was all about. Finding the hit.

Such a nice fellow, Fred.

I invited them over to my house, him and Adele. They started coming regular then.

It was an open house, you see, every night. Everyone dropped by. Me and my brother Ira, the family all around, music all night long. There were drinks, but it was all about the music.

They had a few party pieces, the Astaires, and they were welcome any time.

I said to Fred at that Apple Blossoms *rehearsal, "Well, Fred, we're getting closer to this musical we're supposed to write," and he laughed and said, "We sure are!"*

We'd always said that at Remick's, you see, how great it would be if one day I could write a whole musical for him and Adele.

It was nice to see them up on that stage, in a Dillingham show. They were making the right moves, in the right place, going in the right direction.

La La Lucille *was playing, my first musical, and it was doing well. I was pretty happy. It was before* "Swanee" *– before everything changed.*

The Astaires stayed on my mind, you know. There was something about them, a sort of star quality. They stood out and I knew, if we knocked our heads together, we could tap out something real nice.

Sometime after that Alex A. Aarons came to me, helluva nice fellow, and he said he had a show for me and he was hoping to have the Astaires on board. They were with Dillingham but word on the street was that they might soon be free and ready to do his show.

I wanted to do it, it was definitely on my mind,

but by the times Aarons came back I had already signed up to do Scandals *and that was what I was committed to. That was the thing with musicals, you needed to be in the right time, right place, ready for the right producer, with the right cast ready to go. That wasn't the right time for our musical together. Not then. Not then.*

CHAPTER SIXTEEN

NEW YORK, GLOBE THEATRE, JULY 1920

SWEAT RAN DOWN MY BACK. IT POOLED, soaking the top of my knickers. I lifted the patterned fan I kept with me and blasted it at my face.

Louise, my assistant, applied extra powder to my face in the wings. It did little good. Back on stage, under the lights, with the flurried dances that came one after the other, it streamed in gullets down my cheeks and under my chin.

It was too damn hot.

C.B. called a meeting after the matinee, gathering all of us around the front seats of the theatre. The room was stifling, the smell of sweat and popcorn pungent in the air.

"We're going to take a summer break. You can see for yourselves the audience is dropping to a trickle. It's too damn hot and we can't fight against this weather."

We'd heard of air-cooling being introduced into other theatres. It helped hold the summer audiences, but it had yet to reach The Globe. A bucket of ice with a weak powered fan blowing over it was not doing the trick.

Apple Blossoms on Broadway was at an end. We would regroup for our countrywide tour in September.

I flopped into my chair in my dressing room after the show.

"I'll give C.B. that," I said to Louise, who was just as excited as I was about the impending break. "Timing. He has a knack for spotting when his leading talent is about to expire."

She laughed and we both gripped my skirt and lifted it over my sticky head.

Charles Bancroft Dillingham was a pet. He took a shine to Fred and me when we came to Broadway and he was my favourite producer of all those we had met. We were young. I was only nineteen when we got our first Broadway show and I guess he could sense that in us.

Our youth. How it needed to be protected.

For a producer, he was peculiar fellow. Too nice, I would say. He was like a big jolly daddy. He always signed his telegrams C.B.D. and each time we got one Fred and I would play a game.

"Charming But Dangerous?"

"Crazy But Dapper?"

We put these at the start of our notes and letters back: *Dear Calamitous But Delightful ...*

He loved it. He was funny, you see, a bit like me, cracking jokes, always a little sarky.

Fred enjoyed his humour too. Although my brother could be very serious when it came to work, C.B. brought out the best in him. He made everything light, even when it came to big things like money or contracts or any problems with a show. C.B. shrugged it off, never made us feel like it was our fault, made us feel special. Always, he made us feel special.

We first met him when we were working for the Schuberts at the Winter Garden in New York in 1918. We had been mighty happy to take on that job, it was our first gig after vaudeville, our first high-profile big theatre gig.

But they were very shrewd people, the Schuberts, and as producers they were tricky to work with. We found ourselves signed into a contract we knew we'd be better off out of.

"You kids were great," said Charles, pumping our hands up and down after a show at the Winter Garden one night. He asked us out for supper and we obliged. C.B. had a good reputation. Fred did his usual: all business, charming, but eager to hear why C.B. might be interested in us.

Over the clatter of cutlery and the hum of people talking and laughing in the dark restaurant, C.B. told us he'd like to work with us.

"I see real potential!"

"Could you wait?" asked Fred. "We need a year. Our contracts are watertight but, if you wait for us, we'll be free then."

"I'm in this business for the long term," said C.B. "If you want return on your investment you gotta go long-term. I'm not a short-term kinda guy."

"Well, that's great, Mr. Dillingham."

"Call me C.B."

"What's that stand for? *Clever Boy*?" I asked, smiling.

He laughed out loud.

"C.B. for 'Could Be'," said Dillingham. "I make dreams come true!"

"I'll raise a toast to that!" said Freddie.

We had a good feeling about C.B.

Fred and I stayed up talking for an hour when we got in from our meeting with Dillingham. Mama was interested. She made us tea and listened intently, nodding as we spoke.

She knew how important the right producer was for us.

She knew we weren't going to get it at the Winter Garden.

When we got to bed, it took me an age to fall asleep. I kept playing the conversation over in my mind.

I felt we were on a precipice. That something big was about to happen.

The next morning, Mama woke me, shaking me by the shoulder.

Dappled light spread over the end of my bed, peeking under a gap in my bedroom blind. An autumn coolness was settling in.

I groaned, tired from the night before.

"*Get up*," she hissed. "You need to talk to Frederick."

Frederick. She only called him that when he was trouble.

What could he have done since last night and early this morning to have gotten in trouble?

"Huh?" I moaned, throwing one arm over my forehead and moving it slightly so that I could see her tight, grey face.

"Get up."

She left my room.

I slowly got out of the bed and put on my robe.

We were staying in a spacious apartment – a big upgrade from the apartment we lived in when we first came to New York. We had a bedroom each and a reception area at the front with a valet.

Course, we had a proper wage now.

Fred was at the table in the centre of the room. There were breakfast things laid out and he nursed a coffee cup that looked to have gone cold.

"What's going on?" I asked.

"It's no good," he said. "Don't even try, Delly."

Confused, I sat down and stared at him.

"What's wrong?"

I felt Mama approach me from behind.

"*This!*" she said, her voice terse, hoarse even.

She threw a brown envelope on the table in front of me. It skidded and moved towards the butter dish. It was torn in parts along the top, opened roughly, without care.

I lifted the envelope and removed a small brown card.

My heart dropped.

"No," I said.

"Yes!" said Mama.

I could hear that she was not angry now but upset. She was fighting back tears.

At the top in red print said: 'REGISTRATION CARD'

Below it was a serial number and an order number, Fred's name and date of birth.

Conscription.

Fred had been called to war.

"What are you going to do?" I asked him.

"What can I do?" he said.

"Oh Freddie."

"You could get an exemption," said Mama. "For your show, the show needs you."

Fred laughed. "I don't think the War Office would see it like that! I'm called up, Mama. That's it. Show or no show. If they ask me, I'll go. That's it."

He looked at me, his face solemn.

"That's it, Delly."

We had been watching the happenings in Europe closely, more so in recent times as the casualties grew and there seemed to be no end in sight. Freddie, Mama and I had always been interested in current affairs. She liked to teach us about the world, to understand what was going on outside the rather enclosed globe of stage business.

Mama's family had fled East Prussia because of war. Daddy's family had been high up in the Austrian army. They knew about the military from childhood and he often told us how strict things had been and how he'd longed to come to America, to freedom, ever since he was a child.

Germany, as a country, was quite familiar to us, having grown up in the Bavarian community of Omaha and the language, its customs and its history of brewing meaty beer.

Now we watched as England and Germany fought against each other in France, we read the reports of the numbers lost, and listened to the growing commentary from our politicians that the United States would have to get involved.

The war had a direct impact on the brewing business back home in Nebraska. The Temperance Movement had for years been looking to restrict the sale and production of beer, saying it broke all our good, moral standards and, as the war in Europe raged, they stepped up their campaign. The Government agreed and restricted the use of hops and barley for beermaking. Instead, it would go into food.

Daddy wrote us letters that grew increasingly anxious as the war raged on. We read of ales that were discontinued, how hours were cut at Storz, workers let go. In 1917 the Temperance Movement succeeded in passing state-wide prohibition.

Daddy lost his job.

It was a worry on top of the war worry. We were horrified to hear of the number of casualties, of young, bright men, mowed down in a misty field in France. We were the same age as the soldiers being called up. Our audiences were packed with young men and women and I couldn't help but think, as I looked down from the stage, that just across the water, similar male faces were disappearing day by day, their sweethearts left behind to grieve for what should have been. It was such a waste of life.

Freddie sent back his card and we waited anxiously for news. Three months later reports flooded through that the Great War was over.

Millions of people had died.

But Freddie had been saved.

We finished at the Winter Garden in June 1919. Freddie and I made our way to Charles Bancroft Dillingham's office on the day we finished, an invitation that had been standing for over a year. The steps were narrow and badly lit. I held on to the banister and Freddie walked behind me in case I fell. We were always terrified of injuring ourselves, pulling a muscle or, worse, breaking a bone.

I found if we let ourselves get too tired or didn't rest enough, we could be prone to too sharp a turn, too uneven a landing. We had understudies, of course, but nobody wanted to have to use an understudy.

Freddie worried about injuries far more than me. But that was Freddie for you.

I did my stretches before shows and I swore by cod liver oil. It loosens up the joints. Even though it tastes likes squashed-up rotten fish.

We got to the top of the stairs and knocked to go in.

A secretary greeted us with a warm smile. Her hair was coiffured and blonde.

"Vera," she said and stood up to shake our hands. "Can I offer you tea or coffee? I have cake?"

We agreed to the beverage but not to the treat. I liked to watch my figure. I kept cake for days when I needed a pick-me-up, when I was too tired to move.

Today, I was full of energy.

Already we felt we had moved up in the world. This office was warm, luxurious, with panelling on the walls.

"He's ready for you now," Vera said after answering the black phone which had rung and startled us.

We opened the door into a long office, like an alley you might roll a ball in.

Charles Dillingham was seated at the very end of it behind a mahogany desk.

The room was perfumed with lavender.

He watched us as we walked towards him and then he stood and smiled and came out from behind the desk to shake our hands and kiss me on the cheek.

"Thank you for coming."

"Thanks for inviting us."

"Only took a year!" he joked.

Vera came in behind us carrying a tea tray. She put it down on C.B.'s desk while we all took our seats. Vera poured the tea and C.B. started into the cake immediately.

"So, you've finally left those Schuberts behind?" he said.

"Yes, Mr. Dillingham," said Freddie. "We're all set."

"Well, I'm looking forward to working with you guys, been looking forward to it all year."

"What do you have in mind?" I asked confidently. I was keen to know where he saw us going.

He bent down and rooted in a bottom drawer. When he came up he held up a thick script.

"This! It's an operetta. I think it's the right one to start us off. Going to take a break from all that ragged jazz, go back to being a bit old-fashioned."

"Old-fashioned?" I said. We were young, fresh and new. And C.B. wanted to make us old-fashioned?

"You'll love it," he said. "Trust me. It's something different among everything else that's out there."

C.B. wouldn't tell us the name of the show or the parts we'd be playing in it.

"Now I know how hard those Schuberts worked you," he said. "I want you to take your summer vacation. Starting today. Off you go – we don't need you back here till August – we'll start rehearsals then."

"But, Mr. Dillingham, we're ready to start – we don't need a vacation," said Fred.

It was true. We'd been waiting to start working with C.B. for so long. We didn't need a break – we would have been happy to start right there and then. We were used to working, rehearsals, costume fittings and choreography classes, piecing it all together ahead of the try-outs. But it was true there was nothing doing for the summer – everyone who could would be running from the heat, down to Delaware, upstate to the Hamptons, the lucky few who knew someone with a boat racing to feel the crisp spray of the ocean on their faces.

"Trust me," he said. "You're taking this vacation for me. I want you fresh, relaxed, in tiptop shape. You know any good holiday spots?"

"Well, yes, we usually go with the family to Wernersville," said Fred.

"There you go," said C.B. "Sounds great."

Here, I thought, is a real man, a real man of show business. He was nothing like the Schuberts.

"Say, do you want to take a ride in my Rolls? It's parked right outside. I stole it from my wife for the day. Tell the driver to take you for a spin!"

"Sure!" we said.

We said our goodbyes and waved to Vera as we made our way back down the narrow stairway again.

When we got into the car, I patted the leather seats.

"I like this," I said to Freddie. "We should get one."

He laughed.

Our fortunes were changing.

We had a new producer, a new show on the way, weeks of vacation ahead. We were on the way up.

The operetta Dillingham had been coy about turned out to be *Apple Blossoms*, and it was a gorgeous, classical show. The scenes, set in Austria, were painted by a wonderful artist called Joseph Urban. I felt at times as though I really was in a green, fragrant garden, with bees buzzing and sweet birds chirping and hopping about.

Daddy loved that a Viennese man had such a part to play in our exciting show.

We had two dances and no speaking parts in the show. It meant we were not under pressure and we could enjoy getting to know our fellow cast members, attending gatherings and parties and trying out the new nightclubs that kept popping up and closing down just as quickly to skirt prohibition.

Oh, how I loved a good night club! When our show was over we would get changed and head out for the night. We were fizzing with energy, fuelled by our big production and our prominent roles. I had a range of dresses now, all drop-waist and above the knee and I loved to dance for fun, letting go, grabbing different partners and trying out new steps to the bands that played wonderful, uplifting music.

I loved to let loose after work. Our dances were so choreographed on stage, all stepped and timed, and if I put a toe wrong Freddie would have a face on him. Not that there was room for mistakes at the Globe on Broadway.

Our two dances were perfect, well-rehearsed, as familiar as brushing our teeth. But sometimes if you let your mind wander for a second, if you forgot where you were, if you let someone in the audience spark you, make you think of something else, you could find yourself bang in the middle of a twirl and not quite sure of where you were in the dance.

That was the only time I made a mistake. If my mind wandered a bit. So I had to concentrate, not allow myself to get distracted.

Mistakes weren't worth it. They would make Mr. Dillingham wonder why he was paying you all that money. And worst of all they would bring Freddie's wrath down upon your head. Freddie never made a mistake. He was so set on what he was doing, so het up, he would never, not in a thousand years get distracted by anybody in the audience. He just wouldn't.

It was the difference between me and my brother.

At the night club, free from being watched and our cues and our timing, I would really dance, moving my body just whatever way I felt like it. There were plenty of men to dance with, plenty asking. I danced with Fred sometimes too, because we knew each other's movements as though they were our own, but mostly Freddie was happy to sit and talk, to have a few soda waters and uncurl all that tension from performing.

I wanted to dance forever.

C.B. brought us everywhere, introduced us to everyone.

The thing I liked about him was that he was very refined. He dressed real dapper, stiff collar and tie, and he had the cutest little grey moustache, never a hair out of place. He was tall and well-built and he struck a look wherever he went. We loved being in his company, he was like our showbusiness father, our connected uncle, who could introduce us to the world.

He knew everyone. Everyone! Producers from other theatres, actors and dancers from all the big productions, rich Wall Street businessmen who poured all their money into investing in our shows. He knew politicians and all the people on the council and if you ever needed anything done, well, he knew just how to do it.

We were welcomed with smiles and the red-rope treatment every night. Areas in the night clubs were kept just for us. Sometimes a girl would come up with a pencil and a napkin and ask me to sign it: "*Write anything! Anything at all!*"

Fred and I were bemused by it. We did not feel like celebrities.

We did feel like we belonged, with these dancers and singers and actors who worked so hard all through the years, who spent all their time working to entertain. We were so comfortable in their company. We understood each other. We had the same experiences, the same hopes for our careers and there was a smattering of rivalry, enough of a frisson to keep the atmosphere tense, on edge, exciting.

Still, we did not feel like celebrities.

I enjoyed it. I enjoyed the comedown after every show. I relished the trickle of that first cocktail, the touch of the cool glass between my fingers, the delicacy of the narrow stem, the bitter liquid reaching down my throat.

Hanging out with someone like C.B. Dillingham meant we always got to the parties where illegal alcohol was flowing. It added to the atmosphere. Sometimes he had to give a password – other times it was quick nod and a shaking of hands and we were in.

"Lemme have something new!" I would order from the waitress. And she might come back and say, this is a Sidecar, or a French 75 or a Sloeflower Sour.

I tried them all. "Make it sweet," I'd say.

With the cocktails and the music and the dancing and high of the show, I had never felt so vibrant.

"Isn't this just the finest, Freddie?" I'd say, rushing back from the little dance-pit to our red-velvet booth.

"It's swell," he'd say and he looked happy too.

I could go to a night club every evening of my life.

And, during all that time when *Apple Blossoms* was on stage, that's exactly what we did.

After a long run of the show, with a whirlwind of parties behind us, Freddie and I retreated with Mother and Father to Wernersville, Pennsylvania, again for a vacation. It was a small holiday town with luxury hotels and cool mountain air that invited rest and relaxation.

We had gone on vacation together every summer since we were children, when Mama, despite our often strapped finances, managed to put away enough every year to take us up into the mountains.

Everyone that could escaped New York in the summertime. The place was a furnace, you could barely breathe in the closed-in city streets. It was as if someone had lit a flame under Manhattan and was slowly turning the gas up, day by day.

I brought my knitting to Wernernersville, click-clacking out mittens and socks and vests and bonnets. Mama had taught me how to knit while we waited during rehearsals, but I wanted to improve. Soon, I wanted to move on to more complicated patterns, a large cardigan perhaps or a sweater for Fred or Father.

Mother took her knitting too, and she liked tapestry and embroidery, poking the threads into tiny holes, pulling, picking, yanking at the fibres with her teeth.

We noticed a big difference this year in Father. Last year he had been brighter, more upbeat. More hopeful.

This year, most of that light was gone.

He was such a proud man. He had supported us all these years, sending our keep money religiously, working up his wages, giving everything he could to us.

Now that his job in the brewery was gone, he had nothing.

For a while he'd get an odd shift cooking in a restaurant or a café that needed a cook for a few hours. But we knew that this was a step down, back to the times before we were born, nothing like the good sales job he'd had that had paid our rent, our tuition, the special singing lessons and costumes and dance shoes we needed.

We wrote to him in Omaha, trying to persuade him to come to New York.

The opportunities are better here.

For months he turned us down, insisting he would come when he had his business affairs sorted.

He did not want us to pay his way.

It was Fred who persuaded him in the end. He told him we all missed him and needed to see him and he simply must come and see us on stage.

"You won't believe the reaction we're getting, Papa."

Curiosity eventually got the better of him in April 1920. We paid for his fare to New York and when he climbed off the big steam train and walked towards us on the platform, his appearance, jostled among all the other travellers, caught us by surprise.

He looked old, much older than his years. His skin was leathery, dry and wrinkled, and when he got close we could see his whole nose had changed. It was bulbous and it was red.

A drinker's nose.

Maybe this was why he did not want to come to us. He was too proud to show us what was really going on, and he was probably worried about getting hold of his beloved whiskey here.

Mama kissed him on the cheek but I saw the crinkle in her brow as we all sat into a cab on our way to Luchow's.

Daddy waited to see *Apple Blossoms* for two whole weeks after he arrived in New York. He was saving it, he said. He went to see two other shows before ours, to get himself ready.

"It's good to be back in the big city," he said.

On the night he and Mama were to attend our show, he washed carefully and spent an age oiling his hair and his moustache. The smell of cologne drifted from his bedroom to our sitting room and I smiled and closed my eyes and I breathed in.

I had missed that smell.

We had special tickets put aside at the theatre booth, the best seats in the house.

I was nervous as I got ready, thinking of Daddy out there, watching, seeing us for the first time in such a long time on stage. Daddy was one of the only people who could make me nervous.

In that whole audience that night, it wouldn't have mattered if the Queen of Sheba was there to watch us. The only one I cared about was Daddy.

On stage, I didn't dare look down. Freddie and I put every ounce of energy into our steps, whirling around, concentrating on our tango.

Both of us wanted to impress.

I hoped Daddy would like the music, be taken in by the scenes, by how elegant we looked in our costumes.

Afterwards we changed quickly and came out front, where Mama and Daddy waited in the lobby, all of the patrons filing out, some stopping to pat Fred on the shoulder and touch my hand and say, "You were wonderful, Miss Astaire".

"Well, what did you think, Pop?" said Fred, animated.

Papa was quiet. His eyes glistened.

"You were wonderful. Both of you. I am very proud."

Fred and I smiled and I felt overwhelmed. There were tears in my eyes too.

I moved in to hug my father, a spontaneous movement, and I felt Mama stand back.

He patted me on the back and whispered into my hair, "My little Delly. I always knew you would make it."

In Wernersville, we whiled away hours in the Galen Hall hotel, watching the patrons go by, ordering the odd cocktail and coffee and iced tea. Every night we dined together, ordering whatever we felt like from the menu.

I was never a big eater. I didn't like the feeling of being full, of squashing all that food into my tummy. Still, I liked to try the different dishes on the menu and, even though I wouldn't clear my plate, I appreciated the different tastes and textures.

It was too hot to eat.

Fred played golf night and day. He couldn't get enough of the sport and the back of his neck was the colour of a nut.

He asked Father to come with him, but he would shake his head and say "Not today, son".

"Hey, Pop," I said, "did you hear Walter's Park have a new steam room, where you go in and they have this oil or water on fire or something and all the steam comes out and you breathe it in and it's supposed to do your health wonders? You should try it!"

I took interest in finding out what the sanatoriums had to offer in Wernersville. There were so many of them, all offering different treatments to help with 'ill health, malaise and wellbeing'.

He tried some, but mostly he was happy to sit in the bar, smoking, pretending he felt fine and coughing into his hanky, swallowing it as best he could when we were around.

He had aged a hundred years.

Mama, on the other hand, looked positively beautiful. She relished the mountain air – it made her cheeks glow and she went for long walks every day, all around the town, later filling us in on who she met and who was coming to stay and how we should meet up with so and so soon.

Wernersville was a fine spot to be seen in for entertainers like us. We were in good company. Lots of other actors, singers and stage performers like us took their breaks here.

After weeks of doing nothing much, we began to grow restless. I had read every book I'd brought and many more from the bookshop at the corner of Pearl Street. I was tired of my knitting too: the collection of woolly garments stacked in my room seemed a bit silly in the heat.

We were anxious to get back to work.

Fred was the most anxious and we took to booking the Galen Hall ballroom when it was free to rehearse and try out some new steps he was thinking of. He was so creative, always thinking of new ideas and music that might go with an idea he had.

I didn't have much input but I was happy to practise then, to get my stamina back up, to get ready for the road.

Finally the summer was over and it was time to take our show on tour.

Touring was something we were used to. Having come through the vaudeville circuit, we were well used to travelling and getting out on the road. Touring a show from Broadway, however, was quite different. Now, there were people who organised everything for us. All our accommodation, our bookings, press appearances, breaks, everything was scheduled and accounted for.

Mama came with us, but she was not really needed. Louise my assistant was on hand to pick up anything I needed at all, stockings, powder, sanitary items, a snack.

It was nice to be able to sit with Mama, just to talk, to run over any quibbles I had in my mind. I guess it would have been strange if she wasn't there!

We took *Apple Blossoms* to Chicago, Philadelphia and Providence. In the new year we continued into Boston, Baltimore and Washington D.C. We enjoyed it. We liked getting into a new town, setting up in the best hotel they had, getting out for a wander, meeting new people, seeing new sights. With vaudeville, everything had been so rushed, a night or two here, then back on the train to meet the tight, packed schedule. We were working split weeks and travelling so much, always packing to get back on a train.

On our tour off Broadway, we could play a city for a few weeks.

With the travelling, the new cities and enjoying ourselves at pop-up dance bars whenever we could, the year flew by. Soon it was time to finish up and head on summer vacation again. In the autumn we would be starting a new show, a similar operetta to *Apple Blossoms* that C.B. had planned for us. His thoughts were that we'd been so successful with this run, another similar show would work just as well.

Turns out, those thoughts were rather misplaced.

"Delly, I'm nervous."

"Me too."

"It's just not working."

"It's not."

"What can we do?"

"What *can* we do?"

"I've a good mind to … to …"

"To what?"

"I dunno. Yell at someone. Tell that scriptwriter to write a few funny jokes, actual funny jokes."

"Everyone's doing their best, Moaning Minnie," I told him.

Nobody could understand why *The Love Letter* wasn't working. The same cast from *Apple Blossoms* had been reassembled. C.B. brought in a new comedian and we all worked and worked to perfect our dances.

But it was not happening.

The show was falling flat.

C.B. put on a brave face and made more changes.

Everyone was working to build it into the success that *Apple Blossoms* had been.

But it was like flogging a dead cat.

"Let's try this," said Teddy Royce, the choreographer on the show. He was walking towards us, back from the piano player who he'd just asked to play a marching number, a type of *oompah-oompah* tune.

Freddie and I broke from our huddle at the side of the stage. This was quite a new experience for us. We'd been involved with things that didn't work before. The Wedding Cake act wasn't always great and the Baseball act we did when we came back from our school break when we were young was lame too.

But this time we were adults. On Broadway. With a whole team of professionals around us.

Teddy stood in the middle of the stage.

"Start like this," he said, putting the two of us together, side by side, shoulder to shoulder. He did a little jog.

We followed him.

"Put out your arms, like you're riding a bicycle," he said.

We did, completing our lap.

"Now, faster!" said Teddy.

As the music played we circled, starting small and continuing in bigger laps to the music till we were running all the way around the stage.

It was fun.

"This'll work," said Teddy.

"How do we finish?" asked Freddie.

"Off to the wings?" said Teddy. "When you're done running around!"

The "Runaround" was born.

On opening night we played to a lukewarm reception, a few muffled laughs and the slow horror that we were signed up to a show we were not proud of. The Runaround got a good reaction and, as the nights rolled on, it was the only part that people seemed to like.

We had gone from a hit with *Apple Blossoms* to a complete flop with *The Love Letter*.

Fred and I felt ashamed.

But this was show business.

The curtain was called.

The show was pulled in New York. We would take it on tour outside of the Big Apple to see if the reception was any better.

What would the people of Rochester and Boston think of *The Love Letter*? Broadway or no Broadway, we reckoned they could spot a flop a mile off too.

Just before we due to leave New York, Freddie went to get a new suit. He was a dapper dresser, Fred. Always, even as a child, hated to get dirty or have anything torn. It probably came from our mother, who was always turned out like a proper lady. I liked my clothes too, but Freddie was even more particular.

When he came back, he told me about the tailor who had been tending to him.

"I had a very interesting chat today," he said.

"Oh?" I said.

We were having a cup of tea in our dressing room, a pre-show snack. We didn't like to eat heavy just before the show.

"With Mister Alex A. Aarons."

"And who's he when he's at home?" I asked.

"Well, he was my tailor today," he said. "But we got

talking. He knew all about this show and you know what he said? Said we needed to be going in a different direction. Something more contemporary."

"Did he now?" I said, raising an eyebrow over my steaming cup.

"I was a bit annoyed," said Fred. "I mean who's this upstart giving *me* career advice. But then, you know what else he told me? His dad is Alfred E. Aarons, big composer-producer with Klaw and Erlanger. Alex Aarons knows his stuff. Wants to be a producer too. Even said he might have a show for us."

"Really?" I said. "What you make of that?"

This was news. I put my cup down in anticipation.

"Well, I was still a bit put out but, you know what, since thinking on it I feel he might be right. We're young, Adele, we've got a lot to give. I'm not sure this operetta stuff is where we're at."

I thought on this too. All the reviews so far had noted our comedic ability. Mentioned us as "something different".

Maybe we did need to do something different?

"What are you thinking?" I asked Freddie.

"Well, we'll see. He was talking of getting George Gershwin on board. Now that would be a big deal."

"We couldn't leave C.B."

"We might have to."

"Oh, Freddie."

"Do you want to go on out there with this show?"

"No."

"Let's see what happens. Aarons said he'll be in touch."

I took a slurp of tea and frowned.

It could come to nothing or it could be everything.

But already I was feeling a little sorry for C.B.

CHAPTER SEVENTEEN

THE ACQUITANIA
521 NAUTICAL MILES EAST OF NEW YORK, FEBRUARY 1923

"ARE YOU ALRIGHT?" I ASKED.

"Just about."

"It's choppy."

"It sure is."

Fred looked a little green. Mostly grey, but with a definite tinge of green.

It was our first transatlantic sailing. We had climbed aboard the *Acquitania* with the trepidation of newborn gazelles, stretching our legs, feeling for solid ground beneath our feet.

We gave ourselves over to the waves and the deep, to the captain who would take us and all the passengers to the shores of England.

Mama fared better than us, somehow finding sea legs buried deep within her. She shrugged and smiled at us as we wobbled and gripped for the backs of chairs and railings.

Mama's presence was a dealbreaker.

Aarons had successfully negotiated our first-class tickets from the United States and, at our insistence, had secured passage for Mother too. Sir Alfred Butt, the British theatre impresario who was paying to bring our show to London, was indignant at having to pay for the extra passage.

"*I don't want the mother!*" he roared at Aarons on the telephone which made us laugh no end when he told us.

But mother was part of the deal. And besides, as Aarons put it to Sir Alfred Butt, they could not expect a lady, as young as myself, as in demand as myself, to travel alone. Fred didn't count. I needed a proper chaperone.

Aarons had been as good as his word. He had made the leap from being a tailor into production, still keeping his share in the drapery shop but taking his inherited talent and his ideas to the stage.

We got the wire when we were in Boston with *The Love Letter* and Freddie and I went to meet with him. We had just learned that C.B. was shutting down our show. It was too costly to run, and while the audiences were more receptive than in the more difficult New York, he was cutting his losses.

We were now in contract but without a show.

"The Astaires don't deserve to be in a flop," Aarons said.

We agreed with him. He was full of ideas, full of chutzpah, fresh. We were excited about what kind of show he could produce for us.

But we were torn at the thought of breaking from C.B. He had been so good to us. We knew it would be awful to ask for a release after the failure of *The Love Letter.*

C.B. had put us in classical roles, showing off our dancing skills in tangos and foxtrots.

"You're perfect for musical comedy," said Aarons. "Proper speaking parts. Actually, I want to write the show around you."

In the end, Freddie did it. He went to C.B. and told him that we wanted to work with Aarons.

"What did he say?" I asked when Freddie returned, looking slightly red high in the cheeks.

"We can do the show, but the posters need to say: *Appearing under the management of Charles Dillingham.*"

"Well, that's okay!"

"Yes, that's okay."

"What else did he say?"

"Said he was sorry he didn't have anything else ready to go and that he was very disappointed about *The Love Letter*."

"Poor C.B."

We were his protégés, like his children. And already we had fled the nest.

"Business is business, Delly," Fred said.

But I felt it was like hurting our own papa.

Freddie was able to separate it out. I found it harder.

When *For Goodness Sake* launched on Broadway in February 1922 we knew we had a hit on our hands.

We had big speaking parts, comedic roles. We relished this new dynamic, combining dance with talk, comedy and fun.

We had gone from a flop to a sell-out success in a little over two months.

Talk of London came, even while we in the middle of our Broadway run. Aarons had connections and he had ambition.

"They'll go crazy for you," he told us. "They're maniacal for musical comedy over there. And nuts about anything American. Delly, they will *love* you!"

My popularity had grown with *For Goodness Sake*. I was recognised now most places I went. Fans came to the stage door. We were contacted by companies who wished us to send them a recommendation for a fee.

There was only one problem with us going to London.

We were still contracted to Charles Bancroft Dillingham and he wanted us back.

Going back to C.B. and the type of show he had for us was a step backwards. It was as though hands were holding us down, pulling us in a direction we didn't want to go.

We knew now where we wanted to be – comedy, modern dance, full of fun. We were classically trained but it wasn't where we wanted to be anymore. We were too young to be this old.

When we returned to work on *Bunch and Judy*, C.B.'s next show for us, we found we had little to say and little input into the show.

With *For Goodness Sake*, Fred had a major choreography role. Now he was back to being told what to do.

We opened in November 1922 and knew, after the first night, that we were in trouble.

Fred renamed the show *The Bust and Judy*.

Dillingham pulled the New York run after three and a half weeks. A record even for us.

He sent us on tour, but we all knew what was coming.

C.B. and The Astaires were at an end. Aarons got in touch to say he was in negotiations with Sir Alfred Butt for a London run of *For Goodness Sake*.

We got a telegram from C.B. about arrangements for our last shows.

"*Ciao*. Bye. Done," said Fred.

We both felt sad at how things had worked out.

With a deal done with Sir Alfred Butt for a London run, our passage was booked aboard the *Acquitania* and we would start in the West End in April 1923.

England was getting three more Americans to adore: myself, Freddie and Mama!

Aboard the *Aquitania*, we took great delight in ordering cocktails from the bar, knowing there'd be no rap or tap from a prohibition officer. Mama was in her element. We took afternoon tea with blue-and-white porcelain china every afternoon at four o'clock, nibbling on white bread sandwiches, little bigger than our fingers, tasting buttery pastries and sliced fruits on cream. We dined in the muralled restaurant at seven thirty each evening, eyeing each other in the light of the tall lamps placed on our table, eating lobster and shellfish with potatoes patted into square baked cakes.

We walked in the mornings, up and down the deck, taking in the fresh air, and the salt spit of the sea.

"I can't help but think of my parents," said Mama. "That they made this journey, only the other way round."

"Well, I'm glad they made the trip, Mama, otherwise we wouldn't be here today!"

Would she have enjoyed a life in East Prussia, a place her parents had chosen to leave? Would she be the same person today?

I watched her as she walked over to the side of the deck and curled her hands around the balustrade.

I followed her, wrapping my hands round the rail too.

"You know, before you there was another baby."

I looked at Mama, but she did not look at me.

"Before you were born. It's why your father and I got married. I was only fifteen."

Fifteen. Oh my! We'd always known there had been something a little murky about my parents getting together. Theirs was not a story told with romance.

"What happened?" I asked, tentatively.

"Something went wrong. It didn't take."

"Oh Mama, I'm so sorry."

"Imagine you could have had an older brother or sister. But I feel it was a girl."

I had a special place in the family as the eldest. I couldn't imagine someone else being older than me. What if that older sibling hadn't been able to dance? Would we have ever set out on our journey at all?

"Sometimes I think it is why your daddy drinks," Mama said. "It affected him. The pressures of finding work, settling down."

"What will become of him?" I ask.

"I suppose the same thing that happened to Grandpa. The drink will get him in the end."

I felt so sad and so mournful that right at that moment I wanted to take Mama's hand in mine, climb onto the balustrade and topple head over heels into the swell of the cold sea.

Instead, we turned, both of us, our arms folded against the cool spritz and salt, to go back to our rooms to the warmth and to rest.

As with all cross-Atlantic sailings, the guest list was assessed and anyone with a talent and notoriety was asked to take part in the charity evening for the Seaman's Fund.

"I dunno, Delly," said Fred. "That floor looks mighty slippery and what if it's very choppy?"

Old Moaning Minnie. Fred hated to do anything but his best work in front of any audience.

"Oh Freddie, it'll be fine," I said. I quite liked the thought of putting on a bit of a show for our maritime companions.

As often was the case, Fred's worries tuned out to be true. Not only was it choppy, it was practically topsy-turvy.

We took to the floor and found ourselves moving out of control, slipping down onto our knees and sliding right across the floor. Some dance move that was.

Fred was horrified.

I thought it was hilarious.

I made a big joke out of it and exaggerated all my movements for the rest of the dance, drawing laughs and thigh slaps from everyone watching.

There was nothing for it but to do what we could, all the while being tossed from one side of the ballroom floor to the other, the gravity of the sea pulling us back and forth, this way and that.

We finished to a thunderous applause and cheers.

"London will love us," I whispered to Fred.

"They'll love *you*," he said.

We had bruised knees and the roar of applause in our ears.

We could not wait to see what England would bring.

What a sight London was! Huge grey stone buildings, arches, bay windows, pretty carved decor everywhere the eye could see. We gaped like tourists as double-decker buses drove past, taking it all in – the bustle, the atmosphere, so different to New York.

We took a taxi to the Savoy Hotel and sank into its opulence. We had stayed and dined in all the best hotels in New York, but there was something so very fine about the Savoy. Everything felt so much grander. I loved the drop of the accents in my ears, all round-mouthed and sophisticated.

Everyone told us that *For Goodness Sake* was made for

English audiences. We were not so sure. It had gone over very well in the States and we had travelled well with it. But England was a whole other place.

The night we landed we went to see a show at the Empire with Aarons and his wife and met with Sir Alfred Butt. We took great joy in watching him shake hands with Mother.

"Here's the mother you didn't want," I said coyly, to looks of alarm from Aarons and Freddie. Oh, it was funny! Why not put it up to the man who wanted to leave our dear mother behind?

She was sweet and he liked her and we could see that he was taken by her elegance and beauty.

The show was a revue and it was its opening night. We watched in horror from our seats as the audience failed to get behind it and a chorus of boos and heckles came from the gallery.

"Oh, Freddie," I whispered. "What tough nuts! What if they treat us the same?"

Moaning Minnie's face was pale with worry.

Afterwards Aarons told us not to be alarmed. "That show was no good," he said. "You won't face anything like that, trust me."

We had to trust him. We had little choice.

For Goodness Sake was to be renamed *Stop Flirting* for its London run.

I thought it was a funny name, almost aimed at me. I flirted with everyone. I was born flirting.

I prayed England would flirt with me back.

LETTER TO FRITZ ASTAIRE
4 JUNE 1923, LONDON

Dearest Daddy,

I hope you are keeping well, and you are feeling better now. I hate to think of you unwell and on your own. Do let us know if we can have anything sent to you. Mama is worried about you, I think.

All is swell here. I'm just back from a shopping trip to Selfridge's. It was glorious. Harry Gordon Selfridge himself met me. Refused to take any payment for the cosmetics I got. We had tea afterwards in the resting room. It's a wonderful quiet room for shoppers like me. He keeps the fire going and it has these great big curtains that block out all the sound outside. A tiny haven in London! He likes me of course because I'm American, says he misses the old country.

Pond's have asked me to pose for their new night cream advertisement campaign. I think I will. The money's good. Fred and I don't want to do too many adverts – we don't want to become all about the money. But I do like the cream and I think if I can stand by the product, well then, why not? What do you think, Daddy? You always have a good steer on these things.

London has been everything we hoped it would be and more. We have fallen utterly in love with the place. Sometimes, on my days off, I like to take off walking, all through the streets, or get a cab to somewhere I'd like to see. I don't take Fred, because we would be too conspicuous then. We really are noticed when we go places. Funnily enough, though, when I'm on my own, with my button hat pulled low on my head, I can blend in.

I like to look up at the buildings, they're so tall and ornate, all detailed stonework. I love that everything is so old here. The hotels, the theatres, even the trees along the streets, they're so ancient!

I have it bad for London, Daddy.

Of course, it helps that things have gone so well for us here. Had we come here for a show that didn't do well, that closed early, well, then we might have felt very different about London of course.

We are bigger here than we were in Broadway, Daddy. Can you imagine that?

I've cut my hair into a bob now, which you probably wouldn't like, but it's very stylish and I do like it. The newspapers are calling me impish and a pixie, but it suits me. I know you like long hair, Daddy, but I am 26 now and quite a grown-up!

Every night I look down at the audience and count the bobs that appear before me, waves and waves of young women in the audience. They look just like me! Or at least, they are trying to be me, I guess. (Trendsetters!)

Some bobs rush to the stage door after the show, some leave early to try and meet with us. We have come to know most of our fans by name and we always take time to greet them and autograph their notebooks. We have a stack of teddy bears and handkerchiefs in our dressing room. Sometimes they give Fred flowers and he blushes, but mostly they have come to see me. Oh, it is funny, Daddy!

Mama is doing well, and she enjoys her own time, away from the stage. We have quite a lot of assistance here. I have Louise who helps me with my make-up, costumes and meals and things but Mama stills comes most nights to check if we need anything.

Freddie is good. He's still a Moaning Minnie, of course! He is still pacing up and down before every show, checking the stage two hours before we go on, putting down rosin, checking every surface before we dance on it.

Always, always practising. We have performed this show hundreds of times and yet there he is. What will we do with him, Daddy? Does he take after you or Mama?

I must go, I'm going to have a rest before tonight's show.

Write soon,

Your loving Adele

CHAPTER EIGHTEEN

LONDON, AUGUST 1923

I LIKED AN INTERESTING MAN. Someone who had something about him. I had no time for bores, no time for men who loved nothing better than to talk about themselves. Blathering, blathering, blathering.

A man had to make you *feel* something. You had to feel something when you were with him: an excitement, a flutter in your stomach, a little wince when you met him.

But this feeling was hard to come by.

I was not rude to the suitors that came my way.

There were so many. I enjoyed it of course, it was fun, but it was not real. It was something to play up to and to run away from afterwards. I was looking for a man. I didn't want a boy.

Sometimes production men or theatre directors and some small-time producers would make a move on me, ask me out to dinner, that kind of thing. Dillingham never did that, nor Aarons – they were married and real gentlemen. It was the more lousy types, the guys who'd chase every chorus girl with a smile. Horrible men.

Mama taught us how to mind ourselves. I knew my worth. And we'd been in theatre circles since we were children. She had sheltered us and showed us how to look after ourselves. Now I could mind myself all on my own, thank you very much!

As the shows became bigger and my photograph appeared on advertising cards and in the colour magazines, the men began to swarm.

"Would you like me to do something?" Fred said. "I can say something, get rid of them pretty quick."

Fred was a darling when it came to looking after me. For such a gentle soul, he kept a pool of anger for anyone who upset me. He hated to think of anyone trying to take advantage of me.

There were always so many men hanging around, coming into the dressing room with whoever they could, making jokes, trying to get up close, thinking they could really step out with Adele Astaire.

"No, Freddie, I can handle it, it's alright," I would tell him.

I put up with it a bit. Let them have their fantasy, let them think they had a chance.

But I wouldn't give myself over to just anyone. He had to have something, chutzpah, something special, a real intelligence about him.

Outside the theatre on Shaftesbury Avenue, they erected two huge cut-outs of me and Freddie. Our pictures! Like real people, only giant, out front, looking down on the street all day and all night.

I thought it was so funny. Fred thought it added too much pressure.

"Oh my," he said when we were called out front to see. "Will you look at that?"

I stood back on the street and observed myself, in black

and white and grey – at my face, cheeky and smiling, at the way I held my legs, one pointed backwards, bent up to the sky. Fred was standing still, sure of himself, looking out. I was leaning on his shoulder.

I loved it. Who would have thought, all those years ago, that here we'd be in London, looking down from the Shaftesbury, having people stop and stare and smile and then book tickets for what was surely to be a great, entertaining show.

Our practice run for *Stop Flirting* in Liverpool had gone smoothly – the audience had reacted well. But London was different. London was harder to impress.

Fred wrote home to Father to tell him of the poster cut-outs and that our names were also draped outside in huge big letters.

We wished he could have seen it, but he wrote back that he was sickly. He wrote a different letter to Mama and, when she received it, she made arrangements to go back home to mind him.

"It must be serious," I said to Freddie.

He looked concerned.

"Has she said anything to you?" I asked.

"Not a word."

"I have a bad feeling, Freddie."

"So do I."

We so wished Papa was here to see our names in lights, our cut-outs towering, an international audience cheering us on.

In all our experiences and travels, in all our rehearsals and costume runs and practising of our steps and lines and walk-ons, there was still room for nerves on our opening night in London.

We tried to calm ourselves as best we could, going through our little routines that helped us. For me, it was touching up my make-up at my dresser, lining up all the creams and bottles in the order I needed to apply them. This helped me feel in charge.

If I couldn't find a cream or a lipstick or a powder I wanted, I felt it would bring me bad luck.

Before make-up, I liked to get outside for a while too if I could, feel the air on my face, look at everything going on outside, for a distraction.

Fred wouldn't leave the theatre. He got there real early and he'd pace the stage, shaking his little bottle of rosin, pacing out some of the trickier steps in the exact spot he planned to do it later.

Sometimes he'd call me to go over a part and, if I wasn't there, he'd get real annoyed and tell me off when I came back and say I needed to be around before the shows for this kind of thing.

"Oh, stop your whining," I'd say. "It will be fine! I know just where you're talking about. I'll fix it."

When I had my make-up all done, I would bow my head and say a little prayer.

Thank You for the opportunities that have come our way. Thank You for all that You provide. Please let us do well tonight. Please look after Mama, Freddie and me. Please send Your special healing to Papa. Thank You, Lord.

It had to be this way, for it all to work.

For our opening night in London, I didn't leave the theatre beforehand. My stomach was too tight. I felt that I needed to be around, in case Freddie wanted me, in case I stepped out onto the street and was swallowed up by a great big London hole.

"Five minutes, Miss Astaire."

I look back into the mirror, at the black around my eyes, at my high cheeks, at my mouth lined with pencil, my matt lipstick, dark.

I think how Freddie, Mama, Daddy and I have worked towards this moment our whole lives.

To open to a packed house in a successful show, stars in our own right.

It is we who have been cut out in paper and placed out front, towering for everyone to see.

It is our names that glow above the Shaftesbury's doors.

It is us, Fred and Adele Astaire, who the people have come to see.

My stomach flutters and an excitement rises through my skin.

Go get 'em, I tell myself.

And so I do.

Freddie makes out that he is very coy and innocent and Mama thinks that he has never so much as looked at a woman in his life.

This makes me laugh.

If only she knew. He is very good at hiding it though, from her, from me.

He likes women, but he likes to keep an air of mystery about him too. There had always been rumours going round that Freddie only had eyes for other men, for young men like himself.

But this was rubbish. He was slender and jovial and ever so nice and because he was such a fine dancer people made assumptions.

But I knew. I knew that he was secretive and had been

with plenty of women who would come to his dressing room late at night, who would slip in backstage doors, who he would meet for secret suppers in little dive bars and speakeasies and late-night restaurants.

I could not do this. Mama would be out looking for me, wondering where devious little Delly had gone.

But I did try. And there were ways and means to sneak time with someone you liked, who liked you back, who offered a little bit of excitement on the road, to break up a long run of shows.

There was always a way if you worked hard enough, created a bit of space, the right excuses.

It was all a bit of fun. Girls my age, who I'd been in school with, were married now, most with babies, settled women.

It wasn't what I wanted, not yet. But I did want a man. Someone steady. Someone who tickled my fancy as much as I did his.

I liked the men in London. The way they spoke. The way they held their cigars and cigarettes and blew smoke in the air with their marble-mouth accents.

The parties were glorious.

And we were in demand.

INTERVIEW WITH FORMER PRINCE OF WALES EDWARD VIII, DUKE OF WINDSOR, EXILED TO FRANCE

Recording found among a series of interviews belonging to royal biographer Martin Campbell, donated to The British Museum in 1957

I'd heard about the show from a number of people. "You simply must see it," they said. I was away when it opened, on tour, and so when I was back I made sure to get to see what all the fuss was about. Everyone was talking about the Astaires and I was looking forward to seeing them. It was the start of the American invasion. Talent was coming from across the water and we were glad to see it, I can tell you.

The show wasn't too highbrow – I liked that. It was fun, not too serious. It had a silly storyline actually.

The Astaires brought with them an extraordinary ability to dance. They moved so fast, you barely saw their feet. We were all fascinated by it, by their speed.

Adele has this singsong voice, very coy. At first it grated on me a little and then I got used to it and saw how comic it was.

She was a dear. A true clown. She had this wonderful relationship with her brother, thick as thieves.

I liked Fred. He was a smart guy, dressed well. He fit right in with our set.

I was anxious to get them to the club, to see what they were all about.

Fruity picked them up from their hotel.

I asked Adele if she was too tired to dance and she said she was exhausted and suddenly leapt at me. It was very funny. They really were fun.

The band was very good at the Riviera. I went there as much as I could. I relaxed there, away from prying eyes. They'd section off a whole chunk for my friends and me.

I think I saw the show ten times. Whenever I had a free night, I'd try to go. I'd get them up to the box to say hello during the intermission. They didn't always come out with us afterwards, but if we were going they were invited.

It was a fun time. The clubs were busy, rattling with jazz. I was able to relax, drink, smoke, everything.

It was a free, easier time.

I would ask Adele to come sit with me and just listen to her talk.

I had a penchant for the American accent.

CHAPTER NINETEEN

LONDON, OCTOBER 1923

I HAD A HEADACHE. IT ECHOED ROUND the bones of my head, behind my eyes, passing all the way down my ears, almost into my throat.

Sometimes that happened if we'd been out late and I was tired or had a few cocktails and no water and I got dehydrated, which Freddie always berated me for.

"How do you expect to dance all night with nothing to sweat?"

I had been out the night before.

But it hadn't been too crazy.

I didn't know why this headache had come to strike me down.

I lay in my dressing room, on a chaise longue. I liked to rest with my feet up, whenever I was there. I could have curled up in an armchair, I was small enough, but the chaise longue was so much more graceful.

Our show had been moved to the Queen's Theatre, a gorgeous intimate place, and I asked them to put in the lounge for me when I moved. Why, I was a star now and could ask for things like this!

I let out a moan.

I'd placed a wet cloth over my face, but I wasn't sure it was helping.

A knock on the door.

Freddie.

"Come in!" I hollered from under the cloth.

Outside it was already dark, the fall closing in. One of the things we struggled with in England was the cold and lack of adequate heating and we knew, now that we were going into our second October in the place, that it would only get worse from here on in.

"Delly?" said Fred.

"Yes? Oh, Fred my head is aching! I don't know how to shift the damn pain. It'll be thumping tonight. I know you said to drink plenty of water, but I don't even think that would –"

"Delly," said Fred.

"What?" I said, not moving.

"Can you sit up, Delly, and take that thing off?"

I sat up and whipped the cloth off, holding it in my hand. "What is it, Fred?"

He came and sat beside me on the chaise, my headache rising now as the blood started pulsing in anticipation of what he was going to say.

"It's Daddy. Alfred has just come to me. He had a cable from Mother."

My hand shot to my mouth, and tears glistened all at once.

"Is he …?"

He nodded.

"*No*," I whispered.

"I'm so sorry, Delly," he said and he leaned over and held me as the tears came properly now.

"How?" I moaned into his neck.

"In Wernersville," Fred said through his own tears. "She took him to Galen Hall."

To recuperate. Where we'd enjoyed so many summers.

"But how?" I said. "How could this happen? So suddenly?"

"I'm really sorry, Delly."

My headache heaved. Alongside it came a new pain, in my heart, in my stomach, through the very centre of me.

I bent over, my head down on my lap.

Freddie rubbed my back.

Mama had been writing every few days, saying he was doing well, recuperating. Not in pain. Feeling good. How could he have died then, like this, without warning?

"I knew Mama wasn't telling us the truth, Delly. I knew it. I knew he was very sick."

"I can't believe it, Freddie. Daddy, gone ..."

"Alfred has said we can cancel tonight, but I think we should go on."

In less than an hour, the audience would begin flowing through the doors, all chatter and cackle, tickets and programmes in hand, ready to see us perform.

"Oh, Fred."

"Let's not think about it while we're on stage. Get on with the show and we will see how we feel after. He said he'll cancel for a week or two if we want."

"Do you want that?"

"Not really. What else can we do here?"

"We won't even get to his funeral."

"I know."

I put my head back onto Fred's shoulder and let the tears flow freely.

I would apply extra make-up tonight to conceal my blotchy, tearstained face.

We didn't miss any shows. We thought it would be better to keep working, to take our minds off things.

We went to church and had a Mass said for Daddy.

Sympathy cards and flowers arrived at our dressing room. Everyone was very sorry.

There were days when I could not stop crying but I would have to pull myself together for that night's show.

Fred was suffering too, but he didn't cry, not after that first night in my dressing room.

It was the first real loss we had ever experienced. And we didn't even have Mama to share it with. She was at home, sorting things out.

Two weeks after Daddy died, Mama arrived back in London, weary from travel and in pain.

Her face was pinched and sunken.

We took her home and I helped her to undress so that she could go to bed to rest.

"Would you like me to give you something, Mama, a sedative perhaps? I have half of one put away somewhere."

I watched in horror as she missed the bed and collapsed with a thump to the floor.

"*Fred!*" I roared.

She clutched at her stomach and curled up, like a dog around a tennis ball.

Fred called the ambulance from the telephone in our room.

I was petrified.

She had taken on too much, Mama, travelling back home on her own and looking after Daddy, dealing with his death and funeral.

What if we lost her too? Where would we be then?

We waited anxiously in the hospital waiting room, staring at the painted walls and a dusty oil painting of wilted flowers. What a depressing image for our surroundings!

A doctor came and spoke with us and said Mama was suffering from severe exhaustion, but they were worried about the pain in her stomach. They'd taken an X-ray and had seen something that wasn't right. She was being brought in for surgery.

Within two weeks our whole world had been turned on its head with Daddy's death and now Mama's illness.

"Daddy had cancer of the throat, did you know that?" I said to Fred.

"I wasn't sure what it was," he said.

"She told me, when I was getting her dressed for bed. Whispered it to me. Do you think she's been hiding something about herself too?"

"I don't know, Delly. I really hope not."

After some hours during which we exhausted ourselves pacing up and down the corridor and drinking hot, tangy teas from paper cups, the doctor came out and said Mama was in recovery and the operation had gone well.

She'd had a twisted bowel.

"She will need full recovery, complete bed rest," said the doctor. "I suggest that she is admitted to a convalescence home when she leaves here."

What a relief. She would recover and she would be looked after, not by us, but by a team of trained nurses, who were good at that sort of thing.

"Thank you, doctor," I said. "We will organise that straightaway."

We would put her in the best nursing home we could find, with the most wholesome food and the prettiest of surroundings.

It was the least that we could do for our poor, grieving mama.

Whispers ran through the audience. Like a rushing wind. Louise came to tell me.

"It's the Prince of Wales, Miss," she said, standing behind me at my dressing table. "He's just arrived. The audience are all a-chatter."

"Well, good," I said. "What took him so long?"

I turn to her and smiled. She smiled back.

You could always feel the energy in the theatre rise when there was somebody special in the audience that night. You couldn't get near the wings for the amount of stage bodies hovering, trying to sneak a look out the side.

I spied him too that night, so handsome, as though a spotlight was shining over his head. All eyes were on him.

"He's rather fine-looking, isn't he?" I whispered to Louise.

Having His Royal Highness at the show didn't unnerve me. I found it added a bit of pizazz to the whole thing. It livened everything up.

When I said my lines, I acted as I always did, confident in my delivery and not afraid to make a joke. I did my usual of faux-kicking someone up the rear in jest. When the orchestra made a bum note I stopped and wrinkled my nose at the conductor to get a laugh. Never had I any malice in me. I was simply pointing out what we all heard, what we all saw, made sure to have a sense of humour about it.

The Prince stayed right until the end. That was good, I guessed. He liked the show. The cast were beside themselves, all smiles and giggles and slapping each other on the back.

"It's not every night you get to perform for a prince, is it, Miss Astaire?" said Louise.

"No, it's not," I said.

Freddie knocked on my door and stuck his head in.

"He wants to meet us. And he's invited us for supper, to the Riviera Club."

"Oh God," I said. "Can't we just meet him and go home?"

"Are you going to turn down a prince?"

I sat in my chair and glanced at myself in the mirror. There were patches under my eyes where the make-up had sweated off. The black smoky effect I loved so much was smudged. My dressing gown hung open a little, revealing the flat part between my breasts.

I looked perfect.

Absolutely fit for a prince.

CHAPTER TWENTY

LONDON, MARCH 1924

THE SHOW WENT ON AND ON. Night after night. The audiences did not wane. More more more, encore.

Always wanting more.

Fred and I got tired.

The production toured, out of our London familiarity to Birmingham, north to Scotland, Glasgow, Edinburgh, the audiences cheering and clapping and shouting, chanting our names.

When we came back to London, I felt like we were getting on the merry-go-round again.

We had recorded two tracks from the show for discs which could be played on gramophones. It made people even more eager to attend the show. We had marvelled at the whole experience, singing as loudly as we could into fat potato microphones, and listening to our voices back.

Is that really how I sounded?

"I think I need a break, Fred."

He wanted one too.

It had been a year and a half since we had been on home soil. Our homesickness was growing. We loved England and its people and the success we had there.

But we wanted to rest, and we wanted to rest at home.

Sir Alfred Butt, our producer and sponsor, didn't want to hear about it. He thought the show could run and run.

I began to get upset.

One evening, when I was due to go to theatre, I rolled over in my bed and pulled the covers right over my face. Tears ran down my cheeks. My whole body ached and my toes felt like they had pins stuck through them. How was I to perform eighteen dances again tonight?

"Adele?"

It was Mama.

"I can't," I said.

She was used to my dramatics.

"Get up and get dressed – you'll feel better when you're up."

"I can't, Mama," I said.

My body began to heave with sobs. She came and sat down. I felt the bed shift under her light weight. She pulled the coverlet from my face.

I turned away embarrassed.

She knew it was not dramatics then, that I was not acting up, that I was truly, truly exhausted.

"Get yourself together for tonight," she said. "We will work something out. It will be over soon."

Relief began to bubble somewhere in my stomach, at the thought that Mama would make it alright again. She always did that, helped us sort things out, when we couldn't quite do it ourselves.

Over the next few days Mama and Fred approached Mr. Butt and informed him that I was not well and was in danger of collapse and hospitalisation.

At first he said he would consider cutting some dates to allow a bit of rest.

When Fred pressed him, he began to understand that we wanted to finish up.

Eventually he agreed. The show could end in August.

We immediately went and booked our passage home.

England had been a whirlwind for us, the biggest success of our careers. But we were utterly and thoroughly exhausted. We had paid a price for that success. My body had aged years in that space of time.

We set sail on my birthday, the 10th of September, waving from the deck with white hankies. Members of the press turned out on the quay to wave us off.

In our rooms, telegrams, notes and cards were piled high among flowers.

London will not be the same without you, they read. *Come back soon.*

I was twenty-eight years old. I wondered if I'd have the energy to come back and do it all again.

I'd always liked reading. Like knitting, I found it took my mind from my problems, carried my worries away as I tackled line after line.

In London I had picked up a number of books, recommended by my peers or swiped from shelves at parties if I liked the look of them.

I'd met a lot of writers in London – they were always interested in meeting us. I liked writers. They didn't have the same egos as theatre types. They didn't care much about how they looked. They were more interested in the conversation, philosophy, politics, humour. I had many a great chat with a man of words over a cocktail tumbler, perched on an armchair.

If I read an article by someone, especially a review that

concerned Fred and me, and if I met them later, I would always challenge them. "What exactly did you mean?" I'd ask, acting put out, staring them down and watching them squirm. I did it for fun, just because I could. I have never met a writer who wasn't embarrassed by coming face to face with the subject he had just written about, particularly if it was critical.

After listening to their *ums* and *ahs* and trying to talk their way out of it, I'd hit them on the arm and tell them I was only joking and that I loved the piece and would they like to have another drink, because they looked like they could certainly do with one?

George Bernard Shaw was a beautiful man. I loved his voice and his singsong way of speaking. Every time I encountered him I would sit down and get as close to him as I could and watch how he spoke. I was never sure if he knew who I was, but I didn't care. I just liked being near him, listening, watching his mouth move under that white, spotless beard.

I could have married a man like Shaw. Even though he was more than double my age, I would have gladly offered myself as a wife. I wanted my own Shaw. A gentleman, an intelligent, funny, articulate man. So many of my suitors were brash or full of brawn, ready to argue and fight with all the manliness they carried round with themselves. Others were weak and weary, drips of men who thought the money they had was enough to buy a passage into a marriage with someone like me.

I would wait for a younger George Bernard Shaw. A writer, yes. An interesting man that I would not be able to shake from my mind, no matter how hard I tried.

We stood on deck as the *SS Homeric* pulled into the port, shoulder to shoulder, our hands entwined.

We wanted to see the land of our birth, together, for the first time without Daddy in it.

Mama stayed in her cabin, happy to pack up the last of her things, to give us this moment together.

Tears rolled down our cheeks. I felt as though we were starting to mourn all over again, a different type of grief, knowing that the last time we were on this soil, our father was too.

Fred was quiet.

We were home, but there were only three in our family now.

Despite the sadness of Daddy's passing, our trip home was something of an unexpected triumph and this was apparent by our greeting party on the dock. We had to wipe away our tears and wave to our friends and waiting press.

Camera bulbs flashed in our faces, as we walked down the gangway onto the dock.

"Looks like we haven't been forgotten after all," I whispered to Fred.

We had been worried that our year and a half spent away from the States would damage our career. It was easy to forget a pair who hadn't been seen in so long, hadn't attended the parties, the premieres, hadn't been filling the gossip columns and the fashion pages.

But our success in England had made us even bigger stars. Now, we were connected to royalty.

"*Tell us about the princes!*" shouted a press man.

"*Is it true you and the Prince of Wales are to be engaged?*" shouted another.

I was taken aback.

"Now look here!" I said. "If you think you're going to

get some tabloid headlines out of me, you're crazy. The royal princes were very kind to my brother and me and we won't be talking about them for publicity!"

Fred smiled.

We pushed our way on through, meeting with Alex Aarons and Vinton Freedley who was his new producing partner. They spoke immediately about our next show.

"Golly," I said as we pushed on through, "are you that keen?"

"We are," said Aarons.

He told us about the show they were working on, how it was light and modern and had two pianos players in the pit. All the music was from George Gershwin and the lyrics from his brother Ira.

Finally, Fred's wish to do a whole musical with his old pal Gershwin was going to come true.

"We only have a verbal agreement on this," said Aarons. "You have to sign the contracts. I have them right here. Do you trust me to ruin your lives again for the next few years?"

We laughed at his humour. Amused at the paperwork he produced, we stretched over our trunks in the customs queue and signed on for the American run of our new Aarons and Freedley show.

We would be in rehearsals in less than a month.

You had to take the opportunities as they came.

INTERVIEW WITH J.M. BARRIE, AUTHOR, LONDON

Research on: **The Man Behind Peter Pan,**
by Elizabeth Sherry
Archive Located: New York Public Library of Performing Arts
Status: Published 1946, available on special order

Ach, everyone heard about the Astaires. Especially Adele. She was a real firecracker.

I went to see Stop Flirting *and, as soon as she took to the stage, I thought, just look at her – she'd be perfect. She had this nymph-like look about her, a sprite – she would have been a perfect Peter Pan.*

She was small, real petite. But lithe. A body of a boy in a way.

I sat there, in a trance. I felt there was something truly magical about her.

The audience hung on every word she said.

Aye, I fell in love with her that night. We all did.

I was hoping to meet her, to meet the both of them, but I did'nae expect to meet their mother first. We were both at Douglas Shield's Nursing Home, convalescing. She was pretty poor, Ann, after what happened. I think all those years had caught up on her.

I was getting over a nasty flu that knocked the stuffing out of me, thought I was a goner to be honest. I was happy to go in there to be looked after a while.

And when she was up and better, I noticed her, this glamorous woman, blonde hair swept up, lipstick, really beautiful.

We got talking and soon we spoke about her son and daughter and I could'nae believe it, who she was, and I told her I'd love to meet them and she said of course and a few weeks later I did. When we were both better, both out.

They came round to mine in the Strand, and I had a meal prepared, over candlelight, a great night of fun and flirting, and a good dollop of wine too, although the Astaires were not that big drinkers at all.

I put the proposal to her, I said, "Adele, how would you like to play Peter Pan at the Adelphi? At Christmas? I think you'd be perfect."

Oh, she was thrilled. They all were. Her mother and Fred, they said how wonderful she would be for the part.

And she said, "Oh, Mr. Barrie, that would be wonderful, I would love that."

And off she went back to Alfred Butt and he said no – that he wouldn't release her for Christmas, wouldn't hear of an understudy or loaning her out for the performances. She had to come back and tell me and she was so sorry because she really wanted that part.

And, you know, it would have been good for her, to be out on her own like that, away from Fred, not that there was anything wrong with Fred, just for her to shine, all on her own.

Because she deserved it. She was a true star.

But it wasn't to be. We got Gladys Cooper instead.

But I would have loved Adele.

CHAPTER TWENTY-ONE

NEW YORK, LIBERTY THEATRE, JULY 1925

THE FIRST SIX MONTHS OF OUR NEXT MUSICAL – *Lady, Be Good!* – sold out as soon it was announced that we were the leads and the Gershwins were devising the score.

There was something a bit magical about us and the Gershwins. We clicked. Sometimes I thought George was the brother Freddie never had, even though they couldn't have looked more different.

You'd find them both seated at the piano, George with his cigar hanging like a small tree-branch from his mouth.

Because Freddie was so good on the piano and so musical, they would play bits together, little tunes and melodies. That was the difference with the Gershwins doing our score. The music was special.

They put two pianos in the pit playing alongside each other and against each other at times. Then when you put Freddie up on the stage and his tapping, well, it was like a competition, all against each other, a tit for a tat.

Our feet became pianos too. There was music from every beat and drop and hum. The audience loved when we dropped our singing and had a dance battle with the pianos.

We recorded the songs for gramophone again and the sheet music was selling out everywhere.

The shows kept us busy and there was little time for anything else, but if I was feeling energetic I would head for Fifth Avenue to stock up on my wardrobe pieces. I was going through a pair of silk stockings a day and my shoes wore out each week. I worried about my feet – if the leather couldn't sustain our hectic dancing night after night, how could my poor skin, toes and feet?

I was careful about what I ate. I knew I needed to eat well to have all the energy we required to perform our evening and matinee shows. I couldn't afford to get sick. At times, though, I felt my energy waning. The intensity of the performances began to take its toll a little.

My age was beginning to show.

I didn't want to be an old puss on the planks, aching and creaking and taking God knows what to get me up there to smile and bow and begin the show.

Fred was alright – he could go on forever.

I didn't want to.

Sometimes, it got me down a little, made me fret that I would end up alone, never having known the proper love of a man, lost to a life on the stage.

I batted away the admirers, the hangers-on, the ones who were uninteresting and dull and ever so keen. I was still searching for my own George Bernard Shaw.

And then, just like that, there he was.

He got to me, through his words.

I just hadn't been paying attention.

"*She is no beauty. She makes up her eyes with a pint or two of shoe blacking. She has little colour sense in her choice of costumes.'* This is who you have fallen for?"

"I have not fallen for him, Mama!"

"But you will let him take you out? He is no good for you, Adele!"

"I know, Mama, you've told me."

"Why won't you listen?"

"I am listening."

"But you are still going to meet with him, this – this critical man. This man who says such nasty things. About you. About everyone."

"That's his job, Mama."

"To be nasty?"

"To be a critic."

"He is not for you, Adele."

"Mama, please, I know what I'm doing. Just let me have my fun. I like him. It's not serious."

Mama's face was furrowed and dark. Rarely did I see things annoy her so much. George Jean Nathan had her in a rage.

Oh George. Georgy, Georgy, Georgy.

If Mama thought that I did not take him to task over that review then she was wrong. But she didn't read out the parts where he compared me to Irene Castle. To Marilyn Miller. And talked about my electric little legs!

Yes, I always enjoyed confronting writers when I met them but it was George who pursued me. He had sent a note backstage one night after a show.

Miss Astaire, let me take you out on the town. A girl like you deserves a boy like me.

George Jean Nathan

I was not sure if George and I would marry. I was not sure how my bones felt about it. But I wished Mama, and

Freddie too, weren't so hard on him. I wished they could see what I saw: his magnetism, his absolute sweeping charm and intelligence, his ability to stop a person in their tracks with a sentence.

He was a little bit in love with me.

And I, with him.

"You are still going to meet him tonight?"

"I am."

"I don't like it."

"I know, Mama."

"Why won't you do as I say? Put him off. Tell him you have a new boyfriend."

I laughed: "Oh Mama, because it's not true!"

"He is no good for you."

"So you say."

"Have I ever been wrong before?"

"Have I ever given you cause to worry before?"

"Frederick," said Mama. "Talk to her, tell her to break it off with him, she'll listen to you."

"The hell she will," said Fred.

I smiled at him.

Mama looked exasperated.

"I won't be late," I said, and ran off to my room to add my pint of shoe blacking and spritz my new scent all around my hair and ears and wrists.

"Here, I brought this for you."

"Oh," I said as George flung a battered-looking book in my direction.

"*The Great Gatsby*," I read. "By F. Scott Fitzgerald. Who's he when he's at home then?"

"Dunno," said George, "but I liked it. Reckoned you

might too. All big parties and decadence, right up your street."

I was pleased. Pleased that he had brought me a gift, a thoughtful one at that, and pleased that he was sharing books with me. This great critic of mine.

We studied our menus, glancing up at each other in the dim light. His eyes dark coals, burning.

"Have you reviewed it?"

"It'll be in tomorrow. So you're getting a sneak peek."

"Oh goody."

I couldn't help but smile. I noticed I'd been smiling a lot. Even Freddie said it to me, teasing – *you're like the cat that got the cream*. But it came from the inside out.

I was in love.

"You know my mama dislikes you," I said.

"A lot of people dislike me."

"She read one of your books, the one where you said you wished all girls were orphans. She did not like that at all."

"Oh, that," he said. "Is she an orphan herself?"

"No!"

"Are her parents still alive?"

"No."

"Then she is an orphan, is she not?"

"Mr. Nathan," I said, "don't be silly."

"Miss Astaire, I can only be silly around someone as silly as you."

The scratch of cutlery on white plates rimmed with gold cut through the low sound of the clarinet player, perched in the corner.

"I'll have Chinese vegetable soup and Chicken Chow Mein," I said to the waiter.

It was my first time trying Chinese food and I loved the

sound of the vegetables and the way they were cooked. It was so different, so very in vogue.

"Do you fancy the pictures after this?"

"I thought we might catch a show?"

"Let's go to the picture house. I've seen three shows this week, I want something outside of reviews. The new Chaplin picture is showing."

As a drama critic, George liked to get away from the theatre on his nights off. I, on the other hand, was more than willing to go and visit every theatre in town, to see who was playing and what they were doing. I liked to watch the other actresses perform, see how beautiful they were, what clothes they were wearing and by whom.

But, a picture was grand too. I liked Charlie Chaplin.

"Let's go and see what one million dollars gets you these days," said George.

"One million dollars?" I gasped.

"So they say. One million dollars on one picture. You need to get out of the theatre, my dear, and into the pictures."

"What could you ever spend one million dollars on?" I said.

"Well, we'll see after this," said George.

I picked at my food, eating little bites. I liked the vegetables, but I wasn't hot on the sauce. It was so different and I wasn't quite sure what to make of the noodles. They felt like little worms dancing in my mouth.

We left the restaurant, George holding on to my elbow and both of us felt heads turn as we passed, all eyes on us, even in the dim light.

At the picture house, we were escorted to the top of the queue and brought to an upper box inside, right in the centre of the theatre. We ordered drinks and were huddled head to head, enjoying this time alone together. Perhaps George was right. Perhaps the pictures were more fun.

When the lights dimmed and the film flickered onto the screen, the roll of film whirring, we were disturbed by a couple being escorted into our box.

George tutted. We'd thought we'd be given the luxury of this box alone.

The man nodded to us and we took a second glance as the opening credits of *The Gold Rush* started to roll, casting black shadows across his face.

He was cleanshaven and handsome, and he reminded me of someone I'd seen before.

His wife took her seat, her stomach round, under a lightweight coat.

George nudged me and smiled.

"Guess who that is?"

"Who?" I hissed. I had turned my eyes to the screen.

George pointed at the screen and then at the couple.

"That's Charlie Chaplin and that's his wife, Lita Grey."

My mouth made an O.

We sat and sipped, casting our eyes towards the couple and back to the screen, watching what one million dollars afforded you in a picture.

Maybe George was right; maybe pictures was where it was at, after all.

Maybe Freddie and I should look into it?

PART THREE

OPENING NIGHT

CHAPTER TWENTY-TWO

LISMORE, COUNTY WATERFORD, IRELAND, APRIL 1928

PATRICIA RYAN FELT HER CALVES TIGHTEN as she left the bridge behind and mounted the hill.

To her right, towering over her, the castle loomed, a beacon of stone and razor-cut glass, a place she once believed princesses lived in. She had blonde hair like Rapunzel, her mother had told her when she was a little girl.

For Christmas one year Santa had left a thick book with *Irish Fairy Tales* inscribed in gold on the front. The fairies inside, entwined in trees, tangled in the hair of white horses, had filled her dreams. She fashioned sticks into fairies which she dressed in pieces of ribbon and scraps of cloth, gathered and treasured when her mother cut her Easter dress out on the kitchen table.

The fairy book still perched on the chest of drawers against the back wall in her bedroom. She would never part with it. She knew every page, every drawing, had fingered each tree, fairy and horse over the years. Sometimes she placed paper over the drawings and traced them out herself to shade in with pencil.

It was that book that made her fall in love with castles and the greatest of them all, Lismore Castle, towered right down on top of them in the small village where she lived.

She dreamed one day she would visit.

Her chance had come when she was eight years old. Mr. Mac, the butcher who was very fond of her mother and often called in on them after her father died, was going up to the castle to take an order for a visiting party from Chatsworth in England.

Would she like to go with him?

She raced to her bedroom and took her white ribbon from its drawer, the one she kept for special occasions. Mammy fixed it to her hair, properly.

Walking side by side with Mr. Mac as they climbed the hill, she had never felt such excitement. Not even Christmas could compare to this – on her way to get a look inside Rapunzel's castle.

The first set of castle gates were open, leading to a long narrow avenue. At the end was a tower bridge with another wooden gate, blocking their way.

Mr. Mac knocked on the big wooden gate, and in the middle of it a much smaller gate opened, big enough for only one person to be able to go through at a time.

She went through ahead of Mr. Mac and her eyes swept over all before her. It was hard to take it all in.

It was like a tiny enchanted kingdom.

A flat manicured lawn, green like the weeds that gathered on the pools beside the River Blackwater, was cut into a half circle.

Around the edges were pebble borders of stone, as though laid out by the fairies themselves.

The gravel on the driveway was small, loose, yellow in colour, nothing like the dark black shingle that littered the potholes and roads outside the castle.

Behind the lawn, the building spread out in a square, tall turrets at the corners. A true princess castle. So many windows where Rapunzel could have let her hair down.

She walked with Mr. Mac to the back door, the servants' entrance, and listened to him rap loudly on the wood.

A cook answered, flustered. "Come in, come in, take a seat, so much to do – let's start, will we – we'll need a lot – a lot of dishes to prepare."

While the butcher took the cook's order, Patricia's eyes wandered, over the giant stove and the long narrow table scattered with objects: a large slab of butter, a bowl with broken eggs, a beige earthen bowl just like her mother had, a flour mix, a jug of milk.

The walls were bare, the ceiling tall.

"Four pounds of rashers, three pounds of sausages."

What lay behind that door, behind the cook standing over the butcher writing in his notebook?

"Six kidneys. Fourteen pounds of sweetbreads. Eight pounds of shin beef."

The door opened, a maid coming in, a glance into the darkness of what lay behind.

"Five and a half pounds of fillet ham. And steak. Four pounds. We'll put in the order and if we need extra I'll send a messenger down during the week."

Mr. Mac closed his order book with a big slap. It was a great boost to this week's sales. He was in a jovial mood. Perhaps he might be staying for a cup of tea, but the cook didn't offer. Instead, she went back to her flour mixture in the bowl and he stood up to go.

Patricia wanted to ask if she could have a look, to see what lay beyond that door. What was there in the dark of the castle?

They stepped out the back door into the cool spring air, only then realising the heat that had been in the kitchen.

There was something so ordinary about the room they'd just been in. It was bigger than any kitchen she'd seen before, ten times the size of her mother's perhaps. The stove was bigger, the table longer, but it was still a room with the same foods they had at home. It wasn't the kitchen she wanted to see but the rest of the castle – the rooms were the princess lived – her bedroom, her toys, her dresses.

She was a little bit disappointed that this was all she would be getting.

At the front lawn, gardeners were hunched at borders, digging and weeding.

"Isn't she a fine place altogether?" said Mr. Mac.

She looked up at one of the turrets, the one nearest the River Blackwater. Its window reflected the light, a bend to the glass as though it were not flat. Rapunzel could be up there right now for all she knew, and here she was being shepherded away by Mr. Mac.

He walked quickly, out the gate, nodding to the workers, and she had to run to catch up with him.

She took one last lingering glance before walking through the small wooden door, that would shut and cut the castle off until the next time she could come back again. For now, she would have to lay it down in her memory, into the place dreams come from at night.

It would be a long time before Patricia got to visit Lismore Castle again.

Mr. Mac died the next year, a heart attack, falling to the floor behind his counter of red meats, his sons splashing water on his face, but he was gone.

Her mother was very upset. He had been a very good friend since her husband had died.

Mr. Mac's sons had no interest in taking little Patricia up to the castle any time they had to do an order – they wouldn't understand her interest in a place like that.

It was her mother, in the end, who secured the interview for a housekeeper's assistant at the castle. Mrs. Smyth had heard that Mrs. Keeley the housekeeper was looking for someone respectable, decent, a quiet girl.

"Sure wouldn't my Patricia be a grand girl for the job," her mother said to Mrs. Smyth who was very good friends with Mrs. Keeley on account of them being second cousins once removed.

And the word came back that Mrs. Keeley would like to meet with Patricia, to see if she would indeed be suitable for such a role.

And here she was on a pleasant April day, climbing up the hill, past the Blackwater and the bridge, about to knock on the small wooden door leading into the castle again, eight years older, wiser, no longer a child.

It was different now that she was older. It wasn't quite as big as she remembered. The round lawn at the front no longer resembled an area as big as a football pitch. The buildings did not seem as towering. She could see it for the beautiful, homely courtyard it was.

She knew where to go this time, around to the back to knock on the servants' entrance.

Imagine this could be a place of work, imagine she could be paid to come here each day, to this magnificent solid home?

She waited an age for an answer, the swirls in her stomach

threatening to take over and spew forth her breakfast. Imagine if she did that on the back step? What sort of decent girl would do that?

The door opened and a girl in an apron answered. Patricia recognised her as a girl who lived outside the village and had been in school ahead of her by a few years. The girl didn't smile but went to fetch Mrs. Keeley.

Patricia stood, feeling self-conscious, looking around the kitchen. A cook was peeling carrots.

Mrs. Keeley appeared behind the aproned girl, a woman with a narrow waist but large hips. They formed a round mound beneath her dress, soft. She smiled, but not too brightly.

"Miss Ryan, good morning. I'll take you into my office."

Patricia didn't know whether to smile back or curtsy. She did neither.

Mrs. Keeley led her into a back hall, and down a small corridor.

A large cannonball held a door open, a giant stopper against the green paintwork. She avoided it as she turned the corner in the corridor – it stuck out and could catch an ankle.

And then she was in a small office, Mrs. Keeley's office, and she could feel detergent in her nose.

Papers were strewn across the table – ledgers, order sheets, invoices, a little booklet of stamps. A morning cup of tea had gone cold on its saucer, the cream floating, the liquid beneath grey.

She waited for the questions to start.

Her education, she supposed. Her skills. Her temperament. The friends she kept.

Of course she didn't take a drink or smoke. She was a

decent girl. That's not to say she hadn't tried smoking. In fact, she'd tried it a number of times – little rollies pinched by her friend Deirdre from her mother. She loved to watch Deirdre roll out the tobacco and seal the cigarette with her fingers. The process was soothing and she quite liked the smell and the warmth of it.

Mrs. Keeley sat down behind her desk and looked at Patricia, who was standing, her hands clasped in front of her.

"Miss Ryan," she said and folded her hands into her lap, right beside a big iron ring of keys. They were black and looked heavy, standing out shiny on her skirt. "Mrs. Smyth tells me you're a quiet girl. Never been in trouble."

"No, Mrs. Keeley, never."

"And you have domestic experience?"

"I've worked as a domestic for a few places. I replaced Mrs. Donnelly when she was sick last year at the parochial house. I was there for nearly eight weeks. And the year before that, I was at the Mullens' house as a housemaid."

"And what happened there?"

"Nothing, Mrs. Keeley – just the family, they wanted to move back to England, that was all."

"And have you been looking for work?"

"I have, Mrs. Keeley, but I want to find a good job, a decent job for myself. One that I know I'll like and be good at."

"And what makes you think you'll be good here?"

"I'm very respectable. I'll listen to anything you ask me and do it, without questioning. I'm a hard worker."

Mrs. Keeley regarded her up and down again.

"And school?"

"I went to the Mercy until I was fourteen. I got very good marks. My mother wanted me to go to England, to look at being a bookkeeper, but I didn't want to leave her, you understand."

"I do. Well, let me tell you a little bit about ourselves here, Miss Ryan, and what would be expected of you. This is a very busy estate. A lot goes on behind these walls that you wouldn't even know about. We run the whole estate from here, all the lands, the tenantry, everything is decided here. My job is to make sure the castle itself is maintained and that it's ready for any visitors who wish to come and especially when the Duke and his family wish to visit. We have a lot of staff and everything needs to run smoothly. This would be a very good job for someone like you. I'm looking for someone who has a brain. I don't want a silly type of girl, a gossiper, someone who'd rather stand about and do nothing rather than the work she's paid for. Do you understand?"

"I do."

"At the moment we could probably look at short days, but when the family come to stay, you'd be expected to do extra. It would be all hands on deck."

Patricia remained silent. Her heart began to thump, faster that it had when she'd first met Mrs. Keeley. Was she really about to be given a job at Lismore Castle?

What did she have to say to convince the housekeeper she was the right girl for the job? Was it better to shut up and listen or say something, about her skills, her demeanour, the manners her mother had instilled in her?

"I'll give you a trial, Patricia. We'll see how we get on."

"Thank you, Mrs. Keeley."

"Tomorrow's Friday, so you can start next Monday morning. Seven thirty sharp."

"Thank you, Mrs. Keeley."

They stood and Patricia followed her through the corridor, which seemed lighter now, brighter, and back through the kitchen, where the cook and girl turned to look at her. She couldn't help but smile at them.

Mrs. Keeley closed the door behind her and Patricia managed to keep herself together until she got out, past the lawn, past the yellow gravel, into the avenue, through the little gate.

Had Mrs. Keeley been in the bridge tower, looking down, she would have seen her newest employee jump right into the air and kick her legs together in joy.

It was the best thing that had happened to her since her first visit to Lismore as a child.

CHAPTER TWENTY-THREE

LONG ISLAND, NEW YORK, JULY 1928

HEAT. HOT, HOT, HOT. AGAINST MY FACE. As though I have my face pressed against an oven door. Searing.

I move my head a little, where it is resting, face down on my arms. They are crossed under me, like a pillow. They too are hot. Burned.

The heat is everywhere now, all down my front, my legs.

I pull my head up to see Billy lying on the flat of his back. He must have rolled himself over to quench the flames. He is breathing deeply, his chest rising up and down, like the lapping of the water. Up and down, in and out.

We are lying on the wooden walkway he built at his house, on the lake where he ties up his boats.

My ears are ringing from the explosion.

Small bits of debris are still flying through the air, raining down on us in a slow black shower.

"*Are you alright? Oh my God, oh my God!*"

William is here now.

Billy's wife Xenia is howling, screeching, "*Call an ambulance, call an ambulance!*"

"I'm OK," I say. My skin is too hot to touch.

Don't touch me.

I realise that my clothes have burned into me and that I must remove them or else I am in big trouble.

"Help me to the water," I say, my voice gravelly, not like my voice at all.

"*What?*" says William.

He doesn't understand.

"I need to get this off," I say, gesturing to my dress.

Thank Christ it's July, the sun beating down on us in planks. I could have been wearing stockings.

William helps me, lifting me up by my armpits, and holds onto me as I manage to sit up and drop my legs into the water, perching on the side of the walkway. I need to lower my body down, into the cool, dark water.

It is a difficult manoeuvre for him, holding me like that, trying not to topple over into the water himself.

Ahead of me the boat burns, an orange ball of flames against the cobalt sky.

With one hand I grab the bottom of my dress and pull it up so that it floats around me. I pause for a moment, catching my breath – it hurts to breathe, singeing in and out. With the water lodged in the dress now, I pull it up, feeling it peel away from my skin. It is heavy, a wet sticky bandage, like paper from margarine.

William pulls it all the way over my head. He slaps it onto the walkway and it lies there in a heap.

Under the walkway I can see dark shadows and a lapping sound echoes. What lurks beneath there?

I touch my brassiere. I touch my knickers. I think I am OK.

I want to stay in the water, but I know I need to get out.

William pulls me up and I sit there, sodden, still trying to catch my breath. I look over at Billy Leeds, who is awake, but not really moving and I tell William that they need to wet his clothes, because if they pull them off him now they will surely peel his skin.

Sulphur, in the air, on me. The smell of wood burning now as the speedboat crackles and the paint snaps.

Not what we were expecting from our extended Fourth of July break.

Now what we were expecting at all.

Billy Leeds was the best party host. He was one of those wealthy people who like to share it with others. What was the point of having all these riches and privileges if you were just going to sit at home on your own all day? He reminded me of Philip Sassoon a bit, though he was very American and had none of the pomp that Philip had.

I had found myself often in the company of these wealthy types. It was easier. You could go and stay and have privacy and none of the fuss. Cooks were on hand, but nothing was forced. If you didn't want to have dinner, you didn't. Breakfast could be any time.

Staying in Philip Sasson's home in London or Billy Leeds' home in Long Island was far better than a hotel. We'd lived in hotels for years, with their dry air and their staff always wanting to come into your room. There were rules and checkouts and other people always milling about. Hotels reminded me of work.

These mansion homes reminded me of holidays.

Of legs wrapped round mine, of heady, dreamless, satisfied sleep.

It was easy to sneak away to homes like Billy's. If I wanted to have any privacy I had to.

Mama was already on the case, suspicious. But when I was at Billy Leeds' I forgot about all that.

Now, everyone would know where I was because of what happened. Where I was, what I was doing, who I was with.

I wondered why it had happened to me?

Why had I been the one to agree to go with Billy to see his new speedboat? Why had Xenia, his Russian princess, not come down with us? Why had William stayed at the house, chatting, sipping on a glass of iced tea?

Of course, it was a better thing that they hadn't – there would have been four injured now instead of two.

But still I wondered, why me?

As I lay back in the ambulance that came to pick us up, a man in a white coat taking my pulse and asking me questions, I thought that maybe it was punishment for all the sneaking around.

Maybe God had seen to it that I was taught a lesson. It was sinful to be running around with a man I wasn't married to. It was sinful to be lying to my mother, deceitful to say I was with Fred, when all along I was with William Gaunt in Upper State Long Island, New York.

I thought of Billy Leeds' lovely speedboat blown to smithereens. I had been admiring the smooth woodwork, the way the curve set into the steering wheel. I was thinking maybe Fred and I should buy one between us? Like our Rolls Royce? But Freddie would prefer to put the money into a horse, I knew it.

"You wanna hear it purr?" Billy had said, his eyes glistening.

He loved speed, loved anything that moved fast. This was the latest in his speedboat collection, two others were moored beside us.

All around us were dumpling hills, as though they'd been moulded by his gardener into the landscape. His house, fronted by a gigantic porch, was surrounded by teeming, twitching bushes, exotic flowers grown in greenhouses and replanted to decorate and perfume the front of his house.

"Sure," I said.

I had no real interest in listening to the engine of a speedboat, unless it was during a little trip around the lake. But I liked Billy, he was charming, and I knew he loved to show off his purchases.

We were standing in the boat, my sandals submerged beneath the ankle-deep water that had gathered in the corner. I should have taken them off.

He pulled the engine string.

It backfired.

My dress ignited, a small flame at first, licking at my knees and then it was all on fire.

I screamed, whacking myself down furiously, but fuel must have leaked into the water we were standing in, and within seconds both of us were engulfed.

I felt myself being lifted, tossed hard onto the walkway, thrown like a rag doll.

I screamed again, trying to catch my breath, the pain searing.

I turned my head and saw Billy untying the boat and kicking it hard – it slowly backed away from the walkway.

He grunted as he slapped me down with his bare hands, *whack whack whack*, his blows raining down on me, flattening the flames, beating them into me.

BANG!

I must have passed out, with the pain, with the shock.

Awoke to the heat, to the great heat seeping through my skin.

The ambulance man asked me if I was OK. I was babbling, talking about the lovely woodwork on the boat, how it was all broken up in bits over the lake now, how we'd never even got a proper spin in it.

"Just relax," he said.

And he gave me something for the pain.

It was rare for me to be so attracted to a man. There were so many, you see. So many admirers, so many putting themselves forward. I liked the ones who didn't put themselves forward at all. Who stood back and watched, who let me come to them.

William Gaunt was a cad. Anyone could see it. I knew it, but it didn't put me off.

I felt myself change when he came near, like a jug filling up, fizzing. My skin prickled when he smiled at me.

I met him backstage one night after the premiere of our new show *Funny Face*. It was our third show with Aarons and Freedley, our second with the Gershwins on the score. We had hit on a winning formula, as though we had mixed all the right ingredients and baked a cake for success.

"Look at you, Miss Astaire," he said.

I was still in my costume, sweat drying on my face, my hair flared with the heat.

"Look at you, Mr. Gaunt," I replied, eyeing him suspiciously.

"That was quite a show."

"Thank you."

"Probably up there with the best I've seen."

"Up there?"

"Yes."

"Not *the* best show you've ever seen?"

"Well ..." He held his hands out and smiled, teasing.

"Liar!" I said and pushed past him to head to my dressing room. The corridor was filled with dancing girls, frills, all hugging, saying well done, the sound of applause only now fading away.

He gripped my wrist from behind.

"I'll tell you what my favourite show is later," he said.

"No, thanks," I said and shrugged him off.

His touch sparked through my arm. When I went and sat at my dressing table, I could feel his fingers still pressing into my wrist.

I had a sudden vision of me on top of him, of looking into his eyes, of feeling him, inside.

Mama disapproved of course. Just like George Jean Nathan, my last serious lover, she gave me hell over William Gaunt.

"Why can't you find yourself a nice boy, Adele?"

"He is a nice boy, Mama."

"Yes, he's nice to all the ladies," she said.

I threw my eyes up to heaven.

She wasn't wrong, but I didn't want to know about that. I didn't want to think of William looking at any other woman the way he looked at me. I couldn't bear to think of him making another woman feel the way he made me feel. Why did she have to bring that up, make me feel bad for the affection we held each other in?

The press lapped it up of course. It was on again, off again. And the worst were those anonymous gossip columns where they could say what they liked, print any damned rumour they heard, no matter if it was true or not.

I hated the press intrusion into our lives. I hated that

Mama did not approve. And Fred too – he couldn't stand William Gaunt and that made me saddest of all.

Whatever of Mama's opinions, because she could be old-fashioned and sniffy, it pained me that Fred did not like my William. With Fred, you see, it was as though he were part of me, thought the same thoughts, felt the same way about almost everything. If he didn't like William, then he could see a real reason not to.

And I hated that.

I ignored it as best I could. William was a beautiful man and I only had to look at him to want to jump right on top of him. He filled my thoughts, my sleep at night and when I was on stage I directed my voice and all of my dances to him.

I only had eyes for him.

I could see why Fred didn't like him. That start of our relationship had been a bit ... well ... woozy. Yes, I can see of course why that impacted.

But everyone makes mistakes, right? We don't all sail through life blemish-free?

I did so hate to upset Freddie though. He was a pet and nobody took our stage career more seriously than him.

He was right to be angry with me. I was angry with myself.

I still am.

INTERVIEW WITH FRED ASTAIRE

Background interview recorded ahead of* The Ed Sullivan Show, *promotional tour* Steps in Time, *Autobiography

Broadcast: 28 February June 1959

Network: CBS

Delly never let me down. Never. She was always on time, took pride in it. Sure, she could be lazy, not wanting to rehearse and that, but as for show times and turning up and being where she needed to be, she was like clockwork. Maybe it was our Austrian heritage. All those watchmakers. Ha! I remember once, back when we were young, the producer tried to make out that we had been late to rehearsals and wanted to dock us money over it. The show was a flop, you see. Well, Delly took him to task, in front of everyone, in front of the whole crew and she said, "You listen here, Mister, we have not been late one minute to rehearsals. You might not have noticed, because you were too busy feeling up the chorus girls on that balcony."

Oh, the silence in that room. That was Delly. She

took everyone to task. Loved to cuss out, get herself noticed. Well, the man was furious, but we got our money because we never had been late.

Anyway, this one night, the night after our opening premiere for Funny Face *at the Alvin Theatre, New York, I was there as usual waiting to go on. I liked to be there early, just to relax, to check the stage over, to go through my rituals, chat with Walter my valet, get my water in, that kind of thing.*

I realised I hadn't seen Delly that night – usually we'd have a quick word, especially when a show was premiering and we were still getting used to it.

Word filtered around that she wasn't in the building.

She hadn't arrived.

I went to her dressing room. I guess I had to see it for myself: she wasn't there.

Where the hell was she?

The stage manager phoned her hotel, got the duty manager to go knock on her door – it had happened to me before, I'd fallen asleep and almost missed a show, an afternoon nap, I didn't hear my alarm. It could happen when you were tired.

But she wasn't at the hotel either. Hadn't been there all afternoon, they said. Left earlier, they thought, dressed for a cocktail party.

William Gaunt had picked her up in his car.

That cad. Well, I was fuming. I was so angry. How could he take her out like that, keep her late and this only our second night of the show?

In she walks at twenty-five past eight – twelve minutes till we were on stage. It usually took her least forty-five minutes to get ready.

"Go on now," I said. "Get ready."

I pushed her into her dressing room and went to the stage manager, got them to hold the curtain for five minutes.

I found smelling salts and waved them under her nose.

She didn't like that.

"It's for your own good," I told her.

Our first dance was tricky, not a number you fluffed. Adele was all over the place, woozy, drunk! As she headed towards the footlights, she kept going and I had to lunge out and grab her.

Imagine that for a headline – Leading Lady Dives Right In! *Ha!*

Well, we made it offstage and I held her and I slapped her, on each cheek, "Snap out of it!" I said.

She held her face and looked very sorry for herself and said, "You hit me."

"I did," I said. "Now sober up!"

Later, when she did sober up, I apologised for being heavy.

I had promised her twenty bucks after I hit her, to say sorry.

"Where's my twenty bucks?" she asked.

A drunk lady never forgets!

The accident on Long Island that summer, well, that shook us all. She nearly died. Only for Billy Leeds and his quick thinking – he threw her off the boat and untied it, kicked it out onto the lake before it exploded.

But they were burnt, the two of them, Leeds worse than Adele.

When I got that news, well, you wouldn't believe it, I was actually in a car accident myself that day, in the same place! Myself and Mary Atwill, a sweet girl. We'd been in Long Island and we were driving home and we skidded on some gravel and the car went right over on its side.

Terrifying. We went to the hospital to get checked out, but there was no harm done.

When we got back to our hotel, there were messages to ring Mama and I thought that maybe she'd heard about our crash and I was ready to play down the dramatics and tell her there was no harm done at all.

But she didn't even know about me. It was Adele. A boat accident. A fire. She was in hospital.

Well, my stomach went. Flipped.

She'd always been a worry to me, Adele, always up to high jinks and fooling about, but this? I'd never really thought any harm would come to her.

I had an awful sleepless night – every time I dropped off the road would loom up before me and in and out she went from my consciousness. Adele. At one point, I dreamt she was gone and I sat right up in the bed. A horrible, horrible, nightmare.

In the morning, I organised a lift to the hospital and when I saw her, well, it was a fright.

She was all bandaged up and her hair was singed and everything and she lay in the bed, not really moving, but she smiled when she saw me. She was on a lot of painkillers – she was a bit high.

I felt like crying when I saw her, but I couldn't do that. I needed to hold it together for her, to not let her know how shocked I was by her injuries.

"Minnie!" she said and smiled when I came in to sit beside her, beside Mama.

She said she was OK, but it was shocking to see her like that.

We were due to go to England, to start the run of Funny Face *in London.*

But we had to delay it, put arrangements in place.

When I went back to my hotel, I thought about what it would have been like if Leeds hadn't been able to extinguish the flames. What if they'd been too much, if her burns had overcome her? What if she'd been burned all across her face, her career as an actress wiped out in one minute?

When I got back to my hotel I ordered a whiskey on the rocks and then another and I sat in the bar and downed them and said a prayer to God.

'Thank You for saving her, Lord. Thank You for keeping her with us. It was not her time, not yet.'

And I felt so thankful, that we had our funny, gregarious little sister still with us, still joking from her hospital bed.

I didn't know what I'd do if I ever lost her. She was the other half of me.

Like a twin.

CHAPTER TWENTY-FOUR

NEW YORK, AUGUST 1928

OVER THE NEXT FEW WEEKS IN HOSPITAL, I got a lot of time to think. An unexpected rest.

Unending days of peace, of quiet, of receiving visitors, only if I wanted to, of healing. I began to feel different. I began to look at things differently.

Our success over the previous years had swept us along. There was never time for a real break. We took vacations, but they were a whirlwind of parties and hosting and catching up with new friends and old. It had been a long time since we truly relaxed and let our bodies rest, properly. Fred and I never really sat back and considered anything.

There was too much going on and we were tired all the time. If we did catch a break, the last thing we wanted to do was have a deep and meaningful conversation about where we were going with all this.

We were happy, weren't we? We were more successful than we could ever have imagined. Mama's scrapbooks were bursting, whole journals filled by each show. *For Goodness Sake* in the US, *Stop Flirting* in London, *Lady, Be Good!* all through the States, through England and Scotland. *Funny Face* had a rocky start, old Moaning Minnie was sure it would be a flop, but we got through it with the rewrites and all the improvements and turned it around, into a success. Our US run was over: Philadelphia, Washington, Atlantic City, New York and next up was the British run.

If I wasn't in hospital. If they didn't have to delay it because my injuries meant I had to recuperate and could not perform.

At first I felt terrible, blaming myself for being at Billy Leeds' in the first place, hiding out from the press, from Mama.

It was an accident, but didn't everything happen for a reason? What was in God's plan that saw me standing there, at that very moment that a spark ignited that fuel, ignited us?

As time went on, as I adjusted to the quiet in hospital, I stopped feeling guilty.

Sure, everyone had to wait for our London run of *Funny Face*, but we'd get there. The show would have its British run.

It didn't go unremarked upon that it took a major accident to get us to slow down.

I slept a lot. I would pass out for hours at a time, from the pain, from the exhaustion of being burnt.

They were worried I'd inhaled the flames, singed my whole mouth and throat. If this was the case, my singing and acting voice could be ruined, my stage career over.

But I wouldn't let myself think about that. It was too depressing. Instead, I lay back, took the medication they gave me and let the dreams come. I let myself go quiet.

And I saw some things.

Switzerland. Cool sunset. Burnt orange, the rays on our faces, the sky grey and fading.

George Jean Nathan holds my hand.

George. I haven't seen him in so long, my Georgy.

We sit on our bags on a rock.

I take the walking stick I have, necessary for these stony, slippery slopes. I scratch 'I LOVE YOU' in the snow.

George smiles and squeezes my hand, kisses me on the lips.

"Look," he says after a while.

The sun's rays have melted my inscription, the letters run, dribbling into each other.

George smiles.

A feeling, in my stomach. Niggly. It won't go away. Something's not right. That nagging feeling of Mama's words, of Fred frowning.

What is it?

I will go out. I will go there.

I have to see.

The House of Satan is published. He shows me the book at dinner. I hold it, looking at the soft blue cover, the title scalloped, his name in a smaller font: *George Jean Nathan*.

"Open it," he says.

I flick through the pages.

"Look to the front."

I go back, turn the pages carefully.

There, on the inside, is an inscription. I look closely.

"What is it?"

"Do you remember?"

Remember what, George? How your reviews don't mention me anymore? How you make arrangements but change them last minute? *Sorry, darling, something's come up tonight – let's say tomorrow, shall we?*

I can't make it out.

"Switzerland," he says. "In the snow."

And then I see it. It's the scratching I made. I LOVE YOU, melted, melted now forever, into his book.

"How did you ..."

"I drew it by hand. Got the printer to add it. Isn't it fun?"

Oh George, George.

His words in my ears.

I'm annoying him.

"Where are you going?" asks Mother.

Out.

Out to see, I need to see.

I have my hat on, keep my eyes down. I blend in with everyone else on the street.

Up the steps to the restaurant, the doorman smiling, warm in the foyer, a smell of perfume, plants.

This is where he likes to meet all the important theatre men, politicians, somebodies.

"Can't meet today, darling," he'd said on the telephone earlier. "Paul Claudel is in town. The French Ambassador. Fascinating fellow. We'll meet tomorrow for sure."

I stand at the doorway of the restaurant. The maître d' looks at me.

"Do you have a reservation, ma'am? Oh! Miss Astaire, just a moment and I will see what I can do for you." He goes off quickly, to talk to a waiter, to clear a table. *Hurry, it's Miss Astaire!*

My eyes flit around the room.

Is he here? Is he at our table, the one by the window, the one ...?

He is here.

A woman.

Lillian Gish.

They are laughing, heads close, wine on the table.

The maître d' returns.

"This way, Miss Astaire."

"There's no need," I say. "I'm just here to see someone."

He watches me as I walk past him.

A few heads turn.

Not George's.

He is too absorbed.

I am at the table.

They look up at the same time.

"Adele!"

"French Ambassador," I say and hold out my hand to Lillian Gish.

She is surprised, raises her hand and eyebrows.

"Adele Astaire, pleased to meet you," I say.

Her hand is warm, dainty, not sweaty.

I look at George. His mouth is open, for once no words will come.

I fish around in my bag. I am glad I brought it now. As if I knew.

I throw it on the table. It thuds, the glasses shake. I open the cover and flick through the pages fiercely.

When I come to the dedication, I trace my fingers along it.

"*I. LOVE. YOU*," I say loudly.

Silence around us now, forks down, more eyebrows, up, up, up.

I tear it out, scratch, rip and ball it into my hand. I try to stuff it into his mouth, forcing it in, but his arm is in the way and he stands up, mumbling, grabbing, shouting.

"What are you doing!"

"No," I say. "What are *you* doing?"

He makes a face. Grabs my elbow.

"Stop making a scene."

A drama critic who doesn't love a good scene?

"Goodbye, ambassador," I say to Lillian Gish, her face bright pink.

I walk out of the restaurant, my head held high.

And that was the end of George Jean Nathan.

Fred came to see me a lot, to talk about the upcoming run in London. We were adding more solo dances for him because they brought down the house. I didn't mind. He deserved the applause. He had such good ideas, always working, always trying out new steps, using props for amusement. He wasn't afraid of taking risks anywhere on stage.

Often, he'd wake in the middle of the night with an idea for a step and he'd come in the next day and try it out. The producers trusted him, the choreographer gave him free rein.

He really knew what he was doing, Fred.

Sometimes I wondered whether I was holding him back. The stage had always been mine, our careers led by me. All the reviews talked about me.

When he came to see me in hospital he talked about some new material we might add for *Funny Face* in London. Playing to a London audience was different to an American. You had to give them something new, something real up-to-date.

I didn't feel interested.

All this resting up was making me think. About everything.

I could feel something brewing inside, a longing, for something else. Was this really to be my life, dancing, singing, acting, stage show after stage show, lights, rehearsals, showtime?

I was so tired. Even with all the rest the thought of going back to the stage left me feeling wretched.

"It'll be just swell, Adele, to get back to London. See what they make of us this time around," says Freddie, at my bedside.

"*Mmmm*," I say and I lie back and close my eyes.

"Aren't you looking forward to going?"

"Maybe."

I knew he thought I was saying this because of the accident. He thought I was sore and weary, still in a type of shock. But it wasn't that at all. It was something else.

I needed something else to live for.

I wanted to be happy.

Miss Astaire is a thorough little original. There is no one else quite like her. Everything she does, she does in a style of her own, inspired by a lovely brain, a particular sense of humour and a genius for being different. Her dancing combines perfection of technique with originality of execution.

I wanted something else.

Miss Astaire is, I think, the most attractive thing on stage.

I needed something else.

Adele Astaire. That's all.

That's all. Is this all there is? Is it? Is this it?

William came to see me.

His visits were not as frequent as I'd have liked. I thought he should have been coming more often; if he were a good man, it is what he would do.

"How are you, Adele?"

"I'm alright. Recovering. They've eased back on some of the medication now, so that's a good sign."

"Oh, that's good. And you're eating?"

"A little."

"I brought you these."

He put a brown bag on the table and I opened it to see grapes, black and cloudy.

"Thank you."

He pulled up a seat and I sat up a little more in the bed.

"So you've a new date for the London run?"

"Yes," I said. "November. I should be fully recovered by then. Will you be going over too?"

"Oh, I expect so."

William was from Yorkshire. His father was a wealthy man involved in textiles. He, however, saw himself as a bit more sophisticated than that. He was investing in show business. It was how we'd met backstage in the first place.

I looked at his face, at his smile and I could think of little to say to him.

He was quiet too.

I didn't want to spend my time in England chasing him about, waiting for the next falling-out, for the next screaming match. Our rows were so heated that sometimes, in the pit of my stomach, in the niggle of my brain, I thought he was going to hurt me.

He had jostled me, grabbed me, stuck his face into mine before.

There were times I was terribly afraid of him. Fred knew it. It was why he didn't like him. William Gaunt led me astray, but sometimes I'd wanted that. The excitement of the drama, the highs and the tearful lows.

Now, I felt differently.

The big white clock, with its silver hands and its hospital sheen was the only sound in the room, breaking the silence between us that sat like a wall.

"William, I've been doing a lot of thinking," I started.

I looked at him, judging his face. We had broken up so many times. On again, off again. Reports in the papers, *fiery romance*. It was embarrassing and it hurt, like a wound, inside.

"You have?" he said, and the smile disappeared now. Like he knew.

"I have."

A pause.

"I think it's for the best," I said.

"Is that how you really feel?"

"It is."

It felt good making this decision. There was a maturity about it. For a long time I had thought he was the one for me, the one I would marry. For a short time I'd thought I would marry George Jean Nathan too and now look at me, thirty years old, recovering in hospital and telling the second man I was ever serious about that I was no longer serious about him.

"If that is what you really want, Adele."

"It is."

He stood up, bent over and let his lips brush my cheek.

He looked at me and I back at him, no tears wetting eyes.

The door clicked closed and I lay back on the pillow, a pressure lifted from my chest.

It was the right thing to do, even if it meant I would be left alone and unmarried for the rest of my life.

Better to be left that way than stifled in the wrong relationship, wouldn't you say?

London. Again. The press covered the break-up. There were many comments in the social columns about who had been seen taking me out, now that I was available again.

The admirers were back.

But I had no interest. I'd already gone round with a cad for the sake of it. I swore off men completely.

Fred didn't know what to do with me. I could be sullen and narky and full of bile sometimes. He thought it was all over Gaunt or my emotional trauma after the explosion.

But it wasn't. It was something else.

I felt totally empty, like a barrel, rolling around, dry and hollow.

I was in a terrible flunk.

My hospital stay had changed me. I knew it wouldn't be long before I would be leaving the stage behind. I could feel it, coming down the tracks at me, something different, something new was on its way.

As we danced and sang, went to the parties, did interviews and cut our records, I knew that soon there would be a change.

I didn't know what it would bring and I didn't know how it would arrive, but it was coming.

And that was the only thing that got me through those long, healing months after I was nearly killed standing on a boat.

CARD FROM ANN ASTAIRE NEW YORK, DECEMBER 1928

(FOUND IN AN ENVELOPE OF MOTHER'S THINGS)

My Darling Adele,

I have just been to see the most wonderful show and had to write you straight away. It is an animated picture, of a little mouse, called Mickey Mouse. We saw it at Universal's Colony Theatre. Oh, Adele, it is so dainty, it reminded me of you. You must go to see it when you get a chance, if it comes to London. The picture is called 'Steamboat Willie' and it's by a fellow called Walt Disney. We loved it.

I hope you are keeping well and eating well. Looking forward to seeing you at Christmas.

Your dearest

Mama

CHAPTER TWENTY-FIVE

LISMORE CASTLE, COUNTY WATERFORD, IRELAND AUGUST 1928

PATRICIA RYAN SOON GOT USED TO LIFE in Lismore Castle.

No longer did the great walls and the high ceilings send her blood high when she first arrived in the morning. The avenue and its little gate became familiar to her, the agent knew her name, the gardeners nodded. She was one of them.

The work was harder than she expected. There were so many bedrooms, so many floors, so many fabrics, sheets and curtains. They had no sooner refreshed one wing then it was time to start on another.

Everything was kept ready to go. The main rooms, the large drawing room overlooking the river, was dusted every day and a fire lit to keep it warm and damp-free. It was a breath-taking room, located on the side of the castle which was perched on a cliff edge, the looming window looking down on the River Blackwater where it cut through the fields and forest.

Across on the hills the trees were lush in summer. Patricia looked forward to autumn when they would change to orange, browns and reds. She would stand, if she could get away with it for a moment and just watch, out the window, the pair of swans who had claimed this part of the river for their own. At the handsome horses who galloped for fun up and down the banks. They were used when the family came to stay – they were not work horses like the piebalds that pulled the ploughs.

Sometimes she watched tourists pull up outside on the bridge, in a pony and trap. They'd stop, stand, stare over.

It was that kind of castle. You couldn't help but look.

The door of Lismore Castle opened into an entertaining hall, a good cosy-size room where they had a drinks cabinet set up and sofas around a tall fireplace. They beat the rugs there often and polished the furniture daily. The steps were scoured regularly too, the glass panels polished.

Off the hall ran two corridors, the length of the courtyard, turning at right angles into two more identical corridors. From the east wing, you could stand and look across the lawn at the west wing and see into the south and north. Patricia loved the design, the privacy, the inward-looking cosiness of the castle.

But each wing was large, long and came with its own set of domestic requirements.

The offices were the busiest part of the castle. They took over the whole front part of the building where you came in, and it was where all the estate business was done.

There were always people coming and going, men on horses pulling up, tenants and farmers in flat-bed carts, widowers sometimes dragging children to show their plight.

Paperwork for fishing licences along the River Blackwater were looked after at the offices. Here they decided how much they'd fine anyone caught poaching salmon.

Patricia had seen the cook prepare the big silvery fish for lunches and dinners at the castle, the smell of it sizzling making her mouth water. She knew poaching happened, had even been the recipient of it over the years, especially after her father had died. But that was mostly rabbits. Now, she wouldn't dream of taking anything that didn't belong to her, not when she saw how it was all run up at the castle and the risk you were taking by removing anything from land you didn't have a licence for.

No one cut a tree without getting permission first. Even the berries were watched, a by-law passed that said no one could pick bilberries off the estate.

That didn't go down well at all.

From what Patricia could see, most people came to the offices to apply for rent agreements, housing, house moves, extensions. You could apply to have a new cottage built, depending on how long you'd been a tenant and how badly you needed it.

She watched all the coming and going when she was sent over to the offices to dust and sweep, to wash up all the cups and polish the desks. She enjoyed being over there, acting busy but listening in to everything.

This was the heart of the estate, where everything happened.

She learned a lot listening to the agent with his big guffawing voice. He never noticed her there, only a house girl, a little thing who wouldn't be bothered listening in to all these business dealings and what-nots. She looked at all the papers when she was tidying the desks.

She was always a quick reader.

Probably from reading all those fairy books when she was a child.

Word would come that visitors were coming a few weeks in advance. Some guests were friends of the family and were passing through and wanted to stop for a few nights. Others wanted to come for an extended time of peace and recuperation. Mrs. Keeley warned Patricia about those who were convalescing.

"They expect you to wait on them hand and foot like we're some sort of invalid home and you're forever running with trays and jugs and warm milk and sometimes they're sick and oh, Jesus, I hate to see them coming so I do."

On the odd occasion a young couple would come to stay on their honeymoon and Patricia loved to see them pull up in the horse and trap if they'd come by train with their big cases full of finery. Mrs. Keeley would let her help with the lady's things and she would take an age with the fine dresses, feeling the silk and beads as she lined them up in the wardrobe.

When she was cleaning, she'd touch the ivory hairbrushes and combs and sometimes, if it was really quiet and she knew she wouldn't get caught, she'd sit down at the dressing table and take down her hair from under her cap and brush out the ends.

Rapunzel, Rapunzel, let down your hair!

Hunting parties would come too. She wasn't fond of them – ten, twenty men, all muddy boots tramping in, staying up late in the drawing room and billiards room, drinking all evening, spilling things. They'd have to scrub the rugs after them and fret over stains that might not come out.

Some of the men were hands-on too, reaching for her arse when she was putting a tray down on the bedside locker.

Mrs. Keeley warned her about them.

"If you're bringing something in and they're there with the hands under the covers, get out of that room quick.

Shockin' dirty some of them are, thinking nothing of a young girl like you now – whatever they be getting up to in England, I don't know."

Patricia was learning a lot in this new job.

Lots of cleaning skills, how to work fast, get the work done.

How the estate ran, how the agent had the power and so many people relied on funding to have shelter, work, to eat.

And she was learning how men and women behaved together, how honeymoon couples could stay in bed all day into late afternoon and how older wizened men had the same rabid, sexual urges.

She learned how to mind herself too.

That was the most important of all.

When the Cavendish family came to stay, Patricia came to understand that maintaining the castle was nothing compared to running it when they were in residence.

The family, who normally resided at Chatsworth, Derbyshire, liked to take two trips to Ireland a year. One in the spring, when the weather had begun to thaw and one in October, to get to some race meets and the start of the winter entertainment season.

The first signs that the family were due to Lismore appeared in Mrs. Keeley. She began to simmer. The temper in her swirled, like a kettle on the boil, until she would blow up and let an almighty screech out of her. Nobody could do anything right by her.

Mrs. Keeley had taken a risk by agreeing to be the housekeeper at Lismore Castle. It was just after the civil war over the Treaty and women were reluctant to come into a big estate like that. No one wanted to be seen taking money from the Crown. The troubles had been an awful anxious time for everyone. There were whispers and mutterings and secret meetings all over the place. There were guns hidden in the hills and the crackle of shootouts under darkness.

All cars were suspicious, all soldiers shied away from.

Patricia's mother had particularly worried as it was just the two of them in their house.

"There'll be a knock on the door, wait'll you see," she told Patricia. "Either someone looking to hide or someone looking for them who's hiding!"

Mr. Mac had been a great help to her mother then. He had reassured her and told her no harm would come to her.

After the war, things quietened down and there was no more fighting in the hills, over the winding roads of the bogs. There was an acceptance that the Free State was now here to stay, and slowly the men gave up their guns. In Lismore, they realised they needed to work with the castle if they ever wanted things to change. It was why the offices were always full of tenants trying to sort out their land holdings, their leases, working towards owning their own house and their own plot of land.

Mrs. Keeley in her early days at the castle had to put up with dirty looks and comments whenever she went places. But, as she had decided early on, if she didn't do it someone else would. And besides, as Patricia was learning, the whole of South Waterford was run from the castle. Someone had to do it. You were better off in there, alongside the castle, improving things from the inside out.

Mrs. Keeley was pretty forward-thinking in that respect.

When it came to the family staying, however, there was

no forward-thinking or modern way of doing things. Everything had to be to the standards of a Victorian dinner party.

"I want all that china out, polished and put back before the day is out. Lay it all out on the table, and I want it counted and catalogued. We'll do a different set for the afternoon tea for the first three days and see where we are then. And, by God, if there's any missing, if I find one saucer is gone, there'll be heads rolling here now today."

Everybody scurried. The taut atmosphere meant things were more likely to be dropped or get broken. The tension stretched through the castle. There was no joking or laughing, just heads bent and working, cloths in hands, task after task.

Every pane of glass was wiped down. And with a castle the size of Lismore, this was no mean feat – the men had to get ladders in. When that was done, the floors were cleaned. Swept. Lifting the rugs out to be beaten.

"What's this family like then?" she asked Mary, one of the other housemaids and a small slip of a thing. She had been at the castle a good three years before Patricia, so she always knew what was going on.

"The Cavendishes? Very posh. Very hoity-toity. But they're nice, I suppose, in their own way."

"Do they notice if all this cleaning isn't done?"

"No, they don't," said Mary. "They spend most of their time outside. They love walking and fishing and hunting. They're horse-mad. I've never seen them complain about the cleaning. The weather, yes. But not the cleaning. I think they really like it here actually. A lot."

I wondered what it was like where they lived in England. What was Chatsworth House like compared to Lismore?

Why did they like coming to this backwater in Ireland, when they could stay in England in all their finery?

"Mrs. Keeley's in awful form," I said.

"Sure, she's always giving out, that one," said Mary. "She's like a black widow the way she goes on. It's always worse the day before they arrive. You have that to look forward to."

Patricia threw her eyes to heaven. "Still, I'm looking forward to seeing them, the Cavendishes."

Truth be told, she felt as though royalty were coming. That she was going to see a king and queen with their prince and princesses.

At Lismore, that's what the Cavendish family were to everyone.

They were royalty.

CHAPTER TWENTY-SIX

PORT LYMPNE, KENT, ENGLAND, JUNE 1929

THE SUN BURNED, HIGH IN THE SKY, extracting beads of sweat from the men playing tennis in the court. The *bat, bat, bat*, rattled through the air. I found it comforting, one of my favourite sounds of summer.

My legs were sticky. I could feel the sweat at the back of my knees, trickling to my calf. I'd dragged my safety razor across them this morning, listening to the bristle snap. I preferred it to the depilatory cream, which stank and didn't work half as well. I had been approached for an advert for Wisk's but I said no. I had good legs, it had to be said. I could see why I'd make a good candidate for their magazine campaign.

I had learned to look after myself early. I couldn't rely on doe eyes or lustrous blonde hair like many of my counterparts. I didn't have a face that turned heads, I knew it. I had something else, but I had to learn how to use it.

It was why I studied fashion. Through the magazines, through following the most exquisite designers. It was why I bought only the best clothes, with the most flattering cuts and most modern materials.

It was why people followed what I did.

A waiter came by my lounge chair.

"Iced tea, madam?"

His voice was grand. I loved it.

"Long Island Iced Tea?"

"I can get you one, madam?"

"No, a regular iced tea is fine."

There was something about this place that made you want to drink alcohol at midday.

We had discovered Port Lympne one night after we were booked to play a set as an extra gig during our London run of *Lady, Be Good!*. We sometimes took on extra gigs as favours to a producer, or as a special commission. We'd been hearing Philip's name a lot and were curious.

"You simply must come to Philip's!"

"Philip who?" we said.

"Philip Sassoon!"

That night a car appeared from nowhere and Fred and I were driven out of the city for an hour to his estate at Port Lympne. The house was a neat red-brick affair, with manicured gardens and a pool.

We found out what all the fuss was about. There were parties and there were parties. Then there were Philip Sassoon's parties.

The place was awash with beautiful people. Tall, lithe young men lay about in chairs, smoking, drinking. Some were dressed in light clothes that looked as though they'd been imported from the east. They sat like Indian kings, laughing together, silks wide open against barely hairy chests. Women, smoking, mostly bobbed, joined them here and there, or danced in corners.

I was pretty sure I saw the flash of a breast.

The staff flew in and out, bringing drinks, food. The music blared from a gramophone.

When we got up to sing, I danced on a grand piano that stood below a beautifully muralled ceiling. Later I spotted the Michelangelo himself, crouched beneath the top of the room, on a scaffold, paintbrush in hand and scowl on his face.

He worked as we partied around him.

There was an atmosphere that we had never quite felt before. We were so welcome, so wanted. Everyone was smiling, having a wonderful time. It was different to the parties we'd been to in America, where drink was still illegal and usually home-made. You were never guaranteed what the taste would be like – it could be raw and spiky and you always felt a bit unnerved drinking it. Here, drinking was the most natural thing in the world.

"Freddie, isn't this wonderful?" I said, after we had finished our performance to great applause that echoed through the house.

"It's something!" he said.

We met Philip who was a tall, striking man, similar to the Indian kings who had scattered themselves across his armchairs. He had a cool charm about him, a sense of calm. I liked him immediately.

He liked us too. During our London runs I went out there whenever I could, like now, while we waited for a two-day repair to the Winter Garden Theatre. You could stay over, in one of his en-suite bedrooms, even if he wasn't there. It was like a luxury hotel, a home from home, an oasis of decadence and frivolity.

The waiter came back and put my iced tea onto a wooden table beside me. It had a little umbrella in it.

I took it and sipped, continuing to watch the young men in tight, tiny shorts, diving in and out of the pool. They shouted before they dive-bombed, knees bent, heads tucked in, splashing anyone foolish enough to sit nearby.

It couldn't be ignored how their shapes were identical, how their shoulders were wide, their waists narrow, their pelvis a V. They all wore their hair the same, slicked back, combed. They had prominent noses, striking faces.

I wondered how many were of Sassoon's persuasion. I tried to pick them out, by their gestures, by the way they held themselves. One or two maybe, the rest were certainly straight. But here, anything went. And anyone, I had learned, could be persuaded.

I lay back and listened to the bees buzzing about the lavender. White butterflies were landing on mugwort the same colour, batting their wings silently.

I thought about the end of the show.

Funny Face had one more month to run.

And what would I do then?

Would I come here to Port Lympne to rest and relax, to socialise?

I pictured him on the telephone as I made my future request, in his mauve gown and leather slippers, one leg over the other, foot tapping the air.

"Can I stay with you, Philip?"

"Of course, dahling! Stay as long as you like. My home is your home!"

Would Freddie come too? Probably not. Freddie wasn't as fond of the party set as I was. And life at Port Lympne was one long party.

"Hello."

A man sat down beside me, lay back in his lounger chair.

"Hello," I said. "Nice to see you here."

He looked at me closely.

"Oh … Adele. Adele Astaire!"

"The very one."

I lowered my sunglasses, a pair of Sam Fosters I'd had sent over from Macy's. Harry Gordon Selfridge had admired them the last day I was in, so no doubt there was an order in already. He loved the idea of shielding your eyes from the sun. "Parasols are so awkward," he said. I had to agree.

"It's lovely here, isn't it?" said the man who had just joined me. He was wearing a white suit and I noticed it matched his glistening teeth. He had a lovely mouth.

"It is. I'm just down for a short break, back to the rat race tomorrow."

"Ah, we are here for a few days at least."

"Have you just come from the States?" I said. "Didn't I read about you getting some acting award there, recently?"

"Yes. An Academy Award. A big palaver. You know the Americans. I didn't hang about."

He laughed. I did too.

What a handsome man. He fit in perfectly here with his startling eyes and swept-back fair hair. Nothing like his persona on the screen.

"Well, congratulations. Very well deserved, I'm sure," I said and leaned over to clink his glass.

A shout rang out as a young man leapt high into the air and dive-bombed into the pool, the splash echoing all the way back to us.

Philip came down the stone steps, his mauve jacket flowing against the red-brick background. He rounded the pool and stopped to chat to the water-soaked men. His hand lingered on a shoulder. Wet. Drying in the sun.

"He's some chap," I said, flicking my head towards the pool.

"An unflappable gent."

Sassoon left the pool and made his way towards us. His skin was dark, his hair jet-black.

"*Dahlings!*" he said as he lowered his behind onto the end of my lounge chair. It sagged with his weight and I liked the steadiness it gave to the seat.

We watched the men dive, some of them now tiring and lying prostrate on the grass, water evaporating from their muscled torsos.

"I could live here, Philip," I say.

"Some people do," he joked.

"Oh, it's wonderful. I just love coming here."

"You are welcome any time, my dear. Get that brother of yours down soon, I'd love to see him."

"If we tell him you have racehorses here, he'll be down in a flash!"

"You do that," he said and patted my leg. He turned his attention to my companion, who was now also lying back on the lounge chair and shielding his eyes.

"You'll have to get a pair of Fosters like Adele's, Charlie," he says.

"Yes," I said. "You could introduce them to your films. A bowler hat, black moustache and sunglasses, quite the look."

Charlie Chaplin laughed.

Walter Wanger, a film producer from Paramount, approached us about a screen test for *Funny Face*. He said he thought the show would be perfect for the cinema screen with the mix of songs we had. Freddie had introduced a tuxedo and tails and a top hat to dance to *High Hat* and Wanger said it looked swell. He also loved our final song, which was a bit of a mix-up of the Runaround which we'd been doing for years now – it was our party piece.

Freddie liked the thought of putting our performance on the screen.

We went to a studio where they had enormous cameras, like big black vultures on stilts.

We acted some scenes and shot a dance. It wasn't too alien to us, but we weren't allowed to look at the vulture cameras, which for me was strange as I always tried to catch the audience in the eye.

Afterwards, Wanger brought us into a room where he replayed the footage on a big screen and, well, we looked ridiculous. And my voice! We didn't like it all and told him so.

He reassured us and said it was great, but we didn't feel good about it.

He said he'd be in touch but when he eventually came back to us, the news was that he hadn't been able to secure the movie rights for *Funny Face* and that was that.

"A shame," said Fred.

"Is it?" I asked.

I felt as though the screen was for Chaplin, for others, not for Fred and me, who came alive before an audience, before real heart-beating people. I just couldn't imagine shooting a whole film to those black vulture cameras.

Dancing, singing and performing in the theatre was where it was at.

For me, anyway, definitely.

Funny Face was to close in June. Fred was in discussions with Flo Ziegfeld about a show for us back in the States. I thought it would be a good move, something different. Flo was a bigwig and had been interested in us before. He had once been a great rival of C.B. Dillingham's. Now that we were coming to the end of our third show for Aarons and Freedley, maybe it was time to try something new?

Aarons heard that Fred had been speaking with Flo and hit the roof. He told Fred that Ziegfeld wouldn't know what to do with us. But Ziegfeld was a very successful producer and his shows had a particular flair to them.

There was something exciting about him, something unpredictable. He kept very glamorous company and pumped time and money into the razzmatazz of promoting a show. We thought it would bring us that one step ahead.

We wanted a change.

By the end of June 1929, as we closed *Funny Face* for the last time, there was a sense of something in the air. In six months' time the 1920s would be over and a new decade loomed. What would the 1930s bring?

Look how things had already changed since the war!

As always in our closing shows, tickets were like gold dust. Everyone wanted to see us at our last performance of a show. There was to be a big party afterwards, in a dark, gaslit bar, near to the Winter Garden Theatre. Everyone would be dressed – boas, feathers, pearls and tails – and we would have one last big knees-up, all of us, the cast, the crew and selected guests.

Unusually for me, I wasn't in the mood for going. I was tired. And I was feeling a bit fed up.

It was the end of a long season. I didn't feel like celebrating, I just wanted to rest, to go back to my suite and read my book. I'd had enough of costumes and dancing and putting on a dramatic face. I found myself feeling like this a lot lately.

I think it may have been the accident.

It had changed me.

I sat at my dressing table, looking at my black eyes, thinking how the make-up was simply covering up the dark shadows under my own eyes anyway. Shadow eyes with or without make-up.

Gently I wiped at the soot with a tissue and cream, running the soft material back and forth under my lashes.

"Adele, I'd like to introduce you to somebody."

Behind me stood a small grand-looking man with Fred. I wasn't really in the form for pleasantries. I wanted to get ready and get to the party to get it over and done with.

"Prince Aly Khan," said Fred as the man held out his hand.

"How do you do?" I said politely, not rising from my seat, but holding out my hand.

He bent and kissed it gently.

He was a good-looking man. Dark with petite features.

Behind him stood another man, much taller, striking.

"And this is Charles Cavendish."

I held out my hand to Charles and he took it and kissed it too. His grip was firm.

"It's not too often I have royalty in my dressing room," I joked to Prince Aly Kahn.

"Sorry to disturb you," he replied. "We just wanted to make your acquaintance. You were magnificent tonight."

"Thank you," I said.

"How do you feel, now that it's all over?" he asked politely.

"Oh, you know," I said, waving my hand. "Relieved. A little sad."

"Of course," he said and bowed a little. "We will leave you to make your toilette and hope to see you at the after-party?"

"Yes," I said, nodding. "You will."

He looked happy to hear it.

As the three men left, joking and laughing, my eyes lingered on Cavendish's back as they closed the door.

I was always attracted to a tall man.

I could see why Freddie was hanging around with Prince Aly Khan and Charles. They were all horse-mad. Aly's family had stud farms that bred the most beautiful thoroughbred horses, big graceful animals, all rippling muscles, chestnut and black. Like the Kahn family, they were of Arabian stock.

Freddie had already bought a share in a horse and it was fast becoming his number-one interest outside of the theatre. He knew so much about horse stock, breeding, about brood mares and stallions just out to stud. I enjoyed attending the races too, they could be thrilling if you had a bet on, but standing out in a field looking at the shape of a fetlock or knee, or stalking cold stables sour with horse manure, was not my idea of a good time.

"So do you breed big cup winners too, Mr. Cavendish?" I asked Charles at the after-party. He was so tall I had to stretch to look up at him. Thin, like a poplar tree.

"I try."

"Are your family horse people too?"

"They are. An inherited affliction, I'm afraid."

"Well, I don't know where our Freddie gets it," I said. "There hasn't been so much as a pony in our background. It's such an English hobby, isn't it?"

"I suppose it is. Although Prince Khan might dispute that."

"And where are your family from, Mr. Cavendish?"

"Our home is in Derbyshire, near to Chesterfield."

"Lovely. Is it nice there?"

"Very. You should visit."

"Should I?"

"You should. I think you'd like it."

"And how would you know what I would like, Mr. Cavendish?"

I eyed him over my glass. I loved his accent and felt quite brash beside him.

"You look like you would be at home there."

"Do I now? Well, I say ... let's stick it in the diary!"

Even though I was tired and my back and legs ached, I found that standing here beside this tall, clever man, I was beginning to enjoy myself.

I hadn't wanted to come to this party at all, but now I was so glad I did.

We talked about the countryside, about hunting and fishing, about politics, about writers he knew, about other socialites, about fashion. There wasn't a topic he didn't have a thought on. He kept me engaged, something most men at these parties failed to do.

Usually they wanted to speak about themselves. Or they asked so many questions about me that I felt drained, milked, when all I wanted to do at an after-party was to have a drink and relax. To have a little fun.

Different cast members made their way towards me throughout the evening, wishing me well, saying goodbye. All this time Charles didn't leave my side. I didn't want him to. I liked his presence.

The director gave a speech. Freddie gave a speech. I was called forward to talk too, and I thanked everyone for all the work they'd put in and made a joke about how awful the show had been at the start.

"Thank you for turning this lard of a book into a stomper of a story!"

I drank some cocktails, more than I usually did, asking for another when I'd drained the last flat-top glass. Charles was drinking shorts and as they went in he got funnier and funnier.

When it was time to go, Freddie came to me to see if I wanted to go home with him.

"Yes," I said, a bit merry. Secretly I hoped Cavendish would invite me on to another after-party, a late-night, dark speakeasy-type place.

But he was the perfect gentleman and he saw me off into the safe arms of my brother.

Much to my regret.

CHAPTER TWENTY-SEVEN

LISMORE CASTLE, COUNTY WATERFORD, IRELAND, OCTOBER 1929

HANDS CLASPED. HEAD DOWN. WAITING.

Patricia's collar flapped in the breeze against her neck, tickling.

The courtyard never held a sharp wind, it was too sheltered, but now in October it was chilly. The lawn was manicured like a soldier's head, cut to the quick. She longed to run over and rub her palm against the smooth-cut grass.

They were standing, waiting.

Mrs. Keeley, mouth pursed, glancing at everyone icily. Today was the day.

A soft drone of motorcars came into hearing, then the crunching of gravel on the avenue.

They were here.

Everyone stood to attention, backs straight, heads up.

Through the small, arched gate, the first car appeared, its narrow nose poking through first, its headlamps like bug-eyes.

It drove round the lawn to where the staff were standing, followed by another car and then another.

The cars were shining under the afternoon sun and Patricia pictured the children in the village who would have chased the cars as they drove past. These were vehicles worth pursuing.

Her stomach swirled. What would they be like, these Cavendishes? Would she be run ragged over the next month, left exhausted, expected to work day and night to meet their every need?

Or would they be gracious? Stately?

The footman opened the door of the first car.

An ankle and leg, a wide black skirt, old-fashioned.

The Duchess.

She looked stern, thought Patricia, as she spied her face.

The footman rushed around to the other side of the car.

The Duke. A great big curly moustache. Walking stick. He looked tired. Like an old, aged king.

They came and shook the hands of the staff, one by one.

Patricia curtsied.

The Duke and Duchess's leather gloves were soft, velvety in her grasp.

Her stomach moved again.

Out came more ankles, legs and people.

Dorothy Cavendish, married to Harold Macmillan. He had been an MP up until May when he'd lost his seat, according to Mrs. Keeley. Patricia didn't know much about politics, but Mrs. Keeley seemed to think he was a bigwig.

Rachel Cavendish and her husband James Stuart, who was Scottish. They had two small children left back in Scotland. Mrs. Keeley said aristocrats love to go places without their children.

And the youngest, Anne. She was lovely-looking, fresh, only twenty years old. She was due to marry next month which left only the last single member of the family. Charles.

After a sea of curtsying, hello and how-do-you-do's, the

family made their way into the main hall for refreshments.

A roaring fire raced up the chimney.

Mrs. Keeley put on her singsong voice, addressing the Duke and Duchess about the preparations that had been made.

The Duke waved her away when she came near him, plonking himself into the armchair beside the fire. He was having trouble moving and he looked in pain.

The luggage piled up in the hallway and the footmen carried it to the assigned rooms, a smell of sweat wafting through the air each time they returned.

Tea was served, fresh scones with jam and butter, peppering the china plates that had been counted and polished.

The atmosphere was thick with expectation.

Jackets, coats and gloves were removed, deposited into waiting hands. The items were taken to the rooms where they belonged, footmen and maids scurrying along the corridors, nodding at each other as they passed.

Fresh flowers from the greenhouses had been placed in every room. Dried flowers in netting hung in corners, lavender from the summer bushes that fingered the gravel beds of the flower garden. The pillows had been plumped and the cushions shook out and laundered.

Should a mote of dust be found in any of the bedrooms, Mrs. Keeley had threatened to sack staff members on the spot. So far, everyone was still in employment.

Patricia had never seen such a welcome.

After tea, the family separated, the Duke going to his room to lie down, the Duchess to do the same. The other ladies went to their rooms to freshen up and change into boots – they were going for a walk along the river.

Charles, who was the tallest man Patricia had ever seen, said he would take a walk into the village. His sisters looked at each other and their eyes rolled.

Patricia wondered why.

Patricia's mother loved to listen to her stories from the castle.

"They have boxes of clothes, Mammy, boxes. They have these huge trunks that the footmen had to drag up the stairs and, when I got a look inside, you've never seen anything like it, Mammy."

The first task for the servants had been to unpack everything as quickly and as neatly as they could, to ensure the family had everything they needed at their fingertips.

Patricia had seen different ladies stay at the castle before, but this was something else, five youthful ladies, the youngest not far in age from her, with wardrobes the likes of which she had never seen.

"And they're actually very nice, not as la-di-dah as I thought they'd be. Well, the Duchess is – apparently she doesn't talk to you unless she wants something and doesn't ever say thank you but the ladies are nice. I like them."

"And what of the Duke? What's he like?"

"Oh, he looks very old. Can't go anywhere without his walking stick. I heard Mrs. Keeley tell Mary that's he's aged shocking since the last time he was here. He had a stroke, I think, but no one's allowed talk about it. I'd like to have seen him a few years ago. I'd say he was fierce-looking then!"

Patricia was exhausted after her long days in the castle. She and Mary had been given rooms to stay over in the servants' quarters while the family was in residence so that they could be on hand whenever they were needed. This was the first time Patricia had seen her mother in five days.

"And what do they do all day?"

"They love to go out walking. And fishing. The ladies go out fishing too. And they're going hunting on Friday, with guns. There's people coming over for that, a soiree. We have to have all this particular food ready, little bite-things on plates – the cook is going mad trying to make it all up. They go out on their bikes too. They told me they love to come to Ireland because it's quiet and they can go out and do as they please. I think it's different in England. They read too, a lot of books, big thick ones. I think they're pretty clever. And they sew and embroider. No knitting though. Anne paints, she sets up at the big window overlooking the Blackwater – she's very good. She saw me looking the other day and said she might put me into it – she was joking – she was very funny. Do you know they go to shows in London? Big stage musicals, they said they're just wonderful. They go whenever they can. And they've been to the pictures loads of times too. I'd love that."

"They have some life."

"Oh, they do, Mammy."

"Maybe one day you'll be a lady like them."

Patricia laughed.

"Don't be silly," she said.

As the weekend of Halloween loomed, Lismore Castle was decorated with hollow swedes, their tangy scent scorched by the candles inside. Mrs. Keeley brought some branches inside and had them hung in the entrance hall. It looked quite fearsome. She said she got the idea from a show she'd seen before in Dublin.

The Cavendish family loved spending Halloween in the

castle, listening to tales of ghosts and pookas who would be getting unsettled now, readying themselves for All Hallows' Eve.

"We just don't get this in England," said Lady Anne.

"All the stories are true," Patricia told her as she did her hair for her, pinning and plaiting it before placing a silver slide behind the lady's ear. "My own mother heard the horse's hooves outside the night her father passed away. It was the death carriage come to take him to heaven."

They had sat and shared stories at the dressing table each evening since Lady Anne had arrived. She missed her fiancé terribly and told Patricia she was longing to marry him next month to start her new life.

"I feel as though I have been waiting all my life to grow up," she said.

Patricia thought how young she looked and how similar they were in appearance too. They had the same white skin, soft blue eyes. Instead of beautiful drop-waist dresses, however, Patricia was dressed in her black maid's uniform.

"Patricia," said Lady Anne, "could you accompany us to Wexford tomorrow? We're going to the races and we could do with a lady's maid. Someone to help dress us, fetch us anything we need, that sort of thing. You can help us all pack and then you'll be familiar with what items we are carrying."

Patricia's heart soared. A trip outside of Lismore? With no Mrs. Keeley giving her orders or telling her how everything ought to be done?

"Yes, m'lady. Of course. I'd be honoured."

As she walked down the corridor after finishing the ladies' pre-dinner preparations she thought about how Mary would probably have her nose out of joint at this news. She was longer-serving than Patricia – she'd see this trip to Wexford as pure favouritism.

She made her way to Mrs. Keeley's office and knocked on the door. The housekeeper was poring over menus, a frown line running down between her eyebrows.

"Mrs. Keeley," she said, "the ladies have asked me to accompany them to the races."

"Yes," she said, without looking up.

"Well, I ..." What was she trying to ask? "Is there anything I should know? Anything I need to remember?"

"Just remember to look after them as best you can," Mrs. Keeley said, keeping her eyes on a list of soups and palate-cleansers.

"I'm not sure why they asked me to go?" Patricia said, her hand clutching at her skirt.

"Because I told them to."

"What?"

"Well, who else would be able to hold herself with them? Not Mary for God's sake. She's like a pig knitting, that one. We have no ladies' maid, but you'll have to do, Patricia. Don't let me down."

Mrs. Keeley had paid her a compliment.

The world was turning on its head.

This was the most exciting thing that had ever happened to her.

Almost better than that first ever visit to Lismore Castle.

Patricia had never sat in a motor car before. It smelled of leather and oil and she was terrified, lowering her behind into the seat, right up against the window. Lady Anne sat beside her and Lady Dorothy beside Anne, the three of them, with their knees bent, tucked into the small seat, with a low roof over their heads. Lady Rachael and her husband had decided to stay at Lismore. Harold, Dorothy's husband, climbed into the front.

As Charles started the big Weymann Saloon with a roar, the horror that she would be trapped in a small space with these aristocrats dawned on Patricia.

What would she say? Was she supposed to say anything? How on earth was she supposed to pretend she knew anything of their world? She'd never felt so aware of her circumstances, of her Irishness, of her very otherness to what they were.

The car zoomed along, the trees flashing past, the windy road towards Dungarvan passing in a swirl. For the first half hour, she held her stomach, worried that she might bring up her breakfast.

Lady Anne and Lady Dorothy chatted, about who they expected to see at Wexford, about who they were looking forward to seeing and who they hoped had been carried off into the night and unable to make it.

"Are you hoping to see anyone nice, Charlie?"

Lady Dorothy leaned in, tapping her brother on the shoulder and he shrugged and laughed.

"Not in Ireland."

"*Ooooh*," giggled Lady Anne. "Someone fancy at home then?"

"Some floozy," said Lady Dorothy.

"Dorothy!" said Harold from the front.

"Who is she, Charlie, pray tell?"

"No one. No one at all," he said.

"Rumour has it," said Lady Anne in the middle, "that Charlie has his eye on an actress. A rather prominent actress."

"No!" said Lady Dorothy. "Who?"

"Oh, that'd be telling," said Lady Anne.

"Who?" said Lady Dorothy and she whacked her sister on the knee through her drop-waisted olive dress.

"Adele Astaire."

Lady Dorothy gasped. "No! That's not true, is it, Charlie?"

Charles looked into a small square mirror perched on the windscreen, back into his sister's eyes. He smiled and shrugged again.

"Oh Charlie," said Lady Dorothy, "do marry the girl! This family could do with a bit of glamour."

They got to the country house they were staying in, just outside of Wexford town, by early afternoon.

They'd stopped to stretch their legs on the way, taking a picnic laid out on a flat grassy bank off the road. Mrs. Keeley had packed separate sandwiches for Charlie while he drove and he had two bottles of ale, to help him concentrate.

Patricia was glad to get out of the confines of the car, the smell of the fuel and the stuffiness of five people all jammed into the small machine was stifling. Her stomach was on edge, both from the drone of the engine and the situation she found herself in. She had decided that the only way to get through this unsettling experience was to try to be herself.

She did not need to act like a lady, because everyone knew it was far from it she was raised.

So, when they continued on their way she answered their questions if they asked her any and pointed out things she knew about as they drove past, like a well where it was said Saint Brigid had performed a miracle.

"She's the patron saint of Ireland, cows, midwives and new-born babies," she said.

Lady Dorothy snorted.

Patricia took offence.

When they got to Kilmacthomas she said, "This is where Cromwell rested before the siege of Waterford. He loved slaughtering, he did."

Harold Macmillan cleared his throat from the front.

At the house they were lodging in, the family laid on a great welcome, embracing the Ladies Cavendish when they arrived. The country house was nowhere near the size of Lismore Castle, but it was fancy and stately with well-kept features. Sash windows looked down onto a green lawn, surrounded by boughs of ivy. Patricia felt it was more like a proper house, the rooms laid out neatly – front drawing room, dining room, study room, back corridor, kitchen – unlike the sprawling castle.

Patricia helped with the cases, lugging them up the stairs with the house boy and butler. Lady Anne was sharing with the daughter of the family. Charles had his own room and Lady Dorothy and her husband the best room to the front.

Patricia wondered where she would sleep but did not care either way. No doubt she would have a cot at the very top of the house with the other housemaids and she looked forward to whispering to them tonight, to find out what it was like to work in this house and about its goings-on.

While everyone took afternoon tea, she laid out the ladies' clothes for the evening and prepared their racing clothes for the morning. There was an air of excitement in the house, a sense of anticipation as the owners of the country house, their hosts, had three horses running tomorrow.

She took tea with the staff in the basement kitchen after the wardrobes were done and was summoned to help with evening dress and baths. She felt special in this house, arriving as a lady's maid. No one needed to know that back at Lismore she was only a lowly housemaid.

Patricia was ever so grateful to Mrs. Keeley for recommending her to the Cavendishes.

Already, she had moved up in the world.

The next morning dawned sunny and bright. Patricia watched the rays stream in the small square window in the roof, particles of dust floating in the musty bedroom where she'd slept with two other girls. They were still asleep, one of them snoring gently, as though a flap of skin were caught in the back of her throat.

Last night there had been no giggling, no secrets shared. Instead, Patricia had flopped into her small single bed in a sea of tiredness, kept up late by the raucous, laughter-filled party downstairs, the likes of which she had never before seen. Not from this refined lot anyway.

The whole evening had reminded her of the céilís she'd seen through the years, where everyone, including the women, were drunk on porter and it was all dancing and swinging around, singing and being merry.

She hadn't seen any porter last night but there had been bottles of wine, decanters of whiskey on every surface and black, fat, sherry bottles on the go for the ladies. They held the tiny delicate glasses in their fingers, sipping and sipping and when she went to check that she was no longer required, she nearly got a hug from Lady Dorothy.

As she left the drawing room to make her way to bed, she spied Charles laid out on a low chair, his head right back, and he was snoring. He was perfectly drunk.

She realised that Charles and his sisters were making the most of being away from their parents. Here they were among friends and could behave as they liked. The Duke and Duchess were known to be sober and dour; a scene like this would have been considered a disgrace.

The sound of a cockerel crowing outside seemed to stir the girls and a loud rap on the bedroom door had them out of their beds, still half asleep. They washed quickly and got into their dresses. Patrica wasn't quite sure what she was to do, seeing as this was not her house.

The maids said she was lucky and this was a bit of a holiday for her. She supposed it was.

While they saw to their morning chores she waited in the kitchen and helped with the staff breakfast. The cook remarked that it would be a while before anyone would be up, considering the state everyone had been in last night.

"Probably won't be able to stomach breakfast, neither," she said as she stirred a pot of thick porridge.

At last Patricia was summoned to Lady Anne's room and, when she knocked and went inside, she found the blinds still drawn against two of the windows and two very groggy and tired women.

"Oh Patricia," moaned Lady Dorothy, "you'll need to fetch me a Bloody Mary. Tell the cook to make me one up. She'll know how. Come back to me if they don't know how to make it and I'll give you the instructions. I feel positively sick!"

"I'll just take tea," said Lady Anne.

Lady Dorothy had come to Lady Anne's room for an impromptu review of the night before.

Patricia went back the way she had come and told the cook what the ladies wanted. The cook wrinkled her nose and huffed and puffed as she set out the glasses and began beating eggs.

"As if I haven't enough to be doing!"

Patricia carried the tray back upstairs and was met with "*Thank you, darling!*" and "*Oh, you are a pet!*".

She wanted to laugh at their pained faces.

"My father used to say the only way to cure a hangover is the hair of the dog that bit you," she said. "Would you like me to get you a sherry?"

The ladies laughed.

"Oh Patricia, we'll keep you!"

It took a good hour to get everyone ready and there were many moans and holding heads in hands before they went downstairs to have a proper breakfast with Charles and the rest of the family.

Patricia and the housekeeper watched as they set out for the racecourse in the motor car with a rather grey-looking Charlie behind the wheel. The ladies waved goodbye out the back window. Having heard them talk about it, Patricia knew their spirits would be lifting now in anticipation of the day, the thunder of horses' hooves on the track, the excitement of the crowd. There would be champagne in the enclosure and afterwards a meal served in the banqueting tent.

The family who owned the house did not have a motor car and they left in a trap, four of them tucked under blankets.

Patricia waved and went back inside, a whole day of leisure ahead of her. What was a girl to do in this unusual situation?

They expected the motor car late that evening. The last race finished before seven o'clock and the party would be going to the tent then for food and more drinks. The course was only a couple of miles away.

The host family returned by trap and were soon in bed,

tired after the day's escapades.

By eleven o'clock the staff had started to worry.

Patricia was seated in the kitchen at the table, where the rest of the staff took their meals.

The cook was tired and in a bad mood. The house boy and the butler were playing a game of cards. One of the other housemaids was reading a small square pocketbook, her brow wrinkled, eyes straining at the words.

They could not retire until the race party had returned home and were looked after.

The clock ticked on, *tick tick, tick tick*. Patricia watched a small grey mouse dart under the still warm stove.

"Are they usually this late?" she ventured.

The butler, who was not like the butler at Lismore, nothing as grand, more like a head footman, looked up at the clock.

"Not usually," he said.

At midnight, they were all exhausted and longing for their beds.

The cook laid her head on the table and slept, her back rising up and down, peaceful among the warmth and press of the bodies in the kitchen.

Patricia thought that her adventure to the races had turned out to be a bit of a damp squib. Apart from the motor-car trip and the novelty of staying at a different house, today had been tedious. She wasn't comfortable in her surroundings, and her time off was addled with anxiety. She felt she had nowhere to go. She wasn't wanted in the kitchen. She wasn't going to take on chores when this was not her house. And even the bedroom where she was staying was not hers.

Somewhere, deep in her imagination on the drive up here,

she'd felt she would be accompanying the Ladies Cavendish to the races. She dreamed that they might tell her to put on one of their dresses, toss a feathered hat at her and say, *Patricia dear, come with us, we could do with your help!*

At least back in Lismore, she would be in bed by now.

Before half past twelve, a loud *rat tat tat* came to the front door and someone began ringing the bell. It echoed through the quiet hall and the cook sat up with a jolt, her face lined red where she'd lain against the cuff of her dress.

The butler went to the door and when they heard commotion the staff left the kitchen and rushed to the hall.

Lady Dorothy was standing there, hunched over.

"There's been an accident," said the butler. "Girls, get some water on to boil and strip some sheets, in case we need bandages."

"I'm fine," muttered Lady Dorothy.

She was brought into the drawing room and a brandy placed in front of her.

Where were the others? Where was Charles? Lady Anne? Dorothy's husband?

The cook and housemaids left to go set water on to boil, the cook blessing herself and muttering a prayer as she left the drawing room.

The family of the house had been roused and had come down in their nightclothes and dressing gowns. Patricia stood behind the low sofa and armchairs where they sat and listened to snippets of the conversation.

On the way home from Wexford the car had skidded and overturned into a ditch.

Charlie had received a bang to the head and had been unconscious for a time. The broken glass had cut Lady

Anne badly on the wrist and Harold Macmillan had also received a knock to his head.

An ambulance from Wexford County Hospital had taken the three of them away. They were most worried for Charlie who had come round but was terribly confused.

The motor car was still in the ditch, crumpled and crushed.

Patricia stepped forward when she saw Lady Dorothy was trembling. "Let's get you upstairs, Lady Dorothy," she said.

In her room, the lady sat on the small double bed and looked at the wall.

"Are you hurt, Lady Dorothy?" Patricia asked.

"No," she answered in a quiet voice.

"Let me help you undress."

Her hat was gone and her sleeves looked ragged. There was a blood stain all down the centre of her dress.

"It's not mine," Lady Dorothy said with a wave of her hand at the stain. "It's Anne's."

Patricia undid her dress and boots, removed the corset and helped pull a nightdress over her head. When the nightdress was on, she tugged at her underskirt and removed it from underneath to protect her lady's modesty.

Lady Dorothy lay down on the bed, tucked her legs under her and quietly began to cry.

"Can I get you anything – a cup of tea, something to eat?"

"No, thank you," she said.

Patricia left, taking the bloodstained dress with her for washing, her own blood filling her head.

In the kitchen, everyone stopped talking when she came in.

"How is she?" the butler asked.

The cook gasped at the bloodstained dress and took it to soak.

"She's upset," Patricia said. "But I think she's going to sleep now."

"It was a strange place to crash," the butler said. "On a straight part of the road. It was dry and no gravel or anything. A very strange place to come off the road."

"Let's pray that everyone will be alright," Patricia said.

"Is it safe to go to bed now?" the cook asked, her eyes red-rimmed.

"Yes," said the butler. "We'll get over to the hospital in the morning and see how everyone is."

A straight part of the road, on a dry, clear night.

Patricia imagined the car now, the crumple of metal, smashed glass scattered.

She thought of the fumes, petrol, alcohol, gassing.

She pictured Charles, his face, asleep, snoring last night on the low chair.

Was it the bump on the head that had knocked Charlie out when the car crashed or had he already been asleep at the wheel?

Knocked out by the copious amounts of alcohol from last night and today?

Patricia couldn't help but think it was the latter.

CHAPTER TWENTY-EIGHT

NEW YORK, OCTOBER 1929

THE WALL STREET CRASH OF 1929 ARRIVED with all the aplomb of an unwelcome policeman at the end of a terrific party. Switching on all the lights. Grappling with the gramophone. Shouting at everyone to go home.

The headlines blasted us from every newstand.

Billions Lost. Panic. Black Tuesday. Stocks Collapse.

Freddie came to me with one of the newspapers and we sat in Mama's apartment looking over the print.

"How could this happen?" Mama asked and she talked about how her parents had fled Prussia for the same thing. Money meaning nothing. Bank accounts snuffed out.

Recession.

"Those damn bankers," said Freddie, with venom in his voice.

"Should we take our money out?" I asked.

"Good luck to you getting it," he said.

That afternoon we went for a walk, all the way down to Wall Street to see if there was anything happening. Crowds gathered in clumps. People scurried about, faces wan, everyone worried. Nobody knew what would come next. But we all knew it would be bad.

The banks had closed. There was no access to cash.

We decided to go for a drink to a speakeasy we sometimes went to after a show. A queue of people were at the door and the place was thronged with drinkers, supping down whiskey and shorts and glassy cocktails. They were drinking away their shock. Spending the money they had in their pocket because who knew what would happen to that money now?

We had to wait to see what would happen. We knew the crash might affect upcoming stage shows because most of them were bankrolled by Wall Street backers.

We'd gone ahead and signed with Flo Ziegfeld for a new show called *Smiles*.

"Surely Ziggy will be safe?" I said to Fred over the din of a trumpet.

He shrugged.

"He's too big, surely, to fail?" I said.

I felt if any producer could survive a market crash it would be the flamboyant Ziegfeld.

"It's not the rich, ritzy guys you need at a time like this," said Freddie. "It's the frugal tight bastards you need, the skinflints."

Ziegfeld was no skinflint.

But the show had to go on, right?

"He must be keen to have travelled to Paris to meet you."

"He didn't travel to Paris to meet me, Mother. He just happened to be there."

"And is he keen?"

"Well, I don't know!"

"But you know him well enough to have him escort you around Paris?"

"It was just lunch and dinner."

"Lunch *and* dinner."

"Oh, Mother, stop! I'm not a child. If I want to meet this man I will meet him."

"Yes, Adele, no one tells you what to do."

"Oh, Mother."

Probably what was bothering Mama was that Fred hadn't been with me. She always liked me to travel with Fred, hated when we separated and he wasn't seen to be minding me. After *Funny Face* had closed in London, Fred stayed on in the city while I headed to Paris for a break before we were due back to the States.

I loved all that Paris had to offer: the narrow cobbled streets, the black, bitter coffee, the elegance of the women and the boutiques on the street corners.

I suited Paris.

I was quite amused when I learned that Charles Cavendish was travelling to Paris too, right at the same time. Fred had learned this information through his friend Prince Aly Kahn, so naturally I got in touch. I met with my friends all over the world, whenever I was in town.

Of course, Charlie was different. I knew it straightaway. I knew the minute I laid eyes on him in that tiny café on Rue de la Paix where we ordered strong coffee and beef sandwiches that turned out to be practically raw meat. I scrunched my face at mine. He ate his readily.

I talked, babbled, he was quiet. He listened to me, really heard me. There was no pretending to be interested just so we could step out that night. So that he could say he was my beau.

He didn't need me as his beau. We had equal things about us. He was a wealthy upper-class businessman, I was a wealthy working show-woman.

We were a hit.

We stayed two hours in the café, our coffee growing cold, ordering more. And when it was time to go, I wrapped my fox fur about me and we walked arm in arm and I had never felt so contented as I was with this tall man on my arm.

In Paris, I had no fear of people asking for autographs or popping out from behind corners to surprise me. It was a wonderful break from London and Broadway.

"Do you like shopping?" I asked him.

"It depends on what we're buying," he said.

"Oh, men's clothes are so dull."

"Are they now?"

"Yes."

"Do you think I'm a dull dresser?"

"No, but compared to women's clothes men's are so limited."

"It makes things simple."

"I suppose it does."

We stopped at a boutique with a beautiful mustard dress in the window and the words *Schiaparelli – Pour Le Sport* over the door. We went in, a little bell tinkling as we stepped over the threshold.

I tried on a small hat, balancing it on my head and making a face.

"You're quite the clown, aren't you?" he said, in his lovely English voice.

"Don't you know that by now?"

"I don't really know anything about you, Miss Astaire – you just seemed to appear in my life."

I liked that. I liked that I could reveal myself slowly.

"I'll take it," I said to the lady in a white blouse behind the counter, a gathering of silk at her neck.

She boxed it up and wrapped it in paper and, as I took out my purse to remove my francs, Charles put his hand over mine and took out his wallet.

"A gift," he said. "To remember me by."

I didn't need anything to remember him by. Everything about him was permanent in my head.

I could not get him out of my head.

"C.B.D. is wiped."

"Oh no!"

"Oh yes."

"Oh, poor man."

"Guess I won't be getting my investment back so."

"What investment was that?"

"Well, a loan. He came to me a while back, few years ago. Was strapped. I gave him $15,000."

"Oh Freddie."

"Crushing Big Deficit?"

"Colossal Big Debt?"

He sighed.

We were sitting on two chairs on a stage, looking at the fiasco unfolding before us.

Ziegfeld was nowhere to be seen. We thought he was ill.

Rehearsals for *Smiles* were not going well. The crash a few months ago saw our start date pushed back and back while Ziegfeld sorted out the financial end of things. Now that we were finally rehearsing we realised that finances were not our only problem.

The show was a flop.

We had another disaster on our hands.

After listening to the piano player argue again with the

choreographer, Fred got up from his chair and marched over. He asked the player to stand and he sat down angrily on the stool and began hammering out the song, yelling out steps that would work and that we should be doing.

"*Let's just get on with it!*" he shouted.

Chairs were scattered around, sheet music too. An apple-butt shuddered on top of the piano, beside an ashtray and two cups of cold coffee.

Right at the back, stretched out across the audience seats, hidden, was our composer, Youmans. I knew if you stood beside him you'd hear his snores, coming thick, deep, right up from inside his chest.

He was drunk, of course.

And that's why Fred was at the piano, trying to help out.

I lay back on the stage and felt the stretch on my back. I let out a sigh.

I was so weary. The show was going to be a flop, no stopping it now.

We all knew it. Even with Ziegfeld's great efforts and pomp and all the stars he would bring to the opening night.

You can't make a silk purse out of a sow's ear.

And this show was the bloody pig's ear, trotter and snout.

I thought of Charles and how I would like to have been with him now away from this farce, away from this terrible mess we'd gotten ourselves into. Charlie would know what to say. He'd know how to put an arm around me, make me feel all warm, give me a little kiss, tell me everything would be alright.

He was so handsome, Charlie, and such a catch. I felt awful over here in the States, thinking about him while he lived merrily away in England. I closed my eyes and thought of Paris. What I'd have given to be in Paris right then.

"You have some crush."

"I do not!"

"You do! You should see your eyes when she comes near you. Like this ..." I crossed my eyes and fell right onto the bed. I started laughing.

"Oh, come now," said Freddie. "She's a very beautiful woman, but I don't fall in love with every pretty woman I come across."

"Just this one."

Fred looked exasperated. He glared across at Mother who was sitting at a small desk, writing.

"Talk some sense into her, Mother."

"Is it true?" she asked, looking up from her letter. "Have you fallen for her?"

"No! I have not."

"He has," I said, still lying on the bed.

Fred sighed and sat down on a chair and began unlacing his shoes.

We were in the Plaza Hotel in New York where we were staying while we rehearsed for *Smiles*. I'd been watching Fred fall more and more in love with our co-star Marilyn Miller each day. He was blind if he couldn't see how he was with her. But she was bad news, bad news for him. Ziegfeld was already in love with her and she had another beau on the go. Fred needed to listen to me. She was not the one for him.

"If you must know, I have a date tonight with a very pretty lady. That is not Marilyn Miller."

"Oh," I said, sitting up on the bed. "Do tell, brother."

"Her name is Ginger Rogers."

"Ginger Rogers." I said the name out loud. I liked it. It was a great name for the stage. "And who's she when she's at home then?"

"She's starring in Alex Aarons' new show. They were having a bit of trouble with one of the numbers and I went over to the Alvin yesterday to take a look. Anyway, we hit it off and we're going for supper tonight."

Freddie and Aarons had not fallen out when we moved to Ziegfeld. I was glad.

"Well, well," I say. "Better not tell Marilyn!"

Fred flung one of his shoes right at me and it whizzed by my head.

"*Fred!*" I shouted.

"*Fred!*" said Mother.

He wouldn't have been so touchy about all of this if it wasn't true that he had feelings for Marilyn. Maybe this Ginger woman would turn his head.

"I'm going for a bath," I said and I took Fred's shoe and flung it back in his direction.

"Oh," said Mother, "I almost forgot. This came for you today."

She handed me a letter and I looked at the writing and stamp.

Derbyshire England, blue fountain-pen ink.

It was from Charlie.

My heart soared.

INTERVIEW WITH FLO ZIEGFELD

***In conversation with Terence Whitfield, journalist at* New York Evening Post**
Feature: Show Business Bounces Back from Black Tuesday
(Published March 1930, Paper defunct 1934, New York State Library Archive)

I wanted the Astaires because I know stars when I see them. I had a knack, you see, a knack of shining a light, the spotlight. Course the Astaires were stars in their own right, but I wanted to make them even bigger stars. With all the flamboyance of a Ziegfeld show!

There's no show like a Ziegfeld show, let me tell you that. Everyone who was anyone turned up to the premiere of a Ziegfeld show. And the crowds outside! Sell-outs.

Course you had to work at it. Had to put the publicity in place, play a few tricks here and there.

You wanna know what the number one factor in attracting an audience is? Beauty. You put a nice lookin' man, something about him, a strong jaw, nice face in front of an audience of women and you watch them get all hot under their collars. They'll tell all their friends then and next thing you know, night after night, hordes of women coming back for more.

Same with the women. You get a nice beautiful girl, something about her, because there's a lot of beautiful girls – ya gotta pick a real special one, with charisma, and put her up there on stage, in a nice costume, curves in all the right places, and you make up something about her, something in the news, a romance maybe and then everyone wants to come see the show. Everyone wants to see this girl, to be with this girl and if the closest they can get to her is coming to a Ziegfeld show, then that's what they'll do.

The Astaires weren't beauties, mind. But they had the charisma. And the talent, they had the talent alright.

Course the damn crash happened just as we were looking to see what production we'd do and that set us back. That set everyone back. Damn quiet time on Broadway it was. It took us a while to get going because I had the get the right book, I couldn't just dash them up on the stage with any old book. So I got an outline from Noel Coward – you couldn't go wrong with Coward – and then I got Louis Bromfeld, he'd just won a Pulitzer. I asked him to write the book on Coward's outline, because I thought, get the best, get the best of the best for the Astaires, they deserved a good book, something that would make them real big stars.

Course Marilyn, that's Marilyn Miller, real beautiful actress, been on my books now a while, well, she thinks she knows best, because she's a star of the show too and she says she doesn't care if Mr Bromfeld is a Pulitzer Prize winning author, she wants William Anthony McGuire to write the damn thing, because she knows his writing and knows he'll make a success of it, just like he did Rosalie, *just like he did her other shows.*

Now me and Marilyn got a real special relationship, you see, we understand each other and I just know that if Marilyn wants something real bad and doesn't get it, well, the whole thing will be doomed, so I gave in and I said alright, we'll give the script over to McGuire and let him work on it and we'll see where we are.

Well, now, things didn't exactly go to plan and here we are in March and we should be opened by now and we're not and so we're looking at pushing fall which I don't like, but what's a man to do?

All this toing and froing is making me feel tired. It's just as well the film I have at the minute is doing well, because we wouldn't have any backers for this show right now, if they knew what was really going on.

It's a tough business, show business, let me tell you that. But it's goddamn addictive too.

There's nothing else like it, nothing like it in the world. Ha ha!

CHAPTER TWENTY-NINE

NEW YORK, OCTOBER 1930

CHARLIE'S LETTER ANNOUNCED THAT he was coming to New York just around the time *Smiles* was to open.

He had been involved in a very bad car accident in Ireland and it had changed him. He wanted to take every opportunity the world could throw at him. He wanted to travel. He had secured a financial job with JP Morgan.

I read it and reread it and showed it to Mama.

This was the most unbelievable luck. I had not stopped thinking about him since the time we'd spent in Paris and the fleeting time we'd had together in London.

The fact he was coming all the way to the States, and to work?

It was fate.

Mama didn't complain about Charlie Cavendish like she had done about George Jean Nathan and William Gaunt.

I think she thought there was something respectable about him, something refined.

The day after he arrived he sent a note and came to the Plaza to meet me in the restaurant. I was surprised when he took me and kissed me.

It wasn't what I expected.

A smile wrapped itself around my face.

There it was, that thrill, that feeling in my stomach. There was no one I would rather spend time with than this man.

We ordered food but both of us found it hard to eat.

Our insides were tight with anticipation.

"What do you think they'll be like to work for?"

"Not sure," he said, frowning. "Alright, I suppose. I'm looking forward to seeing."

I liked that he wasn't a writer. Or a critic. Or an actor.

He would have a proper, respectable job.

I liked that he would be working with numbers, making use of his commerce degree. I got the impression he had been floundering.

He ordered a whiskey on the rocks and I ordered a glass of champagne.

We were celebrating. Celebrating our reunion.

The bubbles went straight to my head.

Charlie met Mama for the first time over lunch at Luchow's. Freddie came too.

I was nervous, because Mama had a quick tongue in her head and would cut Charlie down to size, just because she could.

But she was reserved. She could see that already this was a different thing I had going on.

For most of the lunch Freddie and Charlie talked horses, race meets, stud farms, jockeys, new training techniques, a swimming pool for horses.

They laughed, big thigh-slapping jokes, and I looked at Mama over my water glass.

The corners of her mouth were raised in a smile.

She liked him.

Charlie was perfectly behaved. He didn't touch a drop of alcohol during our lunch, although I knew he was tempted.

I was proud of him, I knew he could control it if he wanted to. He just had to *want* to.

Then, after our first lunch meeting in New York, he took me to a tailor's in the Garment District where he took three suits out of the satchel he was carrying. He separated the jackets from the trousers.

"This is my first job to get done in New York," he said. "I was thinking about it on the passage all the way over."

The tailor took the jackets – two with a thin pinstripe, the other a rich tweed and began marking out squares with chalk. Charlie folded the trousers back into his satchel, one of which I noticed had wide thighs, a style that gave the impression he was about to jump into a motor car and zoom off into the countryside. I expected it reminded him of home.

"What are you doing?" I asked, confused.

"Bootlegger's surprise!" he said and pointed at where the tailor was sketching inside the jacket.

"What?"

"Secret surprise! You can pat me down and you'd never find a flask in these pockets."

"But why?"

"Why? Because in this country you have introduced a very very silly law that prevents a good man from having a good drink for no apparent reason whatsoever."

"Oh, Charlie."

"Oh, nothing."

I was alarmed that he felt the need to carry a flask with him. That he took great joy in showing me his ingenious prohibition get-around. He was starting a new job, so why on earth would he risk being caught with alcohol or even feel the need to carry it? It puzzled me.

While Freddie and I waited for rehearsals of *Smiles* to start, Charlie and I took to meeting up at lunchtime or after work, taking long meandering walks in Central Park, stopping for coffee or tea, or oftentimes a swifty in a speakeasy. He somehow knew where they were, no matter what part of town we were in. It was like somebody handed him a list when he stepped off the ship – *here, go find all these drinking joints*. I felt he was taking them down one by one, marking them off some conquest list.

Sometimes I had a cocktail, but most times I stuck to a soda water with lime. I think I was trying to make a point.

I enjoyed walking along arm in arm on our meanders, feeling his height beside me. I loved to look up at him, all the way in the clouds and always I felt great joy when he looked back down at me and smiled.

He went out every night. At first I did not mind but, as I got to know him more, I realised I wanted to spend all my time with him. I did not want him going out without me. I did not want him to meet anyone else.

This feeling began to build. A desperate type of longing, of wanting him to be mine.

One evening we went to 21, a new speakeasy on 21 West 52nd street. It had a big iron grill gate at the front and a sophisticated revolving bar on the inside. They could hide the liquor within seconds if they needed to. It all felt very secretive and naughty.

Charlie loved it.

There was a queue outside, but we went straight to the

door and were brought in by a host who settled us at a quiet table, in a dark corner.

I was feeling a big flighty, a bit excited. Tonight, I wanted to let my hair down.

"I'll have a Sidecar," I said, reading the little drinks menu and Charlie raised his eyebrows.

"I'll have what the good lady is having," he said.

After another Sidecar I made Charlie get up to dance. He wasn't one for dancing, but I told him the least he could do was take me to the floor.

"You know how much I love to dance, Charlie."

He sighed and stood and we went to the small floor, where other couples were pressed, body to body.

I loved to be up close to him like this, in public.

After a Charleston, where he mostly stood back and watched me dance around him, I leaned in to his ear.

"You and I get along rather well," I said above the music. "We ought to hitch up."

He laughed, looked down at me and pushed my head lovingly onto his chest.

"I'm quite serious, Charlie Cavendish!"

He laughed again and we left the floor to sit back at our seats and order another cocktail.

"Need that, do you?" he said.

"Yes," I said. "It's not every day you propose."

We laughed and I felt merry and so sure of what I was doing.

Later, we got a cab to my apartment and he gave me a long, lingering kiss before I tottered to my door.

"Goodnight," he said.

I blew him a kiss, wobbling on my heels. "Goodnight, sweetheart."

The next morning I awoke to a throbbing head and the sound of the telephone ringing in the hall.

Mama came to my bedroom door.

"Adele, Charlie's on the phone for you. Goodness, the smell of alcohol in here!"

She waved her hand under her nose and made for the window to open it.

I groaned and rolled myself out of the bed, staggering barefooted to the hall. My mouth felt like horsehair and my head ached.

"Adele."

I heard his voice. So regal. So familiar.

"You proposed to me last night and I accepted," he said. "If you don't marry me, I'll sue you for breach of promise."

I sank to the telephone chair and laughed. I laughed and I laughed and I felt my headache almost explode behind my eyes.

PART FOUR

CURTAIN CALL

CHAPTER THIRTY

RMS MAJESTIC, NORTH ATLANTIC OCEAN, MARCH 1932

"YOUR TURN."

He picked up the dice and threw it, his eyebrows knitted together, emanating a quiet grunt. He really was a peculiar-looking man.

"*Hmmm*," he said as he moved his checkers, bouncing them along, concentrating. "I fear you are winning."

I smiled. "I told you I was good at backgammon."

A slight smile passed his thin lips. Beside his hand rested a tumbler, bourbon on the rocks. A fat cigar hung from his mouth, the smoke curling up. I liked the smell of it. It was comforting.

"Do you like reading, Miss Astaire?" he asked as he stroked his chin while considering his next move.

He was losing. He didn't like to lose.

"I love reading, Mr. Churchill."

"Good. I like a woman who reads. Everyone should read."

He winced and I wondered if he had been struck with a pain. He was in a terrible way since his accident, even though that was nearly three months before. What a surprise to meet him here, on this voyage. And luck, I supposed. Mama whispered to me earlier that she believed *that man* would be the prime minister of Britain one day. She might be right.

But right now, I was beating him at backgammon.

"What about art, do you like art?" he asked.

"Well, yes, some," I said.

My knowledge of art was not great. I was not going to let myself down by pretending I knew anything much about it.

"I love to paint," he said. "It's good for the soul. For the heart probably too."

"You'll have to paint me some day," I said.

"I'd like that," he said, looking up. The cigar moved as he spoke.

He moved three checkers.

"You'll have to try harder than that, Mr Churchill," I said, as I removed a checker of his from play and placed it in the centre bridge of the board.

He frowned.

"Are you feeling alright?" I asked him, a little concerned.

He took a swig from his glass. "Quite."

"It's a pity about the tour – I'm sure you were very let down."

"My dear, these past two years have been nothing but a let-down."

He had lost too in the Wall Street crash, just like us. But, I feared, he had lost a lot more.

Three months before a car had mowed him down, just after he landed in New York city for a speaking tour. It broke his bones, lacerated his head and left him bruised all over. He was lucky to be alive by all accounts. Mama and I had visited him when we heard. He was not far from our apartment and we knew he would welcome some friendly faces. Even if we were Americans.

Winston was a funny fellow. He was one of the many

interesting characters I'd come across in my time in England, usually at Philip Sassoon's place. Sassoon was an MP and very high up and knew all the politicians. They escaped to Port Lympne for privacy, just like me and other stage stars. It was a heady mix, all those creative and powerful people.

I knew that Winston found me intelligent and engaging and he liked that I had a talent for the stage. He had been to see one of my shows, he told me, but he wasn't a lover of the theatre. He preferred restaurants and quiet bars and painting at home.

"Times have not been easy," I said. "Let's hope the thirties won't be so troubled."

He opened his hands and shrugged. *Come what may.*

"I don't know if I can claw this game back," he said. "I think you have me beat."

I smiled and raised my hand to order a cup of tea from the waiter.

"That I have, Mr. Churchill."

Churchill shook my hand tightly as a queue of people formed to disembark at Plymouth. Mama and I would be getting off at Southhampton, the final dock.

From the window we spied them, a flurry of photographers and press men, gaping up at the ship, moving now as the *Majestic* began to dock.

"Oh, rats!" I said. "I thought we might avoid them."

"Oh, they're for you," said Churchill. "I thought they were for me."

I laughed. I was in no mood to face these men today with their bulbs exploding in our faces, and me trying to shield Mama.

We watched as the gangway was lowered and the press men

rushed past the rope, right up the board and onto the ship.

"For heaven's sake!" said Mama.

"Quick," said Churchill. "Come this way."

We followed him and he brought us into an empty lounge, usually only opened in the evenings.

He looked around and spied a group of tall ferns in yellow brass pots.

"Hide here," he said.

We ducked right in behind the plants, breathing heavily. My heart was beating.

This was quite fun, hiding from the press.

"I'll tell them you've already disembarked and they've missed you."

"Thank you, Mr. Churchill," I said, peering through a fern, feeling like a jungle explorer.

"The very best of luck to you, my dear," he said, smiling, taking out a new cigar to light it.

How many did he get through in a day? No wonder he'd developed pleurisy after the accident.

"You've a good one on your hands here," he said to Mama and she managed a smile from her hideout on the floor.

"Thank you ever so much, Mr. Churchill – we will meet again no doubt."

Mama loved a powerful man.

"Don't drink too much champagne on your wedding day!" he called as he left.

"I won't touch a drop!"

And with that he was gone.

As we sat on the carpet, Mama and I, my thoughts turned to my wedding day and Churchill's words.

Alcohol wouldn't be a problem for me on the day.

But what about Charlie?

INTERVIEW WITH WINSTON CHURCHILL

Background interview with Benjamin Curlew
***Research on:* Churchill's War, A History**
Status: Unpublished, notes and records at London Metropolitan Archive

Adele Astaire. Ah yes, lovely Adele. Great company. I met her a few times in London at dinners, parties, that type of thing. She liked to stay at Philip Sassoon's. Like most of the glamour set. And she came to see me after the accident in New York. That was kind of her.

She and her mother, very kind people.

I happened to be in hospital not far from their apartment. I enjoyed her company, immensely.

Adele was part of the American set who came over to London in the early 20s, bringing all their talent with them. They had to be seen to be believed. We'd never seen such shows!

And she was a big part of that, Adele, a driving force. All legs out and stockings and hair cut up.

Had I been a younger man … well, yes …

Her brother Fred was very nice too. A lovely family.

It was a surprise to meet Adele and her mother on the Majestic. *A most welcome surprise.*

She was going to England to be married.

It was a delight to see such a competent young woman coming to our shores to set up home. And she was marrying into a good family, I told her that.

I'd been to Chatsworth House before, big estate, very fine.

She could do worse, I told her. Marrying into that fine family.

She told me she was retiring at the right time, that she felt she had completed her stage career and even though I thought the stage would be worse off without her, I understood.

There comes a time in a woman's life when it's time to settle down.

She wanted a family, of course she did. Children settled the soul.

I wished her well.

You deserve it, I told her. Happiness. And she did, you know.

A sweet girl. Yes, indeed.

CHAPTER THIRTY-ONE

RMS MAJESTIC, SOUTHAMPTON, MARCH 1932

AT SOUTHAMPTON, THERE WAS NO AVOIDING THE PRESS.

There seemed to be even more of them now that they hadn't caught us at Plymouth.

"It is quite something," said Mama, staring at them out the window.

"We'll scurry past, Mama, keep our heads low."

"It's madness! Why are they so interested?"

I sigh. "Who knows, Mama? A wedding always gets everyone agitated."

I had not been back to England since the close of *Funny Face* in the middle of 1929 and in that time interest had not faded but grown. The fact I was to marry one of their own seemed to send them into a frenzy.

I couldn't wait to see Charlie after our long absence.

It had been torture having him back in England while I was stuck doing first *Smiles*, the flop we all knew it would be, and then *The Band Wagon*, which, thank Christ, had been a success. I refused to end my stage career on a low. I would not go out on a flop. Freddie and I had worked too hard for me to bow out just after a disastrous show.

Flo Ziegfeld was devastated about *Smiles* and we were

all sorry it had been a failure. But everyone could see it had been no fault of Freddie or mine. We did our bit. And even though the show had closed prematurely, we were soon scooped up for *The Band Wagon.*

Charlie had gone back home before Christmas after just a few months working at JP Morgan's.

What had started off so promising had become a bit of a mess. After a few months where he was continuously late to work and altogether grey in the face, they parted ways.

Charlie said it was to do with the crash.

We both knew it was to do with his crushing hangovers.

I missed him terribly when he left.

I missed speaking to him, telling him all the tiny details of my day. I wrote to him every day and on the road. It was the only way I could feel close to him, but it wasn't the same.

He didn't always write me back straightaway and as the days added up, as his letters didn't come, I became jealous and frenzied and swirled in bad humour. I don't think he realised what an impact being engaged and not being together would have on me.

He didn't understand how difficult it was for me to be hearing tales and tattle, of parties and get-togethers, rumours and gossip and all the while I was working, working, working, night after night, dress, make-up, stage, curtain call, applause, encore, goodnight, in a country far away.

Mama tried to reassure me. Fred too. But they couldn't have known what it was like.

Never before had I felt my age so badly.

Charlie was younger than me, he moved in circles where the ladies were younger too, prettier. I daydreamed about their milky-white skin, their pretty shoulders and long hair, giggling, tittering, my Charlie moved by lust unable to keep his hands off them.

Especially if he was drunk.

I reprimanded him, of course. I poured it all out in my letters.

Don't give into temptation. I can't bear it. I won't be long. Wait for me.

He wrote and told me not to be silly and not to worry, but I couldn't help myself.

I was obsessed.

On announcement of our engagement, his family had made it clear that they were none too pleased. His mother needed the most persuading. The fact it had reached the papers before them was against us. The fact that I was an American was against me.

They had expected him to marry another lady with a title, someone with standing, with land and a family history.

A stage star from the mid-west, an uncouth one at that, was not becoming.

I had turned his head, it seemed.

I wondered if his going home to England after our engagement was an attempt on his part to bring them along, or a guise on their part to help him forget about me. I would not give in though. My daily letters proved my love.

I planned my stage exit, telling myself it would all be worth it. After *Smiles* I needed to find something that meant I would not leave the stage on a flop. Not after all these years. Not after all this success.

I pulled back. We pushed Freddie forward, with more dancing and dialogue. We lessened the number of my scenes, set them so that I wasn't the absolute attraction. It was the slow goodbye.

The Band Wagon was a roaring success, different to what we had done before, a return almost to our vaudeville days, but on a much grander scale. The writers put forward a series of sketches and acts which kept the audience entertained and Freddie and I were so at home with that type of work.

Max Gordon the producer would have held on to me for as long as he could, but he knew, once a woman announced she was getting married and was determined to go through with it, it was the end. I was thirty-four and I was tired.

I agreed to finish out the New York run and I would leave halfway through the Chicago tour in the spring.

I would be free to marry Charlie in March 1932.

I marked the calendar, the shows gone by: X, X, X.

Europe was calling me: the green fields, the dark clouds, the wet, fragrant air.

I daydreamed about fashioning our new house, going to suppers and race meets and nestling at night by a warm, roaring fire.

Holding my stomach where his babies would grow.

Seed, stem, branch, tree.

Freddie had been anxious in the run-up to my departure. While he was happy for me and my future, it was a massive upheaval in our lives. We had not been separated since we were children, not in our careers, not from each other in such a permanent way.

And I would be taking Mama with me to England for a while. He would be in America, on his own.

On the afternoon before our last show, I called him to my dressing room and he sat down beside me in a battered old armchair I liked to read in.

"Well, sis," he said, "how ya feeling?"

"Oh, you know," I said. "A bit emotional. It's the end of an era, isn't it?"

"It is. But I'm happy for you, Delly. I really am."

"I know that, brother."

We sat for a minute, taking it all in, this last time we would share a dressing room, ready to go on: our double act.

I could feel tears stinging my eyes and I blinked, worried if I started I wouldn't be able to stop. I needed to hold it all together. This was my decision, it was not being forced upon me.

Why then, after longing for nearly a year and a half to leave and head for England, was I feeling torn? Upset? Sad?

"I got something for you," I said and I reached into my bag, under the dressing table. I took out a small red box.

Fred took it, opened it and smiled.

"Oh Delly, it's just fine," he said.

He took out the thick gold signet ring and tried it on his right hand. It wouldn't fit his fourth finger and he pushed it onto his pinky.

It looked right, like it belonged, like it had always been part of him.

He reached over and we hugged, leaning against each other and I smelt his familiar warmth.

When we came apart, his cheeks were wet, but he brushed them aside, cleared his throat and said, "Well, on with the show."

I'd never loved anyone like I loved Freddie.

He left my dressing room and I sat and looked in the mirror.

Remember this moment, I thought. Remember what it

was like just before you went out to your last audience for the last time.

Remember what it felt like, to be a star.

I think of Fred's signet ring now as I look down at own my hands, at my ruby-and-diamond engagement ring.

"Show us the ring, love!"

"When's the big day, Adele!"

Mama and I have rushed past the press, escorted by RMS *Majestic* staff into a taxi, telling the driver to get us to the train station as quickly as possible.

We look back and see cars chasing us.

"This is crazy," says Mama.

She is really put out by the attention. It does not bother me as much, but I didn't expect it to be this bad.

We are ushered onto the train by a nice conductor who sees to it that we are put in a carriage with other first-class passengers and that the press cannot push past, to snap, to try to interview me.

The other passengers eye me from their books, a hint of a smile on their faces. They do not bother us, in their respectful English way.

Outside Waterloo station, we try to push past the press, but they jostle us and Mama is annoyed. I hold on to her arm.

I look past the press men, over their trilby hats and waving hands, notebooks flashing.

And there he is.

Charlie.

A look of concern on his face. He towers above the crowd and I see him push forcefully through to grab my arm and take Mama by hers.

"*Out of the way, leave them be!*" he shouts.

We manage to move our way out, through the tangle of arms and legs, to the waiting taxi Charlie has organised.

Mama's hat has been knocked off and her cheeks are red. She puts her arm up to shield the flashes coming through the window.

"It's OK, Mama," I say and pat her leg.

I don't like to see her so upset.

I always associate London with this type of interest. When we were in *Lady, Be Good!* and *Funny Face* we were regularly escorted to a waiting motor car to be whisked from backstage home. Opening nights were the worst.

Perhaps this is the opening afternoon for the rest of my life.

Charlie gets back in, looking grumpy, and tells the driver to go, quick.

I lean over the seat, watching the road in front.

He turns and looks at me, his eyebrows knitted together.

"Welcome home," he says.

We burst out laughing and I put my hand out and squeeze his shoulder.

"Don't be nervous."

"Easy for you to say."

"You'll be fine. Mama's a tough nut, but she'll like you."

Butterflies flit in my tummy, making me feel positively sick. I need the bathroom. I'll have to ask as soon as I arrive. I'm going to be watched now for the next three days: how I speak, what I wear, how I sound, how often I go to the damn toilet.

The car turns into the long driveway of Chatsworth House and I gasp as I see the place.

My goodness. Is this really Charlie's home? It's like something out of a fairy tale. He grasps my hand and squeezes it.

I look over at Mama and she smiles.

Her daughter has done well.

Swathes of green lawn stretch out before us. The driveway is winding, meandering, giving a beautiful view of the acreage that surrounds the house. A fountain sprays in front of the house, built into a split-level lawn.

The day is dull, but the stone seems to sparkle.

What a place to grow up!

We get to the front door and I give Charlie's hand another squeeze.

"*I'm so nervous!*" I hiss.

"Shush," he says and smiles. "Treat it like one of your stage performances. Just smile!"

The gravel crunches under my shoes. I've bought a new pair for the occasion, T-bar, patent, mauve leather.

A statue looks down on me with beady stone eyes. I feel as though I am being watched.

I realise that I probably am.

A butler answers, a tall, thin man. He looks very gruff. Well suited to this place, I think.

Still, I smile at him, sweetly.

He takes our coats and leads us through to a very grand room. The ceiling is the height of an ancient oak tree. Thick rugs sink beneath my feet and all around the walls are dark paintings of men and women in white wigs, looking very dour.

Doesn't anyone smile at Chatsworth?

I see Charlie's eyes searching for the drinks cabinet.

Not yet, dear boy, please hold off. We're trying to make a good impression.

Many minutes waiting. I'm too nervous to talk.

Charlie is relaxed, he's at home, although how anyone could feel at home in a giant room like this, I don't know. It's as big as a public library.

"How many rooms are there?" I ask him.

He's lying right back now, his head on the back of the chair, staring at the muralled ceiling.

"Dunno," he says. "A hundred? Two hundred? You'll have to ask Mama. She's the expert on all that."

And then, there she was, Evelyn Cavendish, the Mama, the Duchess.

I jump to my feet. Charlie is still lying like one half of a swastika on the couch.

"Charles," she says, her tone reprimanding.

She is dressed in a tight brown dress, with a wide skirt. She is corseted and has a black veil peeping out from the back of her hair. Victorian to the core.

"Mama," says Charlie and he straightens up and stands. He goes to her and kisses her once on each cheek. "I'd like to introduce you to Miss Adele Astaire."

He throws his arm wide, as though introducing a circus act and I step forward and bow my head and curtsy. It feels right to curtsy.

She puts out her hand and I take it, gripping it and holding on to it like a bishop's. I wonder should I kiss it. I shake it up and down and she withdraws it, and I feel embarrassed.

Maybe I should have kissed it?

"Welcome to Chatsworth," she says. There is no warmth to her voice. No smile in her eyes.

Mama steps forward and I see the Duchess look her up and down. Mama is beautiful and a lady. We may not be from royal stock, but Mama could have been, I'm sure of it. She holds herself well.

They shake hands stiffly, one mother looking like she's from the last century, the other from a future one.

We all sit and look at the Duchess who is studying us. She reminds me of a schoolmistress, a nun, who used to teach me back in high school in New Jersey. She commanded a room, just by looking, by casting her eyes at all before her.

"Where's Papa?" asks Charlie.

"He is in bed. He is not well. I really hope it isn't flu."

The word *flu* makes us all wince, even if it is over a decade since the last epidemic.

"He's been ill since yesterday," she said. "If he's still running a fever this evening, I'll send for the doctor."

We sit in silence for a few moments.

"So you're an actress," says the Duchess, turning her attention to me.

"I am," I say. I almost feel I should add 'your grace'.

She waits, but I am not sure what I am supposed to say.

"A dancer really. I started dancing first and that led to the stage shows. Of course, I'm retired now!"

I laugh.

She doesn't.

"Of course."

Help, Charlie, I think. *Help me*.

"I don't think we've had any actresses in the family before," she frowns. "Although your Grandmother Cavendish was quite melodramatic, Charlie." She gives a thin-lipped smile.

"Yes, she was a hoot," says Charlie. "Threw legendary parties. *Everyone* wanted to be there."

I laugh again, nervously.

Charlie must have inherited his grandmother's esprit, her joie de vivre. Such a spirit never existed in his mother, that is quite clear.

"Have you thought about a date for the wedding?" she asks.

"We wanted to discuss it with you," says Charlie.

"Well, there'll be no London affair."

I sit up straighter.

"I'll not have any more fuss than is absolutely necessary. You can get married here, at Chatsworth, a quiet family gathering."

I had presumed we would get married in London. With all our friends. Charlie practically lived there and it was where I knew. We had so many associates there, so many people I was looking forward to meeting up with again.

"Oh," said Charlie. "Really? Is that what you're thinking?"

"Yes," said his mother. "You can use the private chapel. Mrs. Astaire, you will need to write a letter to the Archbishop of Canterbury to seek permission. I don't see it being a problem."

Mama nods and looks at me.

I think about speaking up. About stating our case for a big wedding party in London.

Charlie puts his hand on my leg and squeezes it.

No. I will say nothing.

So what if his family insist on a wedding here? Chatsworth is truly beautiful. And besides, after waiting so long, I just want to get the deed done. To start our life. It would probably be quicker to do it all here anyway.

"The 25th of April – all the family will be here then," says the Duchess.

"Yes," I say. "We really are keen to be married, we have waited so long already."

Another frown.

"I will write the letter to the Archbishop," says Mama.

"Well, that's settled then," says Charlie and he slaps my leg. "Now, shouldn't we celebrate?"

"I'll ring for tea," says his mother and she reaches over to pull the string of the bell beside the fireplace.

"That would be lovely," I say and I nudge Charlie.

He sighs and flops down into the seat and stares over at the drinks cabinet.

It's just after eleven am.

That evening a gathering is organised with all of Charlie's family, so that I can meet everyone. I don't feel half as nervous about this as I did about meeting with his mother.

I get ready upstairs in a great big yawning room with speckled wallpaper and dark mahogany furniture.

It reminds me of a hotel, but it is dustier, not as used, less life to the place.

If there's anything I like it's a crowd and nothing can be as daunting as facing down Evelyn Cavendish again. I'm quite looking forward to this evening.

Charlie collects me outside my room and plants a kiss on my lips.

"Watch the lipstick," I say.

"You look divine," he says and there's a sparkle to his eyes.

I have never felt so happy.

We walk arm in arm through the corridors and I stop and ask him about the paintings and different rooms I spy. It seems to have washed over him, as though he had never noticed what a magnificent home he lived in.

He shrugs. "I'm not sure," he says, when I point to a very grand grandfather clock with a beautiful carving all down the front. "So much furniture came with the house." He stops and fingers the wood. "You know, our old house, the one before this, was so much smaller. But I preferred it. Not as draughty."

The family hadn't moved into this house until Charlie was an older child, when they inherited it. I could see why living in a smaller home had been cosier for a young boy.

I think about our ramshackle two-roomed house in Omaha and wonder what Charlie would make of it. Then I think of the Duchess and shiver.

Voices filter down the corridor as we approach the grand room.

"Mama is going to bed early," Charlie says. "She won't be here tonight, but everyone else is. Even Papa has roused himself from his sick bed."

What joy!

Charlie opens the door and pokes his head in.

I hear silence fall.

"Everyone," he says. "May I please introduce you to my fiancée, Miss Adele Astaire?"

He opens both doors, throwing them wide. They remind me of a stage curtain, rising.

I see the faces appear, looking, and without even thinking I drop to my hands and turn four big cartwheels into the room.

Think of it as a stage performance.

Gasps. Silence. A cackle. A round of applause and laughter.

Take that, Evelyn Bloody Cavendish!

Charlie takes me over to an elderly man by the fire who is supporting his chin with his hand.

"He's half the man he used to be since the stroke," he whispers.

"Your Grace," I say, extending my hand and dropping down to my hunkers so that I can look at him face to face. "It is a pleasure to meet you. I have snared your son. Apologies for that."

He chuckles and takes my hand, pumping it up and down with more force than I expected.

He has badges and medals on his jacket: a war hero.

"That was quite the entrance," he says. His voice is strained.

"Well, one has to make an impression," I say.

A chair is pulled up and I sit by his side, raising my voice so that he can hear me. At least that's one skill I have from all my years of training: projection.

We talk about the upcoming wedding. I ask him about the estate, and about his former role as the Governor General of Canada. He looks so pleased to talk about these things again and asks me if I've ever been to Canada. He likes that I'm American, I think.

He pats my hand when I break away to meet the rest of the family.

The youngest, Anne, asks after Freddie and whether he will be coming to the wedding.

"I'm afraid not," I say. "He has to work."

She looks crestfallen.

"But I'm sure he will come to visit soon. We are very close."

"We just loved you in *Funny Face,*" says Dorothy.

"We hoped you'd get married in London, that you'd invite the three princes," says Maud.

"Yes, well," Charlie says, "Mama has put her foot down on that. It's to be here."

The sisters raise their eyebrows.

"Really?" says Maud.

"Just wait till she finds out she's Catholic," says Charlie, pointing at me and laughing.

"Charlie!" says Dorothy. "Are you really?" she says, turning to me.

I nod. Was this an issue too?

"Oh, Mama will go crazy!" says Maud.

"And you haven't told her?" says Dorothy to Charlie. "Oh, you charming little fool."

"Is that a big problem?" I ask.

They all laugh.

"We'll sort it out, don't worry, darling," says Charlie and he takes a long drink from his glass.

He turns to talk to his brother Edward who has just sat down beside him.

I feel an overwhelming pang for Freddie. I wish he were here, to talk to, to sit beside me, to support me.

This family is so big, so many people, all vaguely resembling each other, like a little tribe. I have never known a large family. Ever since Daddy died, it's just been Freddie, Mama and me, and even when he was alive it was often just the three of us anyway.

I get a pang for Daddy, a pang for America. I feel so far away from home. A sudden gust of emotion sweeps through me and my eyes fill with tears.

"Are you alright?" asks Maud, seeing that I am getting upset.

"Fine," I say, my voice quiet, desperately trying to hold it together.

Don't cry, I think. Don't cry in front of these people!

What a silly sausage I am. But it's overwhelming being at Chatsworth. I really didn't expect such a palace. And I can't get the image of the Duchess out of my head, her face, unsmiling, dour, looking through me.

If I were different, spoke differently, had a different education, a monied background, then perhaps I would fit in.

And now I'm not even the right religion.

Charlie, still deep in conversation with Edward, squeezes my hand.

It's enough to send the tears back into my eyes and I take a deep breath and they are gone.

This is my new life now, a life that I have chosen.

And life as Lady Adele Cavendish is going to be wonderful, I just know it is.

It has to be.

Doesn't it?

On the Sunday, we have a great big dinner, all of the family seated round a beautiful dark-walnut table, laid out with shining silverware and porcelain plates.

The wine flows and Charlie drinks glass after glass. It barely seems to have an effect on him, he puts away so much of it. I feel quite drunk after one glass.

My body is still tense, I cannot relax here, even though I have tried.

Perhaps, in time, it will come.

Over dinner, the sisters hint that I should dance later, but I refuse.

I am not a monkey here to perform. I want to be accepted as a worthy sister-in-law to them, a woman fit to marry their brother.

Dancing is in my past now, although I may have to employ all my acting skills to get along inside this monied family.

At the end of the meal, the Duke, who looks terribly ill,

raises a toast and says that he is happy to welcome me into the family. I feel that he may be speaking the truth, although the Duchess doesn't smile as we all clink our glasses.

She has such a straight line of a mouth, no lips at all. I wonder what it must have been like for the Duke to kiss her over all these years. Did they ever passionately kiss? The thought makes me giggle and I have to be careful lest I snort wine out my nose.

No lips, no smile. No welcome.

After dinner, we go to the drawing room and Charlie goes with his father and brother to the billiards room. I chat with the sisters and tell them tales of the people Freddie and I have met over the years.

They are fascinated that I know Walt Disney and wonder if I could get them a signed picture?

"Of course," I say. "Isn't he a darling?"

"Oh, I have a Mickey Mouse statue!" says Anne. "It's one of my most prized possessions!"

She is recently married and has a glow about her. I really like her. I think I might ask Walt to send her something special, she is such a sweet girl.

The Duchess rises and says she is going to bed and we all kiss her goodnight on the cheek. She smells of floral perfume, like roses. But there's another smell too, something ancient, like the oils they use at Mass.

Mass. It turns out I'll need to join the Church of England if I wish to marry Charlie. A baptism will be arranged before the wedding. Another change, another turn in the road of my new life.

I relax into my chair when she leaves, as though a lion that we've been trapped in a cage with has suddenly bolted out the door and locked it behind them.

Dorothy laughs at me and shoves me on the arm.

"Don't mind Mama," she says. "She will come round. They just didn't expect an illustrious superstar to capture Charlie's heart. They were hoping for a very fine, very boring, very English girl."

"That, I am not," I say.

"They think a stage star will be up to all sorts – cavorting, drinking, leading him down a dangerous path."

I raise my eyebrows.

"Leading *him* down a dangerous path?"

"I don't think they realise yet that Charlie is quite capable of doing all that himself," says Dorothy. "It's you who will tame him. They really should have rolled out the red carpet for you, Adele, you deserve it, putting up with my brother."

I laugh. She means well.

But a little worry, ignited some time ago, deep in the pit of my stomach, flickers.

Charlie sneaks into my room – it's past one o'clock and I have been asleep.

"You can't be in here," I whisper as he creeps over to my bed and lies down flat, his face on the pillow beside me. The room is enormous but the bed is tiny and so high I felt like I had to take a run and jump at it to get in.

He mumbles something into the bedclothes.

"What?" I say, sitting up.

"A kiss. Can I have one, please?"

"No," I say and whack him on the back. "I've spent all this weekend trying to make a good impression and you're going to ruin it. Out, Charlie, out!"

He mumbles again, sits up and turns round. I know, by the smell on his breath that he is quite drunk.

"My father spoke with me this evening."

I look at him, waiting. Is he going to say his father approves of me? That he likes me?

Have I been accepted?

"He's giving us Lismore Castle."

"What?"

The Irish castle. The beautiful fortress on top of a hill. I've seen pictures of it. Heard about their family gatherings there.

All the way in Ireland, away from Chatsworth, Charlie and I, alone, left to do our own thing.

"I told my father we'd take it. But if you don't want to stay there ... it doesn't have to be permanent."

He is slurring a bit.

"Charlie!" I say and clasp at his nearest hand. "This is perfect. This is fabulous news! Oh, lovely Ireland. Oh, that's just wonderful news!"

I see that his eyes are half closed.

"I wasn't sure you'd want to live in Ireland."

"After this weekend, darling, I'd quite happily live on the moon."

He snorts.

I push him off my bed and tell him to go to his own room immediately, before our wedding is cancelled for impropriety.

He stumbles a little as he goes to the door, but he turns back and says, "Goodnight, sweetheart."

"Goodnight, darling."

I go to sleep and dream of Rapunzel letting down her hair from a great big tower.

I wonder should I grow my hair? Although I'll be married soon. And it's much more respectable to keep your hair short when you're a married woman, wouldn't you say?

CHAPTER THIRTY-TWO

LISMORE CASTLE, COUNTY WATERFORD, IRELAND, MARCH 1932

PATRICIA SAT AT THE KITCHEN TABLE, blowing the steam off a hot cup of tea, enjoying this quiet moment to herself. It's not often she got one. She had just completed the morning rounds of the bedrooms and the cook had gone down to the butcher's, saying she needed to "get out of this godforsaken kitchen". Time for a break.

"Patricia?"

Mrs. Keeley stepped into the kitchen. Her voice cut, shrill.

"Pour me a *cupán* too, would ya?"

Patricia got up heavily and set about boiling up the kettle and adding water to the pot. She knew Mrs. Keeley liked her tea good and strong so she didn't add any extra tea leaves. *Feck her*, she thought.

Mrs. Keeley made a face when she tasted it but said nothing.

She leaned in towards Patricia. "I have some very exciting news," she said, her voice a whisper.

Patricia thought if Mrs. Keeley was excited about another visit from the Cavendish family then she really did need a change of scenery. Another royal visit meant another royal load of work. The glamour of it all had slightly waned for Patricia.

"I've just received word and, Patricia, you can keep this to yourself now while we make the arrangements ..."

She leaned in even closer.

Patricia wondered what on earth the woman could be on about? Could there really be something exciting happening? Who could be coming to stay? Not the King or somebody?

Good Jesus, she thought. They could never handle it.

"We're getting new residents."

"Oh," said Patricia, waiting for more.

Mrs. Keeley let the moment hang in anticipation.

Then suddenly she exploded.

"*Charles Cavendish is to marry Adele Astaire! They are going to live here!*"

Mrs. Keeley's hands wobbled with the excitement and her tea spilled over in a wave into its saucer. A sound came out of her mouth, something she tried to suppress but it escaped. The sound a fox might make if it was caught in a snare.

"Adele Astaire?" said Patricia.

Everyone knew they'd been doing a line – it had been in the papers. Patricia read the *Mayfair Gossip* column every week. A celebrity was going to live here?

"No more cleaning an empty castle, Patricia. We're going to have a proper family living here, making great changes, keeping us all busy. Oh, it's just so exciting, I can hardly contain myself!"

Patricia had never seen Mrs. Keeley in such a state. It seemed she was human after all. There were emotions in there other than anger and frustration and temper-tossing.

"It'll be a big change indeed," Patricia said. She wondered

what the change would mean for the staff. Surely there would be lots of extra work? A permanent couple in residence. And wouldn't a newly wed couple be full of demands?

"Oh, to have a real stage star living here, we'll be the talk of the town," said Mrs Keeley.

It was a bit exciting, Patricia admitted to herself. Certainly a break in the monotony of keeping an empty building clean. She wondered what sort of wardrobe the new Lady Cavendish would bring and whether she might get a look like she did when the Cavendish sisters were here.

"When will they arrive?"

"The letter said the wedding would be on the 25th April, so we'll have a lot to get ready for. They'll be straight here after the wedding, driving over in their motor car."

Patricia slurped her now cooled tea and watched Mrs Keeley's eyes shining in the warm morning light.

Poor Mrs Keeley. She was like a child, with her big excited face. It'd be nice to have a change, but in a way maybe what they had right now was better? Patricia hoped she wouldn't be tied to the place day and night.

She loved Lismore, of course she did. But the castle wasn't hers and it never would be.

Mrs. Keeley seemed to forget that – she acted as if the place was in her command. That's how she went on all the time anyway. As if she owned the place.

INTERVIEW WITH MRS. KEELEY, HOUSEKEEPER AT LISMORE CASTLE

Waterford News & Star Newspaper
Feature: Lismore Castle Says Goodbye to Long-serving Housekeeper (Published 24 February 1954, 'In Conversation With' series)

I'll let you in on a secret. Don't laugh now, because I hate sneers. But I always, always wanted to be a dancer. Not a ballerina now or anything, but a popular dancer, on the stage.

I'm quite graceful, you see. Everyone always said that, my mother especially, she said I had a great athleticism about me.

The first dancer I ever saw was on the stage in Dungarvan Town Hall at a Christmas show. Well, what a sight it was! Merciful hour, I sat there with my mouth open, watching and watching and wishing and wishing I could be like her.

You know, she probably wasn't even any good, now that I think about it, a travelling show it was, more like a pantomime, but I thought she was the most graceful creature I'd ever seen.

She had a hoop, a big hoop covered in ribbon and she did all sorts with it, twirling it, throwing it right up high in the air, swinging it all around.

Sure I pestered my mother for a hoop then and didn't I get it for Christmas? I don't know where she got it. I'd swear she paid Nixie the carpenter to bend a willow branch into a circle or something for me, but it had ribbon on it anyway and I was just made up so I was.

I played with it for months after that, every day, and at the end of the school year that year, I was only eleven I think, we were putting on a bit of a variety show in school and I said I'd do my dance and up I got and twirled that hoop around and did all the moves I had taught myself.

The boys laughed, of course, that's all they ever did, but the girls were envious, I knew by their faces.

There weren't any more shows in school but I never stopped dancing, so much so my mother was forever giving out to me for jigging about. I was stretchy too, you know, I could sit and reach and tip my toes and I could bend all the way back, really far. I was built to be a dancer, I really was.

I had a book too, a book about ballet dancing and I pored over every page. I copied every move they had in that book. Oh, very dainty I was!

I begged and begged my mother to send me to dance lessons, but the only dancing available was set and céilí dancing on Mondays nights down in the parish hall and sure that was no good to me.

And so the dancing never came to anything.

I grew out of my body into a woman and it was

time to go to work and there was no time to think about dancing anymore, not with the back-breaking housework I ended up doing.

Being a housekeeper is bloody hard work so it is.

In the summertime and at Eastertime maybe, if I had my savings right, I'd take the bus up to Dublin, with Mam when I was young and later with Paschal my husband, although he never had the interest like I had, he was just glad to be getting up to the big smoke. After dinner, we'd go to see a show.

We went to the Abbey and the Gate and the Gaiety and I loved them all.

I loved the smell of the theatre, the footlights all hot and I loved the music coming from the orchestra.

And no matter who was up there, what actress, what dancer, I imagined it was me, twirling, swirling, holding them all in the palm of my hand, making them gasp with my abilities to bend and throw myself into all sorts of shapes: tangos, foxtrots, I did them all in my head.

And then before the last bus was gone, we'd go to one of the halls for a quick dance ourselves and I'd close my eyes and imagine that I was on stage and everyone was looking at me and could see the talent I had.

Paschal said I was a fine dancer, but sure he wasn't much of a judge and if you'd ask him about himself he'd say he had two left feet.

My dreams never left me though. I lived for my trips to Dublin, to see the shows. I'd pick them out from the Sunday newspapers and write and send a postal order and get the tickets back in the post. I looked forward to it for months.

I loved reading about the London shows too. I knew all of them, who was in them, which ones were selling out and doing the best.

I dreamed of course that I'd get over there myself someday, to go to see a real West End show.

But it never happened.

And then, like a miracle, like a true miracle sent from God himself in heaven above, a dancer, a real proper famous dancer was coming to my castle. To live.

I was so excited I could hardly contain myself, I tell you that.

I wondered if she could show me some moves. Would she, I wondered, if I asked her like, told her I'd an awful interest in dancing?

She was a very nice woman, she looked like a lovely woman from all the pictures I'd seen and the articles I'd read about her. I just knew we were going to get along.

I did everything I could for her, to help make Lismore the most comfortable castle a woman ever set foot in.

And, oh, what dainty feet! And all the boards they'd trod, the stages they'd seen!

It was almost as good as being a dancer myself, it truly was.

CHAPTER THIRTY-THREE

CHATSWORTH HOUSE, DERBYSHIRE, ENGLAND, APRIL 1932

"Miss Astaire, can you come quickly, please? The Duchess would like to see you."

Flutters. In my stomach. In my heart.

I feel sick.

What did she want? Why had I been summoned?

What had Charlie done?

I walk quickly, down the corridor on the east wing of Chatsworth where I have been given rooms. A small drawing room to myself. A bigger entertaining room where Charlie comes and sits with me in the evenings. I have a desk where I write pages and pages of letters to Freddie, to my friends, about the wedding.

I have not seen Charlie since yesterday. Our wedding is to be tomorrow.

The Duchess is seated, looking out the window over the great lawn leading down to the garden steps.

Her face looks pulled, as though sadness is tugging it down.

My stomach leaps again.

"Adele," she says.

She is using my Christian name.

"Duchess."

I am formal of course. I offer her nothing but the greatest of respect.

"Come sit near me," she says. "Would you like some tea?"

"No, thank you," I say.

Although tea might calm my stomach.

I have been making preparations for tomorrow, overseeing the pressing of my wedding suit, checking my shoes, my tights, my underwear. Packing up all my belongings neatly.

Wrapping my new purchases in crepe paper – the items that will begin my life as a wife. Dresses fit for a country castle, warm, well cut, tweed. Flat shoes for walking. A wool coat.

We are taking flowers from the garden in the afternoon. I have ribbon to wrap around them. I will walk with the head gardener to choose from the greenhouse the freshest in bloom.

The Duchess doesn't speak but continues to look out the window.

I wait.

She sighs.

Then she turns to me.

"Adele, I'm afraid I have some rather bad news."

Charlie. My stomach tightens as though it is noosed.

"The wedding won't be going ahead tomorrow."

Stomach falls.

"Charlie is not well. He is not well at all. We will have to postpone the wedding."

I feel as though I am going to vomit, right onto the Duchess's rug-covered floor.

I knew something wasn't right.

"What's happened?" I ask, the alarm in my voice shrill. "What's wrong with him? Where is he?"

"We had him taken to the Chesterfield Royal last night. With appendicitis. He's quite ill and in a lot of pain. He will undergo surgery today."

I am shocked and bewildered. Why hadn't anyone told me?

She sighs again. "Adele, when I first heard of this romance, I must admit I thought the worst. I thought that you too must be like Charlie. Of the same habits." She pauses. "But since I've got to know you, since your time here at Chatsworth, well, I can see you are nothing like Charlie at all, and that's a good thing. Did you know we sent Charlie to America to save him? From alcohol?"

I think of him the week he arrived in America, taking me to witness the sewing of secret pockets into his suits, the flat flasks he kept there, the merriness in his eyes, the slight colour to his face, always.

I shake my head.

"He had a dreadful car accident in Ireland. Drunk. Could have wiped out half the family. Our American plan didn't work of course. I thought maybe, with their laws over there, with Prohibition, he'd have a chance. Then I thought, because he'd met you, you had something to do with him failing. When he came home, well ... he was as bad as ever."

"I don't really drink, Duchess."

"I know that now. And, in fact, I see that you are very good for him. He loves you greatly."

We are looking each other in the eye.

I feel mine fill with tears.

"I love him greatly too," I say.

I think of myself pottering around my rooms, preparing my wedding items, smiling to myself. Like a fool.

"Why didn't anyone tell me?"

"We thought it was the alcohol at first. We thought he had just poisoned himself. It's happened before. But then we realised it was more serious. It's unfortunate. With the wedding."

"I need to see him," I say.

"It is probably best to leave him for today. He'll be sedated after the procedure. I'll have the chauffeur take you to the infirmary tomorrow."

I think of tomorrow, my wedding day, when I will wake and take the journey to a hospital instead of the church.

"We will move the date of the wedding. This is why I wanted to keep it to a small affair. I didn't anticipate appendicitis of course but I feared some other crisis. I am sure we can find a date in a few weeks that will suit and all will be well."

I can see now that the Duchess was right to insist on having the wedding here. Imagine the fuss had we arranged a London do, what a palaver it would be now!

Tears fill my eyes again. I feel desperately sad, the disappointment whirling inside.

And Charlie so ill.

Could he die?

"It is in the family, you see," says the Duchess. She smiles gently. "It is why his father doesn't touch a drop. Nor his older brother. If I had one wish in the world it would be that Charlie stop drinking. I fear it will be the end of him."

I look down at my hands, at my left hand where my engagement ring sits. I remember the day we chose it in

New York, peering in the window of the jeweller's, picking out the stones from the little bag the jeweller shook. I knew instantly how it would sit on my hand.

"This one," I said breathlessly, picking out a large ruby.

"Fiery like you," said Charlie.

"I think you mean sparkling, darling," I said.

The jeweller said he would make the most beautiful ring from it.

"It is perfect for you, Adele," said Charlie.

I think of him now in a white hospital bed, put into a sleep, too sick to make it to his own wedding.

What was I doing marrying this man? Was it an omen?

I listen to what my heart says, in my chest, beating out of time to the small carriage clock that sits above the white marble mantelpiece.

Tick, Tick, Tick, Tick, Tick.

Charlie is mine, I cannot abandon him. Not in his hour of need.

Not now.

Not ever.

CHAPTER THIRTY-FOUR

LISMORE CASTLE, COUNTY WATERFORD, IRELAND 1932

THE WHOLE HOUSEHOLD HAD NEW UNIFORMS. Mrs Keeley wanted all the housemaids in black dresses with white aprons and frilly lace around the edges. Normally they wore black smocks with dark grey aprons, but she had written to the head housekeeper in Chatsworth and got a list of everything Miss Astaire and Lord Cavendish liked, asking all the details, right down to where they got their uniforms.

The castle would not be a let-down for the newlyweds. It would be a home from home and everything in her power would be *absolutely perfect.*

Patricia watched as Mrs. Keeley's fine behind and rounded stomach reduced over those weeks of preparation. She still took her biscuits with her tea, still munched into her dinner like everyone else. But she never stopped pacing, fretting or worrying.

The anxiety was getting to her.

While there was always a flurry of work before the arrival of the family, this time it felt different. This wasn't a two-week sojourn.

"I know it's a great big deal that they're coming but I'm sure the new Lady Cavendish will have some ideas of her own," said Mary, as they dusted banisters on the great stairwell. "She's putting an awful lot of pressure on herself – Mrs. Keeley – isn't she? Jesus, she's an awful woman."

When news came through that the wedding had been postponed, Patricia thought Mrs Keeley would live up to her name and keel right over on the spot.

"Oh God," she said and sat down at the kitchen table, where she was standing opening the correspondence. Her hand went to her mouth.

Patricia wasn't sure why she was so upset – surely this gave them time to work things out, get things right?

But she realised that Mrs. Keeley was terrified it would not go ahead at all.

She was living for this wedding, for this new couple who would arrive at the castle and make this place a home.

A follow-up letter imparted that a new date had been set for the 9th of May and all plans were back on.

Mrs. Keeley went about singing that day – a slow, bright number.

Her voice was clear. She could have been a singer, Patricia thought. Who would have thought that about Mrs. Keeley?

"*They're coming!*"

Eamon, the youngest house boy, was racing up the avenue, his small pounding footsteps on the gravel, and his roars tipping over the wall.

The staff had been hovering in the hallway for the past hour, ready to form the guard of honour for the new Lord and Lady Cavendish.

In turn, a cloud had hovered over them, threatening rain, and with Eamon's cries the first drops began to fall.

Patricia sighed. They'd get soaked.

Still, they were all dying to get a look at the new Lady of the Castle. Some of the staff had never met Charles either. Patricia felt quite grown-up and mature that she was already familiar with him, that she was acquainted with his sisters and had travelled with them to a race meet all in a motor car by herself. It put her higher up the pecking order for sure.

Mrs. Keeley put her hand out and caught raindrops. "Oh Jesus, the rain, get the umbrellas! Everyone, get an umbrella! Seánie, keep those umbrellas for Lord and Lady Cavendish, they're the best ones – oh Jesus, why does it always rain when you don't need it to? I should have stuck out the Infant of Prague for dry weather, but I didn't know if it would work with them being Protestant."

Patricia wanted to laugh.

But the rain held off after the first spattering of raindrops, and there was no need for the umbrellas.

One by one they walked from the hall, their black uniforms neat against the grey stone of the castle. Everyone had their hair washed this week and their shoes polished. The aprons still smelt from the heat of the iron.

Through the narrow gate, a small neat Ford appeared, Lady Adele herself driving, waving madly from the front.

The head butler rushed over and opened the Lady's door when she pulled up and they watched a small foot dangle and then a petite body appear, a small hat on her head, as neat as her face, as her figure.

She smiled and waved and Patricia felt a rush of good feeling about her – nothing like the Duchess or the rest of the family who had come to stay here before.

Lady Adele took off her gloves to start shaking hands with the procession of staff, while Charles stood by the car, still in conversation with the head butler.

When she reached Patricia she saw that she was taller than her and that she was beautiful, in an impish way. There was much to her face to look at.

Patricia gripped her hand gently, smiled and curtsied.

"Aren't you so pretty?" she said to Patricia, which made her smile even more.

When Lady Adele took Mrs Keeley's hand a squeak was heard, an animal sound again, snared.

"It's like she's meeting the Queen," muttered Patricia to Mary, who had to stifle a laugh.

When it was time to go inside, Patricia noticed Mrs Keeley's arm held high, inviting Lord and Lady Cavendish into their new home.

Her arm was trembling, her fingers quivering, as though they had done too much, and Patricia realised that they were shaking with nerves.

Mrs. Keeley had lost the run of herself.

What a funny woman she was altogether.

"And this is the drawing room, we call it the sitting room. A finer view of the Blackwater I doubt you'll get."

Lady Adele said, "Oh my!" when she saw the view. "This is stunning."

And it was. A large, panelled window, perched above the rock on which the castle was built, looked over the valley, the river below, flowing and cutting through the banks.

Lady Adele spotted two swans, floating along on the river below and she leaned over to look closer.

"We have swans!"

Patricia wondered why she was getting excited about two old swans. She has a lot more than swans. She had a castle. A fleet of staff. A motor car. And a very fine wardrobe tucked into those big trunks on the back of the motor car no doubt.

Mrs. Keeley led Lady Adele back into the small room off the sitting room. Rows of shelves with ancient books were lined up and a writing desk sat at the window.

"Oh, this is beautiful," said the Lady, eyeing up the desk. "I will be very much at home here."

"Now you've probably been told the history so you'll know the castle was built back in the 1100s by King John and then it was remodelled in the 1800s and didn't they do a great job? Those rugs there now are down since that time and we do our best to keep them, beat them regular, and I have a special detergent I got for the older fabrics, the housekeeper at Chatsworth told me about it, we're very careful here at Lismore, mind everything we do. If there's anything you need, anything at all, you just let me know. The castle is very homely but no doubt Your Ladyship is looking to make her own changes and that'll be wonderful, we're all very supportive and will do anything we can to help out, to assist. Actually, I know a good few tradesmen in the village who –"

"Thank you," said Lady Adele, cutting the housekeeper off gently.

She looked over, caught Patricia's eye and smiled, as if to say, *I pity you having to put up with this blatherer.*

Patricia couldn't help but smile back.

The Lady gave a wink and Patricia realised that this new mistress was just lovely and she was going to enjoy working for her.

Maybe she'd put a few manners on Mrs. Keeley. Or at least rein her in a bit. For all their sakes.

That evening Mrs. Keeley came to Patricia and said Lady

Adele would like to see her.

"Me?" she said.

She was in the back kitchen, washing out her white apron that got streaks of black soot on it earlier.

"Yes, you," she said.

The housekeeper sounded disappointed that Patricia had been summoned and not her, for this private audience.

Patricia dried her hands and walked down the corridor towards the large drawing room.

A fire roared in the grate, the lamps were lit low, and the place had a lovely atmosphere. It was as though the arrival of the newly wed couple had brought a whole new sense of warmth to the place.

"Lady Cavendish," she said and curtsied.

"Patricia," she said.

She looked tired.

"Come," she said and she patted the sofa beside her. "Come sit beside me."

Patricia didn't expect to be asked to sit beside her. It was more usual to stand, head bowed, hands behind back.

But she sat, her posture straight, afraid to get too close.

She could smell her perfume, something expensive, something all the way from Paris she expected. Oh, it smelt heavenly!

"I noticed you earlier, Patricia," said Lady Cavendish. "I asked Mrs. Keeley about you and she says you have been here at the castle for some years now."

"Yes, Lady Cavendish."

What had she noticed about her earlier?

"Do you like it here?"

"Oh yes," said Patricia. "It is a fine place to work. I feel very lucky to be working here."

"Mrs. Keeley says you are to be trusted. I'm looking for someone who knows things, who can run and fetch and show me where everything is. Mrs. Keeley will be very busy herself, but I will need a lady's maid. I think I know, by looking at you, that you could do very well in a position like that."

Patricia felt the breath catch in her throat.

"Yes, Lady Cavendish, I would like that. Very much."

Her calm voice belied the joy she felt inside.

"It'll be a trial. We'll see how we get on for a few weeks. If it's not working out, I'll put an advertisement out. But will you try your best for me?"

"I will. Oh, I will."

"Thank you, Patricia. I'll see you tomorrow. I'd like to get all my wardrobe sorted first, everything unpacked and a home found for my things. Then we'll see what I might need while I'm here. There'll be a lot of things to attend to. I've just discovered there's only one bathroom!"

Patricia smiled.

"One bathroom!" says Lady Cavendish. "In a massive castle!"

Patricia thought how the lady was lucky there was a bathroom at all. No one in her row of terraced houses even knew what a bathroom was.

She thought about how she loved her new mistress's voice, her accent, the way her face was animated when she talked. She had so much grace, so much poise, just sitting there, tiny on the big settee.

"See you tomorrow, ma'am."

"Ma'am?" said Lady Cavendish. "That makes me sound ancient!"

"Would you like me to call you something else?"

"No, I suppose not. But if you think of anything better let me know."

"Missus?"

She laughed. "Well, I guess I am a missus now. But no, 'ma'am' is fine."

Patricia left the room, feeling the heat fade from her body in the cooler corridor and thought how she was going to enjoy coming to work now so much more each day.

Lady Adele Cavendish would be a much finer mistress than Mrs. Keeley. That was for certain.

CHAPTER THIRTY-FIVE

LISMORE CASTLE, COUNTY WATERFORD, IRELAND 1932

WHAT A SIGHT LISMORE CASTLE WAS! It was like something out of a fairy book, a palace where ancient kings and queens lived out their refined medieval lives. Which of course they had. The place was over seven hundred years old.

"Bloody hell, Charlie!" I said, when the car crossed the bridge over the Blackwater. "Oh fuck!"

He smiled.

"Welcome to your new home."

He pulled in on the bridge and the young boys and girls, who had been chasing the Ford as it passed, now crowded around us.

We got out to look.

"Hello, Missus," said a cheeky young chappy.

"Hello back," I said.

"Are you famous?" said a girl.

"I am," I replied and smiled.

They put their hands out and touched my coat and I was reminded of nuzzling deer I'd once seen in Richmond Park.

Most were barefoot, one or two had dark, dingy boots on. They were grubby-looking, but all smiles and teeth.

Most of the girls wore their hair in ribbons. I felt a bit like a queen come to meet her masses.

Up ahead on the bridge, two men leaned with their behinds resting on the wall. They looked on curiously from under flat caps.

I joined Charlie at the other side of the car to take a proper look at Lismore, curling my arm into his.

"It's magnificent."

"It's mighty fine," he said. "A lovely piece of engineering – see how it hangs off the rock? Wait'll you see the views from the drawing room."

"I can't believe this is to be our home."

"It's a castle fit for a queen, my love."

I wanted to lean in and kiss him but the children were still surrounding us, firing questions.

"Can you show us any steps?"

"Will you be going to the céilí, my mam wants to know?"

"Where did you get your scarf? Is it knitted? My mam knits but I've never seen her knit anything like that."

"Can we have a go in the motor car, mister, can we, can we?"

We could hear little hands pulling on the door, so we turned and got back in.

"I'll drive," I said. "I'd like to drive myself over the threshold."

Charlie shrugged and searched in his pockets for coins. He threw them to the children out the window and they scampered like pigeons after seed.

We waved at the leaning men under the shade of Lismore, who waved back as if they knew us.

"Beats the press anyway," said Charlie.

We rounded the top of the hill and took a sharp turn into a long-walled avenue.

A houseboy ran ahead of us, alerting everyone to our arrival. A few raindrops splattered the windscreen.

We drove under a small tower bridge and through a narrow gate. I had to take care not to scrape the walls.

Ahead of us staff were gathered, in a long line around a small green manicured lawn.

The castle no longer looked so looming in here, instead it was inviting and cosy, a small courtyard of delight.

"Welcome to the rest of your life, my darling," said Charlie as I pulled up in the gravel and we set about meeting the smiling staff, who would be our closest companions, forever perhaps.

Lismore Castle was very different to Chatsworth. I had expected more of the luxury of the English homestead. Here, everything was a bit more rough and ready. There was a lot of work to be done.

Still, the freedom it offered, a home away from London life, from parties and gossip columns, from press men and photographers, was a whole breath of fresh air in itself.

I started making lists of work I'd like to do. There was the decor and interiors, putting down new rugs, pictures, lamps, things to make the place more homely and inviting. I planned on sewing a lot of the cushions and covers myself and Mama would help too. It would be a project for us.

There were the bigger material tasks: getting in proper furniture for the rooms, new mattresses and beds, wallpapering, woodwork, taking the castle from the early 1800s into the modern 1930s.

My number-one priority was plumbing. We might be living in Ireland, but I had no intention of pissing in a pot for the rest of my days. I wanted proper flushing toilets and baths, tiled and plumbed in. And hot water, lots of it, thank you.

Charlie agreed. He knew if we didn't get the castle up to scratch it would never work out for me here.

Most days I walked outside the castle – on the land, down to the river, over the hills.

Charlie usually came with me and I felt like we were being reborn, I felt my lungs grow and my body relax in a way I hadn't experienced since those young days in New Jersey when we really got a lasting break.

"I love it here," I told him, over and over again, when we got to the top of a hill, surveying fields and forests and our grand, grand castle. He would hold me close and in those moments I felt that this was what true happiness was. I had finally achieved it, after all these years and countries and stages. This is where I was meant to be.

Other days I would go down to the village, to the shops, and I got to know the shopkeepers and their peculiar Irish ways. They were welcoming, but they observed me with a strange otherness. I think they didn't know quite what to make of me.

There were no clothes shops to speak of. I had to go to Dungarvan or Cork city if I wanted anything more than a strip of material. But Cork was where I needed to go to buy proper furnishings anyway, and I travelled there often with Charlie to pick out items we needed.

We had a local craftsman building us furniture too and, even though it was slow, we knew the items would be heirlooms in the castle forevermore.

Before I came to Lismore I feared I would be a bit lonely. Even though I loved Charlie and he was my favourite person to spend time with, I was aware that my life before this had been very different. I was used to being around so many people, lots of company, so much going on. I knew that even with Charlie, I would need more.

My fears were unfounded.

Every day there were callers.

Letters poured in, notes, invites, invitations to suppers and luncheons in person and on paper.

We got to know our contemporaries in the surrounding area – other landed gentry folk with big homes and some with castles too. Most bored the life out of me.

"Oh Charlie, don't bring us here again," I'd say as we drove away from another home where we'd been treated to a ghastly lunch and endless hours of wretched conversation.

I needed to find a couple we could get on with. People who were like us. But, I learned, there was a level of expectation with living in a home like Lismore. It wasn't that it just belonged to us; we were part of a bigger network, a centre of the community, a place where people felt like they could call and expect an audience.

It took some time to get used to.

I determined to find friends I actually liked.

I hoped the lure of a West End and Broadway star would eventually wear off.

I came up with a number of quips whenever the conversation became too stilted, mostly to amuse myself but also in hopes of frightening off the people I found most detestable.

"Can anyone tell where you'd get a good wax around here?" I'd say. "My undercarriage is frightful, I tell you – it's not fit for a newly wed!"

Another favourite was, "What do you do for fun around here? I've heard all you landed gentry types love a good orgy. Do you know what that is? It was all the rage in London."

Charlie would snigger into his drink. I would keep my blank, innocent expression.

We'd laugh about it all the way home.

"You're going to get into trouble one day," he'd say.

"Good," I'd reply. "At least it might be a bit of excitement!"

"You chose to come here, remember that."

"I did. And I'm very happy, my darling. I wouldn't mind an orgy or two every now and then, though."

"Let's wait for the right couple."

"Yes, let's!"

On Sundays we drove down to the cathedral in the centre of Lismore. It was a great big church which opened out into a T-shape, pews lined neatly in rows throughout. It was different to the Catholic churches I knew, bare, cold.

On the morning of our wedding, the second date we had fixed, I had been baptised a Presbyterian at the small private chapel at Chatsworth where I would marry Charlie later that day.

I wasn't quite sure how I felt about giving up being a Catholic.

I felt that I might have been betraying God or something.

Still, it wasn't like I wouldn't be praying to God from now on – it was just that I myself had a different label. Besides, on the morning of my baptism I was worried that something would go wrong again, that Charlie would take sick or another problem would arise and I would be summoned again by the sighing Duchess. I was happy to get the baptism over with, to get through the day, to get to the afternoon, when I would walk down this small aisle again and take his arm. I didn't give the baptism any more thought.

St. Catharge's Cathedral in Lismore was freezing. I wrapped up in furs every time I went, even in summer.

Charlie didn't seem to feel the cold like I did, he was quite happy to sit in his suit, looking ahead or at the pulpit where the minister hung out over the crowd to drone at us. I wondered if Charlie prayed and, if he did, what did he pray for?

After church a flock of people would approach us, all keen to make us feel welcome in the community.

Catholics outnumbered Presbyterians here ten to one. More maybe. *We have to stick together*, they implied with their smiles and invites and compliments as to how well I was getting on.

I was looking well.

Country life was suiting me. I had put on some weight, and I slept gloriously most nights, in the calm stillness of the castle.

Charlie and I were more in love than ever. We made love nearly every night.

I knew that soon I would be pregnant.

It was only a matter of time.

INTERVIEW WITH MRS GREGORY GREGORY GROCER'S, LISMORE

Station: Radio Éireann
Mobile Unit Interview for series* 'Famous Villages of Ireland' *(In conversation with Eugene Murphy, recorded October 1958, not broadcast)

Lovely woman.

A lovely woman.

Oh, she was lovely.

Beautiful. The most beautiful clothes you'd ever seen on a woman.

Cut like … I don't know, cut out and stitched by God in heaven above, you'd think.

She told me she'd got most of them in Paris and London, I think. And New York. Sure she lived in New York.

She had a Yankee accent, you know. Very forceful. Not like the Irish. She was different, you know, the way the Yanks are. Say what they think. Say what they want. No time for nonsense.

Oh, she'd ef and blind you out of it. No better woman. Cursed liked a trooper, she did. At first I didn't like it, but as I got to know her then, you know, I thought ... well, it suited her if you know what I mean. It was part of her personality. It was like she enjoyed it.

Cursing.

And her brother was so famous, oh he was shockin' well known for the pictures. Sure we all used to go and see him when his films were on and we knew it was him and we were looking for the likeness and you know he used to come to Lismore too? Oh yes, sure everyone knows that. He'd come to the castle as often as he could and stay and he'd come down to the village for a pint, oh a lovely man too.

Their mother must have raised them well. I remember her too though not as much – oh she was a beauty too. She lived there for a long time too, I think.

Yes, they were very well liked.

Not like the Cavendish family, you know, all upper class and that, no, they were much more down to earth.

Lady Adele didn't come into my shop now too often, we were more the cigarettes type, groceries, knick-knacks, she was more into the drapery across the road. But sometimes she'd be in, if she needed something and we'd have a chat then.

Sometimes it was hard to believe she was who she was, you know? Famous like. All those shows, up there on the stage in London. The papers would be here sometimes, especially if her brother was coming – they'd run a story. You'd see the picture of them meeting on the ship or whatever.

The husband now, he was a funny one. Well liked

too, you know. Nice man, quiet type.

Very tall, oh his head was in the clouds so it was, you'd see him coming a mile off.

He'd escape down to Foley's when he could. Drank a lot there. Everyone liked him of course, would be all over him trying to get a bit of gossip.

We liked that castle, you know.

It made us special in a way, in Lismore – not many villages that had a big, beautiful castle like that. Tourists came to see it, sure you couldn't blame them, they still do.

It was sad what happened to them in the end.

Very sad.

Sad, because of what could have been, had everything gone their way, you know.

CHAPTER THIRTY-SIX

LISMORE CASTLE, COUNTY WATERFORD, IRELAND 1932

FRED HAD A NEW WOMAN ON THE GO.

A divorcee if you don't mind.

Mother didn't approve. Of course she didn't. Mother hated to see us with anyone, anyone at all. It was a strange part of her personality, but I understood it all the same. She didn't want to let us go.

And I did not want to let Freddie go either.

Not to a divorcee.

Her name was Phyllis Livingston Potter and Fred met her at a golf luncheon in Long Island given by Virginia Graham Fair Vanderbilt. They were put sitting together and well that was that.

It was love.

She really had Fred by the balls. I'd never seen him so smitten. She was pretty, I'll give her that. But very quiet. I wasn't really sure what the attraction was, I thought Fred could do better. Someone with a bit more ... *oomph*.

I knew they'd been doing a line before I got married and came to Ireland. But things were a bit complicated because her divorce hadn't come through yet and if she was seen to be serious with another man it could make things very difficult in court and she might lose custody of her son.

Peter was a dear little boy, four years old, very polite and quiet too.

He was blonde, like Freddie.

Freddie's letters poured out his grief over not being able to make the romance official and his terror that he might lose Phyllis.

I didn't think it would be a bad thing if he did.

Why get involved with someone so complicated? Freddie could have his pick of women. I wanted to see him with someone who had a spark, a go-get-'em personality, a great sense of humour.

I wanted to see him with someone ... like me.

Mama and I discussed our frustration with the romance.

She thought Freddie despondent about all that was going on and I was sad for him. I had gone and left him to handle all this on his own. I felt if I was around, if I was in his ear, I would make him see sense and bring an end to this mad infatuation.

It was dear Phyllis this and dear Phyllis that. He was besotted.

"What are we going to do?" Mama said.

We decided that we would both lean on him heavy, let him know that neither of us approved and if he loved both of us as much as he was supposed to then he would give this Phyllis woman up.

Anyone could see it was the best thing for it.

"Can you see him?"

No answer.

"Charlie, can you see him?"

One of the advantages of having a rather tall husband

was using him as a lookout tower at the port where your brother's ship was docking.

He shook his head.

"*Look harder!*" I roared.

I was impatient. We had been up early, to make our way to Cobh and its cold quayside.

Freddie had just finished the run of *The Band Wagon* in Chicago and had sailed all the way to see us. He had missed our wedding but, as promised, he came to see us as soon as he was free.

I longed to clap eyes on him, to spy his smooth, unmistakable gait.

And there he was.

"Charlie!" I said. "Look, he's there! *Freddie, Freddie!*"

A camera flash. Two press men.

Oh Lord. How did they know he was coming?

He posed graciously and I ran up to him and gave him a big swinging hug. He spun me round to the flash of more camera bulbs.

We held each other for minutes, not caring who was watching.

When we parted, Charlie came and shook his hand and they embraced too, clapping each other on the back, in that manly, gruff way.

"Welcome, brother," said Charlie.

We couldn't wait to show off Lismore and all the changes we'd been making.

We knew Fred would love the countryside, the rolling hills and mountains, the brown, heathered bogs. The landscape was so different to anything we were used to.

"This is something," he said, when we stopped at the viewing point at the Vee, a hairpin bend, on the Knockmealdown mountains on the way to Lismore. "This is really something."

In front of us lay field after field, broken with dark green hedge-lines, rising up to the white, bright horizon. It was a place you had to stop the motor car at no matter how often you passed. It was like being on the edge of the world.

When we got to the castle, Mrs. Keeley met us and I could see she'd been having palpitations all morning. She was white in the face and I thought she might faint when Freddie shook her hand.

Freddie explored the castle with a smile on his face. He ducked in and out of the rooms, stood in the big dining room, in front of grand and giant fireplaces.

"Delly, this is just wonderful."

He was right, it was wonderful.

I was glad that he could see how happy we were here and what a magnificent home we had.

After lunch, he went to the room I had designed with him in mind. It had twin beds and a large, masculine bathroom.

I wanted him to come and stay with me forever.

He picked up a framed picture of us I'd left on the bedside locker. It was from the first show we'd done in London, *Stop Flirting*, and he was holding me in a dance move, looking down at me, smiling. It was my favourite image of us, out of all that were taken over the years.

"We've come a long way, Delly."

"We have."

"Are you happy here?"

"I'm most happy."

"I can see it."

We smile.

He was tired. I could see it around his eyes. That weariness that only a long run of a show can bring.

"Rest," I said. "Sleep as long as you want. The castle is silent, I've never slept better than I have since coming to Ireland. Let us know what time you want dinner – we'll arrange it round you."

"Thank you, Delly."

Over the next few days we went to Lismore and to Dungarvan and for mountain and bog walks. On the last day of his stay, I could sense that he was still quite weary, so we walked through the gardens at Lismore, looking at all the vegetable beds and the small orchard. Tomorrow he would leave for England, where he was meeting Phyllis.

Under the canopy of the yew walkway, a tunnel of entwined, twisted branches, thick with age and birdsong, Freddie told me of his anguish over his love.

"I want to marry this girl, Delly, I do."

"Alright, Freddie, but remember you're still young yet. There's no need to go rushing into any decisions."

"But I want to rush in," he said, exasperated. "I want to rush in and marry her. What if I lose her? What if she decides to give me the flick over all this messing about? I just can't lose her, I can't."

He had it bad.

"I'm not sure about her, Freddie. I don't know if she's really right for you."

I couldn't lie to him, pretend I thought this woman was a suitable match for him.

He was angry. Angry that I wasn't on his side, that I was taking our mother's point of view.

"Why can't you be happy for me? Why do all the women in my life make things difficult for me?"

He was surly over supper and I felt bad that his short time at Lismore had soured.

The next day, when it was time to drive him to the boat, I said, "Oh Freddie, I want you to be happy, I do. But I always say what I think, you know that. Don't expect me to be any different now."

"She is the one," he said.

"Well if she's the one, then so be it. I just want you to be happy, Freddie."

That seemed to appease him a little.

Our car journey to the port wasn't too bad – the mood had lightened and I was sorry that he was going. I had no idea when I would see him again.

At the docks, we hugged again and I cried as I watched him make his way up the gangway.

Freddie didn't walk. He glided.

Charlie sensed my sadness and we decided to go for dinner and stay in the Imperial Hotel in Cork.

"Let's go shopping in the morning," he said.

He knew this would cheer me up.

I would buy dresses, a new fur perhaps and new underwear.

But I would stop by the baby department too.

I would not buy anything. There was no need yet. But I wanted to look at the things, to touch the baby chemises, the soft, velvety blankets.

I wanted to imagine a baby of ours in one of those blankets, curling its fist, lying in a new, white wooden cot.

If you wanted something bad enough, you had to use all your spirit and your might to make it happen.

That was how it worked. Dream your dreams, apply yourself and work hard.

It had always worked for me before.

"Darling, there's something I have to tell you."

"Is everything alright?"

"I hope so," I said.

I wanted to burst into a smile but I used all my years of acting to keep a straight, sad look. I really wanted this to be a surprise.

"Actually, I'd like to show you," I said.

I rang the bell and Mrs. Keeley arrived on cue with the plate of cream buns.

There were three, laid out on a pretty doily.

Charlie looked at the plate and back to me.

"What do you want to show me?"

"Eat first."

"The cream bun?"

"Yes."

"Can't you just tell me?"

"Eat. It's important."

He leaned over and lifted the cream bun, folding it into his mouth, cream peppering the corners of his lips.

He said with his mouth full, "Now can you tell me?"

I leaned over and took the second bun and forced it into my mouth. I hoped it wouldn't come back up.

He watched me as I ate and then I got out of chair and came round and sat on his knee.

I leaned over, lifted the third bun and put it on my stomach. It wobbled and fell, smattering my dress with cream.

"What are you doing?" he laughed.

"What do you think?" I asked flirtily.

"You've mashed a bun into your dress."

"Where is the bun sitting?"

"On your dress."

"No, silly, where on my body?"

"On your stomach."

He still looked bemused.

"Oh, good Christ, Charlie! What do you want me to do, bring you into the kitchen and put it into the bloody oven?"

"A bun in the oven?"

"What would you say if there was?"

"I'd say that's bloody marvellous, darling."

"Well, it's marvellous then, isn't it?"

"Is it?"

"It is!"

"Are you?"

"I am!"

"Oh, that's marvellous!"

I watched as tears came to his eyes and he leaned in and hugged me tight.

We kissed, the cream all over our lips and we didn't even wipe it away.

It had taken nearly a year but now, coming up to our anniversary, I had this wonderful news to tell. I had been doubting myself, worried that my age was against me, worried about everything.

My prayers had worked. They had been answered. All those eyes-squeezed, tight mutterings to my now Protestant God had been heard.

Twas wonderful. Twas marvellous.

Freddie married Phyllis. They wanted to go to Paris but in the end they did it quickly, in the chambers of Brooklyn Supreme Court after Phyllis' extended custody for Peter came through. They cruised up and down the Hudson the next day before taking a trimotor aircraft to California.

Seems neither Freddie nor I were destined for big-deal wedding days.

I had very mixed feelings about it all. On one hand I was glad that Freddie was happy, and he was so happy. His letters to me were gushing. But, on the other hand, I felt that it was still a bad match. I couldn't see how she could make him happy, not in the long run.

Still Mama had come round in the end. She and Fred sat and had a big talk before it all happened and he said she had given it her blessing.

I wasn't so sure. Mama was manipulative like that. I still didn't think she liked her.

But there it was.

He'd spent so much time chasing Phyllis around that he didn't have much time to work on his career.

This worried me.

Now more than ever he needed a hit. He needed to get out there and show them what he was worth. Without me.

Phyllis must have knocked a bit of sense into him, because he made a good decision towards the end of the year and decided to go with a new show called *The Gay Divorce.* It was his first show without me at his side.

When it launched it did well in the States and I was so glad. I'd have hated to see him take on something that flopped. The show was coming to London in November.

November was when my baby was due.

I was excited that he would be near when this was all happening.

Things were working out.

My sickness eased and my belly grew and I was so proud, in that castle, with my handsome husband and the family we were about to make.

I spent hours daydreaming about what sort of child it would be. Would it be silly and funny like me or quiet and charming like its father?

Would any of Fred be in there, Mama, Papa even?

Would it play the piano? Would it be able to sing? Or dance?

I wondered if I could organise lessons here in Ireland for our child. I couldn't imagine any stage schools in rural Waterford, or Cork for that matter. Did I want our child to have those lessons, the same lessons Freddie and I had?

I couldn't imagine not sending our son or daughter to some sort of dramatics.

I would have to look into it all after the baby was born. We would need to wait and see what sort of aptitude it showed.

Secretly I hoped it would show a spark, the makings of a little entertainer, making us laugh, charming the socks off us.

I relished feeling the child move inside me, growing bigger, turning, ready.

I longed for the day it would be emerge, safe, nestled in my arms, a bright new star, into the castle born.

CHAPTER THIRTY-SEVEN

LISMORE CASTLE, COUNTY WATERFORD, IRELAND, MAY 1933

Lady Cavendish was pushy with her ideas. She wanted everything just so and a lot of work happened in those first few months she was there.

She put in bathrooms in every bedroom she could with big free-standing baths and hot and cold water coming out of the taps. Patricia had never seen anything like it.

"King John built the castle, but Adele Astaire plumbed it," said the cook one day.

Patricia thought how the cook would want to watch her mouth around Mrs. Keeley, because if she heard her calling the mistress anything other than Lady Cavendish, there'd be all hell to pay.

Why couldn't she have the bathrooms she wanted? She paid for it herself with her own earnings. The Duke and Duchess over in Derbyshire weren't sending the money for taps, that was for sure.

At first Patricia had trod softly with the Lady. She wasn't sure what to make of her. She seemed friendly, but she was afraid that if she did anything wrong she would cut her to the quick. Patricia wasn't a soft timid person, not like Mary for example. But she wanted to please her.

Everyone wanted to please Lady Cavendish.

What a different castle Lismore was! It was like the whole place had been rebuilt. Not just with how it looked, but how it felt.

As if it was breathing again. As if it had come alive.

One day Patricia had come into the sitting room to find the Lady hanging out the window. She was leaning over at the waist, her shoes in the air.

"*Lady!*" Patricia shouted and rushed to where her mistress was leaning over, holding on to the open window handle, screaming down towards the river.

"*Leave those fucking swans alone!*"

She pulled her head back in.

"Can you see them?" she said, angrily. "There are two men down there with a sack. I swear if they touch those swans I'll hunt them down myself and fold them back into it. *Hey!*"

She leaned back out again.

"*You two! Fuck off!*"

Patricia watched the two dark heads look up warily to where the noise was coming from.

When they saw the petite Lady of the Castle spitting fire from the grand window, they moved off meekly.

Patricia tried to hide her smile.

No one touched any of Lady Cavendish's property and got away with it. Especially anything living. She adored animals, birds, her dogs. She had a pet goat on the farm and a donkey.

Her favourite dogs were Tilly, a gorgeous dark dachshund, and a big mope of gun dog with black curly fur called Sammy.

The dogs were like their children, curled with her and

her husband every night in the sitting room, accompanying them in the car, bounding out before them on their meandering walks.

They loved those dogs like babies.

Patricia was getting to know her ways. At first she hadn't been quite sure what was expected of her, but Lady Cavendish was kind and showed her what she wanted, what she liked.

She had a strict routine, up early, breakfast, bath, dressed. Then she went out for a walk or exercise, she loved to exert herself. She would have run the roads if it was proper thing to do – she had boundless energy.

After lunch, she'd have her afternoon activities, whether it was to do with the castle, or letter writing or shopping. She was always busy.

Most days she took afternoon tea and there'd be a guest to entertain.

She had dinner in the evening with Lord Cavendish in the big dining room where a low chandelier hung over the table. Then they'd retire to the sitting room and play a board game and have a nightcap.

She loved to read too. She always went to bed with a book and she went to bed early.

She was very particular about what she ate, and she didn't drink. Not like himself. She didn't approve of drinking at all, Patricia felt.

Patricia learned to prepare everything for her routine, to run her bath the way she liked, to have her clothes pressed and laid out and how to know the bits and pieces that went with everything.

It wasn't too difficult and it was so much nicer than being a housemaid. The others were jealous of course, especially when they heard what sort of pay rise she'd got.

Let them, she thought. She'd earned her place there. It was a stroke of luck the way it happened but she was well suited to being a lady's maid. So what if they grumbled or said, "Here she is now," when she came into the kitchen.

No one was going to make her feel bad about being in the Lady's special favour.

She was the happiest she'd ever been and she was enjoying her new wages and her new role in the world.

She started to buy some nice clothes with the extra money she had and took delight when the Lady gave her something she no longer needed. She let her borrow her fashion magazines too and Patricia pored over *Vogue* and *Modern Woman* to understand what designs and designers were on trend.

You had to know what you were doing, if you wanted to be a proper lady's maid.

Lady Cavendish knew everything about fashion from all her years on the stage.

She showed Patricia all the products to use on your hair and how to straighten it and curl it. Patricia started to wear her hair with finger waves to the front too and it took a long time for the comments to dry up in the kitchen when she took to the new hairstyle permanently.

"Oh, will ya look, it's the Lady reincarnated!" said the cook.

"Good janey, it's the Queen of Sheba – at least that's who she thinks she is anyway!"

They were sneering, but Patricia shrugged them off.

They were all going through changes; all working their way through this new way of being in the castle.

Everything had come to life. The gardens, the vegetables

beds, the flowers took on a new meaning now that they'd be spread around the castle for the lady to enjoy. The stables were busy, the offices overcrowded as Lord Cavendish took to making his own changes in how things were run.

It was nice to have somebody in charge again, somebody to please, thought Patricia.

They'd struck lucky with Miss Adele Astaire.

Patricia would do anything for her, go out of her way to get anything for her, especially now that she was expecting.

She wished she'd got to see her on stage.

She would have liked to have seen that.

Her mistress, a star.

Different to now.

"Come and sit with me, Patricia."

"Are you feeling alright, ma'am?"

"I'm fine, thank you."

Patricia took a seat on the sofa near to her. She often called her to sit with her in the evenings before dinner.

She was interested in any gossip Patricia might have, about the village, about the castle, but not in a mean way. She wasn't trying to get anyone into trouble. She just wanted to chat.

Sometimes Patricia thought the Lady might be lonely.

She was sewing a large piece of embroidery.

"Doesn't it hurt your eyes?"

"Oh no, I have very good eyes. Do you sew, Patricia?"

"Only when I have to."

"I love to sew. I think, if I hadn't been a dancer, I would have been a seamstress. Imagine if I could cut all my clothes and make them all myself!"

"It would be lovely."

"But a seamstress's work is very hard – all those women in the theatres, they worked day and night making our costumes – it's a tough job."

"Do you miss all the costumes?"

"Not really. They were never ours, you see. I didn't take them home with me. But I suppose I miss … I miss the life, you know. The razzmatazz."

"Yes."

"It's very quiet here."

"It is."

"Sometimes I sit here and think about what's happening in London right now."

"I can imagine."

"Freddie and I used to be invited everywhere, you know, even to Buckingham Palace. The princes are just darlings. They loved to come to our shows. George was my favourite."

Patricia's ears pricked up a little. Real stories of true royalty. Mrs. Keeley would be jealous.

"Bertie is a pet too. And his wife. The princesses are darlings, they really are a charming family. As for David, well, he's heading for trouble, mark my words."

The Lady, for all her coarse language and fits of fury, was very conservative when it came to marriage. She didn't like that her brother had married a divorcee. And, it was rumoured that David, Prince Edward, was stepping out with a married woman called Wallis Simpson.

"She gives Americans a bad name," said the Lady.

She looked out the window and dropped her sewing.

"I feel quite far from everything now," she sighed, rubbing her stomach. "But I suppose I have so much to look forward to."

"You do."

"You won't leave me, Patricia, will you?"

"Sorry, ma'am?"

"I mean if you're considering another position or something you'll tell me?"

"I wouldn't leave. I have no intention of leaving! Why do you say that, ma'am?"

"Oh, no reason, just, well, you know, you're young, you might have a beau, you might wish to go and get married yourself. Or you might go to a new position, it's not unheard of."

"I don't have a beau," Patricia said with a laugh. "And where would I get nicer than here?"

She didn't think the Lady had any idea of the employment prospects around Lismore.

Lady Cavendish smiled. "My mother will be coming in September. She'll be here to help me. I hope you'll get along with her, although you get along with everybody really, don't you, Patricia?"

"I try to, ma'am."

Patricia thought of her own timid mother in their little house down the road. She had become quite frail over the past year and Patricia had taken to going home at lunchtime to check on her. Lady Cavendish didn't mind – she told Patricia our mothers make us who we are.

It was easy to see how Ann Astaire had made Adele Astaire.

"Are you feeling alright?" Patricia asked. "Is everything alright with the baby?"

"I feel fine. I worry, of course, but so far, so good."

So far, so good. Patricia hoped the birth would be as smooth.

CHAPTER THIRTY-EIGHT

LISMORE CASTLE, COUNTY WATERFORD, IRELAND, OCTOBER 1933

I KNEW IT WAS TOO EARLY, I knew it was wrong.

All wrong.

Too early.

Charlie.

Get the doctor.

Will everything be OK?

I don't know.

I'm scared.

Don't give credence to the words out loud.

Pray. Pray to God, to my God, the God I've always prayed to, my Catholic God.

It is too early for the baby to come, don't let it come.

But the waters have gone.

I should have known. I had been feeling unwell for days, something different, below, like a swirling of murky swamp, all thick and moving. Wrong.

Why did I not get the doctor before this?

The doctor takes an age – he is off in Kilbree with an old man who is dying.

Blast that old man for dying.

And now there are pains.

Coming quick, a few minutes apart.

Patricia is here, lovely Patricia and her pretty concerned face.

Mrs. Keeley, doing her bit, taking charge.

I want Mama. But Mama only left for Ireland yesterday. She is sailing on the Atlantic, not even halfway across the ocean.

She was to be here for the birth. Now she will miss it.

I am too shocked to cry. I am too upset to do anything but lie down and hope the pains stop.

They don't.

They go on all afternoon.

I drink a cup of tea, but it comes up again and a bowl is kept beside me as acid vomit leaks from my throat.

Again and again I am sick.

Is it the pain or am I infected? I feel like I am infected all inside.

Finally the doctor arrives.

Charlie is white.

The doctor says the baby will be born today and there is nothing anybody can do about it.

But it's too early.

Let's hope for the best.

The cot is ready, our beautiful cradle we've had carved, soft sheets and towelling to keep the baby warm.

The pains grow. I wonder if they will ever end.

It is night-time outside my bedroom window now, the autumn air settling into the dappled orange oak trees I love so much.

The room is stuffy, people coming and going, all of their faces, concerned, the look of death on them all.

"Can it survive?" I ask the doctor.

He doesn't answer at first.

"I *have* seen it," he says, with an emphasis on the *have*.

A rest. A rest comes over me and then the pains come back, stretching my back, all my insides bruised.

And then, pushing and here she is, on the bed, red, tiny, so tiny, breathing.

The doctor takes her in a towel and examines her.

He puts a tube to her nose and mouth, takes everything out, keeps her warm.

She is breathing.

Charlie is beside me. We are crying.

The baby is not.

Then a mewl. Like a kitten. Weak.

Too early to be born.

The doctor gives her to me to hold and I look her over. She is thin, her limbs long, bony, not like a baby should look.

Where is the fat?

I cry some more.

I try to feed her but she is not able to.

Her breathing is weak, each breath a struggle, like a grunt.

She grows weaker.

She lives for three hours.

Our daughter, gone.

CHAPTER THIRTY-NINE

LISMORE CASTLE, COUNTY WATERFORD, IRELAND NOVEMBER 1933

FRED'S NEW SHOW *THE GAY DIVORCE* opened in London. I told Charlie to go. I thought it would do him good, to get out of Lismore, away from the misery that was the aftermath of our small, sad funeral, of the slow dawning of all that we had lost.

My stomach returned to its normal shape, the stretched skin going back to where it used to be. Soon there would be no trace that she had lived there at all.

We buried her in a plot in the corner of St Catharge's Cathedral, a pink hydrangea tree hanging over the grave.

Pink for a girl.

We put up a wooden cross. There was no need for a headstone.

Charlie said he didn't want to leave me, that it was too soon.

"It's not. Go. I want you to be there for Freddie."

I did want him there for Freddie, but mostly I wanted to be on my own. I wanted to lie in my room and be answerable to nobody.

On the days I felt strong enough, I went outside. The crisp

air helped, the crunch of the gravel under my shoes. The garden was pared back for winter, but I felt the blood running through my veins. I sat in the greenhouse, in the warmth, with the old gardener, silent, watching him pack his black pipe and smoke it.

The smell of bitter tomato plants and tobacco smoke.

Warmth. Life.

Lismore would help me heal.

Patricia was a darling. I loved that she was a no-nonsense girl, always told me what she thought. She was nothing like Mrs. Keeley, who meant well, but was always flustering and flouncing and trying to talk about the stage, or the pictures or all the famous people I'd met.

Patricia didn't care a jot for all that. She cared only for me.

She helped with her small satisfied sighs, with her ready smiles, through all her kindnesses, day after day.

She helped me see that there was a future ahead, that life was beautiful in so many ways.

I did have a lot to be grateful for. I loved my husband dearly. We had a magnificent home, one of the most majestic a woman could ever live in.

I had my mama, still alive, still well, who could come and stay with me and keep me company. I had Freddie now who was in London, doing well, in his own new show.

Everybody was gentle. The papers carried the story and even though I thought people might be shy about it, too awkward to talk about what had happened, they were the opposite. The Irish have an uncanny way of facing down the truth, of referring to it in a matter-of-fact, *sorry it happened to you, m'lady,* way.

It meant our baby was not forgotten, that she had meant something to everyone else too.

Patricia said she would look after the nursery, pack everything away, but that we would keep everything, for the future just in case.

I nodded, but I would not let my mind go there. It was too difficult to think about going through this all over again.

I read book after book, going off into fantasy worlds that were not my own.

I walked twice a day.

I let myself cry.

I wasn't the first woman to lose a baby and I certainly wouldn't be the last.

But why did it have to be me?

Charlie came home full of news from London. Prince George had enquired after me and said he missed my face about London. Noel Coward said he had something new in the pipeline that might suit me, should I ever deign to return to stage. Harry Gordon Selfridge said he had a whole shelf of goods put away for me. Everyone was concerned and full of sadness at our news.

It made me feel a little better.

"Why don't you go over in a few weeks yourself?" said Charlie. "I'll come with you."

"I might," I said.

I was feeling a bit stronger.

Maybe I could face a trip to London to see everybody.

I longed to see Fred, to talk to him in person, to share the pain. It had been a year and a half since I'd seen him. He would know just how to comfort me, he always did.

Mama was very good to me.

She felt awful that she had missed the whole thing.

"It was hardly your fault, Mama," I told her.

I think she had wanted to see the baby for herself, to see the little soul that we had lost.

She organised all the cooking in those weeks, nutritious broths and stews to get my strength back up. I was weak, physically and mentally; I felt like a woman broken, who needed to be built back up, brick by brick.

Mama loved Lismore and its vast gardens. She loved the mulchy air and the dark Blackwater that flowed beneath our windows.

"I feel like I can breathe here," she said.

The castle was big enough to hold her, and I told her to stay for as long as she wanted.

In the evenings, we would both take out our sewing and listen to the radio. Afterwards I would choose records for the gramophone, always avoiding our own. I didn't want to be reminded of all that I had left behind.

One night, as I flicked through the small vinyl discs, a song from *Funny Face* caught my eye. I put it on and found myself mouthing the words. Fred and I sang a line to each other and it felt so good to hear us chatting like that in a song.

I laughed as the crackle of our voices came through the speaker.

I began to sway in front of the gramophone and then I went and grabbed Mama and trotted her around the drawing room like Freddie and I had performed the song on stage so many times – although I spared her the Runaround.

We laughed. It felt good to laugh.

Yes, I would go to London to see Freddie and his new show.

It was time.

On the boat to Liverpool I found that I tired easily. Damn this anyway – was I going to feel wretched for the rest of my days?

Charlie reassured me that I would be fine and that all I had to do was take it easy.

I thought I had gained most of my fitness back, but I had not. I was glad of the pillow I'd brought and slept all the way on the train to London.

Oh, what a sight London was!

I held on to Charlie tight as we made our way through the streets. So many people, but such a buzz too.

After the stillness of Lismore it was quite a shock to the system. A welcome jolt.

We checked into the Savoy and rested and then went to meet Fred for lunch.

My, it was good to see him!

He looked different, a little older perhaps, more mature maybe. He had grown into himself a bit.

Of course, he was a married man now.

Phyllis was with him and she was courteous and sympathetic, but I would have preferred to meet Freddie on my own.

After lunch we did some shopping and I found myself buying lots of things for myself.

"Treat yourself, darling," Charlie said.

He asked if I would very much mind if he went for a drink while I continued shopping and I let him go. We were both treating ourselves.

I wandered around on my own for some time and it was glorious. I got a few glances, one woman even stopped to clutch my hand and say she missed me on the stage but she was going to go to Freddie's show anyway, even though it wouldn't be the same.

That made me smile. I hadn't been forgotten just yet.

I took tea in a small café, sitting, watching the shoppers, in their brown coats, baskets over their arms, small, tight hats pulled over their heads. So many women with children, with babies in large, rectangular prams, toddlers trotting along.

I watched fine ladies in twos and threes, moving along with small dainty steps, feet gliding on the street, no children to be pulled along.

What kind of mother would I be? Would I bring my children out, take them with me everywhere I went, or would I leave all that work to the nanny?

Charlie met me with some colour in his cheeks. He was in good form and wrapped his arm around me. I laid my head on his shoulder.

In the evening we got ready for the show and I dressed in a beautiful cream backless gown by Schiaparelli. It had a bustle on the back and I felt wonderful as I added a fur wrap and drop diamond earrings.

Almost like myself again.

What a reception when we got to the foyer. Lots of hands to shake, the manager to meet, led into my seat, fetched a glass of wine. I was so well treated. It felt good to be back, among an audience, in the theatre – the smell of the electrics and wood and anticipatory perspiration.

The lights went down. The audience quietened. And they appeared.

Fred. Moving like lightning, his voice treacle, magnetic.

Never before had I witnessed Fred like this, all the way down in the audience. I was always beside him, up front.

In my place was Claire Luce, a beautiful blonde, with a slim, lithe body.

Tears welled up and I could not stop them flowing down my face.

I should have been up there with Fred.

Charlie looked at me and I felt him wince slightly. He took my hand and squeezed it.

I looked straight ahead.

Jealous.

I wiped my eyes, glad I'd had the foresight to put a hanky in my evening bag. I would go to the bathroom at the interval to fix myself up, maybe even leave minutes before the lights came on.

I sat waiting for my moment to exit when suddenly the interval came and from the stage Fred announced my name and I had to stand up and take a bow.

Spotlight.

Miss Adele Astaire, the new Lady Cavendish!

Everyone knew that I was there. Everyone knew what had happened to me, all that I had lost.

I felt all of the love in the room and I could not help but giggle, with tears in my eyes.

Of all the times to get a standing, glowing ovation, when I had mascara all over my face!

I sat back down and looked at Freddie on his platform up high. It was sad, but it was how it was supposed to be. I had to remember that.

After the break, after fixing up my make-up and talking to lots and lots of well-wishers, I let myself sink into the show and began to forget my sorrow at being in the audience and not on stage.

Fred was simply wonderful. Had I never noticed how superb he was, or had I always been too preoccupied with my own steps and words and comedy? I simply couldn't take my eyes off him on stage.

When the lights came on at the end, I stood and clapped and clapped till my hands were sore.

"*Encore!*" I shouted.

Freddie looked so pleased as he took his bow, a job well done.

Afterwards we went for supper at Quaglino's in Bury Street and Freddie took out a blue velvet box and handed it to me.

Inside lay a silver charm bracelet with miniature figures all around.

"Here is a lady," he said pointing to a carved woman the size of a ladybird. "For *Lady, Be Good!* This one is a clown for *Funny Face*. I wanted to leave out *Smiles* but I suppose that would be untruthful, wouldn't it, so I got this little girl who looks very sad as a joke. I think she looks a little like you."

I examined the tiny silver girl. She had a pixie haircut and looked like a grown child.

He had put a charm for every Broadway show we'd done, our whole stage life in something that I could wear for ever more.

"Oh Freddie," I said. "Thank you so much."

"You're welcome, sis. I miss you up there, you know. It's just not the same. But we will carry on."

Yes, we will carry on.

We will all carry on.

We went out for drinks and I had two more wines, while Charlie drank his fill. Fred kept up even though he had a show the next day.

"It's not every day your sis is in town, is it?" he said.

I thought I would come to London more.

It was good for the soul. And I needed all the uplifting I could get.

INTERVIEW WITH PATRICIA RYAN LADY'S MAID TO LADY ADELE CAVENDISH

(PERSONAL ARCHIVE, UNDATED)

It was hard not to feel sorry for her.

She tried her best, I think – tried everything she could to stay bright and cheery, but it all got on top of her.

The London trip seemed to do her the world of good at first but, after it, a few days after she came home, well, she went into an awful spiral.

It was hard to know what to do.

I asked Mammy when I was back home, what could I do for a woman in her situation but she said there was only one thing for it and that was to get with child again.

I could do nothing about that so I did everything else I could – bringing her little flowers to put in her room to cheer her up, ordering new books through the newspapers, bringing her lots of cups of tea – she loved tea – fetching her sewing, doing her hair, chatting all the time, filling the silence.

She appreciated it, I think, but she never said much. Sometimes, she smiled at me, a real weak, forced smile. You know.

It'd break your heart so it would.

I think she might have been alright if it hadn't been for how His Lordship reacted, which was the only way he knew how, of course.

It was the talk of the village that His Lordship was coming down from the castle to Foley's every evening and, sure, he had a ready audience, all propped up at the bar, jackeens from everywhere hanging on his every word. Hoping for a measure.

It upset the Lady.

She'd go looking for him, driving off in the Ford, bringing him back with the drink oozing out his pores. She'd be in a foul mood and roar and shout at him and he'd just sit back and take it or else go to his room and slam a door.

She was always looking for a cure, something that would help him give it up and she wrote to doctors in London and in Germany, at wellness spas where they look after that kind of thing.

Sometimes she went with him and sometimes she sent him on his own.

She needed the break I think from him, from the worry and the fighting.

I thought it wasn't much good sending him off on his own, even if it was to a big mountain resort. I thought to myself, if there's drink to be had in those mountains that man will find it. You can be sure of that. No matter what sort of a place it was, with its good alpine air and doctors and all the good intentions in the world.

He was addicted. Make no bones about it, that's what he was.

But she thought he'd get the cure in Germany.

And after that spring, she took him in the autumn too and the next year as well.

She'd do anything for that man to get him right, to do best by him, to keep him happy and sober and vivacious like she was.

But some men aren't built to be sober.

Some men like to be drunk all the time, running away from their feelings and emotions. Living in a pretend world, one that is only a version of the truth.

When he came back from a spa trip, he'd have a fine sober week, looking fresh in the face and all bright-eyed.

But you check back in with him the next week and you'd see the signs.

The signs that he was back on it.

I'd never seen a man so keen on the drink, who would do anything for a drop. The gardener found him in the sheds once, going through all the chemicals for the garden, seeing if there was anything with alcohol at all in it. It was like a disease so it was, eating him up inside. It was as though his blood were alcohol, I'd say if you looked inside him his veins were made of glass. He was like a walking pint bottle.

It was all he ever wanted, all he ever thought about, I'm sure.

And the loss of that little girl didn't help.

It just made things worse.

German spas or no German spas.

We all knew it'd be the end of him, so we did.

CHAPTER FORTY

LISMORE CASTLE, COUNTY WATERFORD, IRELAND, JUNE 1935

WHEN I REALISED I WAS PREGNANT AGAIN, it wasn't joy I felt but a deep pit of worry.

Charlie was ecstatic.

"Darling!" he said when I told him. "That's wonderful news!"

It was wonderful news, of course it was. But, what if? What about all the ifs?

There were no cream buns this time.

When the sickness came and I began to swell, I relaxed a little. The baby was big. My sickness continued. The doctor said things were going well.

Charlie said keeping things normal would help and as long as I rested and looked after myself, all would be fine. We went about our usual business. I walked a bit, but not up hills. Charlie would drive me to a flat part of the forest nearby and come with me. I treasured those rambles, the scent of pine and wet leaves in our nose. Once we saw a mother and fawn and I took it as a sign.

Things would be well.

I loved to watch our dogs Tilly and Sammy roam. They had boundless energy and I smiled as they galloped and raced in and out of the trees. I admired everything about dogs: their wet, quivering noses, their chocolate eyes that said *I love you*. I couldn't understand how anyone could be cruel to an animal, especially a dog. If ever I saw a man or a child strike a dog in the street, I would stop and strike them right back.

It happened once with a horse too.

"*Would you like me to turn that whip on you, you beast?*" I roared out the window of the Ford one day as Charlie and I drove by man on a cart who was lashing into his horse.

The man on the cart looked surprised and tipped his cap at me. He lowered the whip in his hand.

Charlie thought I was a bit soft – he said working animals and racing animals were different.

But how could they be? Did they not have a hide and a skin the same as every other breed? Did they not have ears that could hear and eyes that could see the anger in their owner's face?

Our social engagements continued. We went to the races at Punchestown and Fairyhouse. I sat down at the track, but when Charlie's horse nearly won I stood and jumped, like everyone else.

My tummy grew and grew. It seemed that every morning I got up it had stretched even more.

"I swear I'm three pounds heavier than yesterday, Charlie," I moaned.

"Nonsense," he said. "It's because you had a child before. It's different this time."

"I'm as big as this bloody castle," I wailed.

He could see that my stomach was very large for how far along I was. The doctor was duly ordered.

And there it was.

Twins.

"I am almost certain," the doctor said, listening with his cold stethoscope pressed to my big white belly. "Yes, I can hear two heartbeats. And you are big for how far along you are."

Twins! Oh, my goodness! Perhaps it was God's way of making up for what had gone before. We had lost one baby but now we would have two.

Of course, the whole thing going forward would be fraught with more complications, but I was feeling well and I hoped that this time things would be all right. I couldn't be that unlucky a second time, could I?

"No cartwheels tonight," Charlie warned, wagging his finger.

"Alright, husband," I laughed.

We were just about to go down for dinner at Chatsworth.

I wondered what his family would think if I did try to somersault my pregnant body into the grand drawing room? My very fine bump sailing through their stuffy aristocratic air?

We had travelled to the great estate for a last visit before the birth of the twins. It was October and I knew that I would be cooped up at home in the coming months and it would be the last time I saw anyone for a long time.

And here we were.

The Duchess was more gracious than normal upon our arrival. Perhaps she now saw my vulnerability. She had understood our loss as she too had given birth to babies that did not live past the first few hours. She did not talk about it of course, but she had been kind in her letters to Charlie and to me.

"It is a shock and a loss that will always be with you, but you have time, there will be more babies."

Charlie's sisters were revved up to see me, squealing when they saw the bump. Lady Anne had two little boys now and I relished seeing their sweet faces and wild flyaway hair. She had no problem bringing her boys into the world. She had youth on her side.

It was good for Charlie to get home. He brightened around his siblings, especially his brother Edward and he couldn't keep the smile from his face as headed off to the stables to see the broodmares and the geldings ready for racing.

We had dinner on our first night with plates whizzing back and forth to the kitchen. Duck, quail, roast parsnips and carrot, wine jus, salmon cutlets. It was a feast.

I ate my fill, but the heartburn soared and I had to excuse myself to bed with a jug of milk.

Charlie came up to see that I was alright.

"I'm fine," I said.

He looked concerned and I smiled to show him I was well. It was the journey here that had likely tired me out.

I tossed and turned all night. It was hard to get comfortable in the unfamiliar bed, hard to find a position that didn't hurt my back or my pelvis or to support my enormous front.

The next morning my waters broke.

In the afternoon, the babies came.

Fred. I think of him now as I lie in my bed in Chatsworth.

About how Mama and I went to see his picture *Top Hat* in Dungarvan, just a month ago, nestled with the audience, smiling, laughing, in awe of my fabulous brother who set the screen alight with that siren Ginger Rogers.

How smart he looked in those tails. Even though he hated wearing them, they suited him.

Oh, he was wonderful, he truly was.

The screen loved him. His voice, golden.

I sat there in the cinema, my light summer coat stretched over my tummy, and I imagined that Ginger was Fred's wife. Not Phyllis.

Phyllis and Fred were expecting a baby now. Just one month after our twins were due.

Maybe that's what I got for thinking bad thoughts.

Maybe that was why God had taken our twins from us.

Charlie comes and goes.

He sits by my bed, sighing, and then he goes again.

He doesn't know what to say.

What can he say?

We'll try again?

I don't want to try again.

It is quiet now after all the fuss of the labour, of the birth.

The dawning of the morning after, of my stomach, bruised, sore, empty.

Nothing moving beneath my skin.

No heartbeats. No little arms kicking, punching, gone.

Twin boys.

They had little apple heads, dark like Charlie, dark like me.

I touched their tiny hands and fingered their minuscule feet.

And then I asked for them to be taken away because I couldn't bear to look anymore.

I had lost three babies in two years.

I was thirty-seven years old.

I knew why I couldn't bring these babies to term. It wasn't my age. It wasn't the long walks I took or even Charlie's bad seed from the drink.

It was my insides, you see, from the boating accident. Something happened then, something drastic inside, scarring perhaps, damage to my womb, to my tubes, to whatever parts you need to make and keep a baby inside for as long as it needed to be.

I was missing a part, missing something, and I knew, I knew then in a great big gushing reality that I was never going to be a mother.

I had three babies but I would never watch them grow.

They buried them in the small graveyard beside the private chapel where we married.

Our little girl in Ireland, our little boys in England. Parts of us everywhere.

And now I have to face the birth of Fred's and Phyllis's baby and never a true cousin will it have.

I repeat the lyrics from *Top Hat* over in my mind, singing them out loud when there's no one in the room.

My voice is hoarse from crying.

I imagine it is me in that film, in a top hat and tails.

Wouldn't that look swell, the two of us dressed up again?

Back to our double act.

It is the only thing that gets me through, that keeps my mind from this great loss that has descended again.

Maybe it is time to go back to the stage? Maybe that is what this is all about in the end?

PART FIVE

ENCORE

CHAPTER FORTY-ONE

LONDON, ENGLAND, 1944

"*Adele! Adele!*"

Where is the voice coming from? It is pitch black, every light in the place blown out. I fumble around and suddenly a hand has grabbed mine. I go with it, putting my other hand out to touch whatever might be in front of me. I feel an arm and I clutch at the top of it and go with her.

Running. Stumbling. Plaster and cement falling, bits of brick, wood, glass.

And the noise.

We hear the drone of the planes overhead and for the first time in this whole London experience, I am absolutely smothered with fear.

Outside, bodies rush past us, all running in that slow jog necessary to make it through the streets of debris. We pile out into the middle of the road, where there are spaces where there should be buildings.

Tumbledown bricks and wood, broken and exposed, rubble like hills, a valley on the street.

"*This way!*" she shouts.

We are still holding hands.

Behind us I hear a drop, a slow piercing scream as the

bomb whistles through the air.

There is a slight moment of silence before it lands, as though the building is drawing in its last breath and bracing itself.

We wince, the explosion sending our hands over our heads and our knees to the ground. The force of it so close knocks us, but the realisation that it *is* so close forces us to get up and run on again.

Odd spontaneous screams pepper our ears. Short, sharp, the fall of shrapnel or glass, slicing.

I suppose I have been lucky to have gotten this far without experiencing it like this.

We race by houses blown to smithereens. Tomorrow they will have their wretched residents sitting outside on piles of red brick, cheeks sooty black, white rivers cut through with dried tears.

So far we have been safe.

We have gone to the shelters when the alarms sounded, moving quickly like rats queuing up to dive off a sinking ship, filing, down, down into the underground.

For all the hardship, the cold floors and the hot stuffy air of hundreds of mouths and noses breathing in and out, those nights were not the worst. We came up in the morning, tired, achey, but there was an atmosphere, a companionship, a camaraderie of *we are in this together.* All through the night. Till the morning light came. Till the bombers went home, back across the sea.

When the mood was right, when they called for a singer, when the fiddle player had run out of tunes, I would raise my voice and start.

Ballads sometimes. But mostly comedic songs, parts of the duets Fred and I used to sing.

There were nudges, *That's Adele Astaire*, there were waves from people, smiles. I felt useful, so much more valued here, underground, in wartorn London, than at home.

Home was its own war zone now.

We make it to the station, join the mill of bodies pressing to get down the steps.

The bombers came early tonight, caught us by surprise. Our office, close to where a bomb hit, was shaken, destroyed.

Our dorm, where we stay, rattled.

We are lucky to have gotten out. We are lucky to be alive.

I realise this as we move slowly down the mosaic steps, the familiar scent of unwashed bodies and damp coats and metal tracks coming up from below.

I don't feel like singing tonight. Even if I am asked. I will simply take in what has happened, let the realisation of how near we came to our last night on earth sink in.

I will pray instead, to God, the familiar prayers that I say over and over in my mind for comfort.

Yes, I will pray, for me, for the soldiers, for all the civilians in London tonight. For Mama at home in Lismore, for Fred in America, for Phyllis and Fred Junior, for their new daughter Ava, and for Charlie.

I will pray for Charlie.

Even though he is beyond prayer now.

I realise this.

It is why I left, of course.

The next morning the scenes across the surrounding streets are worse than we expected. Hundreds of bombs have fallen, taking with them buildings, bridges, parks, houses and whole streets.

A church at the end of our road has been hit, a huge

corner of the roof falling off into the street, like a lump of cake.

We survey our quarters, wiping dust from our belongings. All the windows are gone.

Wardrobe knocked over. A glass of water on my beside locker remains, defiant, sporting a proud chip where a piece of debris hit it.

"Unbelievable, isn't it?"

Margaret is another Red Cross volunteer. It is she who led me out of our rooms when everything went black last night.

Today, I feel shaken. I have been here for weeks and while we have duly gone to our shelters, ran when we needed to, taken all the necessary precautions, last night was too close.

I'm scared.

"What's going to happen?" I ask her.

"Well, we gotta bloody win, don't we?" she says. "Nothin' else for it."

She turns over a three-legged chair and kicks it when she sees it will not stand.

"Help me with this," I tell her and we use all our might to force my wardrobe back into a standing position.

I set about hanging up my clothes, although with my Red Cross uniform I don't need much. There is no need for skirts and blouses and coats now. We are standard issue.

"Let's get down to the Corner," she says. "It'll do us good."

She's right. We can clean all this up later. Right now, we want to go and have tea and talk with all the others who are in same position as us.

Vulnerable. Targets.

Who have escaped.

We have all escaped and are alive, for another day at least.

After the loss of the twins Charlie and I returned to Lismore and tried to get on with things as best we could.

Charlie took up a position of positivity. The fact that I had been pregnant twice was a good sign, he said. I could become pregnant again. If I carried a bit longer there was a chance a baby could survive.

But I felt differently. I knew, in my soul, I would never carry a baby to term.

It was my insides, you see. Destroyed.

But when no consuming sickness came, no familiar tug at my breasts, no swelling in my stomach or anything to indicate that I was indeed pregnant again, a despondency set in.

For both of us.

And Charlie began to drink, heavier than ever before.

I researched doctors who could help at special infirmaries in London and more wellness spas in Germany.

We visited alpine ranches bathed in sunshine, with clean, clear water running from glaciers at the top of sky-high mountains. Brown cows munched around us as we walked through wildflower meadows. We breathed in the air, felt closer to the earth, to God, to the sun while the doctors took Charlie and worked with him.

On his body and his mind.

I prayed that it would heal him, that he would see the only way forward.

At first he was enthusiastic. Full of hope. Of determination. But after each trip he became less enthused. He was doomed to fail.

He did not want to stop drinking.

Sometimes, in moments of clarity, on days when the

effects of the poisoning were particularly bad, as he vomited and retched and his skin turned yellow, as the purge began, he agreed he needed to stop.

But it always called him back. Even if he did have a stint of soberness, three weeks perhaps, where he lost weight and the puffiness around his jaw line disappeared, when his eyes became clear and his smile bright, he would always go back to it.

Always, when we returned home, Germany a distant memory, when the lull of Lismore and the dullness of the day got to him.

He simply could not help himself.

I began to despair.

I warned the staff. I told Mrs. Keeley that I suspected somebody was passing drink to Charlie. Where was he getting it from? I kept a watchful eye on him and still in the evening it was on his breath.

I made a big show one day, when I marched out the gate and down the hill to the village.

I could feel the whispers, the mouths behind the hands.

There's Her Ladyship now, where is she off to?

Jesus, she has a face like thunder!

I wouldn't want to be on the receiving end of her!

I went to Foley's and the Great Southern Hotel. I went to the grocer's where you could buy spirits over the counter.

I went into them all.

"My name is Lady Adele Cavendish," I said, if I had not met the person behind the counter before. "My husband likes to take a drink and I am here to tell you that he is under strict doctor's orders not to touch a drop more. Please do not serve him any, even if he comes in here on his knees. Do you understand me?"

The man in Foley's looked back at me and blinked. He

nodded. I took this as an agreement.

The young man in the Great Southern Hotel held his mouth open and said, "Yes, m'lady, yes, m'lady."

The grocer put his hands in the air.

"Right you be, Lady Cavendish, right you be."

But right Charlie was not.

He drank and he drank till be blacked out on the floor and had to be lifted to bed.

Oftentimes he would wet the bed and other times vomit in his sleep.

We had to keep watch, to make sure he did not choke.

It was like minding a child.

Mama came from America and moved in permanently. She said she would try her best with him, but I knew she had come here for my sanity. She knew it was suffering.

She had seen it all before.

Three months after we lost the twins, in January 1936, the news came through that Phyllis had given birth to a son in California.

Fred called me on the phone and I heard the strain of emotion in his voice.

"Delly? It's a boy. A *boy*!"

His voice shook on the word *boy*.

I cried. He cried too.

"I'm so happy for you, Freddie."

I was happy. At least one of us had produced a living child. At least one of us had given our mama a true grandchild.

Charlie hugged me and we had a toast to this new, living baby.

"I want to go and see him, Charlie."

"I thought you might."

"I need to."

"Alright, well, let's go then."

We decided to use the trip to do a big of sightseeing and give ourselves a real break. I'd also been contacted by David O. Selznick who wanted to give me a screen test for his new studio. Fred had been doing so well in the movies and had explained how the process worked.

It would be very different to stage work and it was something I thought I might be able to handle.

Something new. A distraction.

It was nice to climb onto our transatlantic ship and set sail across the ocean. I felt as though the Arctic air blowing down a gale across the deck was cleansing me.

I felt I could breathe again, that I was leaving my troubles behind in Europe.

In New York we decided to take a flight out to California. It was my first time on an aeroplane and I relished the newness of it. I was brave now because what else did I have to lose?

I marvelled at the world below us, at the green fields as we took off, the orange, dusty land as we came towards the west coast.

Fred said life in California was a dream.

I could see myself living there, taking a break from Ireland and its greyness and the sadness that it now held.

Fred met us at the airport, giving me the biggest embrace.

"It is so good to see you, I can't tell you," he said.

We pulled up to his home in Beverley Hills, a large site where he and Phyllis had a built a sprawling Californian bungalow. It was modern and striking, so different to the castle we'd left behind at Lismore.

Inside, he sat me in an armchair and went into another room.

Phyllis emerged with Fred carrying the baby, wrapped in a blue blanket.

Fred Junior.

She laid him in my arms, gently, smiling.

He felt heavier than I expected, solid. I looked over his eyes and eyebrows, his button nose, the flickering eyelashes as he tried to waken up. I kissed him on the forehead and let his scent fill my nose.

He was different to my babies, so much bigger, so healthy looking.

So alive.

I cried, but not sobs. They were gentle tears of joy for this beautiful, beautiful child of my brother's.

Tears that any aunt would shed.

Fred stood behind me, his hand on my shoulder.

Proud.

"He is so sweet," I told them. And he was.

Charlie did not hold him.

He said he feared he would drop him.

As he sat back in his chair, speaking with Freddie, I noticed the tremor in his hand as he lifted it to his head.

"*And cut.*"

I stopped. It was so strange, this acting in front of the cameras. They still looked like big vultures to me, giant black birds staring. Waiting to pick at my bones.

It was hard to perform without a live audience. It wasn't the same in front of these cameras and lighting men checking for all their technical things, not looking to see how you were doing, but more interested in the sound and the pictures and the way their film rolled.

David O. got up out of his chair where he'd been sitting.

"Wonderful," he said. "Wonderful, Adele. Let us get that up and running now and show you. Would you like some coffee while you wait?"

I walked with one of the young film assistants to the little kitchenette down the corridor. Outside, there were bangs and noises coming from what seemed to be a very large warehouse. Almost like a hanger I'd seen at the airport. David O. was renting a small part of this bigger studio for his own new venture. This was where they made movies – giant theatres with no audiences at all. It was all so empty. So cold.

The assistant knew who I was but was far too young to have seen any of our shows. He had a southern accent and I wondered how he'd made it all the way to California.

"So have you met Ginger?" he asked.

"Who?" I said, distracted.

"Ginger Rogers," he said, looking at me as though I was a mad old bat.

"Oh, Ginger Rogers." Freddie had done two films with her now – they were quite the hit. "Oh yes, briefly, a few years ago. She was friendly with Freddie before they shot their first film together."

"Were they?" said the assistant, looking incredibly interested at this news. "Oh, I love Ginger. She is such a beauty. And the way she dances. And it doesn't hurt that she's a Texan belle too!"

This guy would get on very well with Philip Sassoon. I could tell.

"What's she like?" he asked, his eyes wide.

"Nice," I said, staring at the cup of coffee he was supposed to be making me.

"Oh, I'd love to meet her. I keep hoping I'll run into her around," he said, waving his hand towards the warehouse. "It would be a dream to work with her, wouldn't you say?"

I said nothing.

He kept talking. About Ginger's wonderful hair, about how her shapely lips stood out on screen. About her voice, the way she delivered her lines. Hell, he even loved her neat, dainty ankles.

Finally he handed me the black coffee and I took it and carried it back to where the director was working with the vulture men.

"Adele," he said, after fifteen minutes or so. "We have it – come and look at this."

I moved my seat to where they'd set up a projector and screen. The whirr of the wheel filled the room and there was a flicker.

My face was on screen.

Big, puffy. I had gained so much weight.

My lips looked thin and then I heard my voice.

Tinny. Childlike.

Nothing like Ginger, nothing like the blonde bombshell our assistant had just described.

I shook my head.

"No," I said, as the clip finished and David turned to me, a smile on his face.

"No?"

"No. I don't like it. I don't like it at all. This is not for me. I'm not made for the screen."

I put my head in my hands.

"Don't be silly," said David. "You look great up there – you'll be marvellous!"

I said nothing and let his words, which kept coming, wash over me.

He was wrong. I was right.

I said no to the film.

INTERVIEW WITH PATRICIA RYAN
LADY'S MAID TO LADY ADELE CAVENDISH
(PERSONAL ARCHIVE, UNDATED)

If you'd asked me had I ever seen a heart break before my time at the castle, I would have said yes.

I would have said yes. Sure, didn't my mother lose my father when I was only five, leaving her alone to bring me up on her own?

I remember her crying, I remember her being sad.

And then there were always bad accidents happening in the village and surrounds and the war that raged in the hills, when the men were shot at and boys too. There were always sad things happening, always, an accident in a well, a boat overturning on the Blackwater, young people taken before their time. We all remembered the war in France too, so many young lads who never came home to their mothers again.

But the heartbreak I'd witnessed before was nothing to the heartbreak I saw in the castle, because I'd never seen true melancholy up close. I'd never had to live with it, day in, day out, tipping round, watching the cracks, watching her fall apart altogether.

My mam hadn't been like that over my father. Not that I can remember. She would weep into the corner of her shawl and then we'd say the rosary. She might have another weep in the summertime on a warm evening, after she'd be reminded about how her and Daddy used to walk the roads to a dance or go courting in the hay fields. That would make her sad too.

But there was none of this lying in bed. None of this barely able to get up and go about the day.

We had himself half dead from the drink in one room and herself half mad from the sadness in another.

It was a dark time at Lismore.

Mrs. Keeley came into her own around then. Every day she did her best by both of them. She opened windows, cleaned out rooms, made fresh soups and broths and got the cook to do up special recipes of healing to tempt her.

She got out the Lady's bicycle, got it all polished up and said things like, "I've left your bicycle by the back door, Lady Cavendish. The fair's on in Cappoquin today. I know how much you love a good cycle in the summer. Patricia could go with you if you like."

Mrs. Keeley and I came to a bit of an understanding. It was our job to get our employers back on their feet in whatever way we could. Not just for our own sakes, not just for the castle and for all that were employed there, but for Lord and Lady Cavendish too. They were too fine to be knocked down like this, the stuffing taken out of them, their will to live all trampled over.

Not that they'd admit what was going on, but that was the truth. The loss of those babies crushed them. And all their hopes and dreams.

The first year they went on a visit to Germany, I stayed back in the castle and took some time off, moving back in with Mammy and helping her about the house. There were flags on the floors that needed replacing and the house was years overdue a whitewash. The plaster was so cracked in places we had to get a man in the village in to do a bit of job before we could even look at whitewashing it.

I went to Miley's hardware – not there now, long gone – and picked up some paint for the window and we took all the furniture out onto the street, washed it down and gave all the rooms a good sweep-out.

My mother was very house-proud and it was a sparkling house when I was growing up. Now there were cobwebs everywhere, a film of dust on the counter and on the shelves where her lovely ornaments sat.

I wasn't sure whether she had just given up, or she wasn't able.

She loved having me at home those few weeks, Mammy did. And it was enjoyable for a while.

But I missed my Lady. I missed her presence, her smile, her humour and sharp comments.

I missed laying out her clothes, doing her bath and her hair, I missed being around her.

She had become so much a part of my existence I didn't really know what I was supposed to do without her.

She wrote to me and I wrote to her and she said

that Germany was a fine place and the doctor at the sanatorium was very, very good. I presumed that meant he was doing something for His Lordship. I was glad. They needed it, they both needed it, a break from the drink.

I hoped that when they got back he would stick with the lifestyle he'd been leading in Germany.

But I knew it was a fruitless hope, the type when you're staring at an overturned cart and hoping it will right itself again before your eyes.

In 1939 war broke out and none of us could believe it.

Especially Her Ladyship. She found it very hard to reconcile all this trouble between England and Germany and she with such good experiences in both countries.

There was no spa trip to Germany that year.

For a while, not much seemed to be happening in Ireland, us perched in the Irish Sea away from all the politicking and arguing and troops that were marching and sailing towards war.

But the emergency was declared and certain goods became hard to come by. Petrol was one of the first items to go and so the Ford was put away in its shed and covered over.

Cigarettes and flour, rare they got. Everyone started to be careful with everything. Even our coal was rationed and in a big, cold castle like Lismore, that was a big annoyance for us, I can tell you.

We cut down some trees to keep us going and took in turf from the bog. Lord Cavendish gave permission to some tenants to do the same, and a blind eye was turned to anyone out hunting rabbits.

Some lads I knew from the village were all talk about joining the war effort.

Mammy told me about them when I visited her. I thought they were crazy in the head to be leaving safe and neutral Ireland and heading over to sign up. But they were young and there wasn't a lot happening around here and they were looking for adventure.

Lord Cavendish himself would have been in line for duty too.

But we all knew that it would never happen; he would never pass a medical and no army would take him in the state he was in.

He was starting to become very unwell.

Then later on, oh around 1941 I think it was, we got word that a group of wounded soldiers would be coming to convalesce at Lismore.

Her Ladyship was beside herself, getting everything ready, organising rooms and beds and setting up a canteen restaurant in our great hall.

Mrs. Keeley nearly had conniptions, but sure she loved all the fuss really. I knew by her. I was left chasing my tail, running around after Her Ladyship, taking notes for all the tasks she had, getting things done, but not getting in her way doing it.

The Ladyship's appearance became less important as sick and injured men came to Lismore to set up home for a while.

I was scared of what I might see – infections, blood, pus maybe – I'd no stomach for that at all. But in the end it wasn't like that.

Most of the men were very nice, quiet and a lot had injuries that they needed time to get used to, in the body. But in the mind too.

Lismore suited them, with its small courtyard that they could sit in. For the ones more able, they took to the gardens and it was a sight, seeing the ground come alive with men on crutches, in pushchairs, white slings and bandages everywhere.

It was a lovely place to convalesce, Lismore, all its windy paths and that lovely yew walkway, like a big church tunnel. All sheltered. Everyone loved it down there.

And I tell you and don't laugh at me now, because I know you wouldn't think it, but I got a lot of attention myself then, with not many womenfolk around. Oh, they'd have the hand on your arm or squeezing your hand, but there was nothing disrespectful. We wouldn't have stood for that. It was just I could see it in their eyes – how they missed their own wives or their girlfriends, how they missed the touch of a woman, you know.

I probably could have found a husband there if I'd been looking.

The truth was, I wasn't really looking. I didn't want to go down that road, not then. I still felt too young, as though I had another life to lead, something else to happen before I could go and fall in love and settle down.

And I knew if I fell for any of the men, they were almost all English and I'd be whipped off over to England, married and living in Manchester or Yorkshire or Birmingham or somewhere.

And sure wasn't I right?

A part of me would have liked that, though, the experience of it all, the touch of a man and the excitement, but a bigger part of me said not yet.

I knew if that happened it would be goodbye to Lismore.

It would be goodbye to Mammy in her little terraced cottage down the street.

And it would be goodbye to Her Ladyship, to everything she had shown me and given me, everything I'd learned from her, all that experience.

I don't know if she needed me or I needed her.

Maybe it was somewhere in between. Maybe we both needed to stay together, at that time, in that castle, in that place.

CHAPTER FORTY-TWO

LONDON, ENGLAND, 1944

We donated two planes to the war effort. They were called *Cavendish* and *Adele Astaire*.

It was something we could do at least. I could not stop thinking of all those soldiers, putting on their uniforms, marching away from their families, climbing up into the air and, for many, never coming home again.

It moved me to tears.

I listened to Winston Churchill on the radio, imagining him in his chair, with his cane, his low voice droning on.

Mama was right when she said he would be Prime Minister one day.

I found it hard to correlate the man on the wireless though with the fun-loving, jovial man I had played backgammon with on our cross-Atlantic sailing all those years ago.

Now, I thought him arrogant. Self-serving. Ambitious beyond belief. How had things gotten this far?

When the soldiers came to Lismore, things began to change.

Not just at the castle, but with me too.

It had been a long time since I had felt so useful. It had

been a long time since I had felt a spark, glowing, something that lit me up.

Things had become so distant between Charlie and me. We had gotten on with things as best we could – returning to our usual social events, having our suppers and hunt parties, taking trips to Cork and to Dublin.

Sketch magazine came to the castle and set up photos with us fishing on the Blackwater and with Tilly and Sammy outside Lismore. Charlie wore his wide tweeds, and I wore my country suit too. It felt good to have someone take our photos. It reminded me that out there, people were still interested in me, in my life.

But when they were published and the initial thrill of seeing ourselves in print like that faded, I felt a little empty.

What now? And what was the truth behind those images?

We looked happy but were we really?

I had the castle the way I wanted it. All the plumbing work was finished.

I preferred the large drawing room, with its great big fire and bay window over the Blackwater.

Charlie preferred his own sitting room down the corridor. It was more gentlemanly, he said, with its low leather armchairs and papers strewn all about.

Of course, he felt he could drink in peace there.

I had sewn and embroidered, dried flowers and glued bits of paper into pretty pictures, adding tiny bits of colour all over the castle.

I walked the gardens and chose flowers for the hall, for the main rooms, for the bedrooms.

I planned menus with Mrs. Keeley and met with the kitchen staff to discuss any parties or entertaining we were doing.

We took in guests who were passing, invited old friends and new to stay.

But as Charlie's health began to deteriorate, I stopped inviting people over.

I could never tell what state he would be in. What was the point of embarrassing ourselves, to have a guest arrive at a time when he had managed to drink himself silly again? To have to hide him away and make excuses?

Oftentimes he would refuse to stay away and would accost our guests, challenging them to drink with him and slur his way through an animated, expletive-laden conversation.

If it was a friend of mine, they would look over at me helpless. If it was a friend of both of ours, they would look at Charlie, puzzled, wondering how the vivacious and charming man they knew had turned into an old, cranky, fusspot, spewing vitriol and often incoherent mutterings about some small matter or grievance.

I was falling out of love with him.

He was not the man I married.

And I began to retreat into myself, to wonder how on earth I could change things for myself and this life and marriage I had signed myself into.

When the soldiers came and I held vibrant, colourful conversations with men of all backgrounds, their accents northern, southern and in between, I found myself coming back to life again.

They lifted me with their tales of bravery in the face of fire, surviving bombings and raids and falling from aeroplanes with only parachutes on their backs.

I wanted to *do* something.

I wanted to help more.

I wanted to go to London, to be at the heart of things, to feel really alive.

I booked a ticket and sought my visa to go over.

I was dying a slow death in Lismore anyway.

"You have such a way with people, Adele."

"Why, thank you."

"Once they get past your foul, coarse mouth."

"Oh, do kindly fuck off!"

"You see!"

I laughed. I threw my head back and let it escape. I heard it over the clinking glasses, over the hubbub of all the other drinkers and smokers.

Kingman Douglas leaned over and put his hand on my knee.

It felt good. Warm and steady. I did not push it away.

He was a tall man, like Charlie. He was sturdy in stature, someone I had to look up to, to talk to. I always liked that about a man – that presence. Charlie had it in spades; at least he used to have.

It was hard to see it now, the way he curled in bed.

"You could be very useful in the war effort," said Kingman.

"Could I?"

I suppose he thought I'd dance for the troops, put on a show, get everyone singing, dancing, telling jokes. Back to entertaining.

"I'm think I'm past all that now."

"Nonsense," he said. "You're a youthful woman. There are plenty of jobs going, but you could do something special, be a ... I dunno, a point of contact. A morale booster."

"Morale booster! I like the sound of that."

I smiled. He made me feel vibrant. I liked his blue eyes, the way he looked at me, as though staring through me. He had no fear of me the way some men did.

"You should consider it," he said.

"I have a husband at home, dear man. I don't think coming to London permanently is an option."

"Well, you're here now."

"Yes, I am."

We were jostled, a couple pushing past in the busy, small pub.

"I'll give you my address and if you change your mind, write to me."

"I'll do better than that," I said, opening my bag and rummaging through the contents.

I took out a piece of Lismore notepaper and wrote our telephone number on it.

"Give me a call, whenever you like."

"I'll do that."

"Now ... get me a fucking drink, please."

This time he threw back his head and laughed.

He got up and swayed through the throng and I thought how strange it was that this was the happiest I'd felt in such a long time. Things were bad when it took coming to the middle of wartorn London for a break.

Maybe Kingman was right.

Maybe I should come to live in London for a while, do what I could to show my support.

All hands on deck.

Spades, club, diamond, heart.

Rainbow Corner, the social unit of the Red Cross, was a mishmash of all sorts. The men came through in their droves, sitting, standing, talking, chatting, laughing, holding cups of coffee and tea. Some sat and stared, and they were left alone, because sometimes a solider needed to sit and think. To recollect his thoughts. To find himself again, amongst all this madness.

Freddie thought it was so funny that I had managed to find a position in the midst of a raging war – being a socialite to soldiers.

"Only you, Adele!" he laughed.

But I loved my job. It brought joy to the soldiers and, of course, to me.

I had a purpose again. And I was good at it.

Kingman and I had begun telephoning each other when I got back to Lismore after my first visit to London. I had gone back to mind Charlie, but I could not shake the feeling that I would be better off in the centre of the war effort.

Where Kingman was.

At first they were short chats here and there, light conversation, joking and catching up. Then they developed into a more regular rapport. He liked to talk to me, I think. In between his work.

I wasn't quite sure what he did, but I knew it was top secret. He was very high up in the force.

He appealed to me. And I liked that he was American. We had an understanding, a certain knowing where we stood, seeing as we had both been born and raised in the same country.

Slowly I told him about Charlie.

In our early conversations I made out that all was well. I didn't feel it was right to bring up our issues or to talk about Charlie's drinking problems. It was easy to pretend that Charlie was still the man I had married. That he was a good sport and a great conversationalist and that he was always happy to see me.

I started using a version of the language of Mrs. Keeley, a whole code of sentences to convey a covert meaning.

"*His Lordship is in good form today*," meant that he had enough to keep him going and all his symptoms at bay, that he was not particularly sick and might be lucid. They were the good days now.

"*His Lordship is feeling very tired*," meant that he had taken his fill and was likely passed out and needed to be kept a close eye on.

"*His Lordship is in a mood*," meant that he was belligerent and aggressive and it would be best if I kept out of his way that day, because he liked to take out his fury on me in particular.

Kingman was going through a divorce. He too did not want to talk about his affairs or to air his dirty laundry with me.

Neither of us wanted to show each other our faults.

So we met somewhere in between.

I looked forward to the ring of the telephone, to the shrill tone of the receiver in the hall.

I would rush to it, ready to take the handset from Mrs. Keeley, who always answered before me, even if I told her I was expecting a call.

The sound of his voice would soothe me, make me smile, standing in the great hall of Lismore, leaning on our big black walnut table, which I had long cleared of being a drinks cabinet.

I would pick at the flower petals in the vase beside me, swirl the telephone wire round in my hand. Laugh, loudly.

"Lady Adele!" he said one morning. "You told me to keep an eye out and I have found it, the perfect job for you.

Could you tear yourself away from Ireland and that husband of yours and come to work for us in London? I can't think of anyone else who could do this job like you could."

The job was at the Rainbow Corner canteen, a drop-in centre for soldiers, near Piccadilly Circus. It was where they went when they were off duty, to socialise and relax.

Kingman had discovered that they needed a letter-writer, and as he read and liked the letters I had sent him, he said I would ideal.

"Besides, I don't know any woman who can curse like a trooper as you can."

And so that was that. I organised my small case, my visa, my passage to London and I left Lismore.

Mrs. Keeley would look after the castle.

Patricia would look after Mrs. Keeley.

Mama would look after Charlie.

And I would look after me.

I was tired of seeing my husband's sunken face, his white pallor, his stubble and dribble and vomit and tears.

I was tired of repeating myself, of telling him how much I loved him, of pleading with him to try and get better, so that we could go back to the life we used to have.

I was tired of being the wife of a drunk.

Charlie was beyond help.

I knew that now.

It was a slow awakening.

London simply brought it all into focus.

I wore a green uniform, standard attire, although I was missing the badge. I was not official Red Cross. I was something in between.

A hybrid.

My American accent was welcomed at the barracks. They said it was *music to their ears*.

I danced with the soldiers of course.

Each day, I sat at my desk and worked through the line of soldiers before me. Letter-writing was a free service provided at Rainbow Corner – a help to those who weren't sure what to put in their letters home, to those who found it difficult to read and write, or to those didn't want to have to go to the bother of purchasing paper and stamps.

I developed a method where I got each solider to tell me three pieces of news about themselves and I would put them into short sentences.

I would sign them '*Written by Adele Astaire (sister of Fred Astaire)*' and this pleased the soldiers no end. No wonder there was a queue. I had to set a time limit for letters in the day as I worried I was damaging my hand.

At night I played piano but everyone preferred when I danced.

I stayed in a dorm house with other Red Cross workers. Somehow I managed to get a tiny annex to myself and I enjoyed the comings and goings of everyone, while having a small space of privacy for myself.

The will was good. Everyone was trying to help.

We were all trying to win the war.

Mama's letters from home were getting worse. She was worried.

Eventually she told me to come home.

I was angry at Charlie for being sick.

I felt I had achieved more in just a few weeks here in Rainbow Corner than in my whole decade renovating and entertaining at Lismore.

But I applied for the travel visa and I went home.

Mama was grave in the face when I saw her and I thought that maybe this was all too hard on her.

But Charlie loved her, they had their own connection now and, having not seen his own mother in so long, she had become a surrogate.

"You look wonderful, Adele," said Mama.

I was in my uniform and she said she was proud of me.

"Is he really bad?" I asked.

"He is the worst yet."

"Oh, Mama."

"I've arranged for the doctor to come by this evening to speak with you."

"Should I go to see him?"

"He's expecting you."

I didn't know what to expect myself.

He was lying in a half-awake state. His eyes were open, unblinking. He made soft moans as his breath went in and out. He was in pain.

"Charlie," I said as I reached his bed.

I sat down on the chair that Mama had placed there, where she must have sat herself for hours, beside him, nursing.

Another soft moan.

"Charlie, darling."

He turned his eyes to me, but his face did not move.

He was not recognisable. His eyelids drooped, swollen. His skin was tinged yellow, like a rotten buttercup. His hair had greyed all around the temples and it was long and matted at the sides when it used to be short. His jaw was drawn up towards his nose, like he'd been clenching his teeth.

A smell of bleach in the room.

"Darling," he said.

His voice was hoarse.

I reached over and took his hand.

"You're back."

"I'm back, darling."

"Are you a solider?"

I saw him looking at my uniform.

I laughed. "No, silly. I'm helping soldiers. With the Red Cross."

"Daddy was a soldier."

"I know, darling."

"A good one. I wasn't a good one."

I thought he might start rambling now.

"How are you feeling? Mama says you haven't been well at all?"

"I love your mama. She is better than my own mother."

"Don't say that."

"It's true."

His words came out slowly, dribbling out of his mouth, it was such an effort for him to speak.

"I'm dying, Adele."

"Don't say that, Charlie." Tears sprang to my eyes.

He was always morbid, Charlie, but this time I thought he might be speaking the truth.

"You can get better, darling."

"It's too late."

"It's never too late."

"I'm sorry."

"It's alright," I said, my voice quivering now.

"It didn't work out like we planned, did it?"

I put my head on his hand and I let the sobs come. I didn't think I'd be this emotional. I didn't think I'd feel this sad. He was still here but I felt that he was gone.

"If they had lived, maybe it would have been different," he said.

I didn't think this was true. I think Charlie would have broken his soul with drinking anyway.

"I have organised all my papers. Your mama knows where everything is."

"Charlie, please don't speak like this – it is so upsetting."

"It is so good to see you, Delly."

I looked up and caught his eyes and in there, through the bloodshot yellowness, through the swelling and fluid and all of the pain, I saw, for a moment, the Charlie I had always loved, the man I married, the lovely, funny, charismatic man.

"I love you, darling," I said.

But his eyes were closed, back into a dreary sleep, his breathing in and out, his stomach extended, looking like mine when there were babies inside.

I left the bleached-out room and went to find Mama where I let her take me in her arms and hold me as I cried.

When the doctor came that evening he told us something I had not expected.

"Weeks, possibly months."

"What?" said Mama. "But he is so ill."

"Months?" I said.

He told us that the disease was unpredictable. "He is very ill but, going on my examination, I think that he will live for another number of weeks. It is a slow end, I'm afraid."

When he left, Mama and I sat in silence.

Mrs. Keeley brought tea and Patricia came and asked if she could do anything for me. I had missed her kind face in London. She could sense my pain at this whole damned situation.

"No, darling. Thank you. Please go home and I'll see

you tomorrow. I plan on going for a long walk then – perhaps you can accompany me."

"Of course, ma'am," she said and left.

I looked at Mama and our eyes met, the fire crackling in the great drawing room of Lismore.

"I can't stay," I said firmly.

"I know."

"I can't watch, Mama. I can't stay and watch him go piece by piece, losing one faculty after another."

"It is alright, Adele."

"Would it be terrible if I went back to London?"

She shrugged. "If the doctor said days, that would be different. I don't think anyone expects you to stay and nurse when you can be doing a lot more in London."

"I can't do it, Mama."

"I know. I am here, Adele. Don't worry."

And so I returned to Rainbow Corner, to continue my duties, to look after soldiers who were white in the face and brightened with a smile when they saw that Adele Astaire was there to pen a letter home to their family.

I got so many kisses on my cheeks.

Mama sent letters and I telephoned when I could.

Charlie was hanging on, his symptoms changing, some days were better than others, but he was bedridden and we all knew he would never get out of his bed again.

Four days into March, Mama telephoned me, the call coming through in the morning, an hour into my shift.

"He is gone," she said.

"I know," I replied softly.

I had felt it that morning.

His soul had left our world.

CHAPTER FORTY-THREE

LISMORE CASTLE, COUNTY WATERFORD, IRELAND, APRIL 1944

PATRICIA OBSERVED MRS. KEELEY'S AGONY, catching her crying into her apron, trying to get on with her duties, but having to stop and wipe her eyes and take a minute to gather herself together. She was a big softie really.

They were lucky that Mrs. Ann Astaire had been there to see to everything, to all his needs. She had been a wonderful nurse and she attended to important things too, on the estate. She took charge.

It was different having her nursing rather than Mrs. Keeley or one of his manservants.

She was his equal.

For Patricia and all the staff, Lord Cavendish's death brought a conclusion to the long months of waiting at Lismore.

It felt as though the castle let out one big collective breath it was holding.

They had all been waiting for the end.

In the days after he died, activity at the castle reached fever pitch.

Patricia was called down to the office to help with the hundreds of workers and tenants who came into the offices to pay their respects. There was a big book for all their condolences, and there were callers of every type to the house. Friends, acquaintances, other big house owners, business owners, priests, vicars, councillors, horse people, racetrack goers, ladies in fine dresses who carried little white hankies to sniff into.

When Her Ladyship came home, Patricia thought her heart would break with the sadness at seeing her.

Her face was all white, and they gave her time with him alone.

Patricia thought, *Just look her at now, three babies lost and a husband too.*

She was glad she had her war work in London. It was doing her good.

Although she worried what would become of all of them in the castle now.

On the day of the funeral, thousands of people poured into the village. Motor cars from all around descended through the hilly streets, their engines purring, sending diesel-smoke plumes into the air.

People gathered like black bees all the way along the streets, swarms, waiting, taking their caps off as the coffin passed, Her Ladyship and her mother in front, senior staff behind.

None of his family came from England.

It was too difficult to travel with the war, they said.

There was a great sense of sadness in the air, of a life snuffed out, of a warm, unusual man who had gone too soon and had brought it all on himself.

It was as though a prince had died and the village mourned.

Patricia went into St Carthage's for the funeral, even

though she'd never been in a Protestant church before. It was very different to her own small church, in the layout and the bareness of it all.

She wasn't sure if it was a sin to be in there, but she wasn't going to wait outside. God would understand, surely.

After all the words and blessings, the coffin was carried the short distance out the front door and around to the special grave in the corner. It was the best plot in the whole graveyard.

And all it held was the tiny body of their lost little girl.

It was hard to get back to the castle, through the crowds, through all the handshakers and head-nodders.

It was the biggest day out Lismore had ever seen.

"God rest his soul."

"A great loss."

"You'd feel sorry for Her Ladyship all the same."

Mrs. Keeley sobbed non-stop into her sleeves and hankies, crying harder than Her Ladyship herself.

Patricia managed not to cry even though she felt awful, awful sad inside.

Everything would change now, she knew. No matter what, things would be different.

She just didn't know how different and her stomach ached with it all.

The week after the funeral was a whirlwind too, with all the comings and goings and visitors and an estate now that had lost its master and all that came with that.

Everyone was on tenterhooks, muddling their way through.

Patricia stayed in the castle to help Her Ladyship, checking in with her and letting her know she was there whenever she needed her.

She assisted her with a mourning wardrobe, all the black clothes she could find, got them washed and pressed and laid out so that she didn't have to think too much about it.

Lady Cavendish held it all together very well. She was quiet, but warm and welcoming to all that came to pay their respects.

Something had changed within her though. Patricia could feel it.

A few days after the funeral she was called to her room.

"Thank you, Patricia," she said. "For everything."

Patricia didn't think she had done anything at all.

She nodded her head.

The Lady looked weary.

"I'm going back to London, the day after tomorrow. Will you organise my case for me?"

"Yes, ma'am."

"There will be a great deal to sort out, but it will have to wait. The war continues apace."

"Yes, ma'am."

"Are you happy to stay here, to wait for me? I don't know how long I will be gone, but I would hate to lose you. It is a comfort to know you are here at Lismore."

"Of course, ma'am. I'm not going anywhere."

It was a relief to hear these words from her. Everyone was worried about their position now.

"You can attend to Mama. I fear she will be very cut up in the coming weeks. She loved him like a son, you know."

"She did. She is a great woman."

"I would invite you to London with me, but I fear you would fall for a soldier, and then I would lose you!"

"Maybe you'll fall for a solider too?"

The words were out of her mouth before she knew what she was saying, and she gasped and put her hand to her lips.

"I'm sorry, ma'am, I didn't mean anything ..."

"It's alright."

A moment of silence as they both thought over their predicaments.

"Please wait though, Patricia. I will be back at some stage. And I couldn't bear to come back to a castle without Charlie and without you."

"I will wait."

"Thank you."

Patricia left her room and wanted to slap herself for the stupid flyaway remark in the midst of all this funeral palaver. Maybe it was tiredness.

How could the lady fall for a soldier and her husband not even cold in the ground?

It was unthinkable.

Altogether unthinkable.

She was lucky she hadn't been sacked on the spot.

CHAPTER FORTY-FOUR

LONDON, AUGUST 1944

FREDDIE CAME TO LONDON.

He looked so handsome in uniform and we laughed at the sight of us both, decked out in our khaki green.

"We're in matching costumes again," I joked.

He held me in a hug and said, "How are you, Delly?"

I shook my head and didn't answer.

I didn't need to.

He understood exactly how I felt.

He was quite the celebrity now with nearly fifteen films behind him. I was so proud to be on his arm in London, with everyone stopping us to wish him well and shake his hand.

He was coming from Belgium and France where he had spent three weeks touring with the United Service Organizations.

He was tired, he said, but it had been a lifechanging experience.

"I'm so glad I got to be part of it," he said. "To help in some way."

Freddie had wanted to come to support the war effort for years, but the studios could not release him until now.

Everyone encouraged us to do something together, dance a few steps, sing a song.

But it was Freddie's gig.

He was the star. And he was too rehearsed, too light on his feet.

I felt like an old stomping mare.

It was wonderful to see him perform. It was different to seeing him on screen. I could feel the electricity from him, that I too used to feel on stage. The smarting of the live performance, the unpredictability, the liveliness of it all.

It reminded us what we were fighting for. For the joy of living. For freedom. To remember that there was triumph in the gloom, that we could be happy, when we came together for entertainment.

"What's going to happen to you now, Delly?"

"I don't know," I said.

"Don't be afraid to be happy," he said. "You deserve it."

The war ended with its jubilant scenes on the streets. White flags fluttered madly, like large butterflies abuzz in the clutching hands of Londoners who had survived bombs and blasts and blackouts and the blitz.

We all celebrated, getting drunk on what alcohol we could find. Couples kissed on the street, many matches made in moments of passion.

I listened to Churchill crackle through the wireless and I couldn't get rid of the image of his big head wavering among the green fronds of the fern pots on our ocean cruiser, as he hid my mother and me from the press. Who could have predicted what lay ahead for both of us?

It was the most magnificent street party I'd ever seen.

All those smiles, and tears too. For those who would be coming home, for those who wouldn't.

After a week of gatherings and impromptu parties, I got a longing for Lismore. I wanted to see Mother and the green fields and rolling hills and the beautiful swathes of trees that would now be taking on their autumn coats in County Waterford.

I met with Kingman and he held my hand and kissed me on the cheek.

"Can I visit you?"

"Yes," I said. "When things have settled I would love to show you Lismore."

I returned to Ireland, to face the estate, to look after the will and my inheritance and the tricky path to a new future I had to cut for myself.

I didn't know whether I would stay in the castle or look to do something else.

I loved that home, but what was a home on your own, with no one in it to love?

I had to think about things.

I had to think about everything.

CHAPTER FORTY-FIVE

CALIFORNIA, 1973

SHE ENJOYED THE CAR JOURNEY, along the green fields, cows spread out across hills, standing, looking, heads bent to grass.

After a day and a half the fields became noticeably more dry, dusty, the western soil taking over, desert plants encroaching on green leafy roots.

Soon, she would be home.

Her mind whirred as she drove, with all that she had seen, the characters she had met. Many of them had such direct links to the Astaires that it would be easy to write those chapters, she thought. She had all she needed to go on now and so much more.

Her eyes left the road for a moment and flickered to the folders placed on the passenger seat. Her stomach still bubbled at what they contained, all those news articles, clippings and cuttings, photographs, programmes and even letters in their own hands that would help so much with the voices she wanted to portray. She had so much background now, so much understanding of their roots.

When she got back home she would follow up on the other calls she had made, her enquiries.

She guessed she might need to go to London, to see

where the theatres were.

And she would need to go to Ireland. Finally, after all these years, she would get her chance.

She would have to save – this wasn't something she could do soon. The Omaha trip alone had cost a lot.

Of course, she could use the money her mother had left her, small sum that it was. But she felt as though she should save it. For what, she wasn't sure.

Kirk had been supportive at first, urging her to go when she told him of her plans to go to Omaha.

"Sure, honey, when are you thinking of? Let me know so I can pop it in the diary."

He was interested in hearing her talk about the project, all the letters and diaries she had found in her mother's things, anything related to Adele Astaire. But after a while his interest waned.

"When did you say you were going away again?"

Her mother hadn't liked him of course – she rarely did with her boyfriends. But Kirk – well, Kirk really rubbed her up the wrong way.

How she missed her mother. There were things she missed about her that she didn't ever think she would. Her quick jibes, her remarks and gloomy way of speaking. Her propensity to put everything down, even when her daughter's manner was positive and outgoing, sunny like the Californian sun under which she was born.

It was her mother's six-month anniversary that changed things.

The estate was being finalised and the apartment was due to go on the market. To ensure it reached its full selling potential she had to clean everything out and spruce it all back up again.

It was a task she was dreading in the grief over her mother's death.

She shed many tears as she separated out clothes into bin bags, put small possessions into her car to go to charity, helped the man in the big van who called to take away the furniture.

It was all the paperwork that was the hardest though. Photographs, letters, a menu from her parents' wedding reception.

A picture of her mother and Adele on the wedding day. Smiling.

As she sifted through the memory boxes it became clear that her own life, her own achievements were her mother's greatest pride.

Her mother hadn't been a woman for compliments, for gushing about how well her daughter had done, first at school and later setting out on the path in journalism that saw her keep steady jobs, growing her name and reputation, climbing the ranks to where she was now, features editor of the *Los Angeles Times*.

She had never told her how proud she was of her. But here in the boxes she found all her work, scrapbooked, laid out like a journey, dated.

She was reminded of the recordings she had taken over the years, hitting start and play on the Dictaphone when her mother was speaking.

Her mother had laughed at her, waved her hand in the air in dismissal.

"Whatcha want to be recording me for?"

Time and again she came back to her time at Lismore Castle. To her memories of Ireland. Of her great mistress Adele Astaire.

Listening to her mother's tales of what it was like when she first came to America, as a companion to Adele after her marriage to Kingman Douglas never held much interest for her when she was younger. It was simply her mother's background – how she came to be in the United States.

But towards the end of her mother's life, she spoke about it more and more.

"No one remembers. No one knows what it was like. Everybody knows Fred, but nobody remembers Adele. Would you write about her, would ya? Put it in the paper. I'd love to see that. Love to show her. It's been so long since we spoke."

After her parents married, her mother had stopped working for Adele, but they'd kept in contact as friends and confidantes over the years.

Gradually they'd lost touch. One year the Christmas cards stopped. Neither was sure where the other lived now.

"It's something I'd like to see," her mother told her one day, when she was in the bed, resting, her most recent stroke rendering the whole right side of her body useless.

At the time, she was busy with her features desk, with news stories that kept sparking other new stories, with research and planning to be completed and pressure from her editors above her.

An old woman's story was of no interest to her for nostalgic reasons.

Even if she had been famous once. Wasn't Hollywood full of old, retiring stars?

When she took a call from a hospital worker at Christmas to tell her the worst of news, that her mother had passed in the middle of the night, suddenly she felt as though something huge, strong and powerful had kicked her in the stomach.

Her mother gone? No more words to be spoken between them? No chance to even say goodbye?

She took a week off work to organise the funeral, but she could not bring herself to sort out her mother's things and over the next few months threw herself back into work to forget.

In a way, she forgot to grieve.

And then, there among her mother's papers, among all the college newspaper articles she had written and her school reports and medals that she didn't even remember winning, were the letters to Adele Astaire.

"Would you write about Adele, would ya?"

Adele. The person she was named after.

"She had no children of her own so I wanted to honour her. It's a lovely name anyway. And it suits you."

The by-line of her articles flashed in front of her: Adele Morgan. Daughter of Tom Morgan, a most lovable man. Daughter of Patricia Ryan, a fierce Irishwoman.

She thought about it. She could put together a feature for *The Times*.

They'd find the space, find something of interest to keep it newsworthy. But she wanted more. She wanted something else, something that took in her mother too.

She would write a book.

She would tell Adele's story and, in turn, her mother's.

"Great idea, honey," Kirk had said. "I love it. You're full of good ideas!"

And so she took all the material her mother had, all the letters and correspondence, news articles and clippings. She listened back to recordings, to the crackle of her mother's voice on the tape, laughing and crying at the same time hearing her mother speak again.

She went to the library, found what she could on the Astaires and she rooted out the last address her mother had for Adele.

I'm sorry to tell you about the passing of my mother. I know at one time you were great friends. She always spoke so highly of you. One of my mother's greatest wishes was that I would write about you. You may know that I'm a journalist. I know it's a long time since you've done any press but would a project like this be of interest to you?

And so she continued. Researching in her spare time. Tracking down sources, collecting clippings, audio recordings, visiting entertainment archives. She realised she would like to travel to the places Adele lived, to get background for her book.

She had never really left California. Maybe it was time?

On the long drive back home to Los Angeles she thought about all this. About how far she had come, how she felt her mother was with her, strangely, on this trip.

What would it be like if she went to Ireland? How would she feel if she got to visit Lismore?

It was evening time when she pulled up at the small house she and Kirk shared. The sun had just set and the sky was dark, black, the last remnants of the day's rays dipping off over the horizon.

It was good to spy her house and she looked forward to getting inside, running a bath, telling Kirk all about her trip. She hoped he'd cooked up something, some fried rice maybe – she was starving.

She had made good time on the road back, better than she expected.

When she put her key in the lock she heard voices, a woman's laugh, the TV on.

She walked through to the sitting room and discovered the source of the laugh.

A petite brunette was curled up, her arm around Kirk's neck, throwing her head back at the comedy they were watching.

"*Hello?*" Ellie said, her voice a squeak, the cold realisation of the scene in front of her dawning.

Kirk leapt from his seat, the girl falling right down onto the floor.

"*Ellie! You're back ... I ...*"

The brunette stood and gasped. They all waited in shock, to hear the words that Ellie was going to say.

Nothing came. She could only stare.

At last the brunette rushed past her and ran from the room, the sound of the front door slamming behind her.

She was gone.

Ellie turned and ran up the stairs into the bedroom she and Kirk shared. The bed was dishevelled, the sheets in a tangle, the room musty with sweat. Another woman's sweat.

An ashtray lay on the bedside locker, four butts stubbed out, two with pink lipstick, smudged.

Kirk was behind her.

"I can explain," he said, holding out his hands.

Without a word Ellie pushed past him down the stairs and into the kitchen.

She held onto the table.

What could she do? Should she get back in her car and drive – somewhere? Anywhere?

But why should she leave? Shouldn't he go? Follow that

slut of a girl, whoever she was, however he'd met her?

The phone was ringing, at the wall.

Kirk's footsteps were on the stairs.

Ring ring ring ring!

"Hello?"

Her hand automatically lifted the receiver to stop the noise. *Stop!*

"Hello, is that Adele?"

"Yes?"

Kirk is in the kitchen, his face white.

"Adele, this is Adele Astaire, your namesake! I was so sorry to hear about your mother. So sorry, she was just my favourite, she really was."

Kirk walking over, gesturing to her to hang up.

"Oh ... yes ... oh, thank you. Yes, I'm d-devastated," she stuttered, hanging on to the receiver, turning her back to Kirk.

"I ... I loved her, you know."

Tears sprang to her eyes. Shock. Pain. And now her project, the subject of all the work she'd been doing, live on the telephone.

"And you want to write a book about me! Well, isn't that wonderful! Of course I'd love that! Love that. I've been thinking for years how I'd like to go back over it all. I'm not getting any younger, you know!"

Kirk is shaking his head, staring at her.

"Oh, I'm glad you like that idea," she said, her voice shaking. "I wasn't sure what you'd think."

"Why don't you come to visit me? I'm in Arizona. Although I'll be going to Ireland in the summer. Have you ever been? I haven't seen you since you were a child. I'd just love to catch up."

Kirk's hand is on the wall. He wants her to hang up, he looks as though he is about to press the button on the phone down.

She slams her hand into his chest, pushes him away.

"Oh yes, I can come. I can come to you. That would be wonderful."

"Great. Then I can tell you all about me. And what happened to me. To me and Freddie. It's a wonderful story, you know."

"I know."

She looked at Kirk, who was now backing away in defeat.

"I know," she said again. "My mother always told me you had a wonderful story to tell."

Headstand Books
381 SW. Grant St.
Astoria, NY 11103
2 September 1978

Dear Miss Morgan,

Thank you for your submission of *Adele* to Headstand books.

We liked your story and believe the manuscript has promise.

We wish to arrange to meet with you to discuss this project further.

I will be attending a conference in Los Angeles the last week in September.

Would it suit to meet then?

Yours sincerely

Jacob Waller
Commissioning Editor
Headstand Books

THE END

AUTHOR'S NOTE

Adele is a work of fiction based on fact. It is what I like to call a bio-fiction. Almost all of the book is based on true happenings, but of course there are characters, conversations and plotlines that came entirely from my head! To be fair to the people that once lived or are still living, it is right for me to clarify a little as to what I have written here.

The character of Ellie Morgan, who we meet at the start and the very end of the book is a fictional character, as is her mother Patricia Ryan. However, I do know anecdotally that Adele Astaire had an Irish maid who became a close friend and went with her to America and settled there, never to return. I was also told that she did have a little girl and named her Adele in honour of Adele Astaire. I have not researched or tracked this person down to confirm this, but I did like the sentiment of it and found it a hook on which I could base my story.

All of the interviews and snippets of extracts, some with rather well-known people are fictional, although based on real relationships that Adele had.

The housekeeper Mrs. Keeley is entirely fictional and I have no knowledge of the real relationship Adele had with her housekeeper at the time, as I didn't find anything in the letters I studied.

As with any historical fiction work, research is key to discovering your character's motivations, personality and drive. This story is derived from a number of sources.

Fred Astaire's autobiography *Steps in Time* is a wonderfully written book and provides plenty of insight into the special relationship the siblings shared. Richard MacKenzie's book *Turn Left at the Black Cow*, gives many anecdotes of Adele in later life which show her gregarious character. The book which provided the most comprehensive and overarching information on which this novel is based is Kathleen Riley's biography *The Astaires*. I got in touch with Kathleen while writing this novel and she kindly shared further information with me including documentary footage which was most helpful.

The Howard Gotlieb Library in Boston, USA, houses the Astaire archives and I was lucky enough to visit to research the Astaire's personal collection. It's a fascinating array of scrapbooks, photographs, personal diaries and interview materials and gave me a huge insight into Adele's personal thoughts and feelings. It is from this source I was most able to extract the scenes with her great love, Charlie.

I was also lucky enough to visit Lismore Castle, in County Waterford, Ireland, where Adele spent the years of her first marriage and visited every summer until just before her death. From here I was able to track down sources who knew and worked with Adele and these were the small details that allowed me to build a complete picture of her. The swan story is true!

In fact, almost everything relating to Adele and Fred here is true, from the smallest details about the apartment they stayed in in New York, to the timeline of their shows, to the anecdotes around the gifts they gave each other to the complicated but loving relationships they had with family and colleagues.

I did of course create many of the conversations and small plot points featured throughout because we have no way of knowing what was really said at a point in time, if it wasn't recorded.

Adele Astaire did sit down with her friend Helen Rayburn in later years to record a series of interviews with a view to publishing a biography of her life story. The interviews indicate that the book was to be written in story form. Although it was never published, the interviews remain and give one of the best glimpses into the thoughts, memories and personality of the charismatic, gregarious, and of her time Adele Astaire.

I'd like to think that even though it is nearly forty years later, her story is now being told, even if it is by an author who never met her, has limited showbiz connections and can only dream of 1920s life, one hundred years ago.

May she live on in spirit, forever dancing, in our hearts.

Now that you're hooked why not try

also published by Poolbeg

Here's a sneak preview of Chapter 1

Chapter 1- *The Discovey*

From its hiding place in the grass, a ladybird clung to a stalk that had narrowly avoided the chop. It waited to see if another blow, a downward shunt of metal, was to come. When it did not it moved up slowly over dewdrops, making its way to the tip of the blade of grass, a vantage point to see where to go next.

On the newly uncovered earth stood a man and his son, his wife behind them holding a tea tray.

"Do you think it's a treasure chest, Da?"

"It could be," said the man. "Doesn't smell too nice, does it?"

"No," said Aidan.

They were staring at a suitcase, a dour smell escaping

from it and filling the air around them.

The man kicked it with his boot. It was spongy and soft, wet earth dislodging where his toe had hit the leather.

They were working on potato beds. They would sow a large crop, to give an abundance in late summer. The man had no experience of growing anything, but he had a battered book he'd found in one of the second-hand shops where they'd picked up some baskets and creels for the new house. It was called *Gardening: Vegetables and Seeds*, and he had read the whole thing twice, folding down the pages where it detailed how to grow the things he wanted. Cabbages, lettuce, turnips, summer strawberries.

Now that the house was shaped up, now that the rooms were fresh and aired out, the shed fixed up and the hedges peeled back, now that the front drive had been cleaned and all the stones and broken plaster removed, he finally had time to turn to the garden.

He'd been looking forward to planting spuds for months, ever since they bought the house. "Balls of flour they'll be!" he said as they dug.

Aidan jumped on the spade with enthusiasm. He had grown since they'd come here, filling out, his cheeks turning pudgy and soft. The countryside suited him, where he could run for distances, safe, across green fields. He could hang from trees, upside down, till the blood in his head pooled.

The wheeze that he had lived with for all of his eleven years had mostly disappeared. The woman had always known that the damp tenement block they'd shared with fourteen other families had been the cause of his bad chest. She had worried that the green mould that grew down the wall was growing inside him too.

He had taken to gardening with gusto, following his father around with a wheelbarrow, his willing assistant, proud of his status as the only son. While his young sisters happily played in the house and front garden, he and his father had got to work, preparing the ground for potatoes and vegetables, pulling great clumps of strong rooted grass from their maze of earthworms, clay and small stones, hacking at briars that scratched the skin from their hands, and flattening and lifting the devil's bread that flourished around the banks of the garden.

It was Aidan who'd made the discovery, the blunt edge of his spade hitting something hard and flat, deep in the earth. He'd leaned on the spade at first, trying to push it through, but when his weight couldn't force it any farther he bent down and rubbed at the soil to reveal a dark wet surface.

"Look, Da!" he called. "Something's buried!"

The man came to see what the boy had found and his wife too who had just come from the house with a tray of tea and sandwiches. The three of them peered at the thing he had uncovered.

With their hands, the man and the boy cleared the flat surface, revealing more and more of what appeared to be a leather surface. When they found an edge they dug beside it, throwing wet clumpy clay up onto the mound of earth they'd made.

The man bent and, grunting, managed to dislodge the edge from the soil. It didn't take long before they could pull the object up from where it had been buried.

The smell, which was now permeating the air, had quelled any hope of buried treasure. Aidan pinched his nose and grimaced.

"Will we see what's inside?" said the man.

Aidan nodded, his mother standing back to give them some operational room.

With his spade the man knocked at the catch, which was caked in solid earth. It took three attempts before the clay moved and loosened.

The boy squatted down and fiddled with the catch, forcing it apart.

He pulled back the lid slowly and they all recoiled as a powerful stench filled the air.

Inside the case lay two small bodies, babies, the glint of a bone visible, their clothes dark and stained, their skin a dark grey pulp.

The boy jumped back, gave a short sharp yelp and burst into tears.

His mother dropped the tea tray with a rattle to the ground and put her arm around his head to shield him.

In fear, they ran, the man, the woman and the child, up the garden and into the back of the house, slamming the door behind them.

The case lay stinking beside two freestanding spades, where a white butterfly flitted about, watched by a ladybird who clung tightly to its drying blade of grass.

See Poolbeg.com for more . . .